"A powerful, sweeping story; epic science fantasy at its best."
SUNYI DEAN, BESTSELLING AUTHOR OF *THE BOOK EATERS*

"Kritika H. Rao returns to the SFF scene with a fury in her
sequel, *The Unrelenting Earth*. Intricate worldbuilding and a
labyrinthine magic system weave together to form the foundation
for a gripping plot filled with twists and turns, sky-high stakes
(literally), and heart-breakingly relatable characters."
M. J. KUHN, BESTSELLING AUTHOR OF *AMONG THIEVES*

"*The Unrelenting Earth* is a powerful epic of heartbreak and
hard-bought triumph, of anguish and enduring hope, woven with
complex magic, intricate worldbuilding, and deeply felt humanity.
A stratospheric sequel that truly raises the stakes!"
MELISSA CARUSO, AUTHOR OF THE SWORDS & FIRE TRILOGY

"The first novel of The Rages trilogy was a masterpiece of
worldbuilding and creativity, and *The Unrelenting Earth* doubles
down as Rao ratchets up the pace and the stakes. It does not
suffer from "middle book syndrome" in the slightest. Rao is a
phenomenal new voice and deserves a place alongside authors like
Arkady Martine, N.K. Jemisin, and Adrian Tchaikovsky. I can't
wait to see how she wraps up this epic series!"
S. B. DIVYA, AUTHOR OF *MACHINEHOOD* AND *RUNTIME*

PRAISE FOR *THE SURVIVING SKY*

"Enthralling and highly imaginative. *The Surviving Sky* is a richly crafted story set in a fascinating world... I loved the protagonists and their relationship, fraught with tension and secrets, ambition and desire."

SUE LYNN TAN, BESTSELLING AUTHOR OF
DAUGHTER OF THE MOON GODDESS

"Breathtakingly inventive, *The Surviving Sky* is a twisty, cerebral journey through a fractured marriage, a world plagued by storms, and the question of what it means to be human. This is a book to get lost in."

TASHA SURI, WORLD FANTASY AWARD-WINNING AUTHOR OF
THE BURNING KINGDOMS TRILOGY

"Kritika H. Rao crafts an inventive and cerebral debut, reimagining South Asian culture in a wonderfully different world. A story about love, duty, power, as much as it is about fascinating lore and costly magic."

R. R. VIRDI, BESTSELLING AUTHOR OF *THE FIRST BINDING*

"Intensely imaginative and heartbreakingly human, *The Surviving Sky* paints a brutal, unforgiving world and the life that tenuously exists above it... this is a story that is hard to put down."

ANDREA STEWART, BESTSELLING AUTHOR OF
THE DROWNING EMPIRE TRILOGY

"This wildly imaginative book explores a fracturing world through the deeply painful lens of a fracturing human heart. At times brutal, often beautiful, *The Surviving Sky* offers a thrilling glimpse into a flawed society scrambling to survive... Don't miss it!"

LUCY HOLLAND, BESTSELLING AUTHOR OF
SISTERSONG AND *SONG OF THE HUNTRESS*

Also by Kritika H. Rao and available from Titan Books

The Surviving Sky

THE
UNRELENTING
EARTH

KRITIKA H. RAO

TITAN BOOKS

The Unrelenting Earth
Print edition ISBN: 9781803365275
E-book edition ISBN: 9781803365282

Published by Titan Books
A division of Titan Publishing Group Ltd
144 Southwark Street, London SE1 0UP
www.titanbooks.com

First edition: June 2024
10 9 8 7 6 5 4 3 2 1

This is a work of fiction. All of the characters, organizations, and events portrayed in this novel are either products of the author's imagination or are used fictitiously. Any resemblance to actual persons, living or dead (except for satirical purposes), is entirely coincidental.

A CIP catalogue record for this title is available from the British Library.

Printed and bound by CPI Group (UK) Ltd, Croydon CR0 4YY.

For those of you trying to do the right thing.

1

AHILYA

The tracker locket in Ahilya's hands lay silent.

She fidgeted with it, running the chain through her fingers, rubbing her thumb over the glass screen, resisting the urge to glance at it. She had once used similar trackers to mark yakshas, but the other half of this particular locket was not attached to one of those massive, mysterious creatures. The last time she had seen its counterpart, it was hanging around her husband's neck. He had been atop a gigantic, monstrous falcon-yaksha. That had been two months ago.

She stared toward the jungle, imagining the wild foliage past Nakshar's briar dome. A part of her could not believe she stood in this tiny clearing within the outer ashram, the twittering of birds filling her ears, afternoon sunshine dappling through Nakshar's tall trees. She could almost hear Oam preparing for an expedition. She could almost feel Dhruv pull her aside to discuss the price of a council seat. And she could see him, Iravan, accompanying her into the jungle. She'd lost all of them, in unique, immeasurable ways.

Ahilya swallowed, a heaviness in her throat. Her palm pulsed with the imagined rhythms of the inert tracker. The device had been chiming for the last ten minutes, as it had intermittently through the two months since landing, an indication it was being charged Ecstatically. This time it was Iravan charging it, close enough to the landed ashram to appear as a red dot on the screen. By the time Ahilya had arrived at the outer copse, the dot had disappeared. The chiming had stopped.

Naila stood next to her, shifting weight from one foot to the other, surreptitiously watching her from the corner of her eyes. The Maze Architect was dressed in full uniform, a brown knee-length kurta over embroidered trousers, her translucent robe belted over, sharp and regal. She had graduated from Junior Architect during the recent turmoil, yet there was deference and worry in her posture. Naila had followed Ahilya through Nakshar's morphing paths but she did not speak, as though unwilling to interrupt her thoughts.

Sighing, Ahilya turned to her. "How much time do we have?"

"None at all." Naila's veins glowed blue-green with the power of trajection, as vines and creepers articulated themselves over her brown skin. Perhaps she was trajecting the ground they stood on. It would explain why the copse didn't change, even though the rest of Nakshar was undoubtedly altering into flight architecture. "Nakshar and Reikshar have almost fully merged. Nakshar's council will convene soon. You can't be late for the takeoff. Chaiyya-ve will hold that against you."

It was not Naila's place to direct her—Ahilya was a member of the council now—but the Maze Architect had been trained by Iravan for years to occupy the very position Ahilya now occupied. Naila knew the weight of seemingly inconsequential actions far more than Ahilya could after her mere months of councilorship. Ahilya had expected rancor or hostility from the Maze Architect, but Naila had come to Ahilya after her initiation to offer her services most humbly. The woman was nothing short of her lieutenant now.

Naila's face drew into a frown. "The lull was longer than ever this time, but another earthrage was inevitable. Why does that bother you so?"

"Is this earthrage a new cosmic being dividing itself? Or the same one Iravan and I trapped?"

"Does it matter?"

It mattered. Two months before, Ahilya had discovered the truth behind the earthrages in a discovery that had shaken all her assumptions about their culture. The images still haunted her—the furious split of a cosmic creature, the painful separation of a yaksha and an architect, the desperation to choose annihilation over erasure. She and Iravan had nearly been destroyed while trapping the cosmic creature within the Moment.

"If it's the same being," she said, "then the rift we closed won't hold, not by the measures I know. We might never be able to end the earthrages. And if it's a new one..."

"You fear retribution?"

"We know nothing about those beings except that all architects came from them. They're more intelligent, more powerful, more advanced than we can imagine. Maybe we've angered them by trapping one of them, denying them new life."

Naila's fingers curled around her robe. She gazed toward the briar wall as though she could see the beginning of the split occurring. Somewhere out in the jungle, a yaksha existed, formed or formless, that belonged to the Maze Architect. It might even be one that Ahilya had tagged so long ago—the tiger-yaksha, or the bear-yaksha, or the elephant-yaksha.

Ahilya nodded at the tattoos glowing over Naila's veins. "Is trajection still difficult for you?"

"An earthrage is going to occur soon. It's normal." Naila's eyes tightened, but she didn't look away from the jungle.

Ahilya didn't probe. Trajection was known to be harder during an earthrage, but Ahilya had learned that only architects who had denied Ecstasy in their past lives found it so. For Naila to feel it, as she so clearly was—

"I can't be an Ecstatic," Naila whispered, evidently following the same train of thought. "I... I haven't felt anything like you said Iravan-ve had."

Iravan's symptoms of Ecstasy were not the only ones, but Ahilya did not say so. Instead, she reached out a hand and lightly touched Naila's elbow, bringing the younger woman to meet her gaze.

"I won't let you be excised," Ahilya said softly. "Not you, not any of the other architects. I promise you I will speak of this at the Conclave."

As a councilor, the weight of excision hung heavy on her. Four Ecstatics had been discovered in Nakshar in the last two months alone, a statistic both unusual and alarming. All four captured architects currently awaited their excision within the sanctum.

But, unlike they had once thought, excision did more than merely cut an architect away from their trajection. It destroyed an architect's chance to unify with their yaksha. It mutilated the sentient part of their personality. It rendered an architect insensate.

On her return from the jungle, Ahilya had told the council everything that had occurred there, but even that had failed to stay their hand in wanting to excise the Ecstatics. To prevent the atrocity from occurring, she had divulged her information to all of Nakshar— an action that had confused non-architect citizens, but won her Naila's loyalty. It had earned the wrath of the other councilors too, yet Ahilya was planning to enrage them even further by announcing the same news to the Conclave. The meeting with Nakshar's sister ashrams was to discuss precisely why trajection was getting harder. With innocent lives at stake, Ahilya could not stay silent.

Beyond the copse, the briar wall began to curl into itself, growing thicker, approaching them more quickly. Soon Nakshar would need to take to the skies again. The Maze Architect glanced at Ahilya, and she nodded. They turned away from the jungle toward Nakshar proper.

Ahilya tucked the tracker locket back into the pocket of her kurta. Among all the rudra bead necklaces and bracelets she now wore, her due as a councilor, the locket was a heavy burden, confusing her mind. Yet she couldn't bring herself to leave it at home. Iravan was somewhere out there, and he hadn't said goodbye; he had *deliberately* not said goodbye. How could she leave this device that connected him to her? Especially now? She needed him, not just to corroborate everything she had said to Nakshar, but for herself.

Her hand drifted to her stomach. She could feel her pregnancy in the twinges and tucks by her pelvis—but fear gripped her. Was her pregnancy growing at all? The last few weeks had brought her terrible, sudden pain, and Ahilya had not dared to examine it too closely. Instead, each time she was in the throes of agony, she thought of what she had done by chasing after Iravan in the habitat, by leaping after him into the vortex. She had saved the both of them, and the world, but at what cost? This pain… what did it mean? What would Iravan say?

She and Iravan had parted in love, but there was still so much left unsaid between them. A fragile dream filled her mind of a home with him, of toddling children, and a world that was finally fair, where Ecstatics were free to unite with their yakshas and non-architects had their rightful place. She and Iravan could make such a world. They could find happiness. She had to believe it. She pictured him like she had seen him last, a mere speck in the sky.

She and Naila emerged from the copse directly at the base of the rudra tree. The architects had decided to use Iravan's ellipsoidal model to conserve trajection, though much had been altered to match Reikshar's architecture as it merged with Nakshar. During landing, Nakshar had tentatively expanded and stretched itself, but now that they were making ready to fly again, the rudra tree *was* the ashram, holding all of its citizens in its boughs. A winding ramp led up from the base and disappeared into the foliage. Ahilya couldn't see it, but she knew that far above the topmost tier, a dome covered the ashram—a dome that would soon become Nakshar's outermost shell.

For a moment an image of the rudra tree flashed behind her eyes, of how it had looked a mere two months ago, shriveled, burned, a near desiccated corpse, rendered helpless by the combined damage sustained from Bharavi's Ecstasy and the falcon-yaksha's attack. Nakshar's landing had allowed the core tree to heal, but it would not have been possible without Reikshar's Maze Architects.

Perhaps that explained the tree's current design. Thin gray vines crept over its dark, almost black trunk—vines that belonged to Reikshar's bael tree. The ashram had been the first to respond to Nakshar's distress call, the first to accept Nakshar's invitation to the Conclave. Ahilya imagined the rudra tree held up by the bael, like one person supporting another.

She and Naila started up the ramp that wound around the wide tree trunk. Through the foliage, Ahilya glimpsed platforms built from branches circling the tree, like rings hidden in the boughs. Hushed voices rustled within the whispering leaves, guarded and tense. Naila briefly trajected, and through the light of her skin, Ahilya noticed citizens crowded together, shoulder to shoulder, barely an inch of space between them. A child's face peeked out from the dark leaves, but a woman pulled them back. Her cold gaze swept over Ahilya before she was lost to the darkness again, and Naila continued to climb.

Startled, Ahilya followed more slowly. She did not know the woman but there was no denying her hostility. Things had changed so much in the last two months. Ahilya's ascent to councilor had been welcomed by non-architects, but their regard had changed into suspicion ever since she'd defended the Ecstatics. Nakshar's citizens carried such grief for all they'd endured and lost. They did not trust her anymore, and in truth Ahilya could not blame them. Was she really *their* councilor?

A few tiers higher, tiny sungineering glowglobes blinked at her, their twinkling caught among the leaves. The sounds changed too, a laugh here, excited chatter there. Ahilya stopped, and spun slowly, gazing past the waving leaves, taking in the carved railings of the platforms, the seats trajected from healbranch, the faces of the citizens she recognized—citizens who were all married to architects, Reniya, Vihanan, and Lavanya, Senior Architect Chaiyya's own wife. Off-duty architects sat together with their families, as though this were a park. Ahilya bit the insides of her cheek in sudden rage. Where was Ahilya's sister Tariya, now that Bharavi was gone? Where were Kush and Arth, their children? If Ahilya had not been a councilor, would her place under this new design have been down there in the darkness and crowds of the lowermost tiers with other non-architects?

"What's wrong?" Naila asked. She had come to a stop a few feet away.

This had been one temple under Iravan—one space with the same safety for all, whether a citizen was an architect or a non-architect. To see it like this... this design that was so clearly prejudiced—

With effort, Ahilya worked her jaw, trying to relax herself. "Iravan once told me that the quality of trajection depends on how far it is from the core tree, but did he mean the Architects' Disc?"

"The Disc has always been a part of the tree... but yes, that's probably what he meant."

"But now the Disc is at the topmost tier, and the citizens at the lowest. Is that safe?"

"Not as safe as Iravan-ve's original design," Naila admitted. "At least not right now, when we're pressed for trajection energy."

"Do the citizens even have healbranch to help them through the flight?"

"Our healbranch has not grown as fully as we'd hoped, and..." Naila's skin lit up as she entered the Moment. "You're right, I don't see any down there."

"How is that possible? He told me healbranch grows everywhere in the ashram. That it's an unalterable permission embedded into the core tree. Not even Senior Architects can change that."

"They can't... but..." Naila's skin grew a touch brighter. "I think within this architectural design, the lowermost tiers are not recognized as a part of the ashram at all. They've manipulated the design so they can restrict the healbranch to only the highest tiers."

"Where the architects are."

"I think they're trying to reassure the architects—especially Reikshar's—that they are still a priority. With Iravan-ve and Bharavi-ve gone... well, we are taught the council must always have more architects than not. Now that there are only two on Nakshar's council instead of five... I know many architects find it troubling. This is clearly some kind of overcompensation."

Horror and anger churned in Ahilya's stomach. That's what they had chosen to do. Not recognize non-architects as people, as part of the ashram, at all. With her defense of the Ecstatics, she had been party to this. She had served the architects, Ecstatic or otherwise, before those of her kind. No wonder the mother in the tree had studied her with such resentment.

"I know this is wrong," Naila said, breaking the silence. "But the enslavement of architects for their trajection is a true fear, even more so after what happened to Airav-ve. It's why we were taught the council must always have more architects."

"Architects are already enslaved," Ahilya bit out. "But not all of them see it."

Naila nodded and rubbed her arms as though suddenly cold. The foliage thickened the higher they climbed until the ramp straightened, to be replaced by a short corridor of thick bare wood. The two stopped at the end, facing a wall of black moss. Ahilya brought up her wrist, but Naila cleared her throat. The sound was deathly quiet in the tunnel.

"Perhaps I should accompany you?" she asked.

"You can't. You're overseeing construction at the solar lab. Besides, this is for the council only."

"Yes, but the council—how they treat you—how you stand there—" The Maze Architect broke off, eyes lowered in embarrassment.

Once, Ahilya would have thought that Naila was embarrassed for her. But she had spent enough time with her to know that she was embarrassed on behalf of the architects of the council—specifically, Senior Architect Chaiyya. In that, Naila was unlearned—but Ahilya had once been married to a councilor. She hoped she still was. She had known the games they played. She had known the consequences and the contingencies of accepting the offer of the council seat, of divulging everything she had to Nakshar.

It was no secret that Chaiyya already regretted inviting Ahilya to the council. Clearly, the woman had thought Ahilya's proximity to the architects, her pursuit of Iravan in the jungle, her cooperation with the council, all indicated her consideration for architect welfare. She must have thought Ahilya would make a good puppet for the changes occurring in the ashram, and a good scapegoat if matters went awry. She hadn't known Ahilya well enough. By announcing to the ashram everything she had learnt in the jungle, Ahilya had disabused the Senior Architect of her illusions. Unsurprisingly, Chaiyya had mounted a full offensive against Ahilya and her plans. There was no safety in the council for Ahilya. Only traps and machinations.

"I can take care of myself," Ahilya murmured.

"I know you can," Naila said. "I just... I wish they treated you better."

Ahilya shook her head. She couldn't fully blame Chaiyya for her hostility. The consequences of being so open with her discoveries in the jungle had already made themselves apparent in non-architect citizens. Architects had been affected even worse. Yakshas intrinsically connected to architects? Cosmic beings that caused the earthrages? Ecstasy that ought to be encouraged instead of being excised? Architects were growing confused about their loyalties. Some, like Naila, had offered greater allyship to non-architects. Others had grown hostile, angry at the changes. Some continued to fear Ecstasy like they always had, but many more had been vocal about desiring it. Ahilya's news had brought discord already. By sharing it at the Conclave, she would change their entire culture.

She made to tap at one of her many rudra bead bracelets, but the Maze Architect touched her arm.

"Ahilya-ve," Naila said. "Please remember. There is precedent for councilors to be dismissed. A vote of no confidence can be passed. For Senior Architects, it usually precedes excision. But non-architects can be dismissed if they do not comply with the wishes of the council or have at least one Senior Architect supporting them through their critical decisions."

"Don't worry—"

"Please, Ahilya-ve. I know you are relying on Airav. But he can't traject anymore, not after what happened with the battery. Chaiyya-ve could argue that he does not count as an architect at all. His influence may not be enough."

Ahilya's chin trembled. It was because of her that Airav, a Senior Architect, could no longer traject. She had forced him into using the battery.

"You don't want to lose your position, Ahilya-ve. You'll be powerless again, and the architects need you, *all* of us need you, to set the record straight about Ecstasy. You won't be able to do that if you're no longer a councilor."

"I—"

"Please," Naila said again, and there was a tinge of desperation there. "There has already been so much chaos. The architects are not taking to it well. Risks in the council must be carefully assessed, and your news has challenged the need for material bonds. Iravan-ve tried to do that too, you know—challenge the bonds—but he understood what the consequences of such change could be on the architects. He was... circumspect."

Ahilya nodded slowly. She had once accused Iravan of being imprisoned by his material bonds; she'd thought he'd wanted a child simply because of those, not truly believing he would use his power to change the world.

But Iravan had picked his battles carefully. He'd progressed to a Senior Architect without having children. He'd wanted Naila, who had then been a mere Junior Architect, to become a councilor—not merely a woman who had no children, but one who was not married, her selection as big a challenge to the importance of material bonds as his own.

Iravan *had* tried to change Nakshar, but he had taken a winding course to it, typical of an architect. Ahilya had come in with her news and obliterated the need for such a course at all. She had created Chaiyya's hostility. She'd made her own position on the council tenuous.

Ahilya closed her other hand over Naila's and squeezed. "I'll be careful, I promise. I'll see you afterward."

The Maze Architect didn't move, biting her lip in worry, but Ahilya turned away. She tapped at one of her rudra bead bracelets. The curling leaves in front of them parted into a doorway, and murmurs rose from within. Ahilya entered the chambers, determined and alone.

2

IRAVAN

The silence of unity rippled through Iravan.

It threaded through him demanding attention even as the world prepared for another death, another annihilation.

He sat upon the falcon-yaksha, his shoulders tense. Under him, the falcon was rock still, a gigantic bird perched on an earthy outcrop. An expanse of jungle spread out in front of him, a construct of soil illuminated by afternoon sunlight, green clutched in a birthing storm.

Leaves curled and withered. Bark groaned and crackled, crumpling from the inside. Wind rustled, fierce and gusting, lifting seeds that poured out of trees, carrying them away in a promise of new growth. The sounds of destruction filled his ears, but Iravan sat motionless, aware only of the silence that occupied his heart.

The silence was not his, not truly; it belonged to the falcon—

But then he grinned, a tight twisted smile—for weren't he and the yaksha part of the same being? There was no other sign of life in the immediate jungle, no birds, no squirrels, neither animals nor humans. For two months, he hadn't even seen any other yakshas except for his own falcon. Those had disappeared far from the habitat, and he had spent his time with only himself for company. He was still unaccustomed to the deathly quiet of loneliness. It was more marked now than ever before, with the full fury of the earthrage imminent.

He sank his fingers into the falcon's silvery feathers that, after all this time, still smelled like smoke. He and the falcon had burned together when they had separated into an earthrage. Iravan had forgotten it once. He would never forget again.

That was the silence—a memory he had repressed far too long, angry and vast and relentless. There was no forgiveness in what they'd done. No absolution. Shame formed a tight ball in his throat. It embossed a lasting image on his heart.

The earthrage built like a long drawn out scream.

The yaksha's silence remained.

Iravan took a deep, shaky breath.

All his instincts told him to nudge the yaksha, to leap into the air where it was safe, but he had not landed here of his own accord. They had been gliding in the open skies, and the falcon had brought him to this outcrop. He knew it would not leave, not until it had shown him what it wanted.

Iravan waited, embedded in the Two Visions of Ecstasy. He and the falcon watched the storm come in their first vision. The ground trembled. Tree trunks burst like overripe melons. Massive balloons of dust rose, racing toward them from all directions.

In their second vision, within the infinite velvety darkness of the Deepness, Iravan and the Resonance fluttered around each other. The Resonance was the falcon's form in the Deepness; he would forever think of the silvery molten particle in those terms. The thing had haunted him for so long, but it was still familiar, more familiar than the creature whose feathers he clutched. What was it doing?

Why was it waiting? In his first vision, Iravan gripped the falcon tighter and licked his lips.

Under them, the jungle roiled, a deep tremor.

A trembling dewdrop reflected a ring forming around the falcon's eye.

Powered by the yaksha, the tracker locket around Iravan's neck began to chime. A thrill rose inside him.

Silvery light emanated from the Resonance in the Deepness. The particle summoned the Moment, a globule of stars reflecting the possibilities of all the lives of their world. The Resonance aimed its jet of light toward the globule, its ray invisibly thin. Fibres leached from the source, like branches attached to a stem, reaching toward the part of the jungle where Iravan and the falcon were perched. The yaksha was creating a web of supreme complexity, Ecstatically trajecting the jungle from the Deepness into the Moment.

The jungle changed.

All around them, the dust stilled as though it had come up against an invisible barrier. The wind stopped. The churning lessened. They waited there, man and beast, gazing around them, as for an instant, a brief blink, the falcon held back the storm wall in a perfect circle, freezing the earthrage itself.

Awe filled Iravan. The silence was overwhelming.

Is this what the falcon had wanted to show him? Iravan hadn't seen it traject through an earthrage yet, but he had been studying the bird since their union, learning from it. This trajection was more complex than any he'd seen before. Was the yaksha showing him this technique so he could replicate it? The infinite blackness of the Deepness was its territory, like the stars in the Moment were his—Iravan was no master here.

But he was no beginner architect either. He was an Ecstatic now.

Goosebumps prickled his neck. He had accepted his own Ecstasy, but lifetimes of conditioning did not make it easy to reconcile with the idea that this was his natural state. Sometimes, at night, he still jolted awake, sweating and trembling. The nightmares had come true, he was an Ecstatic now, an outcast. He had become what he had been taught to fear, to eradicate—

The frozen storm around them trembled.

Iravan tasted wet earth. A crack appeared in the invisible barrier, then more fissures, like glass splitting. He blinked and nudged the falcon with a toe. The falcon could traject in an earthrage, but Iravan was mortal. The storm could kill him.

The falcon didn't react.

Dust flicked at Iravan, then shards of jagged twigs. Wind whistled through the gaps, bringing in stray leaves and rain. Iravan nudged the falcon again, more urgently, fear replacing his awe.

Finally, the yaksha cocked its head. Uttering an angry yarp, it ruffled its feathers, unfolded its gigantic wings, and leapt into the storm, abandoning the barrier of the circle.

Wind rushed at Iravan at once, making his eyes water. Branches lashed, and grit filled his eyes, blurring his first vision. In the Deepness, the Resonance fluttered around him, and he caught a glimpse of himself over its mirrored surface, a reverberation of cold calculation that thrummed through the ever-present silence.

Iravan ducked low, wary of giving the yaksha any more instruction. The silence filled him again, a void ready to consume him. Twigs scored his skin, as the yaksha flew even lower within the storm. They entered a hurricane of thorns. Boulders streaked past Iravan. He sunk his head into the smoky feathers. He had thought once that he could control the yaksha, but how foolish he'd been. The creature might be a part of himself, but it was a stranger nonetheless, a higher being, complex and eternal. They had identified each other, perhaps even accepted one another. They had not yet understood each other.

That, perhaps, was why the yaksha had brought them here. That, perhaps, was the reason behind its torturing silence.

His own quiet had grown in him ever since he and the yaksha had repaired and remembered themselves in that vortex within the habitat. At first, the falcon's silence had been considering but now it built into a roar in his mind and he knew it contained lifetimes of anger, lifetimes of reprisal. The yaksha was wild and feral. It had lived alone for thousands of years, but it had not forgiven him, and it had certainly not forgotten its own pain. The silence was not peaceful, it was punishment. Iravan's only answer was regret.

He lifted his head slightly. A whipping branch filled his vision, and he ducked again to see it carried away by the earthrage. In the Deepness, the Resonance bobbed as though in laughter, and Iravan recognized in its fluttering a bitter satisfaction at making him flinch. Ahilya flashed into his mind. She had attacked him too when they'd left Nakshar together for her expedition. Had that only been a few months ago? He could hardly believe it.

"Enough," Iravan growled, as another flying branch nearly took his head off.

The earthrage was coming, the split of another cosmic creature, and here they were performing what could only be described as self-flagellation.

He gathered his own energy in the Deepness, pointed the beam in the Moment—

The Resonance smashed into him.

The ray he had carefully aimed bounced past the star he had targeted. It hit something else, another star, and Iravan swung himself away from the Resonance in the Deepness, terrified.

What had he hit? What had they done? Had he hit the possibility of an ashram? Of a *person*? He spun around angrily in the Deepness toward the Resonance, but before he could gather his energy, the silvery particle trajected, and a stray vine looped itself around Iravan's neck, choking him.

"Wh—" he gasped. *What in rages?* His hands scratched at the vine, scrabbling, even as they flew amidst the fracturing trees and the rising maelstrom. He couldn't breathe. Tears sprang in his eyes. *What the fuck are you doing?* he screamed, spinning in the Deepness, trying to gather his desire to him.

But the Resonance knocked him away again, too easily.

He scratched at the vine around his throat, pulling it, but it only tightened. The creature could traject Ecstatically far better than he could ever hope to—it had thousands of years of mastery over him. It had held back the *earthrage*. Its Ecstasy was sharp enough to fly through the storm, trajecting and releasing each part of the jungle it flew through.

Gasping, Iravan darted in the Deepness, made to enter the Moment. The Resonance blocked his path, its flutters overtaking his second vision.

Iravan's body seized. He coughed, grit filling his nose and his throat. He couldn't *breathe*.

A memory flashed, of when his Two Visions had merged. He had become the magnaroot. They had tried to rip themselves apart. They had tried to kill himself.

His eyes closed against the horror. It was happening again.

The darkness began to take him. He pulled desperately, one weak tug, then another, his strength waning—

The vine came free in his hands.

Iravan wheezed, still atop the falcon, his Two Visions collapsing. The yaksha glided lower in a lazy circle, and swept down to a courtyard—the habitat, Iravan groggily recognized. His Garden. The creature came to a rest at the ledge outside the walled enclosure Iravan had built all those months before. It shook its wings and Iravan slithered down to the grassy floor, away from the beast.

The yaksha tilted its head to one side, its gaze cold and victorious. It snapped its beak once.

Then, in a rush of wings, it was gone again, beyond the habitat into the earthrage. The glittering green dust of pure possibility—the everdust—rippled where the bird left the habitat's safety. Iravan glimpsed the screaming face of the birthing earthrage, visible now from inside the habitat, attempting to break through the barrier of everdust. A slight terror gripped him. The habitat was no longer the degraded version he and Ahilya had once found. Their actions had mended this place, keeping the earthrage out. Yet there was no telling how long that would last.

He staggered through the jagged hole in the rock wall. A chair waited inside, one he had trajected for himself weeks ago. Iravan collapsed onto it, rubbing his neck, his vision swimming. He coughed, throat burning, and snatched the sungineering locket from around his neck. His fingers ran over at the ridges where the vine had pressed the chain of the locket into his skin.

Gasping, Iravan entered the Moment.

His visions split again, but unlike the ever-darkness of the Deepness, the Moment was a vast universe, full of giant floating stars, each star a possibility of consciousness. Here was the firethorn in its bud, suspended within one star; a few stars away, it climbed over grass, in the manner of the most insidious predator. One star contained the rileweed, white and glassy, poised over a pond. In another, the rileweed grew over the forest floor, slithering like a worm. These plants of the jungle were nothing like those of the ashrams. Out here, life warred with itself, unchecked, until an earthrage erased all progress and the plants began anew.

Iravan knitted a few short constellation lines together, connecting the stars of dewy grass to the wild pothos in a pillared lattice. The grassy mound of earth in front of him rose into a column. Dew bubbled over it like a fountain. He leaned forward, cupped his hands, and drank deeply. When he was done, he severed the constellation lines. The leafy post collapsed back into the ground.

Head in his hands, Iravan started to shiver.

What had the mad creature done? It had never performed such violence, not on him—and surely, they had never met in another life? *You tried to kill me*, he thought—but had it? The yaksha had flown expertly through the earthrage, keeping Iravan balanced on itself even as it tried to strangle him. What had the creature hoped to achieve? Iravan had no more lives to reincarnate into. He might not have been what the yaksha wanted, but unity, imperfect as it was right now, was neither reversible nor repeatable.

The silence grew in him, dark and heavy, the falcon's manic satisfaction echoing in the corner of his brain. The creature had already trajected him, multiple times. What else could it do? Take over his mind? Iravan buried his head in his hands again, trembling uncontrollably. He was losing himself. There was no one to ask if this was what happened to all Ecstatics. His past selves had denied themselves true Ecstasy, and the Ecstatics who had once united had long since died. He was one of a kind, unique, exceptional. Alone.

After a long time, he looked up.

The Garden stared back at him, this place that was now his ashram, his temple, his kingdom.

A short set of stairs led down to the courtyard he had created for his wife on the day she had saved him. A stream gurgled within the Garden, and trees burst with fruit. A bone-white sungineering battery peeked from under a bush. It had once brought Ahilya to him, and he treasured it even though it no longer worked. He breathed deeply, and he smelled her through the jasmine that grew profusely on one wall. If he tried, he could believe it had been mere moments since he had returned her to Nakshar. All this beauty and life—for whom? He alone witnessed it. He had asked her to stay, and she had refused. He had decided to stay, but for what? The falcon? Iravan had thought the unity would help him find himself. This... *this* was who he was? Hysterical laughter built in him.

He ran his hands through his grit-filled hair. It was longer than it had ever been, reaching past his chin to his shoulders. He had become a wild creature of the jungle now, his beard overgrown, his clothes a mere memory of what they had once been, held together by the mending he'd trajected on them.

What would Ahilya say if she saw him like this? He closed his eyes, and he could see her, beautiful and intelligent, her hair rippling in long dark waves, her mouth turned in a sardonic smile. An ache for her grew so strong within him that Iravan gasped aloud. He needed her— desperately now, the more he learned of the falcon. If the falcon took him over, how far would he lose himself? She was his balance and without her now... An emptiness yawned in him, deep within his heart, exposing a place of stark reflection. Exposing the terror of clarity.

An image conjured itself in his mind, one he had imagined many times, of two children with his dark skin and her fierce beauty. He had made so many mistakes with her. He wanted so badly to atone for them. But more than that, he wanted a second chance. To show her how much he loved her. The dream glimmered in front of him, his final hope for happiness in this life left to him.

Green dust swirled around him, responding to his desire, its *own* desire, for her. He had circled Nakshar so many times in the months before, hoping to see her. Yet each time he had glimpsed the ashram, he had changed his mind. He was an Ecstatic now. He had no place there. Not unless he figured out how to make amends to the citizens, for everything he had done as a split cosmic creature and as an architect.

At the thought of this, another vision grew behind his Two Visions. The Etherium hovered between his brows, superimposed, ever-present. Iravan did not fully know what it was, but images flashed within it, cloudy, gray, colourless. Ahilya heavily pregnant, irritated that her round belly was getting in her way. Nakshar flying in the sky, a flat city, luxuriously built. His fathers holding each other, his mother laughing with them. Bharavi—and Iravan's breath caught in his chest in despair—hugging her grown children, Kush and Arth. The same series of images had flashed in his head since his unification, a hundred of them, a thousand, from this life and others remembered.

He had thought the Etherium a vision of guidance. It had once shown him his choices. It had provided the method to trap the cosmic being in the Moment, shown him how to unify with his yaksha, shown him his history.

But these images... these couldn't be true. Iravan had murdered Bharavi. She would never play with her children again. She would never laugh again.

Amends. He had to make amends. To Ahilya, to the falcon, to the citizens of the ashrams whose backs he had stood on to get here. He had to stop the earthrages. That was his purpose. But how? Another one had been inevitable, but the Etherium hadn't yet shown him the tear within the Moment where the rift was occurring. Without its help, he could wander the Moment forever, never to find the breach, even if he could feel the bleeding of another cosmic being seeping into life, even if he knew where every star was.

Besides, even if he found the opening, he could never close it alone. He needed Ahilya. It was the same thought that had troubled him through all the trajection he had done in this habitat. Frustration created a pounding in his ears. He was useless here. Architects weren't supposed to be useless, and he was the most powerful architect in the world. But if he couldn't do *anything*, what was the point of his power?

Abruptly, the Etherium sharpened.

Iravan sat up.

A mass of Maze Architects on their knees screamed at him in the Etherium—and more, so many more in cages. He had sent Manav to a cage like that once. He had *killed* Bharavi in one.

Deathcages.

The architects were going to be excised, cut away from their trajection and their yakshas forever. Horror hammered in his chest.

He had circled Nakshar from afar for the last two months, trying to find a way to go back, building the arguments in his head about how to reveal the truth of Ecstasy. He had demurred, always to return to his Garden out of cowardice and fear—but *this*, if this were a true vision of what was going to happen—

It had always been at the back of his mind, the knowledge that excision was surely occurring in the ashrams while he was confined to the jungle. Yet faced with it now, so starkly... How many architects had already been separated from their power because of his delay? How much damage had Iravan caused in two months of silence?

The images became sharper in the Etherium. Nakshar appeared in his third vision again, this time smaller, more fragile than it had ever been, a bark oblong floating in the sky. Nests of green approached his ashram—no, *his* ashram no longer—and he watched them come from all directions, attaching themselves to Nakshar.

So.

A Conclave.

It made sense; after all, the sister ashrams had stared their own extinction in the face. What had happened to the other cities, the ones that existed in the bands above Nakshar? Inkrist, Karran, Erast, and the others. Had they survived? Nakshar and her sister ashrams were of the lowermost bands, and Iravan had only focussed on them while ending the earthrage with Ahilya. As a Senior Architect of Nakshar, he had only ever cared about the sisters; the others had not really existed for him, beyond his attention on different altitudes. Had he forsaken them by his negligence and ignorance? Were the sister ashrams all that were left of humanity? The thought was terrifying.

The vision in the Etherium faded. The older colorless images reappeared, Ahilya heavily pregnant, Bharavi with her children, Iravan's three parents holding each other.

Iravan stood up.

The silence within him clamored, his guilt and rage bleeding into it. He did not know what the Etherium was, or what it wanted him to do, yet he had no choice but to trust the third vision. He had avoided Nakshar and the other ashrams, despite his aching need for Ahilya, despite his terrible desire to make amends. No more.

Jogging down the steps, Iravan began trajecting in the Moment, changing the architecture of the habitat, expanding the Garden beyond its intimate structure into something bigger, wider, more welcoming of the many people it should belong to. He would build apartments, and sungineering chambers. He would invite others into his home, making it their home too. As soon as the yaksha returned, they would make their way to Nakshar. Next time, when he came back to the habitat, he would no longer be alone. Perhaps then… the silence would not be as loud.

3

AHILYA

Despite the ashram's successful launch from the jungle, no celebration echoed within Nakshar's council chambers. The circular quarters were situated within the topmost boughs of the rudra tree. Tiny glowglobes twinkled from within the murmuring canopy. The only sounds came from the whirring and clicking of sungineering devices and the occasional chirp of a quiet bird. Ahilya had entered to see the other councilors already at their posts, a light blinking impatiently at her bio-node.

Each of the councilors was positioned at a separate station. They had watched Nakshar's ascent in silence, and none spoke even now. Kiana and Laksiya, the two Senior Sungineers, stood barely visible behind a dozen holograms depicting energy usage. Airav, in his wheelchair, continued to monitor Nakshar's merging with Reikshar. Chaiyya, her dark skin glittering blue-green, coordinated with the Architects' Disc. Ahilya tracked the citizens through their citizen rings.

The canopy susurrated around her as she studied the cluster of dots on the glassy screen. Each dot represented a citizen, all of them non-architects. In her mind, they huddled together, frightened in the darkness of the lowermost tiers of the rudra tree. How were they managing without healbranch? The plant was necessary to provide healing and comfort; it was imperative to flight.

Ahilya glanced over to where Chaiyya stood, her glowing skin the brightest thing in the dim chamber.

Kiana caught her eye past the holograms. The bespectacled woman muttered something to the other sungineer, then circled around the rudra tree's trunk to make her way to Ahilya. Chaiyya looked up as the sungineer passed her, her eyes traveling from Kiana to Ahilya. Her jaw moved, a tight grinding motion.

Ahilya turned away, back to her bio-node. She and Kiana had become allies—something Chaiyya did not like—but though Kiana was a sungineer, and therefore could not traject, she was not Ahilya's friend. The sungineer had agreed to support Ahilya; she had even been the one to tell Ahilya about Chaiyya's decision to excise the Ecstatics, thus prompting Ahilya to divulge all her information to the citizens of Nakshar. Yet in return, Ahilya had conducted several expeditions into the jungle during the lull. She had extracted minerals from jungle rocks, returned with dangerous plant samples within deathboxes, hunted for a yaksha to capture, all so Kiana could continue her experimentations with Ecstasy.

Ahilya had only herself to blame. She had begun down this road with Dhruv, with her expeditions and her ambitions and her smuggling. Even if her activities were all above board now, she knew it was treacherous. Kiana had found a way to extract the technology from Dhruv's tracker locket to create the energex, a device that *used* Ecstatic energy. She was looking for a way to replace the dependence on trajection with a dependence on Ecstasy. Ahilya had practically told her to do that a few months before, driven by her desperation to rescue Iravan. Knowing what she did now, about the architects and yakshas being parts of the same whole, Ahilya had been grateful to find no yakshas in the jungle. Yet each day of failure had brought the council closer to trying the energex on one of the architects in the deathcages, instead.

Naila's voice echoed in her mind. *Enslavement of architects is a true fear.* It was every architect's worry, one that the council had tried to mitigate by informing Nakshar that Ecstatic trajection was different from normal trajection—but the very premise of using Ecstasy created a need for Ecstatics, to harness them instead of releasing them. It was even more dangerous to their culture than Ahilya's own plans.

What was the Senior Sungineer attempting, really? How had she convinced Chaiyya to let her pursue this? She was as much Ahilya's ally as she was Chaiyya's, playing her own clever middlegame. Already the ashram was divided into those who wanted matters to return to how they had been, and those who coveted change. Either one, in isolation, was dangerous.

Kiana neared Ahilya and studied her with piercing gray eyes. "You're troubled."

"What makes you say that?"

"Please. I was the first non-architect in Nakshar to ascend to the council. Do you really think—"

"All right," Ahilya said. "I'm troubled."

Kiana nodded and adjusted her leg-brace. "Because of this architectural model?"

"Whose idea was it?"

"You know whose."

Ahilya met Kiana's gaze, then glanced at Chaiyya again. She moved, intending to confront Chaiyya, but Kiana put out a hand and stopped her.

"Think for a minute," the Senior Sungineer said. "Of why."

Ahilya pulled her arm away. Naila had already told her why, but that was not what Kiana meant. If this design was truly to show architects they were protected, especially architects of Reikshar, then Chaiyya had chosen it specifically to undermine Ahilya and her stance at the Conclave.

Her hand curled into a fist. They had barely escaped extinction—they didn't even know if all five hundred ashrams had survived—and Chaiyya wanted to play *political* games?

Nakshar had sent out messages to her sister ashrams, and while all had responded, no messages had been received yet from the ashrams that floated at higher altitudes. Perhaps Ahilya was being impatient, wishing so desperately for their reply. But why hadn't even Inkrist or Karran or Erast replied? Of all the ashrams on those bands, these ones were the most communicative with Nakshar—though usually, even that communication was once in seven or so years. Before recent events, Ahilya had never paid their existence much mind. They had been only names to her—all trade occurred between sisters, that was the way of the ashrams. But her world had grown since she had become a councilor, and Iravan had only confirmed Nakshar's survival those months ago when they had emerged from the vortex. How many of the higher ashrams had already crashed and burned into the earthrages? They had no news.

"Reikshar is stable," Airav called out in his deep voice.

The Senior Architect—still an architect, no matter what Naila had said—sounded exhausted. Then again, he had sounded so for a long time. The dark bald man, a stubble of gray on his head, had lost much weight. Once he had been the seniormost in the council, his word a law unto itself, but now his rudra beads hung loosely over his spotless white kurta. Ahilya's belly cramped in guilt. The image was seared into her mind: Airav bucking in his chair, his mouth open in a soundless scream of horror.

Airav caught her look, and gave her a small nod. The Senior Architect had been surprisingly willing to support her intention to speak at the Conclave. Did he think that if Ahilya succeeded in convincing others of the good of Ecstasy, it would benefit him? That unity with his own yaksha—legally and carefully—would restore his trajection? For all Ahilya knew, that was possible, though the only man who could know for sure had disappeared, quite literally, off her tracker. The locket in her kurta pressed against her thigh.

With Airav's trajection gone, Chaiyya had become the head of Nakshar's council. She had taken no time off after the birth of her twin daughters two months ago. Sometimes their meetings had occurred with Chaiyya nursing her babies within the council chambers, the little girls falling asleep while the councilors discussed food supply and Bharavi's vacant seat and the creation of new plant species. Though Chaiyya still appeared matronly, her round face had developed permanent frown lines. Her once-thick braid had more gray in it. Ahilya approached her, and Chaiyya froze for a long, telltale moment.

Ahilya hardened herself. Chaiyya had done everything to remind her that despite being a councilor, some things were still not for her to know. Even for normal city logistics, Ahilya was given no access to the architects' archives. When she'd asked, Chaiyya had stared her straight in the eyes and said it was privileged information.

The shame of it still heated Ahilya's cheeks. Iravan had never once mentioned Chaiyya being unreasonable, but then again, he had never been a councilor in times like these. He had never been a non-architect. This game was entirely different for him. Ahilya watched the Architects' Disc on the bio-node in front of Chaiyya, marshaling her words.

The Disc, a hidden ring circling the rudra tree, was a large dim chamber grown one tier below the council. This was where Nakshar was created, where it was maintained. If the rudra tree was the spinal cord of the ashram, the Architects' Disc was its brain. Nearly seventy Maze Architects sat around the thick trunk on a floor of soft moss, legs folded underneath them. Their bodies glowed like Chaiyya's, except trajection tattoos of vines and creepers crawled over their arms and necks, up to their faces. All their eyes were closed, in profound meditation even as light emanated from their bodies. As Ahilya watched, some architects stood up to leave, while others entered the chamber. Shift duty had grown shorter if more frequent since it had been recognized that trajection was becoming harder. These architects, required to sustain the ashram, had been flirting dangerously with their attachments. How much time had they spent with their families, to strengthen those bonds that kept them from becoming Ecstatics? *Yet Ecstasy is your true nature,* Ahilya thought. *You don't know completion yet. You don't know freedom.*

One of the bio-nodes blinked. Chimes sounded from it.

Airav sat up. "They're coming," he said tersely. "That's Yeikshar's call."

A series of blue-green trajection tattoos grew over Chaiyya's skin. Tight coiled spirals relaxed like a flower blooming. In concert, the tattoos of architects within the Disc began changing. The council chamber expanded. The rudra tree groaned, and Ahilya took a couple of hurried steps back. Foliage shuddered, then expanded like lungs breathing. Somewhere a bird squawked in alarm. A window creaked open in the bark by the rim, then more windows, shafts of afternoon sunlight pouring into the chamber.

On the holograms by Senior Sungineer Laksiya, a dozen lights blinked. A map of Nakshar replaced one of the images. The oblong ashram was opening up, as though it were a massive dragonfruit, nodes forming on its crust outside. Thick root tentacles stretched in uneven layers connected to hundreds of gigantic bark petals.

On the screen, Ahilya noticed glittering dots, plants of Nakshar, that blinked away, inactive. One of them was healbranch.

"What's this?" she asked sharply. Her voice came out loud in the quiet chamber. "Are you taking healbranch away from even the higher tiers of the tree? Is Nakshar itself to no longer be considered an ashram?"

Chaiyya's eyes ran over Ahilya, a subtle darkening filled with disdain.

"This is an essential maneuver for an ashram that forms the heart of the Conclave," Airav said. "We're retracting all the plants that form our barrier in flight. If we don't, then those plants will mistake the plants of the other ashrams as contaminants. The rudra tree will fight the Conclave's merging."

"So, the Architects' Disc *is* Nakshar?"

"The Disc and the council chambers," Airav corrected. "Only until we've merged. Retracting these plants leaves us temporarily vulnerable, but it is necessary. The other ashrams are doing the same thing to some degree, even if they don't form the heart of this model. Conclaves are no easy constructions, Ahilya-ve; there is a reason they are called only in times of true need." Airav shook his head. "*We* called the Conclave, so *we* must form its heart. It is tradition, but there is great architectural effort required to do it accurately and we are already weak."

Chaiyya turned back to her screen, a tight smile on her round face. "Considering how perilous our situation is, perhaps you will re-evaluate speaking your theories at the Conclave."

Ahilya stared at her. "I took a veristem test, Chaiyya. They are not theories, they are facts. Besides, the healbranch oath I took as a councilor allows for it. I have the right to speak to our sisters."

"A right, yes—but not one exercised by tradition. Only the lead councilor speaks at the Conclave. Each ashram provides a united front. By speaking of all this, without the rest of us seconding it, you will show our sister ashrams how divided we are. Nakshar will lose its authority in front of the others."

"We don't *have* to be divided," Ahilya said. "You could agree with my position. You could support my ideas."

"Your ideas endanger all architects, especially now when we're already defenceless."

"No. They endanger this way of life. Why don't you see, Chaiyya, that stopping the earthrages and releasing the architects into Ecstasy is the only way to survive?"

"That is not what our wisdom tells us," Chaiyya snapped. "None of our lore or history, none of our evidence, none of our theories or principles speak of this. Our lives are in the sky—this is where survival is. As for Ecstasy—you are no architect. You don't know how dangerous it is. Ecstasy is to be condemned, not celebrated."

Ahilya's stomach tightened. Once, Iravan had said the same things. All architects had been brought up to believe this. He had changed his mind after the events in the habitat, but even so it had taken first-hand experience. All Chaiyya had was Ahilya's word.

"Yeikshar is in position," Airav said quietly. "Lakshar and Renshar are approaching, as are the Three Southern Sisters."

On the floating hologram map, a flat ashram with a netted dome flickered and stabilized, waiting by one of the nodes of Nakshar's open petals.

Ahilya took a deep breath trying to calm herself. "I've told you before," she said evenly to Chaiyya. "What I saw in the jungle, what I experienced—"

"That *you* ended the earthrage?"

"Iravan and I both did. Together."

"You're delu—"

"I'm not delusional," Ahilya snapped. "I saw the histories that have been buried, the truth that has been forgotten. Architects once knew that Ecstasy was their true state. They chose to fly to the skies, to continue perpetuating the earthrages, rather than believe that they caused the rages in the first place. They did it for power and control. Your entire history is a fabrication. Our lives in the skies are built on a lie, Chaiyya, and that lie is going to cause our downfall. It is going to break our survival."

"It is not those *lies* I see as the cause, Ahilya, it is your stubbornness to share what you saw. Look at what has already happened. You blurted out these things to all of Nakshar, and now half the Maze Architects refuse to show up for their duty, afraid of becoming Ecstatics. The other half who do show up *want* to be Ecstatics—and we can't afford for them to lose touch with reality and destroy the ashram. Even though we've successfully taken off from the jungle, I dare not release permissions of trajection beyond the rudra tree to enable common citizens to mold the architecture to their desires—not when their desires are so convoluted. Our entire survival was based on the fact that we could use the desires of the citizens to augment the trajection of the architects. But if both architects and non-architects are confused about their roles now, where does that leave survival? Where does that leave safety?"

Another silence grew, this one harder. The other councilors exchanged guarded looks. Between her brows, Ahilya received a sudden glimpse of her husband when they had been in the vortex together. She had held him. She had poured her strength into him. Pain lanced through her, shaking her knees. Her palms grew sweaty at the memory of the cosmic creature attacking her. Her being had ripped apart into tiny pieces, but she had held, *rages*, she had held. Why did her will suffer now, when it was imperative she hold her stance? Chaiyya's words made all too much sense. Ahilya had spoken of her experience to provide the Ecstatic architects with a reprieve, but she had created several unintended consequences.

"Seventeen of fifty ashrams are in position," Airav called out. "The Seven Western Sisters are approaching."

More ashrams appeared on the map, waiting by Nakshar's nodes—ashrams shaped like round leafy nests, some in the form of misshapen boulders, others like tulips with bark petals open to the skies. Those that hovered above Nakshar were already beginning to form elevators, while those alongside created bridges. All of them were smaller than Nakshar—a construction Ahilya knew was necessary so the sister cities could dock with her own ashram. What did the citizens inside these other cities think of this accommodation they needed to make for Nakshar's call to the Conclave?

"Chaiyya, please," Ahilya said quietly. "If the earthrages are back, it means that even though we closed the rift, it did nothing to dissuade the cosmic beings from splitting. It could get much worse. Those Ecstatics in the deathcages, we need to send them to the habitat I found, to allow them to unite with their yakshas safely so we can end the earthrages."

"Is this the habitat you cannot show us?" Chaiyya countered. "Where is this magical place? Why haven't we seen it?"

Ahilya clenched her teeth, knowing she was losing the argument. During the lull, she had directed the sungineering probes to the habitat in the jungle, the very habitat where Iravan now lived, but they had failed to retrieve any images. That was not surprising— sungineering equipment had been unable to pierce the habitat before. But where in rages was Iravan? Why hadn't he appeared to corroborate her? He had said his plan was to release Ecstatics safely and tell the ashrams of the truth behind the earthrages. He should be here, doing exactly that. Ahilya's revelation had kept the Ecstatics from being excised—but she did not know how much longer she could do it, not without him.

"The Seven Western Sisters are in position," Airav rumbled. "Nilenshar, Auresh, and Katresh approaching from the Northern Sisters."

Nearly all the nodes at Nakshar's map had ashrams waiting by them. The Conclave bobbed, waiting to be merged, a massive collection of plant-made cities floating in the sky to become one united entity.

Chaiyya turned away. "You'll only embarrass yourself at the Conclave if you tell them all this."

"You're scared," Ahilya said softly. "I can understand that, but—"

"You will do irreparable damage, not just to architects but to your own kind. Nakshar was one of the first ashrams to induct non-architects in its council, Ahilya. There are ashrams out there, many you will meet now, who have none on their councils. If you shout about these stories from the jungle, you'll only convince them that non-architects cannot be taken seriously. That they don't belong on the council." Chaiyya's round face hardened. "You will regress us even further. You have no idea what you're doing."

"Nilenshar and the others are in position. The last of the sisters approaching now."

Ahilya frowned at Chaiyya's back. The Senior Architect had a point. Ahilya knew her own reception at the Conclave would be nothing more than indulgent. What consequences would it have for others who would come after her? The child flashed in her mind, the one she had seen in the lower tiers of the rudra tree, hidden in darkness.

In the council chambers, the rudra tree groaned. Golden sunlight fell in wider shafts combining with Chaiyya's blue-green trajectory and the pale holograms floating in front of the sungineers. On the map, the sister ashrams slowly drifted closer to Nakshar.

"Everyone is in position," Airav called out. "Communicating boundaries now."

Nearly fifty ashrams surrounded Nakshar, blinking on the map, each of their shapes unique and beautiful. Each ashram was slightly different, some stony, some covered with vines, others in bark and thorns, each of them favoring their own safest construction. In the Moment, the Conclave undoubtedly appeared like a maze of supreme complexity with a billion constellation lines attempting to intersect as architects of all the ashrams coordinated with each other. Nakshar hovered in the center as the nucleus, its nodes open and inviting.

Kiana and Laksiya murmured to each other. Ahilya laid a gentle hand on Chaiyya. The woman glanced at her, startled.

"Chaiyya, you know the Conclave will believe me once I retake a veristem test," Ahilya said softly. "Rumors will spread from our citizens to theirs about everything Nakshar knows. Isn't it more important that you side with me and we create a plan together for our futures? A future where your daughters can be safe?" A weary note entered Ahilya's voice, and there was nothing she could do to stop it. "This is the reason the Conclave is gathering—to assess if we can continue living in the skies. To study alternate methods to trajection and survival. To discuss why trajection has become harder. I *know* why trajection has become harder, why it has *always* been becoming harder. I have an alternate method of survival. My news is pertinent."

"You are new, Ahilya. There is so much you don't understand. You can't brazenly walk into the Conclave and tell traditionalist architects that non-architects are *complete* and can save them and have some hidden power to end the earthrages, even if you use veristem—especially if you use veristem. Nakshar might use the plant for many things, but several ashrams don't even countenance its *mention* for truth-telling; architects argue about its use constantly in academic circles. You'll antagonize them by trying to turn their own invention against them. You'll anger them if you so much as imply they've been subduing non-architects let alone announce they once caused earthrages themselves. Half the Conclave will wonder why you're on Nakshar's council at all. The rest will treat you as a joke. And *all of them* will want to know why you're not more grateful to architects for your own survival in the skies than you appear to be."

"Then, teach me to navigate this. Ally with me. Your plan is to pretend the things I learned in the jungle never happened, but we ought to be working toge—"

"What's that?" Airav's voice rang out sharp.

Ahilya and Chaiyya turned to look at him. Airav pointed at his bio-node and through the magnifiers, Ahilya noticed a flying object come straight for them.

"Looks like another ashram," Chaiyya said.

"It can't be." Ahilya frowned. "It's moving too fast."

"And all the sisters are here already," Airav said.

They continued to watch as the object flew in closer, faster. It was like no ashram Ahilya had ever seen. Subtle webs of gossamer surrounded the object, waving in and out like mist. If it weren't green, Ahilya would have thought it was a cloud, heading toward Nakshar.

In the tense silence, the locket in Ahilya's pocket began chiming.

She pulled it out slowly, her heart beating fast, even as the rest of them turned to look at her. The sungineering tracker muffled in her cradled hands, but on its glassy screen—clear for everyone to see—blinked a bright red dot, approaching ever closer.

Laksiya pursed her lips. Airav's eyes went wide. He looked from Ahilya's tracker to the misty green cloud.

"Iravan," Kiana said quietly. "He is returning."

"How?" Chaiyya's voice was sharp.

"The falcon-yaksha," Airav said, slightly panicked. "It has to be. We are vulnerable to its attack again—all the ashrams, the entire Conclave! Our defenses are down. We haven't established boundaries or merged fully yet."

The council chamber broke out in flustered cries. Chaiyya's skin began to glow iridescently. Through one of her bracelets, the Senior Architect barked out terse instructions, to the Disc and other architects on standby. Airav's hands flew over the holograms, enlarging the image of Nakshar's architecture. Laksiya hurried over to assist him.

Ahilya looked up to meet Kiana's gaze, but the woman's face was still, calculation in her gray eyes. The concerns of the architects were surely important, but for all the flurry of sudden activity, Kiana had never truly believed Iravan capable of hurting the ashram he loved, even if he was an Ecstatic now. That was the one thing she and Ahilya had agreed on when they had assessed the risk of Iravan's return in whispered conversations.

No, Kiana's look was for something else, something the others had not thought of yet.

Usage of Ecstatic energy had not begun yet, not because there were no Ecstatics but because the councilors were undecided on the wisdom of using the energex on people, especially since Ahilya had let out her news. Everyone had counted on finding yakshas to harness, but they had found none, despite Ahilya's archeological endeavors in the jungle.

Now Iravan was returning, bringing a yaksha back—the one thing they needed that they did not have. The one thing that could delay all their troubles.

Ahilya stared at Kiana, her heart turning cold in her chest.

4

IRAVAN

They flew through the open skies, heading for Nakshar.

Droplets of rain slashed at Iravan like incessant tiny knives. He was drenched, the cold soaking into his bones. He could have trajected a cover to protect himself against the elements, but a raw excitement seized him to be so free. He was returning. The ambiguity of the last few months had been torture. Now finally, for better or for worse, he had decided, and the falcon had not shown displeasure at leaving the jungle. Iravan laughed in relief for the first time in months.

He had thought to change his appearance to match the civility of the ashrams, but when he'd attempted to trim his beard using a bark blade, it had only resulted in jagged unkempt cuts. He had tied his hair with twine before leaving, but already it was a windblown mess. His clothes were all living plants, made of vines and moss and soft bark. Had he used normal trajection, Iravan would have had to maintain constellation lines to keep this living costume intact, but he had changed the nature of those plants with Ecstasy, converting their stars in the Moment to form his attire.

Now, instead of rudra beads, he wore bracelets and a belt made of carefully cultivated seeds. Instead of the translucent robes of the architects, a heavy cloak billowed out behind him, fashioned out of silvery-gray yaksha feathers. He knew what the effect would be, wild and frightening, as if he were a creature of the untamed jungle. Did they even know he was alive? Would they be surprised? It didn't matter. He was no longer a respectable member of society. He was an Ecstatic. At least this way, he looked the part.

The feather cloak blew around Iravan as he leaned low over the yaksha. The falcon, relishing the rhythms of flight, streaked swiftly through the sky. Iravan whooped as his belly dropped and the falcon climbed into the air. In the Deepness, the creature's exhilaration mirrored his own. The Resonance danced in his second vision, and his own giddiness reverberated back at him. He and the particle zoomed around each other nervously, playfully, for once feeling the same emotion: freedom.

Iravan nudged the yaksha with his knees and shifted his weight. The creature swung eastward. For now, it followed his instruction, but there was no telling when it would change its mind. Their communication was far from perfect. The falcon was Iravan's only method of arriving at Nakshar—no matter his Ecstasy, he could not fly alone, not without a core tree.

His heart skipped a beat. In his mind's eye, the falcon dove down into Nakshar, manic in its rage and pursuit of him. Bodies fell out of the sky, and Nakshar split into two, a part plummeting into the jungle. All that had happened only two… three months ago. Iravan had once held goodwill in the ashram. Would anyone remember that when he arrived with the creature that had attacked Nakshar? His plan was simple: to take the Ecstatic architects away with their families, back to the habitat, so he could train them to stop the earthrages. Somehow, he doubted it would be simple in its execution.

The people in the ashram knew Ecstasy was a different energy signature to normal trajection. If they were monitoring Ecstatic energy—and Iravan would have advised that as a Senior Architect—all his planned stealth now would mean nothing. Moreover, Ahilya had already told Iravan how she had suggested the ashrams look for a way to harness Ecstasy from the yakshas. He was likely flying into a trap, one he and his yaksha might not escape. His grip tightened on the falcon; he made himself release the feathers and pat the creature.

Between his brows, the Etherium sharpened. Once again, he saw a dozen, no, a hundred architects fallen to their knees, screaming. The image changed, the same architects waited trapped in deathcages. This, *this* was why he was taking such risks. The Etherium had shown him many things, but none of the visions had led him astray yet. He had to trust it.

The yaksha changed direction again, looping in a wide circle. There in the far distance, like a minuscule rock bobbing in the sky, was Nakshar.

Iravan entered the Moment.

Immediately, he was surrounded by infinite stars, each frozen, each containing the possibility of a life. He zipped through the universe, searching for Nakshar's maze.

When he came upon it, a grief so sudden, so strong, seized him that, for an instant, Iravan couldn't breathe. This had been his home once. He'd had a life here, a family, friends, a wife. He had wanted children here.

Nakshar's maze sparkled at him, a thousand constellation lines crisscrossing each other, replicating the design of the ashram as it appeared in the sky. Undoubtedly, Maze Architects were patrolling the design, creating and repairing constellation lines constantly. Iravan hovered far from them, so he would not be detected, but he could still see the rudra tree's stars, overbright and large. A dozen other stars were connected to the rudra, core trees of other assembled ashrams, Reikshar's bael, Katresh's neem, Auresh's peepal. The Conclave had already assembled, though the architects had not yet defined its boundaries. He had counted on that; it would allow him to enter Nakshar without having to meddle with the permissions of the core trees.

The yaksha completed its circuit and headed toward the Conclave again.

In Iravan's first vision, the structure became bigger—a gargantuan collection of fifty ashrams. Nakshar hovered in the center like a great sun, and ashrams closed in from all directions, some flat, others shaped like flowers and nests and boulders. Yeikshar had chosen a bark-domed design, Katresh a wild maze that connected first to its Northern sisters before moving gently toward Nakshar. The construction was complex. Within the Moment, the Maze Architects had tied and tightened a billion lines, one star to another in knots and loops carefully created to allow for boundary flexibility.

This was no single construction. It was the lives of a thousand, a hundred thousand people. The Senior Architects of Nakshar had chosen an archaic design, one that Iravan could tell even from this distance had compromised the safety of its citizens. Merging was occurring even while Nakshar remained open to the elements in several directions, as though the councilors were trying to be subservient to the Conclave while still maintaining their dignity and sovereignty. He would never have countenanced it, if he had been, if he still were—

I am, he thought furiously. *I am* still *a Senior Architect and a councilor of Nakshar. I am not dead yet. I am not excised.*

He could not afford to discount himself, not when his entire purpose was to approach the Conclave and make outrageous demands.

The ashrams bobbed, growing bigger the closer he came. A yearning seized him, a tug on his heart. Iravan leaned forward on the falcon, half-standing so he might get a better view.

There had never been a full Conclave like this when he had lived in Nakshar. At most, Nakshar had traded with its closest sister ashrams, Reikshar and Kinshar or one of the others. A full meeting, with all the councilors—he could remember it occurring only once, when he had been a Junior Architect of Yeikshar, before he had emigrated to Nakshar. It had been a time of youthful friendships and dalliances with foreign architects, of laughter and song and daredevilry when the problems of survival had belonged to his betters, not him.

Under him, the falcon cried out, a high-pitched blood-curdling yarp. Iravan darted in the Moment, toward the stars of the seeds he had looped around his wrists and waist.

Constellation lines whipped out of him in the universe, and he knit them around the stars, twisting and darting, tossing lines then sinking them into intricate knots within seconds. Thousands of hair-thin filaments, green and shiny, emerged from the seeds on his belt, reacting to his trajectory. The filaments extended around and above them, connecting to each other like a web of green. Gloom surrounded Iravan and the falcon instantly. Blue-green light from his own trajection reflected off the silvery feathers of the yaksha. Sunlight streamed into this little misty nest he had trajected, but it was diffuse, like they were within a green-webbed storm cloud.

Iravan sensed amusement from the falcon. They had practiced this trajection before, but the falcon had dissolved it in minutes, boredom overtaking it. Iravan sent a fervent wish to the silence at the back of his mind where the creature had taken residence. *Not today. Let us land safely today. We need to avoid detection.* There was no answer, just the yaksha's brooding silence.

Through the web, Iravan glimpsed the Conclave closer. He had already identified a landing area, a large terrace courtyard within Nakshar, open to the skies yet secluded from the main ashram by tall trees. No dust motes of architects seemed to be patrolling it, but that was not strange. Nakshar had been having troubles with patrolling even when he had lived there. Besides, the Disc had to be busy creating its boundaries for the Conclave.

Even so, the courtyard looked too perfect for his needs. Very carefully, keeping an eye out for wandering dust motes of architects, Iravan began trajecting Nakshar's stars.

The falcon circled lower, approaching the courtyard. Within the misty nest, its wings flapped a few times. Then, finding its position, it began to descend. The trees within the courtyard grew a touch taller, their canopy bushier. Iravan could barely see this change through the mist of his cloud, but his constellation lines on Nakshar had connected. Trajection would render his design on the foliage. He and the falcon swooped silently below into the courtyard, minutes from touching down—

In the Moment, Iravan paused, glancing around him.

Something wasn't right.

Stars twinkled, thousands of them, but as the yaksha dropped the last few feet onto the courtyard and ruffled its feathers, the universe blinked. The stars in the far background disappeared. Iravan spun, confused. He couldn't feel the rudra tree anymore. Had the yaksha taken control? Was it affecting things from the Deepness? But no, when he darted into the Deepness to check, the Resonance fluttered at him curiously, no stream of light emerging from it toward the Moment.

It hit him like a slap.

In his first vision, past the misty green webbed cloud of his own design, Iravan glimpsed golden shimmers rising from the ground.

Deathchamber.

Someone had activated it, and given that he had seen no patrolling architects, the activation had occurred remotely. He had entered its bounds already. Deathchambers formed a barrier around the Moment, creating a separate pocket Moment. That was why the stars had blinked out, all save the ones of the grass he had landed on and the seeds he carried. Only plants that had been trapped with him in the deathchamber were visible in this separate pocket Moment.

Right. He had anticipated something like this.

Iravan clutched the falcon-yaksha at its neck, and pulled at the feathers in a painful grip, directing the creature to fly. A deathchamber had no physical boundaries. They could still leave.

The falcon fluttered its wings, curious. It obeyed—but even as they began to ascend, Iravan noticed his own unshaven face staring back at him past his misty green nest. *Glass*, he was looking at glass, he heard a *whisk—*

This was no ordinary deathchamber. This was a death*cage*, where ashrams imprisoned an Ecstatic architect to await excision.

The falcon ascended a few feet and its wing tips touched the confines of the deathcage. Glass—thick heavy glass—surrounded them in all directions. The yaksha shook its feathers, and settled back down to the ground.

No, Iravan thought, horrified. They couldn't be captured.

Deathcages worked on stone. They could not be created on grass; to have plants as their base negated their entire purpose. How had the sungineers done this? Why hadn't the Etherium warned him of it? Foolish, foolish, to rely so much on a strange third vision. He had not seen himself and the yaksha trapped within a cage. He had assumed he was safe.

He dove back into the Moment and slashed at his constellation lines. His misty nest disintegrated, even as the falcon settled itself.

With the obstruction of the mist gone, he saw what he hadn't before: Maze Architects stepping forward from behind the trees. Comprehension burst within him. They *had* been patrolling, but not in the second vision like he'd expected. They'd done it simply by physically being here. He had relied too much on his power.

They approached carefully, a dozen of them dressed in their brown kurta and trouser uniforms, their translucent robes pushed back over their rudra beads. Their skins began to glow iridescent, patterns of vines and creepers glittering.

Iravan stared at the Maze Architects. Gaurav and Megha, Karn and Viana, his colleagues, his friends, his students. Gaurav bit his lip, his eyes wide. Megha clenched her jaw, one finger poised over her rudra bead bracelet. She and Gaurav were the seniormost here, Iravan could tell at a glance, though from the looks of it, Megha had activated the deathcage. The woman shifted on her feet, her lips pursed. Iravan imagined what he must look like, a wild creature from the jungle, sitting atop a massive falcon-yaksha, glaring down at them through the confines of a glass deathcage.

"What are you doing here with that beast, Iravan-ve?" Gaurav called out, a quiver in his voice.

"What am *I* doing? What in rages are you doing? Release me, at once."

"I… we can't do that."

Iravan frowned. "I am still a Senior Architect of Nakshar, Gaurav. Don't test me."

Gaurav glanced at the other Maze Architects. "Technically, that's true. He is still part of the council."

"Don't be an idiot," Megha snapped. She raised her arms in front of her, blue-green tattoos vivid on her dark skin. "We're following Chaiyya-ve's orders, and he is—"

Iravan didn't wait for her to finish.

Anger flared in him, hot and molten. He dove back into the velvety darkness of the Deepness, and the Resonance perked as it recognized his emotion.

How dare they try to trap him? They could not contain him. Bharavi had supertrajected through a deathchamber during his Examination of Ecstasy; she had trajected Ecstatically past multiple layers of deathchambers and a deathcage when she'd been trapped in one. She was untrained. He was not.

You have no idea what I am, he thought, his fists clenching over the falcon's feathers.

In the Deepness, Iravan summoned the Moment—the *entire* Moment—and the globule appeared. The deathcage may have cut off access to the universe, allowing him only a pocket Moment, but it could not affect the Deepness.

He shot a thin ray of light into the globule. Beyond the glass deathcage, the trees began to shudder. Branches broke off from the trees, then sharpened into spears and jagged arrows. He aimed them toward the glass to crack it, a hailstorm of blades rushing toward himself and the yaksha.

Several architects screamed and ducked, covering their heads. Tentacle-like roots whipped up, pushing the earth, slamming against the deathcage, responding to Iravan's Ecstasy.

The glass was strong, he *knew* how strong, but it could not hold a non-stop barrage. Iravan would use as much force as he needed. He would not be trapped. He would not be excised. In the Deepness, the Resonance fluttered around him, watching, its mirrored surface thoughtful and considering.

Then, a jet of silvery light flowed from it into the Moment, joining Iravan's own Ecstatic trajection.

The ground shook under them. Wind churned, and leaves stripped off branches. The Resonance had seen Iravan's trajection;

it had understood he wanted to be released, and it was helping. Dust flew everywhere, as the architecture of Nakshar changed.

The yaksha was trajecting the entire ashram. It would traject the core tree.

"*NO*," Iravan bellowed, whirling to the fluttering Resonance. Rage everything, he was trying to be careful, but the yaksha would not bother with subtlety. The creature would destroy Nakshar, perhaps the entire Conclave, in its brutish attempt at *helping* him. Iravan gritted his teeth. In his first vision, his nails sunk into the falcon's feathers. "No, damn it, *NO*. Leave this to me."

The Resonance stilled in the Deepness.

In their first vision, the yaksha tilted its head.

The churning of the courtyard stopped.

Maze Architects rose to their feet, their faces scared, as they looked around at the damage. Their skin lit up again as they entered the Moment, and Iravan knew they could see broken constellation lines littering Nakshar, perhaps other parts of the Conclave too.

Gaurav stared at him in shock. An angry buzz began among the collected architects. They did not know it was the falcon that had done this, they did not understand its powers. Rages, *Iravan* barely understood the creature, and it was a part of him. The Resonance fluttered in his second vision, curious and waiting.

Iravan took a deep breath. He had no idea how the falcon would interpret his desires, but it was too dangerous to find out, and he could not stay behind the glass.

"You have to let this barrier down, Gaurav," he said quietly. "Before it gets worse. Please."

Gaurav glanced at Megha, and took a step forward.

She pushed the Maze Architect away. "Enough," she said and crouched to the ground.

The other architects moved in unison, arranging themselves. Maze Architects surrounded Iravan from all sides, their hands reaching into the broken earth. Whatever they were doing, they had trained for this.

Thin layers of glass began to rise where the architects touched the earth. Each pane was separate, unconnected to the other, but there were a hundred panes rising, higher and higher, taller than the deathcage, the architects standing between them. A forest of fragile-looking glass grew over the courtyard, open to the skies yet refracting sunlight, throwing rainbow colors out where the blue-green light from the architects touched it.

The Deepness shrank.

The velvety darkness constricted.

Iravan felt true terror.

He raced through the darkness of the Deepness, but for the first time ever, his dust mote came up against a barrier. He summoned the Moment, yet instead of the globule, a shard appeared, jagged and broken. He had no more access to the rest of Nakshar, or the Conclave, or—horror hammered in him—the jungle. He could affect nothing but this shard Moment containing the plants within the glass labyrinth. Neither from the Deepness, nor from the Moment.

Sweat drenched his skin. "What did you do?" he said softly.

"We call it a deathmaze." Megha stood up and brushed the grass off her clothes. "An enhancement of the deathcage by the sungineers. It's supposed to stop the movement of Energy X from Ecstatic architects. Did you really think, Iravan-ve, that we would not be prepared? That creature killed half of Nakshar."

They had managed it, so quickly. How? Where had they found the resources? The deathmaze was a true maze, its glass panes arranged puzzle-like, with multiple dead ends and perhaps only one path that led to his cage at the center.

Iravan flew through the pocket Deepness, claustrophobia building in him. He should never have come here. Bharavi had shown them that she could traject through a deathchamber—of course they had prepared. The sungineers must have designed this... this *deathmaze* as a priority. It's what he himself would have suggested had he been on the council.

"We don't want to harm you, Iravan-ve, but—"

The falcon uttered a chilling cry and slammed against the glass cage.

In the pocket Deepness, the Resonance shot out a complex ray toward the Moment shard.

Megha's arms dropped to her side. Her mouth went slack. Her eyes darted around in horror. She dropped to her knees, shuddering, a silent scream emerging from her. More architects dropped to their knees on the courtyard, their bodies seizing, writhing.

"NO!" Iravan screamed.

The falcon was trajecting them.

Within this deathmaze, he and the yaksha could only affect the stars of living things trapped with them, but those living things included the architects. Had the sungineers not thought of that? Iravan would never have dared to touch the architects—the thought made him nauseous—but the falcon had no such scruples.

Iravan crashed into the Resonance with all his strength, and the particle spun around to face him, abandoning its supertrajection for an instant. On its mercurial surface, Iravan detected a cold intention. He could almost hear its thoughts—it would be so *easy* to remove these people who would trap them, to destroy them, kill them—

Iravan aimed for the Resonance again, but it spun away. An angry burst of lights released from it, all aimed toward the Moment shard.

The falcon smashed against the cage. The glass rattled ominously, but it held. Architects raced over the courtyard, activating more panes. Glass whisked up from the earth, and the pocket Deepness shrank further, just a dark room with a tiny shard of the Moment hovering within it, imprisoning, nauseating. The falcon darted its head, rings around its eyes, and men and women fell to their knees, screaming, as grass within the deathmaze grew harder, tripping them, trapping them.

For fuck's sake! Iravan thought furiously. *Stop! Let me handle this!* He dashed in his second vision through the pocket Deepness. He rammed into the Resonance again and again, but it slipped at the last second each time, mercurial, too fast. Silence built in the back of his mind, fury and storm, mingling with the yaksha's agony at being ignored and unheard for a thousand years, the rage overwhelming—

In desperation, Iravan focussed on the Etherium, and it sharpened, an image of Megha and Gaurav and all these Maze Architects lying on their backs dead, while Iravan and the falcon flew through lightning and thunder, high above the Conclave. He glimpsed the face of the earthrage in his third vision, screaming through the rain. What was the Etherium showing him? What was the falcon doing?

"Iravan-ve," Gaurav screamed. Past the flurry of feathers and the roiling earth, the man held onto Megha, helping her up. "Stop what you're doing, Iravan-ve. I'm warning you!"

"You stop what you're doing," Iravan screamed back, still jostled by the yaksha. "You're enraging my falcon."

He could see in the Etherium, how much worse it was going to get. The face of the earthrage screamed at him, lightning strikes for eyes, a jagged mouth flecked with rain. Iravan saw himself and the yaksha facing the storm, minuscule compared to its size. He blinked and the Etherium receded, raging between his brows.

Soil ruptured outside the cage, flinging up chunks. Maze Architects screamed, their skins glowing. This could not go on for much longer. Someone would get hurt, most likely the architects. The yaksha smashed against the glass again and again. Iravan held tight, slipping as a flurry of silvery feathers blocked his first vision. Roots and vines ripped from the ground, trajected Ecstatically by the falcon. The creature was half-insane. It wouldn't stop. He had no control over it.

"For the love of Nakshar," Iravan yelled. "Let me out of here!"

The architects screamed back, defiance and rebellion.

It was going to hell too quickly.

Then through the clamor, a woman's voice rang out. "Maze Architects, stand down! On my authority!"

Ahilya.

That was Ahilya.

Perhaps it was Iravan's realization the yaksha responded to. As soon as Ahilya's face appeared in his mind, the Resonance stopped Ecstatically trajecting. It spun away, to a corner of the dark pocket Deepness, watching him from the other side sullenly.

Under Iravan, the yaksha stilled. It ruffled its feathers, and Iravan leapt down from it. His legs shook so hard it was all he could do to remain standing. He let his Two Visions collapse. The images in the third vision of the Etherium muted to a dull buzz.

Dust settled beyond the cage. Foliage floated, torn from the earth, then was carried away by the breeze. Reflected a dozen times over on the still-erect glass panes, Iravan saw the councilors of Nakshar standing by the copse of trees. His eyes met Ahilya's.

She was dressed more extravagantly than was her style. A white embroidered kurta flowed to her knees over tight narrow trousers. A green and golden scarf circled her neck loosely. Dark rudra bead necklaces spilled over the scarf and more beads dangled from her wrists. Ahilya's thick wavy hair rippled over her shoulders. His wife stared back at him, her big intelligent eyes considering him, a heavy sungineering locket clasped tightly in her hands.

How had she done it? Commanded the yaksha, when he himself could not? Commanded the architects, when he had no authority? Relief and admiration poured into him. He placed a palm on the cool glass, breathing hard to steady himself, drinking her in with his eyes. The ache he had embraced in her absence flared again, and he thought, *She's here, my tether, my sanity, she's here.* She would save him from himself and the falcon. She carried in her his possibility for fatherhood and salvation.

Chaiyya grabbed Ahilya's arm, muttering feverishly, but Ahilya shook her off, her gaze still on Iravan. Her voice rang out again. "I invoke my Right of First Contact. Will you deny me, Chaiyya?"

First Contact.

A slow smile grew on Iravan's face. *Clever, clever Ahilya.*

She was clearly a councilor of Nakshar now, if those rudra beads were any indication. She had learned of this archaic law.

The Right of First Contact had been created to emphasize the material bonds of architects. If ever an architect was accused of Ecstasy, it was the right of their spouse to speak to the Ecstatic architect first, before anyone else could. No one had used it in centuries; it had existed in a time when architects were only allowed to marry other architects, and they had thought to reverse Ecstasy.

The people around Ahilya froze. Several Maze Architects seemed confused, though Gaurav and Megha exchanged wary glances. Chaiyya looked like she had been struck.

Iravan's smile grew wider.

Everything hung in the balance.

Finally, Chaiyya raised her hand. The Maze Architects retreated. Several of them grabbed their friends, helping them out of the labyrinthine glass columns, stepping over wounded earth, some of them limping.

Beside Iravan, the falcon thrummed, a purr. Ahilya's eyes fixed on Iravan, an intense unblinking stare. He could almost hear her ask him not to do anything stupid.

Then, his wife broke the gaze and turned back to the others.

The councilors of Nakshar put their heads together, whispering.

5

AHILYA

Ahilya tried to focus on the councilors.

Sunlight ricocheted off the glass Iravan was trapped within, and she resisted the urge to look at him. He flickered in her mind, tall even though he stood next to the falcon, his almost black eyes glittering with intensity. Iravan had always been reckless, but the jungle seemed to have stripped away the leash he'd had on himself. Ahilya had only to study the ruptured earth of the courtyard, the limping architects, and the torn leaves to know this.

"You must be pleased, Kiana," she observed dryly. "The deathmaze is a solid invention. It holds even with all this chaos. None of the glass has shattered."

The Senior Sungineer blinked behind her spectacles. "I'm not sure what you're implying. That glass is the strongest material in Nakshar, and all of Nakshar has been primed to release deathmazes at the command of the council."

"The council?" Ahilya laughed coldly. "I think you mean the sungineers and the architects. You have prepared for this. In ways I was not told."

"As have you," Chaiyya cut in, her voice hard. "Who told you about the Right of First Contact?"

"Not everything is a part of *privileged* architect records," Ahilya shot back.

When Chaiyya had denied her access to the architects' archives, Ahilya had gone hunting for information in her old archeological records. She had requested Reikshar for their citizen chronicles, gleaned information from disparate accounts, detected hints and suggestions for any laws and history that might help her. Hidden among treatises exalting architects, she had finally found mentions of the Right of First Contact. If she weren't an archeologist practiced in reading between the lines, she would not have known what she was seeing. As it was, she did not know how accurate her understanding was. The Maze Architects had stood down at Chaiyya's gesture. Not at her own command.

"What do you intend to do with him?" Laksiya asked. The other Senior Sungineer was a tall slender woman, with gray-brown hair and narrow, calculating eyes. "We have a clear protocol in case of another yaksha attack."

"To attempt to harness them for their energy?" Airav asked. His image hovered over Chaiyya's communication bracelet now, as he joined their discussion through the sungineering device. He had not rushed with them to the courtyard on Iravan's arrival. Instead, the Senior Architect had remained in the council chambers to oversee the establishment of boundaries and the merging of the Conclave.

"You do not know Iravan if you think he will allow you to touch his falcon," Ahilya said.

"Then we imprison him too," Laksiya retorted. "That is our protocol."

"Yes," Airav said. "But he is no ordinary Maze Architect awaiting excision. Until he is excised, he is still a Senior Architect."

"He is an Ecstatic," Laksiya said.

"He is my husband," Ahilya snapped. She turned to Chaiyya. "I've invoked my Right of First Contact. Are you going to deny me?"

The round-faced woman glanced around them. Ahilya knew what Chaiyya was thinking. First Contact was created to emphasize the importance of material bonds, the one thing architects always upheld. To deny that, in such a public gathering, would create shockwaves—especially now when Chaiyya fought so hard to maintain the old way, when architects themselves were unsure about their bonds. *Do it*, Ahilya silently dared. *Deny me my right to see my husband, and find out what happens to the ashram and your own plans.*

Chaiyya's glance fell on Ahilya. "Very well," she said softly.

Laksiya snorted. Kiana looked thoughtful, a small smile in her eyes. On the communication bracelet, Airav had fallen silent.

Ahilya turned back to Iravan. Reflected in the glass columns, he paced the deathcage, his feather cloak swishing behind him. Occasionally, he patted the falcon that had settled itself, its head tucked beneath a wing as though sleeping.

She took a step forward, but Chaiyya held up a hand.

"Not so fast," the Senior Architect said. "Remember, Ahilya. You are a member of the council now, not merely the wife of a would-be councilor. You'll need to connect your communication bracelet to us, so we can hear your conversation."

Would-be councilor. Regardless of what Airav had said, Chaiyya had not yet decided about Iravan's position. She could ask for a vote of no confidence at any instant.

Ahilya raised her arm where a bone-white bracelet glinted on her dark skin. Shortly after she had divulged the secrets of excision and the cosmic beings to the ashram, the council had directed her to wear one of those bracelets.

"You don't trust me," she said. "But I swore a healbranch vow as a councilor—to protect the council's secrets. Do you not trust that either? I'm pregnant. I am hardly going to break my vow and endanger myself or my child."

"Pregnancy didn't stop you from endangering yourself before," Chaiyya returned evenly. "You flew after Iravan to rescue him, remember? Besides, Ecstatics can traject higher beings. Look at what Iravan did to these Maze Architects. You could break your vow and suffer none of the consequences if Iravan healed you."

Violating a healbranch vow instantly poisoned the oathbreaker. Iravan had once done it; the memory flashed in Ahilya's mind, of his healbranch bracelet growing thorns to pierce his skin when he'd told her how excision rendered an architect senseless. But he had been an Ecstatic architect, capable of healing himself. Chaiyya was right—if Iravan trajected Ahilya, he could undo the harm of a broken healbranch vow. Still, the thought of being trajected set the bile rising in Ahilya's throat. Healing or not, she would never allow it.

"It will hardly be First Contact with the rest of you looking over my shoulder," she said.

"How do you intend to find your way through *that*?" Chaiyya asked, waving at the glass columns. "You need a sungineer or an architect to provide you instruction."

The glass maze glittered, reflecting the clustered Maze Architects, the councilors, the falcon, and—every now and then—a still-pacing Iravan. It did not look like her husband was trajecting anymore. His skin was as dark as it always had been, no tattoos forming on it.

Ahilya tore her gaze away from him. She could ask Chaiyya to give her a map, but the rest of the council was nodding along. They were not about to let her go in there alone, First Contact or not.

She nodded tightly and adjusted the scarf around her neck. Tapping at one of her rudra bead bracelets, she strode forward to the glass columns.

Under Kiana's instruction, Ahilya made her way through the deathmaze. Echoes of golden sunlight bounced off the panes. She turned a corner and began down a glassy corridor. Her own image surrounded her from a dozen angles, brown skin and worried eyes, and beyond those, the images of the waiting councilors and assembled Maze Architects. Feathers winked in the shape of a man. Sunlight sparkled, like a roaring falcon. Ahilya blinked and tried to concentrate on Kiana's instruction, winding her way.

Her sungineering locket had been a giveaway, of course. Had it not been for its chiming, perhaps Iravan would have been able to land in Nakshar discreetly, like he had when he'd returned her from the jungle. Now, because of her, he and the falcon faced terrible dangers.

Iravan did not know it yet, but he was imprisoned in no ordinary deathcage. The massive box could be connected to an experimental Ecstatic battery. The sungineers of Nakshar had known that even if Ahilya found a yaksha in the jungle there would be no way to transport such a massive creature to the ashram, let alone use the energex on it. They had enhanced the prototype battery that had once been used on Airav to create a new kind of battery, this one to store Ecstasy. Yet without being able to test it, the new Ecstatic battery remained experimental. If Iravan did not cooperate, the situation could get ugly quickly. She needed to navigate this carefully.

I told them about this, Ahilya thought, guilt clenching her belly. Nausea rose in her and she breathed deeply to contain the sensation. She could still remember it—nearly three months before, when she had bargained with the council. Iravan had been deliberately silent about sharing that information even with her, but she had disclosed to the council that yakshas could traject Ecstatically, that Dhruv had created the means to detect and use such trajection, that Energy X was Ecstatic energy.

Now, her husband was trapped in a cage of their own making.

Deep within the maze, the reflections in the mirrors glittered, silver and gray, a massive eye, a whisper of feathers, the skin of a tall dark man. She reached the end of the maze. Kiana's voice fell silent, the instructions complete.

Iravan stood next to his yaksha, resplendent in his green clothes. Her husband's head was tilted to the skies, baring his neck around which he'd hung necklaces of seeds in the approximation of rudra beads. He dropped his chin, his gaze meeting hers. She walked forward, so they were face to face separated only by the glass pane of the deathcage.

"Hello, Iravan," she murmured. "It has been a while, hasn't it?"

A smile cut his dark face, at this echo of the words he had said to her once. Iravan snorted and tapped the glass. "Is this any way to welcome your husband, my love?"

"You certainly know how to make an entrance."

"This wasn't my idea." His eyes searched hers. "You look good."

"As do you."

"Let me out of this," he said, tapping the glass again, "and I'll give you a closer view. Maybe even a kiss, my heart."

His tone was teasing but Ahilya bit her lip.

She was not lying. Iravan did look good. His almost-black skin shone with vitality and health. His salt-and-pepper hair had grown longer than she'd ever seen, and he sported a beard now. The glass prevented her from smelling him, but she could imagine his scent, eucalyptus and firemint. Were they his scents anymore, when he no longer belonged to the ashram? What jungle plants had replaced those in the last few months? She had parted in love with him, but what had life been like for him in the jungle all alone? There was so much about him that had changed since his Ecstasy, so much she could no longer rely on.

Iravan leaned forward and his face grew serious. "Ahilya, what is going on?"

She fingered her communication bracelet. The others were listening to every word. How was she to answer this question? Iravan's secrets as a councilor had once nearly destroyed their marriage. She did not want hers to do the same. The bracelet twirled around her wrist over and over again.

Iravan's eyes followed the movement. He sighed. "You can't tell me, can you?"

"Not everything."

"No, of course not. I'm not speaking merely to my wife. I'm speaking to the rest of Nakshar's council. You're here as their spokesperson."

"I can't confirm that."

"You don't have to," he said, beginning to pace again. "I know their ways. So. Since your rudra beads are still working, and those Maze Architects could still traject from between the glass columns, I take it that this *deathmaze* only contracts the Deepness. But not the Moment proper itself? Clever. How did the sungineers design it, if they don't know of the Deepness? Another lucky accident by Dhruv?"

She followed him with her eyes. *They know of the Deepness*, she thought. *I told them that.* She had needed to, in order to convince everyone that Ecstasy was not a dangerous unknown power, but the natural state of all architects.

"It was not an accident," Ahilya said. "They combined the existing technology from tiered deathboxes with the fortification of solid glass. That became the deathmaze."

"They were able to test it? Without an Ecstatic architect?" Iravan glanced at her. "Or perhaps you have more Ecstatics in Nakshar now."

Ahilya pursed her lips. Nakshar did have four trapped Ecstatics in its sanctum, but she could not tell him that, not unless he was confirmed as a councilor of Nakshar, a decision the others had not made yet. She had already said too much.

"Iravan," she said instead. "This cage, it's dangerous for you and the falcon."

"I know that already."

"No—you don't understand—"

Ahilya cut herself off.

Iravan stopped pacing and frowned at her.

Ahilya blinked. *Did* he understand? He could not know about the Ecstatic battery that Kiana and Laksiya and the other sungineers were experimenting with, but he knew about the battery Ahilya had forced Airav to use. He knew Dhruv had accidentally created technology that used and detected Energy X. Iravan had pushed for the battery himself. Perhaps he understood more than she was crediting him with.

"You need to let us out," he said. "Something isn't right." Again, he gazed toward the sky, his brows furrowing.

"You must surely understand why the council fears you? Why Nakshar fears the yaksha?"

"I'm not here for the council. My business here is with the Ecstatics. To take them away to the jungle with me."

Ahilya kept her face still. She knew, as well as he did, that their conversation was a performance for the council. Each word they spoke would be weighed and analyzed.

Yet, she could not help the stab of hurt that went through her at his words. He was here for the Ecstatics. Not for her. Nor for their child that she carried. It was too early to show, but did he even remember she was pregnant? Did he care? Her stomach spasmed as it so often did, and she buried the horror of the physical pain she felt. In her mind's eye, she leapt after Iravan. She heard him say, *Ahilya, you don't know what that vortex did to you!* He had warned her that she would damage their child. Sudden tears burned the back of Ahilya's throat.

"Take them away," she repeated hoarsely. "You mean stop them from being excised?"

Iravan shivered. "Yes, but also to teach them to be properly Ecstatic. Do you remember those carvings we saw in the caves in the jungle?"

"A hard thing to forget," she replied.

Two months earlier, when they had closed the rift in the Moment while in the jungle, Iravan and Ahilya had seen the history of their peoples laid out in carvings on rock. The pain felt fresh, like a weight in her heart. So many architects had been excised, so many citizens deprived, all to keep the terrible secret that architects had once caused the earthrages themselves.

Behind the glass, Iravan nodded, a tight gesture.

"I've been thinking so much about those carvings," he said softly. "I stand by what I said. We were never meant to find trajection, we were only meant to find Ecstasy. It is our natural state, but for thousands of years we set arbitrary limits of trajection upon ourselves and now the path is twisted." Iravan's voice grew harder. "I remember my past lives, Ahilya. I saw my own history. When I had been Nidhirv, my husband and I lived in a time when Ecstasy was known and revered, even if I never reached it. Yet somewhere along those thousand years, Ecstasy was outlawed and maligned. Trajection became our only power, a deliberate trap so we'd never be tempted to put an end to earthrages. But it's not Ecstatics who are the real enemy. It's the rages and the cosmic beings."

Iravan's gaze flickered to where the other councilors waited and listened.

He might not know of the dangers of the Ecstatic battery, but he'd known what his welcome here would be like. Perhaps he understood that speaking this now corroborated everything Ahilya had herself told the council. Perhaps he understood the implications.

"So, you want to dismantle trajection," she said, practically hearing the question from Chaiyya. "You want to replace all architects with Ecstatics."

"That's a fool's errand," Iravan replied, catching the lead she was throwing him. "This world works on trajection. I know that. But as long as you have trajection, you will have architects becoming Ecstatics. I'm here to take *them* away. Ecstatic architects will have to unlearn the limits of trajection safely. If they don't, they could overextend themselves. Their veins might incinerate. They could lose themselves in their Two Visions while uniting with their yakshas. They could damage the architecture of the ashrams. Worst of all, they could try to traject a higher being. I want to take them away before they can do any of this, to train them in the safety of my Garden in the habitat."

Ahilya watched him, the determined set of his jaw. "You say it like these events are inevitable. But you did not go through them."

Iravan shook his head. "When I ascended to Ecstasy, I had Bharavi watching me. I had the forced break of the investigation—a time where I wasn't trajecting at all. But it was difficult despite that. These Ecstatic architects—ones hidden and scared within your ranks even now—they will have none of these limits. Even with vigilance, this is a risk. The ascension is quick once it starts." Iravan tapped at the glass cage again. "I haven't come to make trouble, Ahilya. I've come with a proposition. You don't want Ecstatics in the Conclave any more than I do. But there are architects here close to Ecstasy already. I saw this happen in the Etherium."

"The Etherium tells you the future now?"

"Among other things," he answered. His gaze returned to the sky, considering and confused. "There's a storm approaching."

Ahilya followed his gaze. Afternoon sunlight still shone in a cloudless sky. "Do you mean that literally?"

"Yes. I should be out there, examining it. You need to let me out of here."

She studied him as he craned his head back at the sunlit sky. He sounded so reasonable. He looked *so* in control of himself, despite his cryptic warnings and his tempestuous attire. If anything, the grass-woven kurta, the soft-bark trousers, and especially that feather-lined cloak, made him look majestic as he stood next to the gigantic falcon. But Ahilya detected a darkness in his eyes, one she had never seen before. It felt like loneliness and shame. It bled like regret.

They were having two conversations, one for the councilors, and one between themselves, but her next question Ahilya asked for herself. To know if he was still the man she loved, the man she had married.

"Iravan," she said, her heart beating fast. "Did you traject those Maze Architects?"

He froze. His dark eyes flickered to the falcon then back at her. "No," he said quietly. "I stopped it."

Relief broke over Ahilya, leaving her knees weak. She opened her mouth to ask another question, but Iravan shook his head imperceptibly. He didn't want to speak of it, not with the others listening. She'd have to wait to discuss this.

The falcon ruffled its feathers. It popped its head out from under its wing, and fixed Ahilya with its glinting eyes. She felt like she was being scrutinized by something far more intelligent than her, something terribly foreign. The falcon seemed to be looking past layers she did not know she contained. It was one of the most ancient creatures in the world, after all, a split half of one of the original cosmic beings, harbinger of one of the very first earthrages. How could Iravan be so nonchalant around it?

The creature grunted, then shook its feathers again. Its head darted to the sky, and it pecked at the glass cage, making it rattle.

Perhaps Iravan meant to cover this pause up, or perhaps he really wanted to know. His eyes traveled to Ahilya's waist and to her belly. "Ahilya, how are you and the—"

"Not now—"

"But—"

"Not now," she insisted.

Iravan grimaced, then rubbed a sheepish hand over his beard. "I've missed you," he said softly. "So very much."

He traced her jaw on the glass, and Ahilya met his eyes. *I've missed you too*, she wanted to say, but the words were caught in her throat. He had wanted to know about their baby. He had wanted her to stay with him back at the habitat.

She could not explain the hurt and anger that flowed through her now. Her husband had always wanted children, far more than she had, perhaps. Why was it that now, when they were finally pregnant, they were divided by this gulf of politics and necessity? Her stomach squirmed, and a dull pain throbbed in her feet. She was pregnant for the first time, and Iravan would not be there for her or their child. No, he would be busy saving the world. That had been his choice, *their* choice. Resentment shot through her, at their circumstances, at themselves. She could do or say nothing to express it. It would give

Chaiyya another thorn to wedge between herself and Iravan.

Her husband's expression grew withdrawn. He had seen the passage of emotions on her face. He opened his mouth, perhaps to respond, or to give her comfort or an apology, but Ahilya cut in before he could speak.

"This earthrage," she blurted. "Is it the same cosmic being?"

Iravan rubbed a hand over his beard again. "It's a new one. I've kept an eye on the other. That creature is still trapped in the rift. But the cosmic creatures are evolving, Ahilya. We need to end this earthrage before something terrible happens."

"The last time we had to use your power and my will combined."

"And the possibility of the green dust—everdust as I've named it." He moved a shoulder. "It would be the same equation this time too. Those are critical elements."

"Everdust," Ahilya repeated. "Could you use it now? Here?"

"I could," he said slowly. "Despite this deathcage, I can sense the stars of the green dust everywhere, both from the pocket Deepness and the pocket Moment. But I'd rather not use pure possibility frivolously. It would be dangerous for all of us, and I mean no harm to the ashrams."

Dangerous how? she thought, but Iravan's dark eyes glinted, and she knew that this was another question he was unwilling to answer right now.

The falcon straightened and shook its feathers again. It uttered a soft impatient cry. Iravan's skin began to glow with blue-green light. Rings formed around the falcon's eyes.

Ahilya glanced back through the glass columns. The assembled councilors reflected a dozen times over, Chaiyya's considering face, Laksiya frowning, Kiana adjusting her leg-brace thoughtfully. They had all heard this exchange, word for word. How had they interpreted it?

Iravan had made it sound so simple—offering to take any Ecstatic away from the dangerous confines of the ashram. But the idea of a race of super-architects with tremendous unknown powers—it sent a chill down Ahilya's spine.

The council would not tolerate that, and it would never pass through the Conclave either. Iravan might believe in the power of his conscience and desire, but the council would not allow Ecstatics to live merely by the dictates of their morality.

Besides, no matter their differences, Chaiyya was right. The skies had been the home of the ashrams for a thousand years. As much as Ahilya wanted humanity to return to the jungle one day, it was not going to happen, not without great cause. Even if the architects believed trajection was ultimately doomed to fail, they would seek an alternate source of energy to remain in the skies. Ecstatic energy was that source. They were not about to let Ecstatics leave so easily, not when they could be an answer to all their problems.

"There might be a way," she said at last. "For all of us to have what we want. But I need you to trust me."

"I trust you," he said, without missing a beat. His palm touched the glass. "You should have been a councilor all along. You've taken to it so easily."

"You did, too."

He shook his head. "I made too many mistakes. With them. With us."

"And I will learn from your mistakes," Ahilya said, her voice catching. She placed her palm over his. She could feel his warmth despite the glass barrier.

Iravan smiled. He stepped back and turned away to the falcon. He placed a foot on the wing, then leapt up to seat himself on the bird. His eyes darted around the cage, then settled back onto the sky. "I trust you, Ahilya, but you need to release me now. Something doesn't feel right about all this."

The way back through the maze was much faster. Ahilya's mind buzzed with possibilities and machinations, the things she was intending to do and say, the dangers and the pitfalls. The others were already discussing the conversation by the time she returned to them.

"—is clearly of sound mind," Kiana was saying. "He is not an Ecstatic in the manner we understand Ecstasy."

Airav's face bobbed over Chaiyya's communication bracelet. "I agree. It has always been hypothesized that Ecstatics can balance material bonds while being in Ecstasy. Iravan seems to have found a way. We can't treat him like he belongs in the sanctum with the other Ecstatics."

"There are *two* Ecstatic architects here," Laksiya countered. "We have a battery to trial, and we need to show the Conclave an alternate source of energy. That is why we called the Conclave in the first place, is it not?"

"No," Ahilya said, joining them. "Not if you plan on draining two sentient beings without their consent. That is not the way of the ashrams."

"Katresh will support us using the energex to extract Ecstasy," Chaiyya said. "As will Nilenshar, Auresh, and the rest of the Seven Northern Sisters. They amongst all have the greatest aversion to Ecstatic architects."

"But Yeikshar wouldn't," Airav said. "Iravan hails from there, Chaiyya, he is their shining son. They sent him to Nakshar *expecting* him to become a Senior Architect. Besides, they are our greatest allies. If you touched him without his consent and word got out, Nakshar would get no help from our sister ashram."

"Then we have the falcon."

"I think," Kiana said dryly, "we have established that he won't allow that. He's *riding* it. This is no wild yaksha."

Ahilya shot a glance at the gigantic creature. Did Iravan have control of the yaksha? He had implied that the creature had trajected the Maze Architects. Megha still looked shaken, her limbs trembling. Gaurav and the others hardly seemed to be faring better. What must it have felt like—for their bodies to no longer respond to their desires? The Maze Architects had been little more than marionettes being manipulated by the yaksha.

She turned back to the councilors. "Neither of them belong to Nakshar. Even if we discount the other ashrams and their reactions on learning this, we have no jurisdiction to hold and imprison them."

"Yakshas have no rights under the Conclave," Chaiyya began, frowning. "As for Iravan, he is an Ecstatic who is also a citizen of Nakshar. He must be treated like the other Ecstatics. Caged and awaiting our decision."

"If you consider him a citizen of Nakshar, then you recognize that he is a Senior Architect until a vote of no confidence is passed and he is excised. You can't have it both ways."

"What's your point?" the woman said, her eyes narrowing.

"We release him," Ahilya said, immediately. "If we need to check his intention regarding the safety of Nakshar, we conduct an Examination of Ecstasy."

"The Examination is moot now with the invention of the radarx. And we can't release him. He is covered in jungle contaminants and those cannot be allowed to seed themselves in the city. They could infect all the ashrams of the Conclave."

"There are ways around that and you know it," Ahilya said. "He can discharge all his contaminants into the sky. We can trap those in individual deathboxes. We can cleanse him—"

The falcon screamed, a terrifying sound.

Ahilya's stomach squeezed. Nausea returned, compounded by her pregnancy. The Maze Architects jumped to their feet. Megha shook Gaurav off, her face determined. Atop the yaksha, Iravan stared at the sunlit sky.

"Ahilya," he called out, voice heavy with warning. "Do it now. There's no more time."

She whipped back to the councilors. Their eyes were on her husband. The denial began to form on Chaiyya's lips. Ahilya could almost see her intention—to ask for no confidence in Iravan, here and now.

"I call for a formal vote," Ahilya said, before the Senior Architect could speak. "We vote whether to release him. Now. At once."

The falcon rattled the cage again. The sound echoed in the courtyard.

"I vote no," Chaiyya said, lifting her chin.

"As do I," Senior Sungineer Laksiya said.

"I vote yes," Airav said quietly, over Chaiyya's bracelet. "Ahilya is right, Chaiyya. We cannot imprison him. He is no ordinary Ecstatic. We must consider the truth of what he is saying, the truth of Ahilya's own testimony."

"*Ahilya!*" Iravan called out, louder. "Release me *now!*"

"Iravan and I vote yes, too." Ahilya took a shuddering breath.

"Iravan doesn't get a vote when the decision is about him," Chaiyya shot back.

It had been worth trying, but now they were two for two. Ahilya swung to Kiana to break the tie. The woman stared back, her gray eyes calculating.

The falcon rose inside the cage. Glass rattled. In her mind's eye, the earthrage shook the jungle during the expedition. Oam dove for the satchel, and Iravan screamed at her to return. Ahilya grabbed

Kiana's arm. "Vote yes. Please."

"I'm not sure I should," the sungineer said, implacable. "The falcon is still our best shot at the Ecstatic battery. If we let them go, the sungineers have nothing again."

Ahilya threw a glance back at the falcon. Its silver wings beat heavily against the glass. Iravan's skin was glowing blindingly. His head tilted to the sky. Blue leached out of his eyes. He seemed to barely have control over the yaksha. If the creature trajected the architects again, they would lose all leverage. Their only bargaining chip now was Iravan's apparent sanity and his hold over the creature.

"*AHILYA!*" Iravan bellowed, anger and fear in his voice.

"Vote yes," she said, her grip on Kiana's arm tight. "I promise you. Everything you are trying to do with sungineering, I will find a way to help you."

Chaiyya frowned. Kiana smiled, a calculation hidden in the depths of her eyes. "Agreed," she said. "Release him."

Chaiyya drew in a sharp breath. "Very well," she said. Her fingers danced over her many rudra bead bracelets in a complicated pattern.

The columns of the deathmaze retreated into the earth, disappearing. The deathcage opened, the glass whisking down.

Iravan and the falcon erupted from it, a heavy beat of wings that sent the wind rushing, blowing Ahilya's hair around her. Then the falcon was in the air, casting a massive shadow over the courtyard.

Ahilya watched it rise. The Maze Architects murmured around them. Iravan guided the falcon lower, studying the courtyard. His gaze met Ahilya's. His skin darkened again, and his eyes returned to their almost-black shade. It appeared that whatever danger there had been was averted. They had freed the falcon, and it would no longer traject the assembly.

Then lightning flashed in a cloudless sky.

Iravan's head snapped up.

Maze Architects fell to their knees, screaming in agony. Their veins flickered with blue-green light, then flared into blood red, widening crimson cracks on dark skin. They crumpled to the moss, writhing.

"He's trajecting them," Chaiyya breathed, horrified. "I told you he's dangerous."

But Iravan's skin no longer glowed, and there were no rings around the falcon's eyes either.

"This isn't him," Ahilya whispered.

The ground shook under them. Ahilya clutched Chaiyya as the ashram groaned, seizing like in an earthrage.

6

IRAVAN

Lightning cracked in a sunny sky.

The Etherium overtook all his visions. Images seared through Iravan.

Bharavi dying as he let go of Oam.

Nakshar in pain, in Ecstasy, infected.

Crimson instead of blue, blood instead of green.

A dozen screaming faces lurched toward him, gigantic, shapeless, mere wisps in the air.

The Etherium subsided, and Iravan realized the falcon had shot into the sky, diving upward. Rain poured, slicking his hair back. His clothes were already drenched. Wind screamed at him, and he glanced back to the Conclave, but the entire structure was a speck—he and the falcon had flown too far. What had that vision in the Etherium been, so raw, so real?

He summoned the Moment from the Deepness. The globule appeared, and for a fleeting instant, he felt deep relief to be out of the deathmaze, to be free again. A shaky laugh formed in his throat.

The globule quivered.

Within the Deepness, the Moment trembled like a fragile dewdrop, readying to fall away into nothingness.

No, Iravan thought, laughter turning to ash. A cold horror grew in his heart.

He spun around in the Deepness, searching for the Resonance, but the silvery particle was nowhere to be seen. This was not the yaksha's doing. This was something else.

He dove into the Moment. Stars surrounded him as he'd expected them to, but the universe *thrummed*, vibrating unlike ever before. Cracks appeared in the possibilities of living beings as Iravan broke out in a sweat. He streaked through the universe, past splintering stars, toward Nakshar and the Conclave. What would happen if the cracks widened?

The Etherium answered. Between his brows, the stars disintegrated, cracking like limestone, powdery, gone forever. Ecstatic trajection changed the nature of the stars within the realm of possibility, it did not destroy them. *This*, whatever it was, it was removing the possibility of lives altogether. He had never seen anything like this—

Iravan froze, shock arresting him.

It *had* happened once before.

It had happened to him.

Pain flowed through his veins at the memory. The cosmic being had unravelled his own existence in the vortex. Ahilya had barely saved him. The creature had ripped him apart, taking away the possibilities of his future, *erasing* him. It was going to do the same thing to Nakshar. It would do it to the Moment itself.

We have to go back, Iravan thought, frantically, tugging at the falcon. They needed to return to the Conclave to help. He clutched at the falcon, but the yaksha ignored him, still diving upward into jagged lightning.

Iravan raced through the Moment, unaided. The Conclave appeared in his second vision, a construct of great complexity, ashrams connected to each other through constellation lines like lace embroidery. Even as he watched, the lines shattered, collapsing into the universe. The Moment *thrummed*, the force of the vibrations shaking the lines like spiderwebs in a deluge. Cities collided, their merging imperfect, their boundaries unestablished. Rain streamed down from clear skies.

Establishing boundaries during a Conclave was complex. Each trajecting architect of every ashram simultaneously carried a separate pattern of constellation lines fastened to a different plant. Merging allowed those plants to coexist with their counterparts. Without it, Nakshar's healbranch would poison Kinshar's amelaus. Yeikshar's mediweed would eradicate Katresh's yararoot. People would die, ashrams would weaken. Iravan could not let that happen.

Come on, he thought furiously, tugging at the falcon, trying to force it to turn. *We can't fly away like cowards.* The silence in the back of his mind grew grim, a cold anger, not his, *truly* his. The yaksha continued to ignore him. Lightning cracked angrily, too close, momentarily blinding Iravan. He cried out, squeezed his eyes shut.

In the Moment, architects of Nakshar struggled to establish control. At the center of the activity, Chaiyya hovered weakly, a dozen glittering constellation lines emerging from her. She was surrounded by a tight netted sphere of a thousand intertwining constellation lines. The Senior Architect controlled the orb, forming the nucleus of the Conclave. Without her, none of the architects would be able to communicate their permissions to each other's ashrams. It was an exhausting, delicate endeavor at the best of times, but now? Chaiyya was no Ecstatic. The effort would scar her permanently—it would kill her. Iravan sped toward her, just as the Senior Architect spotted him across the netted sphere. *Let me help*, he thought, wildly. *Chaiyya, you have to trust me!*

The Moment *thrummed*.

She could not hear him in the Moment, but they had once been colleagues; they had even been friends. One of her constellation lines snapped, ricocheting like an angry snake before dissipating. The sphere around her juddered. Somewhere, an ashram disconnected and wobbled dangerously in the sky. In her flustered movements, Iravan detected deep terror and exhaustion. Rain splashed down his face, as the yaksha climbed higher, its wings beating a gale.

Iravan soared toward Chaiyya, his intention clear through the fluttering of his dust mote. *Let me help! You can't handle this.*

He directed his constellation lines toward hers, reaching through the netted sphere, desperate, asking for the transfer of power. He could see her make the calculation, to turn over the Conclave's merging to an Ecstatic, the dangers of it, the suicide. He thought wildly of what he was asking her. He could be struck by lightning any second. The falcon could steer him into danger. He and Chaiyya stared at each other, both of them struck with doubt at his ability, at his sanity.

Another of her lines snapped. One ashram crashed into another, healers and poisons fighting each other within the plants. The Moment shivered, frozen stars blinking. The falcon swung, barely avoiding a bolt.

Then, with great effort, as though in slow motion, Chaiyya disconnected her constellation lines from her dust mote and unleashed them toward Iravan.

He spun through the Moment, catching each of them, tying his own lines to hers. The falcon screamed, a high-pitched echoing sound.

Constellation lines snapped together.

The gravity of the Conclave pulled at Iravan.

At once, he was surrounded by tight constellation lines glistening in every direction. He hovered at the center of the orb now, taking Chaiyya's place as the Conclave's nucleus.

Maze Architects came to a standstill, fear and wariness in their dust motes as they viewed him through the netted pulsating orb of light. Iravan's lines connected to theirs, and by extension to the rest of the architects in the Conclave.

Chaiyya had turned over the power connecting all the trajectors in the ashrams to him. He held it now, the point of the Conclave's merging. In the skies, the falcon swerved, avoiding another errant lightning strike, nearly throwing Iravan off. The skies rippled, the air twisting like a tornado, heavy and oppressive, shimmering though there were no clouds.

The vibrating Moment felt like a current running through his veins. If he could feel it, then Chaiyya had been holding on by a mere thread. She quivered close to him, her dust mote just beyond the ball of constellation lines, ready to intervene. Admiration filled Iravan. She was desperately exhausted, but she was a Senior Architect, through and through.

He could not fail now.

The Moment vibrated, stars skewing, but Iravan secured himself in his second vision, held by the gravity of the Conclave. Constellation lines flew out of him, changing the anchor-points of the trajection within the orb. The design Chaiyya had constructed was flawed—it relied too much on one Senior Architect to form the delicate nucleus. Iravan altered it, attaching nodes to the trajection, checkpoints to fasten the energy. He dissipated the sphere of the orb into smaller parts. Chaiyya hovered, alarmed, but he wove in and out, releasing tied knots, creating multiple smaller orbs, intending to throw them back at the Maze Architects for a decentralization of control. In his first vision, he clung to the falcon, eyes tightly closed, the storm in the sky filling his senses. He was almost done, a few more to go, the core nucleus loosened—

The falcon stopped abruptly.

Iravan looked into the sky below them. The yaksha had ascended over the unnatural lightning, but they were still besieged by the inexplicable rain. He turned his head, to where the yaksha looked.

The face of the earthrage screamed, inches away.

Sky cracked open, and wind buffeted them. The falcon swayed against the gale, facing the cosmic being. Eyes appeared like stormclouds, jagged rain within an open mouth like sharp-filed teeth. The earthrage roared, another gust of wind chilling Iravan. The cosmic being was massive, taking over the entire sky. He and the falcon were minuscule in comparison. A shimmering twister of air surrounded them. They were in the eye of the storm, and beyond the air rippled further, ready to eat the skies in its hunger, dust and clouds swirling in a fierce tornado.

In the Moment, Iravan paused as the cosmic being's shrieking shook the universe. Stars around him chipped. The dust motes hovered anxiously. Iravan sped up, unweaving the nucleus at breakneck speed, one knot then another, loosening the central power even as he tied constellation lines more tightly into nodes.

The earthrage attacked, sizzling bolts emerging from its mouth, heading straight for them.

The falcon cried out, swung at the last instant, blurred wings, shards like arrows missing.

Iravan raced through the Moment, disconnecting more lines, creating more nodes, frantic. Chaiyya hovered outside of the nucleus, watching. She had understood. She was ready.

And then the Resonance was next to him in the Moment, fluttering furiously. Over its mirrored surface, Iravan detected impatience and anger. He knew what it was going to do, and in desperation, he flung the distributed nodes to the surrounding Maze Architects, flung the loose orbs back to Chaiyya, just as the Resonance slammed into him, pulling him back to the Deepness.

The velvety dark surrounded them, the globule of the Moment shivering.

We need to return, Iravan thought, panicked. He had thrown the nodes to the architects, but what if they had not caught them? What if Chaiyya could not handle it? They needed to go back, he needed to—

The Resonance shot a silvery jet of light into the Moment. Filaments emerged from the light in an intricate pattern. Fibers leached from the beam, creating a net of Ecstatic trajection aimed toward Iravan's stars—more complex than any other trajection the yaksha had done on him before.

The awareness of the falcon within him burst into a shout of silence. In the rainy sky, the yaksha swerved, avoiding another onslaught of lightning shards. Iravan cried out, but the silence in his mind was too loud. A blinding pain seized his head. The yaksha was trajecting him. The Etherium flared, and Bharavi died colorless again. In his first vision, the face of the earthrage screamed, shooting jagged arrows of lightning at their flying form. The Moment, and its concerns, retreated to the back of Iravan's mind.

No, he thought, horrified, even as the falcon trajected him. *What are you doing?*

The silence in the back of his mind exploded.

The yaksha conquered him.

7

IRAVAN

Within the velvety darkness, the falcon watched him, this simple creature it was tied to, so full of angst and infinity.

The creature, this… *man*, shuddered and stilled, a jagged thing hovering blindly out of control. He had never known the darkness, no matter how much the falcon had tried to teach him. He did not learn fast enough. If it took any longer, the falcon would have only one choice.

Within the velvety darkness, the falcon lifted the combined webbing of their power and directed the rays far from the trembling droplet of lights. It—*they*—saw themselves: man and bird, raging in the sky, drenched in blue-green light. From a far distance, the man listened, understood. He thrust his hands out, and lightning shredded itself into golden dust the same instant the webbing in the darkness reached its target.

Air burned. Lightning weakened.

The storm thundered, furious, but the falcon focused their power into the blackness, it aimed deep and true.

The lightning splintered, sparks dissipating.

In the velvety darkness, the man-shaped melody shuddered, unable to hold onto their power any longer. He was weak; if only they held, they could web this now, fully, forever. They could—

But it would kill the man, this fragile thing.

The falcon would have to think of another way.

Resigned, the falcon released him, absorbed his pain. The hurt lanced through it, amassing atop lifetimes of agony, and—

it, they, no, *he*

came to himself in

s-h-a-r-d-s

that affixed themselves back into his shape—

Iravan slammed into his body.

His visions split. He was back in the Deepness. The Resonance was gone. The Moment had stilled. Rain continued to fall, but softer, calmer. Within the Etherium, Ahilya stared at him from Nakshar, horror on her beautiful face.

His last view was of the falcon engulfing him in its silvery wings. They dropped from the sky, losing consciousness.

8

AHILYA

Iravan fell from the sky.

Ahilya saw it happen between her brows, like a nightmare she couldn't dispel. Her stomach seized, even as Nakshar trembled beneath her feet. Was it real? Was it truly happening? Lightning cracked in clear skies, and the storm rained on her, like tears down her cheeks. The ashram shuddered again, and Ahilya lost her balance.

Senior Sungineer Kiana shot out a hand, steadying her shoulder. They still stood within the copse of trees, the council of Nakshar huddled together under the flimsy cover. Five minutes had gone by since Iravan and the falcon had flown away. Five terrifying minutes. Ahilya had counted each breath.

The courtyard was a mess, a violently desecrated scene as though ripped by an earthrage. Several of the collected Maze Architects had fallen to their knees, red pulsating on their dark skin like a horrible infection of trajection tattoos. Each time one of the councilors had moved to help them, another shuddering had overtaken the ashram. Chaiyya had quietened, her mouth open in a small O, her eyes glazed.

The Senior Architect still glowed blue-green. Ahilya's knees shook in relief—but something was deeply wrong. Laksiya was pouring instructions into her communication bracelet where Ahilya recognized Dhruv and Umit and Reya, their faces troubled. On Kiana's rudra bracelet, Airav's face hovered, horror plain on his features.

"The Conclave," he gasped. "The establishment of boundaries is not complete, yet. We're sitting prey for another yaksha attack, for an Ecstatic malfunctioning. What in rages is happening?"

"We don't know," the Senior Sungineer answered. "Chaiyya is in no condition to speak."

Ahilya tuned them all out.

In her mind's eye, she watched the falcon drop like a stone through a fading air tornado. *Wake up*, she thought. *Wake up, damn you.* Her hands shook as she connected her own communication bracelet to Naila. The Maze Architect appeared instantly, her image bobbing over Ahilya's palm.

"Ahilya-ve," Naila breathed. Her hair was in disarray, a streak of mud on her cheek. Blue-green trajecting tattoos climbed up her neck. "What's going on? Are you safe?"

"Naila, you have to enter the Moment. You have to find Iravan. Where are you?"

"Still at the solar lab. But the Moment isn't—"

The ashram shuddered. The courtyard rumbled, and rocks sliced up the earth between the whimpering architects. Naila's image wobbled. Ahilya staggered, bile climbing in her throat. What if Iravan wasn't in the Moment? What if he was in the Deepness, or not trajecting at all? They would never find him. He could drop down into the earthrage, and she'd never know.

"What in rages is Chaiyya doing?" Airav said, over Kiana's bracelet. "Is she altering the construction of the boundaries—of the Conclave itself?"

Sure enough, Ahilya glanced over to the Senior Architect and saw the patterns on her skin change. Blue-green vines still crept over Chaiyya's dark skin, but they seemed to break apart and join each other in a dizzying array. Chaiyya's eyes moved to catch Ahilya's gaze. The Senior Architect raised a slow, trembling hand to her mouth, her skin still furiously glowing.

"What do you mean, she's changing the construction?" Kiana demanded.

"The nucleus," Airav said incoherently. "She—the nodes, distributed—this is not how a Conclave should merge. I need to communicate this to the other councils." His brows drew together in concentration. Ahilya imagined him in the council chambers within the rudra tree, surrounded by floating holograms, swishing rapidly from one to another.

In her mind, the falcon continued to fall. The ground roiled again, dust flying everywhere. Maze Architects writhed in pain, their skins cut by a terrible red light. Grit entered Ahilya's mouth, and her eyes watered against the dust.

She coughed and shook Kiana off her. Stumbling a few more steps forward, she raised her chin to the downpour. She could see nothing. Where was Iravan falling? Where was this happening?

"Naila," she whispered, turning back to her own bracelet. "Please. You have to do something."

The ashram shuddered, a groan that reverberated deep in Ahilya's bones, chilling her—Lightning cracked, several bolts slashing the sky— Air rippled like a scattering tornado, and—

Stillness.

A strange silence grew over the courtyard. Dust rose and fell, but the ground no longer moved.

Then, Ahilya realized, the architects had quietened. Their skins were dark again.

"The Moment," Naila said, her eyes wide on the hologram. "It's—it's back to normal."

Ahilya staggered through the ruptured earth, picking her way past broken roots and slippery mud. She squinted up into the rain. She could make them out now, just barely, a speck falling furiously fast. In her mind, the falcon grasped an unconscious Iravan in its talons. It opened its eyes, though the effort seemed too much.

Ahilya raised her wrist, back to Naila on her bracelet. "The third quadrant," she said urgently. "The eastern terrace courtyard on the seventh level. That's where we are, Naila, and I see them, they're dropping fast. You have to catch them! You need to traject the plants! We can't have them land in another ashram."

"That's Iravan?" Kiana asked. Both the Senior Sungineers had joined her, staring at the falling speck as well.

On the hologram, Naila's face grew taut with worry. "I see them through the magnifiers. They're closest to your location, Ahilya-ve, but they're still too far. Our plants will never reach them."

In her mind, the falcon unfolded its wings and careened toward Nakshar. She saw the falling stone in the sky change direction, hurtle toward them. Its eyes blinked, then closed again. They could all see it now, the falcon, lurching, weaving, coming too fast.

"It's headed for us," she breathed. "We can do this."

"They're going to crash into us," Laksiya said, horrified.

"*Naila!*" Ahilya commanded.

"I see them, I see them," the Maze Architect gasped. The tattoos on her face changed. Around them, the plants morphed in a wave. Roots grew from within the ruined earth like thick tentacles, reaching upwards into the rainy sky. Ahilya teetered back to the copse, as roots formed right by her, barely avoiding her, combining with the ones reaching up.

Awe eclipsed her worry. Naila was likely doing this trajection all alone. The Maze Architect could not see the falcon fall, not directly. She was following the yaksha's hurtle through the magnifiers, aligning her trajection remotely while tracking the people in the courtyard through their citizen rings. What kind of coordination did that take? No wonder Iravan had picked her to be his apprentice.

An arm touched Ahilya. She turned to see Chaiyya. "He's covered with jungle contaminants," Chaiyya whispered. The effort seemed to take all her energy, but the tattoos on her skin had simplified. The Senior Architect shook her head, her instruction clear. *We can't allow jungle plants into the ashram.*

Ahilya spun toward the two sungineers, still standing where she had left them. "The deathcage. Command Naila to form it around us. A massive deathcage."

"We'll be trapped within it," Laksiya called out.

"It doesn't matter. They're unconscious. They're barely holding on. They can't hurt us."

Kiana nodded, a snap decision. She tapped at her rudra beads and Ahilya watched as she transferred the permission to Naila.

The Maze Architect's eyes focused on the hologram. "All right. The deathcage is rising far beyond the courtyard. As soon as I catch them, I'll close it from the top. You might want to get out of the way, councilors. This will be rough."

A thick glass pane grew on the side of the terrace courtyard that remained open to a sheer ledge, rain slicking across it, but little else changed. Chaiyya's skin still glowed. Airav's image continued to hover over Kiana's wrist, slashed by the rain. The sungineering equipment worked without the pocket Moment of a completed deathcage. The rest of the glass was far behind the courtyard, surrounding them from all sides except the one open to the skies.

"Laksiya, with me," Kiana said sharply. The two women began to weave across the damaged courtyard, helping the sobbing Maze Architects back to the relative safety of the copse. Kiana was barely managing, with her leg-brace and half limp. Ahilya tried to move, to help them, but her feet seemed frozen. Within the copse with Chaiyya, her eyes tracked the yaksha coming straight for them like a comet.

Above her, Nakshar's roots combined like two giant brown hands joining, ready to catch the massive falcon. The thick roots stretched, reaching. The yaksha tilted—they could all see it now. Its eyes blinked, and closed, and Ahilya knew. The creature had provided direction, aimed for Nakshar and the courtyard, but it had no control over its descent. It was up to Naila now.

On the hologram, Naila gritted her teeth.

The roots thickened, growing tighter. They reached higher, almost there.

Then the falcon wrapped its wings around itself.

It smashed into the roots, in a burst of twigs.

Naila screamed, even as the roots encircled the creature, trying to slow its momentum. The falcon hurtled toward them, toward the copse and the councilors. Ahilya watched it come, in relief and horror, unable to breathe. Wood and feathers filled her vision, a comet that would crush them. The roots groaned, trying to slow it down, but it was too fast, it would hit them.

Laksiya shrieked. Kiana yelled. Ahilya staggered back.

Then glass whisked across the sky, connecting to the deathcage, slicing through the roots.

Active trajection immediately cut out. Naila and Airav blinked away. The roots unraveled instantly. The falcon dropped the last few feet, sliding over the mud, a gigantic creature slithering to rest in the center of the courtyard. Dust and earth swirled everywhere, but through it Ahilya saw the massive falcon's wings unfold. A bleary eye opened and closed.

Nestled amid its talons, Iravan was motionless.

Ahilya made to move toward him, but Kiana caught her arm. "Nakshar's council cannot be trapped within a deathcage with two Ecstatic architects. The falcon is semiconscious. We need to leave, now."

"He's hurt. They're both hurt."

"It doesn't matter. We cannot hold ourselves hostage to their whims. We are all that stand between Nakshar and its destruction by the falcon."

Ahilya clenched her fist. Already, Laksiya was ushering out hobbling Maze Architects beyond the copse where an open glass pane shimmered. They were clearing the deathcage, before the Ecstatic architects regained consciousness. Ahilya's eye met the falcon's bleary one across the dust. *I'm sorry*, she thought and turned away. Kiana led her through the trees, waited until everyone had emerged, then tapped at her rudra bead bracelet.

Glass whisked back up, trapping Iravan and the yaksha again.

Vertical glass swam across shards of soil. The boundaries of the deathcage grew closer. Injured Maze Architects limped away, while more uniformed architects appeared, marching resolutely through the trees toward the courtyard. Kiana had activated the battle protocol. Ever since the yaksha's last attack that had broken Nakshar into two, the attack where Iravan had been taken away, several processes had been established. Architects had been trained. Now, everyone moved in synchronisation aware of their roles.

Kiana connected her rudra bracelet to Airav again and dropped her hand. The four councilors huddled beneath a tree, rain still splattering them. Against a tree trunk, Chaiyya slowly sank to the moss floor. Pale white healbranch vines grew from the ground, entwining her. Ahilya and the others dropped to their knees, concerned, but Chaiyya waved them away.

"I'm all right," she whispered. "Iravan—he—" She shook her head, then gazed at where Airav still blinked over Kiana's bracelet. "The boundaries. Are they established?"

Airav's voice was troubled. "The other councils are furious you changed the architecture. What possessed you to distribute the nucleus? The boundaries are connected, but the entire construction is fragile. The Conclave is no longer a single unit with Nakshar at its heart. It is a cluster of barely connected ashrams. We can't reverse it, not now, and the danger—"

"I know this," Chaiyya said, irritation on her features. "I couldn't hold the nucleus any longer. Besides, decentralizing wasn't my idea. It was Iravan's. He... I gave over control to him."

Ahilya drew in a sharp breath. Raindrops dripped down her back, chilling her.

On the hologram, Airav's face grew appalled. "Chaiyya, do you mean to say you gave over the trajection of the Conclave to an *Ecstatic* architect?"

"You weren't there, Airav," Chaiyya snapped. "I made a judgement call. I'd have been knocked out of the Moment altogether if he hadn't helped." Her face spasmed. The Senior Architect closed her eyes. "Iravan did something to the Moment. I've never felt anything like it. It... it *moved*."

"That's impossible," the other architect said. "The Moment is a frozen reality. Even an Ecstatic cannot do that."

"It's not impossible," Kiana said, her voice measured. "We don't know the extent of Iravan's power, let alone that of the falcon."

Chaiyya only shook her head again. Rain pattered down on them. The two Senior Sungineers exchanged a glance.

Ahilya bit her lip. The council had allowed Iravan to leave the deathcage only for this to happen. They would excise him and drain the yaksha. Iravan, undoubtedly, would fight. What would that do to the construction of an already weakened ashram and Conclave? To the truth of architects' history Ahilya wanted to share? Iravan would become a liability; his anger and fear would ruin both their chances of ever releasing the Ecstatic architects and returning to the jungle.

Yet Chaiyya had turned to Iravan for help. If the Conclave ever found out, she would have to defend her decision. The Senior Architect could easily claim she didn't have a choice, that she was manipulated into it by the Ecstatic architect, of course, but if Ahilya could avert that altogether…

A plan formed in her head, dangerous and profitable. She had told Iravan there was a way for all of them to achieve what they wanted. It depended on one thing—the Conclave and Iravan agreeing to the terms she laid out. She had never played both sides. When the sides were her husband and all of Nakshar's sister ashrams, the people who had invented this game… The thought made her part giddy, part terrified. So, this was what the council did. This was how it had changed him, too. She would not make his mistakes.

"We don't know that was Iravan or the falcon at all," she said softly into the silence.

Chaiyya's eyes snapped open.

Laksiya snorted. "This again? As soon as they returned to Nakshar, everything went to rages. The Moment twisted, the Maze Architects warped. He clearly trajected them as soon as we released him from the deathcage."

"No," Ahilya said, shaking her head, dispelling raindrops. "No, that's not how it happened. I saw—*you all* saw—that the architects burned with those red tattoos when neither he nor the falcon were trajecting. There was urgency in his call for us to release him. He saw this in the Etherium. He said a storm was coming."

"That means little," Laksiya began.

"You know I'm right," Ahilya said, ignoring the Senior Sungineer altogether. She leaned forward, her eyes on Chaiyya. "Why would Iravan help you with the establishment of Conclave boundaries, if he was the one who instigated the shuddering of the Moment in the first place?"

"We don't know if he helped," Chaiyya said. She untwined a few healbranch vines from her arms. "He could have attacked the Moment and decentralized the Conclave's nucleus for his own reasons. He could have deliberately told us about a storm coming, just so we'd believe his innocence."

"You trusted him to help you. You gave trajection over to him."

"Because I had no choice."

"Chaiyya, please," Ahilya urged. "I am not arguing semantics. I am pointing out that in your moment of crisis, you trusted Iravan. You still do. You can't deny it. He was one of you. Perhaps he still is. I know you're thinking it."

The councilors fell silent. Kiana nodded thoughtfully. On the hologram, Airav swept a hand over his face. Rain pattered down, loud in the sudden silence.

Chaiyya met Ahilya's gaze. "Trust," she said softly, "is an overstatement. I did what I had to do."

"Maybe he did that too." Ahilya swept a hand back to where he lay unconscious. "Once before, all of you blamed him for something that was not his fault. Something that needed greater investigation. Will you do the same again?"

"What exactly are you asking?" Airav said, over the hologram.

"I'm asking you to give him a chance," Ahilya said. "Let me deal with him. Let me find out what happened to the Moment, why the architects' tattoos burned crimson. I am a councilor of Nakshar, and I'll speak with your voice. Besides, I'm the only one with the expertise and knowledge of yakshas. I can negotiate peace between all of us, the Ecstatics, the Conclave, the sungineers, the citizens, and Iravan. You saw this promise in me when you made me a councilor. Let me do my job."

The councilors exchanged glances. Airav *hmm*ed on the hologram, the sound a rumble through the rain. Chaiyya shook her head, readying her arguments as Ahilya had expected her to. She was not about to give her sole authority to deal with Iravan, not when Ahilya had so patently announced her support for architects to *become* Ecstatic.

Ahilya took a deep breath and threw down her final card. "Let me do this. And I won't speak at the Conclave about what I learned in the jungle."

The others stilled, eyebrows raised. They all knew, in the end, it came down to the two women. What they said would decide how the Conclave responded. They would decide the fate of the ashrams, the fate of Nakshar's own future within the sky. Ahilya could see the others weighing the decision. She was giving up her right to speak at the Conclave, to announce everything she had so passionately argued in the last two months, in return for what? To spend time with her husband? To defend him?

In her heart, Ahilya felt the weight of the gamble.

By relinquishing her position at the Conclave, she was staking the justice and fairness she sought for the citizens. She was choosing to become just another puppet and mouthpiece for the council's decisions, whether regarding the yakshas or the Ecstatics trapped within the deathcages. The child flashed in her mind again, hidden within the rudra tree. Iravan said, *I trust you*, and Naila said, *The architects need you*. Ahilya's stomach tightened; she could feel the twinges of her pregnancy, aches which she knew in her heart were not normal. *There is a way*, she thought again, desperately this time. *For all of us to get what we want.*

Chaiyya leaned forward, eyes narrowing. "You want sole authority to deal with Iravan. What happens if you find out he is not as safe as you think he is? If he is, in fact, not in control?"

Ahilya stared at her.

She recalled the darkness in his eyes, the shame and loneliness. He'd said he hadn't trajected the architects, and Iravan did not lie... but what if he had changed? What if she was mistaken, if he truly *had* endangered all the people within the Conclave? Could she shield him? Would she make that choice yet again, to choose Iravan over the rest of the world? *You two deserve each other*, Dhruv had said once. But not like this. Not like this.

A coldness descended over her. What was her alternative? If Iravan truly had no control over his Ecstasy, he was a danger to all of humanity, to the child and the future she carried in her womb.

"If that happens," she said, her voice hollow, "then he will no longer have my defense. If that happens, I will stop Iravan myself."

"Agreed," Senior Architect Chaiyya said at once, her eyes sharp.

"Agreed," the others murmured in unison.

Ahilya's knees shook under her. Chaiyya extended a hand, and both of them stood up. The others backed away, making space.

"I suggest you find what you need to before the Conclave's discussion, Ahilya," the Senior Architect said. "I will have to explain to them why I changed the architecture of the Conclave. They will need to know that we have the technology to detect and use Ecstatic energy. The architects from their ashrams all undoubtedly noticed the disruption in the Moment, perhaps even noticed the falcon's flight. Agreement or not, this is all dependent on where those conversations lead us."

"I understand."

"Good." Chaiyya leaned on Kiana, then ran her gaze over Ahilya one last time. "Give him my thanks," she muttered. "Whether he caused the disruption in the Moment or not, Iravan saved the Conclave by taking over the nucleus. For this, he has my gratitude."

The Senior Architect turned away. The three women disappeared around the bend, leaving Ahilya by the knot of trees, rain still splattering on her through the leaves.

She turned back to look toward the courtyard. Beyond it, Iravan was likely still unconscious, and the yaksha too, both of them trapped in the deathcage. But she had seen before how Ecstatics could heal. She would be no use to them now. Besides, Iravan would ask questions—he would demand explanations. Ahilya walked away from the trees, preparing her answers.

9

IRAVAN

He awoke to the sounds of rain plunking on something solid.

Iravan's eyes fluttered open to complete darkness—the darkness not of the Deepness, but of imprisonment.

They had put him back in a deathcage.

He frowned, accepting but not understanding. How had they done that? He had been in the skies. He had escaped.

He shifted the falcon's wing off him and rose unsteadily. He didn't bother to traject. He stood there, gazing into the darkness, waiting for his eyes to adjust. It was nighttime, and far above he discerned twinkling stars, so like the Moment yet completely different. The skies were clear, which meant the rain was unnatural, like the lightning he and the falcon had flown through, like that face they had seen in the skies. His head pulsed, a throbbing ache that threatened to become sharp and piercing at any second. The last thing he remembered was the creature trajecting him. After that…

He shuddered. After that, things had become murky.

Iravan knelt slowly, his hands in front of him, reaching for the gigantic inert shape by his feet. The falcon felt cold, but surely it was not sleeping? Not when it was so sensitive to danger all the time. Tentatively, Iravan felt for the silence in the back of his mind, but it was weak, barely present. Something had happened to the yaksha. Something terrible. He shook the creature, feeling the beginnings of tears behind his eyes. The memory flashed, of the falcon trying to strangle him in the jungle. Had they tried to kill themselves again? Had they succeeded?

Wake up, he thought in anguish, but the falcon remained inert and the silence in the back of his mind remained small. Under his fingers, the yaksha was unmoving, though Iravan detected its breath, shallow and irregular.

Still trembling, Iravan entered the second vision of Ecstasy, but there was no waiting Resonance. Instead of the infinite velvety darkness of the Deepness, he found himself within what felt like a tight claustrophobic room—the pocket Deepness.

Of course.

The deathmaze.

They would not have simply trapped him within a normal deathcage. They had cut him off from the Moment *and* the Deepness, leaving only pockets of each to be manipulated. He had to understand this technology. Until then, it was a weakness, one that might well kill him and the falcon.

He slid from the pocket Deepness into the pocket Moment.

Immediately, a dozen stars surrounded him.

Plucking a jungle seed from his belt, Iravan trajected without truly knowing he was doing it. Blue-green tattoos formed on his skin, and vines grew from the seed in his palm. Thick thermogenic moss flowed from the vines and covered the inert form of the falcon, cushioning it from all sides, covering it entirely within minutes so it seemed that Iravan faced a small green hill. The silence at the back of his mind flickered slightly. The thought occurred to Iravan that he could heal the yaksha by trajecting its stars, but he had never attempted anything as complex. What if he made a mistake? He could damage the creature forever. He had trajected the yaksha before, but it had been under duress and in ignorance; perhaps that had encouraged the falcon to traject him in return. Besides, even if the yaksha were awake, they still had to find their way out of this cage. That was where he ought to focus.

Led by his own blue-green light, Iravan began pacing. The cage was tiny, barely large enough to fit both him and the falcon. It seemed to work as it always had, creating a pocket Moment containing only the possibilities of the plants trapped within it while blocking an architect from physically leaving. Yet the sungineers had seen fit to no longer use stone for its base. Instead, Iravan walked on soft grass. The glass far underneath him prevented him from sowing any of his jungle seeds permanently—which meant they had found a way to embed it into the fabric of Nakshar.

Why had Chaiyya and Airav allowed this? Did they not understand how the other ashrams would view it? Sungineering devices had always been a part of the ashrams—glowglobes appeared based on a desire for light—but all of it was strictly controlled by trajection. Now, by embedding glass, it appeared the council was allowing *sungineering* to control trajection. The effect to an unpracticed eye was the same, but the implications to an expert were manifold. Was this solely as preparation for his inevitable return? Or were they in fact preparing themselves for a world that no longer relied on trajection? A world that instead explored sungineering's depths? If so, Iravan could use it.

Blue-green light reflected off the glass, the light of his own trajection. Iravan glimpsed himself, dark skin, harried eyes, naked shame.

Overwhelmingly, he was reminded of Bharavi when she had been trapped in a similar cage.

He could almost see her, her short dark hair, her diminutive frame, her piercing brown eyes as she told him once again to grow up and become the man he was supposed to be. Grief rippled through him, clutching at his heart. Iravan swept a shaking hand to his face.

Bharavi had died—he had killed her—but was that not a better fate than if she had been excised? She would be reborn again in another time. That was the way of consciousness. She would have another chance at uniting with her yaksha. He knew this; he had studied the depths of consciousness as a Senior Architect. Had she been excised, she would have been ripped apart from her trajection, divorced from her yaksha. What would have happened to her... depth-memory? That ineffable substance that formed and nurtured her *life*? Consciousness was vast and deep, but could that severance affect rebirth too? He had no way to know. The councils had callously excised so many architects. They could excise him too.

I have to get out of here, he thought, sweat breaking out on his forehead. He needed to be free so he could make amends. He needed to be free so he could create a world where Bharavi's future Ecstasy was possible on rebirth. Where she could unite with her yaksha.

Golden light glimmered beyond the glass. A face appeared and murmured something.

A second, bright golden light shone from all directions cutting through the comfortable darkness.

Iravan suppressed a cry, shielding his eyes. Shapes moved beyond the glass: Maze Architects, dressed in their brown kurtas and trousers and translucent robes. "He's awake," one of them said. "Let her know."

He lowered his hand and looked around. He appeared to still be in the courtyard where he had first landed, the rain plunking heavily, but now tall thick trees surrounded him as though the council had hoped to hide the cage and its inmates. The stars above were completely obscured by sungineering light that shone from the trees. A dozen Maze Architects surrounded his cage, reflected over and over in the tall glass columns of the deathmaze, standing within the different layers. The yaksha lay in the center of it all, a shapeless mound, but Iravan did not hasten to it. He would learn nothing in the light that he had not known in the darkness.

"What happened?" he asked the Maze Architects, his voice raspy.

The architects looked at each other. Their reflections flickered within the glass columns. Viana, a tall gangly woman closest to the deathcage, shifted on her feet. She opened her mouth, but then closed it again.

Of course. They had been instructed not to speak to the Ecstatic. Yet, these people who had been set to watch him were *architects*, not jailers. Once he had been a Senior Architect, perhaps he still was. Iravan stepped closer to Viana, held her gaze, and did not repeat his question.

Viana grew abashed. Her eyes darted away then returned to him.

"You unleashed a… a *sky*rage," she muttered, at last.

Skyrage.

Iravan recoiled, his heart beating fast. Memories flashed in his mind: the yaksha trajecting him, and the image of himself through the Resonance's eyes. The Resonance had always looked like a mercurial floating particle to him, but he had appeared like a jagged splinter, broken and harsh. Was that his true form? All trajecting architects inhabited the Moment as dust motes, but that had more to do with their training than any reality. Beginner architects were *taught* to imagine their form as dust, and that image carried into their trajection. Did his true shape even matter?

That face in the sky... he could make sense of it now... that was the cosmic beings, certainly. The yaksha had taken him over to try and stop the lightning. The Resonance had shot the combined webbing of their trajection away from the Moment but there was nothing else in the Deepness. What had it aimed toward? What would have happened had they not stopped the lightning? Iravan reached with trembling hands for the seeds at his belt and scattered them.

Skyrage. Yes, that was a good name for it—that twisting shimmering of air that had taken the shape of a jungle storm, of a raging tornado. What else could damage a yaksha that had lived for a thousand years and had survived hundreds of earthrages? It had knocked the falcon into unconsciousness. The silence in his mind twitched, a feeble movement.

"That was not us," he said, his voice low. Vines grew from the seeds he had dropped, curling into long sharp runners. His fear and anger simmered under the surface, fingers curling into fists.

"You mean it was the cosmic beings." Viana seemed unable to stay silent now that she had begun speaking. Around her the other Maze Architects shifted, made hushing sounds, but she ignored them.

"You know about them?" Iravan asked.

"We all do."

"Then why are we in this cage?"

"We take our orders from Chaiyya-ve, not Ahilya."

No respectful suffix for his wife, Iravan noted. It meant the ashram was in flux, a patent rivalry present among the councilors. It was dangerous in a flying city that worked on the consolidated desires of its citizens, but Iravan was no stranger to the politics. When he had first become Senior Architect, several Maze Architects had accepted his ascension with scepticism, choosing to align themselves with either Airav or Chaiyya. Iravan had learned to speak with the council's voice to solidify his own support, but that had ruined his marriage. He had hoped to speak to Ahilya now, but clearly the "she" they had meant to call was Chaiyya. The low fury of resentment and disbelief coursed through Iravan like fire in his veins. The plants he was trajecting grew thicker, tentacle-like, slamming against the cage.

He had been so naïve, so *optimistic*. A few lonely months in the jungle had washed away all his training as a Senior Architect. Of course they were not going to simply relinquish the Ecstatic architects to him. Excision was a time-honoured tradition. Everyone knew that if ever an architect achieved uncontrollable power, they would be cut away from their trajection. Excision kept architects accountable to the citizens of the ashram. He was an unexcised Ecstatic architect. His word meant nothing more than the ravings of a lunatic.

He stood there, staring at the prone shape of the yaksha, staring at nothing at all.

We need to get out of here, he thought again, desperation building in him.

How would he do it? Deathcages created a pocket Moment. And he had learned that this latest technology of the sungineers—the death*maze*—could contract the Deepness, creating a pocket too. Yet the yaksha had Ecstatically trajected the Maze Architects who stood *within* the deathmaze. It had done so while accessing a shard of the Moment—which meant that a pocket Moment and a shard Moment were different. While the pocket Moment did not include the Maze Architects within it—outside of the deathcage but inside the maze as they were—the shard Moment did. And the architects did not know of this weakness. For all of its innovation with this new technology, Nakshar was still uninformed of its dangers.

Could he do it, too? Use the shard Moment to Ecstatically traject his jailers now, just like the falcon had trajected them earlier? The thought chilled him—to take away their control over their own bodies in such a horrendous way, to commit such an atrocity—he couldn't, he *couldn't*. But what was his choice? Chaiyya would arrive any minute. She would excise him and the falcon.

Manav's drooling face floated in his mind, then Bharavi in the cage as the spiralweed strangled her. He took a deep breath, listening to the sounds of the roaring rain, trying to anchor himself in the present, but the images came faster, Nidhirv and Askavetra, Bhaskar and Mohini, all the men and women he had once been who had failed to make the right choice in their lifetimes, who had been cowards, who had not sought their Ecstasy, who had contributed instead to a world where Ecstasy was outlawed. Now it was up to him to redeem *all* of his selves, to make amends not just for this life but all those he had lived, while the world thought him a madman, while he was *trapped*—

"Iravan," Ahilya said quietly. "Stop scaring the children."

He spun around.

She stood just beyond the deathcage. She had made her way through the glass columns without him noticing. Her face was tired, her rudra beads a jumbled mess. Her white kurta was muddy, and she no longer wore the scarf. Dark circles loomed heavy under Ahilya's eyes, and her hair was in disarray, but she had never looked as beautiful, as reassuring. Iravan's heart skipped a beat. He took two long steps forward only to be stopped again by glass.

He growled in frustration.

Ahilya smiled wanly. "Now that's not going to help, is it?" She gestured with a hand. "Want to stop, so I can come in?"

It was only then that Iravan realized the vines he had been trajecting had climbed high all over the deathcage, their tentacles sharp with thorns as though attempting to pierce the glass. He glanced at the surrounding Maze Architects still standing within the columns of the deathmaze, their skins lit up in defense, their faces awash with terror and wariness.

Ahilya's greeting suddenly made sense. He had scared them with this unintentional display.

Iravan sighed and severed his constellation lines. The vines retracted swiftly, back into the fallen seeds. He stepped back.

"Councilor," Viana said. "Are you sure?"

Ahilya smiled again, her gaze still on Iravan. "I'm sure. I'd like some privacy, please. If you would all step outside the maze?"

The architects exchanged doubtful glances, but none of them moved.

Ahilya's voice became sharper. "Viana. You can pay attention to me, or I can have Chaiyya repeat her instructions to allow me to conduct this negotiation. She has a lot on her mind. I don't think she would appreciate being interrupted."

They obeyed this time. Soon, the Maze Architects were mere shadows in the trees, visible only through their blue-green light. The harsh sungineering lights dimmed into something serene. Iravan watched as Ahilya tapped at one of her many rudra beads. The glass pane closest to her whisked up, and she crouched and entered the cage, shutting the pane behind her.

As soon as she straightened, Iravan seized her.

He crushed her to him, so tight that she gasped out loud. Iravan buried his head in her hair and inhaled. The scents of jasmine and sandalwood wafted to him, *Ahilya's scents*, and all his fury, shame, and loneliness poured out of him. He choked back a sob and squeezed, trying to derive strength from her, this woman who had been his stability, without whom he had truly seen who he was in the last few months. Desperation clawed at him, to be closer to her, to feel *safe* again. He needed her so much.

When he let go, Ahilya stumbled back, a surprised laugh emerging from her. "You *have* missed me," she breathed.

"You have no idea," he murmured, preparing to seize her again.

She anticipated him this time and took a step back. Iravan paused, confused. Was she not happy to see him? But no, he noticed what he hadn't before. She was carrying a satchel, so like the ones she had used for her expeditions, and was only setting it down.

"Before we say anything more," she said, straightening, "I need you to traject."

Iravan's brows furrowed, but he obeyed. He entered the pocket Moment. Wild white jasmines bloomed from a couple of scattered seeds, growing rapidly over the glass cage end to end, so that in minutes all the walls were covered with the intoxicating flowers.

Ahilya watched them sprout and shook her head, amused, but then she tapped at a couple of her rudra beads and said, "You should know, my love. Everything we say here is now being recorded for the rest of Nakshar's council. No secrets."

He froze, raising his eyebrows. Of course. What else was he to expect? She had needed her sungineering beads to work within the deathcage; it was why she had asked him to traject.

"We could lie," he said slowly. Once he had been conflicted about his loyalties to the council and to his wife, but Ahilya had said she wouldn't make the same mistakes. Then why had she chosen to activate the beads so quickly, before they could have a proper conversation, unhindered by listening ears? Why hadn't she chosen… *him*?

Ahilya didn't blink. "You don't lie," she reminded him quietly.

Iravan said nothing, his jaw clenching.

That had been true when he could afford the luxury of such scruples. No matter the differences in their marriage, that was one thing he had always held to. He had never lied to her, nor lied in his position as a Senior Architect either, but did that matter? He did not lie, but that hardly made him a good man.

He watched her now, her expression quiet, assessing, as though his reply would flip the scales toward a decision she hadn't quite made. Iravan shrugged and turned away. He trajected the same seat that he had made for himself in the habitat in the jungle. With the profusion of jasmines and the sounds of rain, he could almost believe he was back in the Garden. Back *home*.

Ahilya nodded in silent understanding. She strode over to the falcon, and bent to her knees, hands hovering slowly toward the creature.

The silence in the back of his mind grew louder, then emboldened as she patted it. The yaksha did not stir, but it was waking from a deep realm of exhaustion and defeat. Ahilya was doing something—but what? She had no powers of trajection. Her consciousness filled his mind, the exquisite beauty Iravan had seen in the Etherium when they had floated in the vortex together. She was a complete being, never having split into a yaksha. He knew she had power, but the way she could see inside him, inside the falcon… Iravan watched, his breath shallow, as she continued to pat the creature, perhaps desiring its recovery, perhaps desiring his own.

Warily, he trajected another seat opposite his. She looked up, rose slowly, and joined him.

"How did we land here, Ahilya?" he asked in a low voice. "The last thing I remember… we had flown into the skies."

"You fell," she said. "I saw you. In… in my Etherium."

Iravan frowned and nodded slowly. His Etherium had linked with Ahilya's when they had ended the earthrage together, but he had not expected that connection to still work. He had attempted to open it in the lonely months of being in the jungle, but what did it mean that it worked now? Was it only in times of great desperation? Or did Ahilya have control over it that he didn't?

"Tell me what happened," she said.

Iravan swept a shaky hand through his hair. The silence of the yaksha had grown dim again, though there was another restful quality to it now. Where should he begin? Those months of… *living* in the jungle? The number of times he had tried to return to Nakshar? The visions of the Etherium, the yaksha strangling him, the discordance of his unity, the lightning storm, his regrets and shame, the way the falcon had trajected those architects, the way the falcon had trajected *him*?

"The skyrage," he gasped. "That wasn't us. I know the others think that the falcon and I made the skyrage happen, that we trajected the architects and shook the Moment. All of that was the cosmic beings. They have always been able to affect the Moment, but now they can affect the architects in the Moment too. The falcon and I stopped it. We forced the cosmic creatures back."

His fingers still clutched his hair as he remembered how the falcon had shot a webbing into the dark of the Deepness with their combined powers. It was the same pattern the creature had used while holding back the earthrage in the jungle, the same pattern it had tried to teach him. Where had it aimed this time?

Ahilya's fingers tangled with his own in his hair. She pulled them down and stared into his eyes. "Yes. I thought as much."

Iravan stared back. "You believe me?"

"Of course. Why wouldn't I?"

Iravan shivered, then shrugged.

"I believe you," she repeated quietly. "But belief doesn't help us now. This is not about what is true. This is about what is convenient.

Iravan, I've already told everyone in Nakshar everything we learnt in the jungle. I took a veristem test. They believe me but they still oppose me, because believing me doesn't allow for their way of life in the sky—"

"Their way of life is *wrong*," Iravan interrupted, frowning. "Bharavi knew it, and I know it now, too. You saw the carvings in the habitat— the erasure of complete people, the tyranny of the architects. Ahilya, this way of life is an attack on both architects and non-architects."

"Yes, but we have nothing to replace it with," she said. "We can't dissolve our structures just on pure intentions, and say we need to return to the jungle. They will never accept that, no matter the truth. What we need is to find a compromise. We need to build something new together. We need to plan."

"I'm not sure we have the time." Iravan stood up and began to pace. "I'm trying to do what's right. I'm trying to make amends, but Ahilya, this has never happened before. The Moment shivering, the crimson color to the Maze Architects, a freak lightning storm, now this inexplicable rain? It's going to get worse. I don't know how, and I don't know when—the Etherium gave me only the briefest warning, and it isn't reliable. There is a pattern to it I haven't figured out yet. But the skies are no longer safe. All of this only means one thing. The cosmic beings are evolving, they are—"

"Retaliating," she finished.

He stopped pacing and stared at her. "Yes."

She gestured for him to go on. "You said that before. What do you think is happening?"

"I've learned about them in the time I was in the jungle. I am trying to understand them—because in the end, they are the true enemy." Iravan crossed the distance and returned to his chair. "They are dangerous, Ahilya, more dangerous than you can imagine. The cosmic creatures are a hive mind. The one that you and I trapped…

I think it has communicated to the others through the hive mind, and those creatures now know that people like you exist—complete beings who can stop them from splitting in the first place. Perhaps they had always known. You and I were not the first people ever to stop an earthrage. There were others, you remember, rebels who did that who we saw in the carvings. But this attack on the architects—I think the cosmic creatures realize that we're attempting to stop them from splitting again after so many centuries. Maybe they realize that we're not just interested in ending individual earthrages, but ending forever the phenomenon. The architects are clearly in danger, and I think complete beings like you are vulnerable too."

"They cannot hurt non-architects, Iravan. I stood as a shield against the cosmic creature."

"Yes, but—"

"And people like me hold the key to ending the rages."

"I am counting on that. It's why I need to take not just Ecstatics but also complete citizens."

"Yet you will get neither," Ahilya said softly. "Until the council—the Conclave—cooperates."

Iravan paused.

Ahilya grimaced, and her hand snaked around her waist. She closed her eyes for a long second. A quiet sigh escaped her.

It hit him then, what it must have been like for her, a councilor who was neither an architect nor a sungineer—a woman, who had no partner around her while she was pregnant. Pain wrenched through him and he pressed his head again wearily. Would the guilt never end? His choices pulled him in different directions, yet no matter what he did, he hurt her. That is what he had given her, the legacy of their marriage.

He dropped his hand to find her watching him. The Etherium flashed brightly, the scream of the cosmic beings.

"All right," he said tiredly. "I'm listening."

Ahilya's lips turned up into a small smile. "What we need," she murmured again, "is something that can work for all of us. You and I are asking the council for the same thing. We both want Ecstatics to be released so they may unite with their yakshas and help end the earthrages. But even if the rages did come to an end, I'm not sure people would truly want to live in the jungle."

"The skyrages might give them a reason to," he said dryly.

"Yes, but you ended that today. Ecstatic architects could end earthrages and skyrages altogether."

Iravan wasn't so sure. He couldn't even end an earthrage alone, he needed the falcon and Ahilya and the everdust to do so. The skyrage was a totally new variable. At best, he and the yaksha had delayed it. He glanced at the prone shape of the falcon. How had the creature known to do that trajection? If they could delay a skyrage together, could they delay an earthrage too? Iravan had not considered it, but the falcon knew so much more than he did.

The silence in his mind twitched, then settled. Between his brows, the Etherium sharpened. For a second, the falcon swerved through a haze of arrow-like lightning even as ashrams wobbled in the skies, ready to crash below. The image was so clear that a chill went through him. It was incongruous, him and his wife sitting here so calmly, discussing the end of their world and civilization, an event that could occur any second. The weight of inevitability grew in him. The clock was ticking, one raindrop at a time.

"What do you have in mind?" he asked warily.

"A compromise," Ahilya said. "You want to train the Ecstatics, and I can convince the council to allow you to do that—not in the habitat, but right here. Once you've trained them, you take them down to the jungle. You end the earthrages, then return the Ecstatics to the ashrams."

"I can't end the earthrages without complete beings though."

"We can arrange that too. The families of the Ecstatics, maybe their spouses, could help like I helped you." She made a dismissive gesture. "These are logistical details. We will work them out. The important thing is that you train the Ecstatics here, in the skies."

Iravan frowned. "I'd have to use supertrajection to do so. Is that what you're offering me? Authority to move freely in the ashram? Aren't you afraid?"

"The sungineers are trying something. Even as we speak, they are embedding Nakshar with deathmazes. Kiana believes the height of the glass columns is secondary to inhibiting Ecstasy. What matters is that they are *there*. She intends to insert the pattern underground, within the structure of the ashram. We wouldn't see the mazes but they will still control your Ecstatic trajection. You'll be free, in a manner of speaking, only able to supertraject when and where you're allowed to—but you *will* get what you want. The ability to end the rages with the ashram's Ecstatics."

Iravan studied her, his wife, the mother of his unborn child, a councilor of Nakshar through and through.

"I see," he said quietly. "And in return for this? What does the council want from me?"

Ahilya met his gaze. "We already have the means to use Ecstasy, but our Ecstatics are out of control. *You* are not. I want you to cooperate with the council."

He would already be doing that by training the Ecstatics. In theory, they could one day replace non-Ecstatic architects in the ashrams—but that was not what she meant.

"How do you mean, exactly?" he asked slowly.

Ahilya took a deep breath. "Help us make an Ecstatic battery, one that can store and retain supertrajection."

Iravan recoiled. "Why in bloody rages would I do that? They'll never let me out. They'll never allow me to take the Ecstatics away to end the earthrages."

"As long as Ecstatics are useful, they won't be excised. That's what we are trying to prevent."

"You don't need an Ecstatic battery to do that. I could simply train the Ecstatics—they could power your devices with Energy X like trajection has done before."

"I have made promises to Kiana, Iravan," Ahilya said wearily. "The creation of Airav's battery, the embedding of sungineering within the ashram right now—sungineers have never before had the freedom to create freely. They have a stake in the future of our survival too, a stake in *their* relevance. Kiana is especially interested in an Ecstatic battery. Your cooperation will allow them to create their inventions."

"By trapping Ecstatics here? Never letting us fulfill the purpose of Ecstasy? By creating a battery that would only be dangerous to us?"

"By rebuilding you," Ahilya snapped, irritated. "By showing them Ecstatics are reasonable and willing to help. By showing them that Ecstatics don't need to be excised, but can be a willing, functioning part of society as it continues to evolve."

Iravan pulled back from her, staring. Ahilya sighed, as though at the end of her patience, but she reached for her satchel again and pulled out what appeared to be clothes.

Iravan accepted them, shaking them out.

She had brought him a kurta and pair of trousers, black as night with blue-green swirling embroidery on the cuffs of the sleeves and collar. The work was exquisite, rich, more suited to the council chambers than the deathcage.

Iravan looked up at her slowly. Rebuild Ecstatic architects, she had said. She was giving him an identity. The one thing he did not have. With the clothes, with his cooperation, with his *performance* as a reasonable Ecstatic architect, Ahilya was setting him up as an integral part of the ashram. No one existed in the ashram without contributing to its survival. The citizens got to pick vocations, but perhaps Ecstatics could do more. They could be neither dangerous nor a deadweight. *There might be a way*, she had said to him. *For all of us to have what we want.*

In one stroke, she had found a way to do everything: assist the sungineers with their battery, train the Ecstatics, end the rages, appease *everyone*.

All he had to do to make it work was be reasonable. Show the councilors that for all his wildness, he was still a civilized man, capable of being a functioning part of society.

The silence flickered in his mind, and Iravan glanced at the yaksha, whose traits had already bled into him. The fury, the hurt, the shame, it burned just a heartbeat away from unleashing. Civilized. That's what he and the yaksha had to be. Laughter bubbled in him at the difficulty of Ahilya's ask, at the necessity of it.

"This is a dangerous game, Ahilya," he said. "Ecstatics do not have the status normal architects do. This is why I wanted to prevent anyone knowing about Dhruv's invention. People don't like Ecstasy. They barely understand it."

"This is why we need your help. Iravan, I am trying to imagine a world where Ecstatics are reunited with their yakshas but are still useful to the flying ashrams. Who knows—if you help us make a battery, maybe they will even allow you to take away the Ecstatics permanently—as long as every once in a while, the Ecstatics returned to recharge the batteries. But for now, this is the only way the Conclave will allow Ecstasy to go unexcised—if we make Ecstatics indispensable to our survival in the skies." Ahilya sighed, and her voice dropped. "I know it's dangerous. But I'm trying to find the best way for everyone to win."

The best way for everyone to win would be for him to first take the Ecstatics away to unite with their yakshas and end the earthrages with their families, then train them when everyone had safely landed in the jungle. Yet ever since that time in the vortex, Iravan hadn't seen a single yaksha in the jungle. He did not know the form non-corporeal yakshas would take, but the corporeal ones? Had the creatures abandoned the habitat simply because he had now become its resident? Had they bowed to the falcon's superior will? Iravan could sense the urgency rise in him, a racing heartbeat. Rain still fell, and the wind whistled behind the foliage and the glass cage.

The Ecstatic trajection he and the falcon had done in the skies had delayed the skyrage, but what if the cosmic beings broke through the paltry defense? Iravan didn't even fully understand what he had done. He certainly couldn't teach that trajection, not even if another Ecstatic architect happened to unite with their elusive yaksha while they were still up here in the skies. It was only a matter of time before the webbing he and the falcon had built collapsed. With a complete skyrage, the Conclave would fall to the earth.

Besides, for all of Ahilya's dreams of compromise, the battery had always been one step away from enslavement. Iravan himself might have suggested it as a Senior Architect, but he had meant the battery for normal architects—those who could not be touched, who were revered too much, who had seats on each ashram's council. A battery for architects would have been dangerous, but there were safeguards to it.

But unlike normal architects, Ecstatics had no rights, no place, no belonging. They were vilified in every ashram.

What happened if Iravan could not find a way to train the Ecstatics to the satisfaction of the council? What happened if the sungineers found no way to store Ecstasy? Would they still let him take the Ecstatics away, especially when they had means to use supertrajection, battery or no battery? Even if the Ecstatic battery worked, what reassurances did Iravan have that they wouldn't simply use the device to drain the Ecstatics? Ahilya was trying to give them an identity, but faced with extinction, with a brand of dispensable Ecstatics at their disposal, the Conclave's morals would go to the rages. Iravan was looking at not just his own enslavement, but that of all those like him.

His doubts must have reflected on his face, for Ahilya leaned forward. "I have something else, too. As a show of good faith from the council."

This time she handed him her entire satchel, waiting for him to look within it. Iravan's hands brushed against instruments of civilization: a comb for his hair, a mirror and implements to shave, and another set of clothes. She had thought of everything—but then his hands touched bark and papers, and he froze.

He inhaled sharply as he withdrew a dark notebook. In his mind's eye, he saw her—not Ahilya, but Bharavi—holding this notebook, reading from it. *You could change the very definition of Ecstasy*, she had said to him once. *You could show the council how Ecstasy is beneficial.* Tears sprang unbidden to Iravan's eyes. He reached a trembling finger to flip the pages, to see Bharavi's careful, precise handwriting.

"H-how?" he asked. "Wh-why?"

"Bharavi bequeathed her research to you," Ahilya said quietly. "It never made its way to you because of everything else, but I've brought it now. Everything she discovered. All her hypotheses."

Iravan closed his eyes for a long moment. He took a shuddering breath.

Admiration and aversion filled him. He was being manipulated, an entirely new experience when he had always been the one doing it before. Once, he had brought rare books to buy Ahilya's trust; now she was doing the same. She was becoming one of them so quickly. Something had changed in her since she had come to the jungle to rescue him. Something had broken and grown and had allowed her to become herself in a way she hadn't before. Was he losing her? He had lost himself already, even as he'd seen who he really was.

He nodded, to indicate his acquiescence. What choice did he have? Iravan did not know when the next skyrage would occur, but perhaps before it hit he could train the Ecstatics enough to let the council store some of their energy for flight and allow him to take them away. He had been a teacher in the Academy once. He could do it. Rages, he *had* to.

Ahilya relaxed at his nod. She smiled. "You'll have to swear on veristem in front of the others to confirm you were not behind the skyrage."

"All right," he said, sighing. "But Ahilya, this thing you're attempting, it is noble and beautiful, but the tiniest slip could lead to devastation. I need to know what happens in the Conclave."

She stiffened, her finger circling a healbranch bracelet on her wrist.

"You can't tell me?" he probed.

"I'm not sure," she said. "I should be able to. Chaiyya said that you belong to Nakshar. She gave over the trajection of the Conclave to you in her time of need. We even considered you in the vote we took, and the council is delaying passing a vote of no confidence in you. I should be able to tell you things, since my healbranch vows are to the council of Nakshar, not to any individual person."

"But?"

"But it is terribly dangerous. They haven't truly made up their minds about your status. This entire situation is unprecedented.

What happens if I tell you, and it breaks my vows to the council? Perhaps the poison will be slight and the bracelet will remain intact. But I will still be poisoned, and I cannot afford to be, not even a little bit."

"Then don't," he said at once. "I don't want you to endanger yourself."

She smiled, and stood up, and he mirrored her movements.

"Keep the beard," she murmured, lifting a hand to his cheek. "We don't want to take the jungle entirely out of you."

They stood there for a long moment, staring at each other. Iravan reached for Ahilya's waist, down to her belly. It felt as flat as ever, the pregnancy not yet visible. A dozen questions choked his throat, questions about her and their child she carried, the opportunity she had seized, the changes she planned to make, and the things she intended to say in the council. But Ahilya rested her head on his chest, and he breathed her in, unable to break this fragile peace.

"If this cage is to be the falcon's home," he said at last, heaviness in his chest, "then I can't leave it, Ahilya. Not unless I have assurances that the falcon won't be harmed."

Ahilya pulled back immediately. Her face was unreadable, but her eyes flickered in understanding. He was telling her he couldn't live with her in her home in Nakshar. They had come together only to be apart again.

"I wouldn't have it any other way," she said. "But you should know that material bonds holding strong is the only condition to Ecstasy that everyone might challenge at this stage. I will send word to your family to come visit you from Yeikshar."

Her words were like a slap on his face. *You are my family*, he thought, but how could he say it when shame overwhelmed him so much that he could not ask about her welfare? When the falcon and the Ecstatics and the cosmic beings pulled him in different directions so he felt torn apart instead of being rebuilt? He was going to be a father, at last, but he had never imagined it would leave him so heartbroken. He had never imagined the both of them would be so estranged.

Ahilya turned to leave the deathcage, but he grabbed her arm before she could go. He could not let a chasm open between them, not now, not when his sanity depended on her and the child she carried within her; the only material bonds that mattered, which tethered him to reality. He wanted to say he was sorry. He wanted to tell her he *knew* any apology was inadequate for everything he had done. It choked him, how badly he needed to make amends to her.

"Please," he said. "Please don't go—not yet. We haven't… We've barely… talked."

She stopped. He detected coolness and anger and resentment in her gaze. Her hand drifted to her stomach then dropped as she noticed his observation of it.

"What do you want to talk about, Iravan?" she asked carefully.

"About you. How you've been. Your pregnancy."

"Now? When all this is going on? When more important things are—"

"Nothing is more important," he said, his heart breaking, because in that second of shame he could not truly say whether those words were spoken for her welfare or his own. His voice grew soft because there had been a warning in hers, a warning and immeasurable hurt. "Ahilya, please. I just want to know. All this, what we're doing—I need to know there is a future with you and me and our child. Especially if your plan works—I need to know that it will end well between you and me. That *we* will still be." He gathered his courage, meeting her gaze. "I know you're still angry with me."

"Of course I'm still angry," she snapped, but the heat left her voice immediately when he flinched. She took a deep breath. "Rages, Iravan, we still have so much left to sort out between us."

"Then let's begin. I don't care if the council is privy to this conversation, Ahilya. We keep putting it off. I still want us. I want you and a family."

A long silence followed his request, his demand, his unspoken apology.

Ahilya remained very, very still.

Then her eyes flickered down to her rudra bead bracelet and she came to a decision. Her palm caressed his cheek and his neck, a gesture of cool affection. "I'm sorry," she said quietly. "But now is not the time for this, Iravan. Get some rest. It'll be a long few days."

She turned before he could find the words that he could not say, that he cared about her, that he needed to know not for any comfort her explanation would give him, but because he needed to know *her*. The glass whisked, flowers tearing, and Ahilya was gone.

Iravan stood there, the warmth disappearing, alone with his selves in the cage, ripped jasmines floating down to the grass.

10

AHILYA

The Conclave met in Nakshar, amid whispers and worry, beneath a cascade of rain.

All councilors of Nakshar had arrived early in the morning, each of them dressed in their full uniforms. The two Senior Architects wore white kurtas over narrowed white trousers, with translucent robes billowing behind them. The Senior Sungineers were swathed in colors of burnt orange and yellow, rudra beads completing their look. Ahilya had spent agonizing moments wondering how to appear in front of the Conclave. She had no uniform, and non-architect though she was, she could hardly claim to be a sungineer.

In the end, she had worn black, the same combination she'd given Iravan two days before. She'd draped a thick green and gold scarf around her neck, the colors she chose a nod to all the parties she was associated with. Yet for all that harmony, when she'd stared at herself in her mirror, she'd seen not her own face but that of Iravan.

I need to know it will end well between us, he'd said. It was what she needed too, but how could she give him that assurance? Every day she swallowed herbs to dull her pain, and though the medicines would work, she knew the pain would be back tenfold soon enough. In the last few days, she had even bled—bright red streaks on her underclothes before she had worn absorbent bandages. In a horrified part of her mind, she knew what such blood and agony meant. If what she suspected were true about the pregnancy... If it... if it really were true? *How* could it end well between them? Anger and grief lanced through her. He had always wanted to be a father. What if the pregnancy was damaged because of her actions in the vortex? She had saved them all. This couldn't be punishment for it.

She had been close to hyperventilating—but as the herbs began working and the pain abated, she tore herself away from what was happening to her to focus on the Conclave. The Maze Architects of Nakshar were putting the final touches to the circular theater, raising wooden benches in tiers, working in tandem with the sungineers. A glass dome had sluiced through the downpour, supported by thin veins of branches and twigs, so that it appeared they were under a translucent canopy with rain providing a constant melody. Glowglobes grew through the benches, providing a soft light to the dim chamber. The design was possible only because glass was now embedded within the ashram, and Ahilya had thought it promising—never had sungineers and Maze Architects worked in such synchronicity together.

But that was before the other councilors of the fifty sister ashrams had arrived.

She studied them now, the architects from Auresh, Katresh, and Nilenshar, murmuring and shaking their heads as their eyes traveled to the veined glass dome. The sungineers from Yeikshar and Kinshar leaned forward, studying the architecture meditatively, while the councilors of Lakshar and Renshar sat stiffly, their expressions unreadable.

The hall buzzed with mutters and whispers, yet despite the expansive theater, a claustrophobia gripped Ahilya. Yellow glimmered occasionally, but nearly all the councilors collected were architects. Over the last two days, ever since her bargain with both Chaiyya and Iravan, Ahilya had studied the dossiers on each ashram. She had collected and practiced every argument. She had conferred with Naila about the decorum expected of her, the nods and silences, and how every action now would be weighed and judged. Even so, she was aware of how she was the only non-architect or non-sungineer citizen among the three hundred people. Ahilya tried not to fidget between Chaiyya and Airav.

The councils had spent the morning in quick ceremony, announcing themselves and taking their seats on the tiered benches, whereupon Chaiyya opened the Conclave by laying out the purpose of the meeting. The Senior Architect had spoken about trajection getting harder, the dangers of having more Ecstatics on hand, the need to find an alternate method of survival—but even before she had truly finished, Senior Architect Basav of Katresh had leaned forward and tapped harshly on the wood.

"You will undoubtedly first explain, Chaiyya," he said in a gravelly voice, "why you changed the architecture of the Conclave from what had been mutually agreed."

Basav was a thin man, and his dark eyes were narrowed in disapproval. His night-black skin was a sharp contrast to the short gray hair and the white of his uniform, yet far more intimidating was the fact that he led Katresh, the ashram that formed the head of the Seven Northern Sisters, the most influential of the ashram collectives.

Next to Ahilya, Chaiyya sat very still.

Ahilya could sense the nervous energy rolling off her in waves. Surely, Chaiyya would not admit that Iravan had changed the construction? Apart from the fact that she had agreed to let Ahilya deal with Iravan, admitting to the Conclave that she had handed over the trajection to an Ecstatic would derail the entire meeting.

Chaiyya pointed a finger to the glass dome, where heavy rain still pattered down through increasingly stormy skies. "You all saw the skyrage," she said, her voice even. "It disrupted the Moment—an event that all trajecting architects experienced. I had no choice, Basav-ve, but to adapt the construction."

Basav snorted, and around them mutters filled the theater.

"We do not think it is this *sky*rage that disrupted the Moment, Chaiyya. We think it is you and how Nakshar is being run. Ashrams are supposed to revere architects—that is the way of life. Yet time and time again, we have seen Nakshar defy this. If anything, *you* are to blame for the disruption of the Moment, for this *sky*rage."

Chaiyya frowned. "This is unfair."

"Is it?" Basav said, his cold smile a snarl. "Earthrages are created because of a conflict of consciousnesses on the planet. That is why we left the jungle in the first place—because there was no order, no cohesion, no discipline. But you took our safety in the air for granted. You chose to break our rules, our methods, our *laws* by experimenting with things you do not know. You disrupted consciousness in unknown, untested ways. If anyone is to blame for this skyrage, it is Nakshar. Already our architects have burned crimson because of you."

Ahilya frowned but didn't speak. Senior Architect Basav was presenting the old theory of earthrages, one that she had disproved already but could not share under the terms of her agreement with Chaiyya. Would the woman speak it instead? It didn't seem likely. Katresh was one of the traditionalist ashrams Chaiyya had warned Ahilya about, and Basav was not a man to be swayed by new evidence. Ahilya pressed her hands close together, and took a deep breath. Wind rang outside the chamber, like a long drawn-out wail.

Chaiyya shook her head. "Nakshar did not cause the skyrage, councilors, I assure you."

"Can you attest for every effect of your battery?" Weira cut in. A big woman, with her salt-and-pepper hair cut short, Weira led Auresh's council of grim-faced architects. Her gray eyes glittered behind thick spectacles. "Can you say for certain it was not the disruption of consciousness caused by your battery that resulted in this skyrage?"

"No," Chaiyya said. "But—"

"Pray tell, Chaiyya," Basav said. "Who within your illustrious ranks sanctioned the creation of the battery in the first place?"

Ahilya squirmed, but Chaiyya's response was neutral. "The council of Nakshar did, Basav-ve, though the idea came from a Senior Architect."

The heads in the Conclave swiveled between Chaiyya and Airav, who gripped the table in front of him tightly, the only indication of his unease. As with the Conclave's construction, they could hardly admit Iravan's involvement.

Still, keeping Iravan out of it did nothing to mitigate the tension.

Senior Architect Basav shook his head and slapped the table in front of him with a loud palm. "What else are we to expect from a radical ashram like Nakshar?" he sneered. "Did you ever stop to consider what this will do to our world? If all the ashrams need is the power of trajection and not its skill, then architects become a mere energy source. You are bringing about a shift from a place of prosperity into a culture of slavery. What kind of a world is Nakshar intending to build?"

"One that is equal for everyone, councilor," Chaiyya said tightly.

"How is it equal if power shifts to the sungineers?" Weira asked, pointing to the dome. "You have clearly allowed your sungineers to meddle in your ashram's most basic building blocks. With this battery, the architects can be enslaved."

"Please, Weira-ve, there are safeguards to that."

"Safeguards like the council seats?" Basav jeered. "Tell me, how many architects are a part of Nakshar's council currently?"

Ahilya stiffened, and next to her Chaiyya froze for an instant, too.

"Three," Chaiyya said, finally. It was a cagey answer, Ahilya knew, with Airav being unable to traject and Iravan an Ecstatic.

"Three," Basav repeated. "And two sungineers. A council is always supposed to have *more* architects than not, yet your newest councilor does not wear white." He turned his cold gaze upon Ahilya, and she felt the weight of all the eyes in the chamber on her. She took a deep breath and tried to keep her hands from shaking.

Senior Architect Basav consulted the notes in front of him. "Ahilya, is it? You are what? A Senior Sungineer? A Senior Architect? What exactly is your expertise here?"

"I am a citizen of Nakshar," Ahilya said, her cheeks warming. Chaiyya had warned her not to speak at the Conclave. By tradition, only the heads of the council were considered speakers. Yet she could not ignore a direct question.

Chaiyya shifted on her other side. Her hand squeezed Ahilya's arm discreetly in warning. A buzz of mutters grew over the chamber. Architects and sungineers leaned forward on their seats to get a better look at Ahilya. Lightning cracked above the glass dome.

"So Nakshar's council is open to anyone, these days?" Weira asked, an eyebrow raised.

"She is also an archeologist, councilor," Chaiyya replied, her grip on Ahilya's arm tight. "If it wasn't for her, we would not have known that yakshas can traject Ecstatically. We would not have known that the energy signature of trajection is different from Ecstasy. She has contributed to the survival of Nakshar in many different ways and has earned her seat on the council. Without her, we would never have invented the battery."

"The battery that shackles architects," Basav said, snorting. "Tell me, Airav—can you traject at all? We have heard rumors of your condition. Was it this citizen that brought about your ruin? How magnanimous of you to sit here rubbing elbows with her."

Airav inhaled sharply, but it was again Chaiyya who answered. This time her tone was sharp.

"You forget, Basav-ve, that an architect's consent is necessary to the use of the battery. Our sungineers could strap their cords into you right now but unless you entered the Moment and trajected, it would be useless—the battery would do nothing. This device does not replace architects. It helps to *sustain* constellation lines, not create them. We still need architects to build the pattern. We need them to cooperate. Airav volunteered to save us because of our dire situation two months ago."

"To what effect?" Basav replied, folding his arms over his chest. "He cannot truly traject anymore. The power is but a memory to him. Better to die than to live like this."

A silence descended over the theater, broken only by the rush of wind. The child in the rudra tree flashed in front of Ahilya's eyes. Tariya and Kush and Arth smiled at her in her memory. Senior Sungineers all around exchanged glances, but no one said a word. All the ashrams of the Conclave depended heavily on the Seven Northern Sisters for trade. Ahilya choked back her anger.

Next to her, Chaiyya took a deep breath. She glanced around her, meeting the eyes of as many of the assembled people as she could.

"Rest assured, councilors of the Conclave," she said loudly. "Our using the battery was an act of desperation. We do not intend to repeat it. We have decided it is too dangerous—but what we do intend to do is alter the technology to store *Ecstatic* energy. As we speak, our sungineers are conducting their experiments. They have already found a way to use Ecstasy, through a device we call the energex."

"If you have this technology," a new voice asked, "why haven't you used it yet?"

It took Ahilya a moment to find the speaker amid the congregation. Garima of Yeikshar was a petite woman, her thick brown hair tied in an intricate braid. Her skin was as dark as Iravan's, native to the Yeikshar ashram, and her features were sharp. She was both stunning and intimidating, her voice cool, her mouth set in a hard line.

Chaiyya acknowledged Garima with a nod then took a deep breath before addressing the Conclave. "Nakshar has decided that we cannot make decisions about Ecstatic architects without first hearing from them."

Ahilya held her breath. This was what she had bargained for after her conversation with Iravan. She had outlined to Nakshar's councilors the same plan that she had told him, a method for all of them to achieve what they wanted. The council had been as wary of it as Iravan, but at least they hadn't dismissed her. It depended entirely on how the Conclave received it, and—

Basav's derisive laughter reverberated around the glass dome, a harsh counterpoint to the rustle of the rain.

Ahilya opened her mouth, but Chaiyya's grip had grown painful and now the other architects in the Conclave were laughing too. Chaiyya said nothing, though the corners of her mouth drew tighter.

Nakshar's council sat there, in silence and humiliation, as gales of mirth rang out around them. Hot shame choked Ahilya. She blinked back sudden tears and stared resolutely in front of her.

From the corner of her eyes, she noticed that Garima and the other councilors of Yeikshar were not laughing, though they had put their heads together to whisper urgently.

"Councilors of the Conclave," Basav said, flinging out a contemptuous hand. "It would appear our sister ashram is in need of a reminder."

He dropped his hand, and his eyes took in Nakshar's council. The humor had gone; his gaze passed over Ahilya coldly, dangerously.

"Ecstasy," he said, enunciating each word as though speaking to a child, "is *evil*. It is when an architect renounces all bonds to family and ashram. It is when an architect forgets all allegiances to survival and reality. It is when an architect breaks the world. Ecstasy is chaos and disorder, it is terror and madness, it is an architect's greatest shame. Is Nakshar so lost to good sense that it wishes to give Ecstatics *power* to decide the fate of the world?"

It was more than Ahilya could take.

Iravan flashed behind her eyes, caged and pacing, worried about the skyrages, anxious to save all the ashrams, sacrificing his fatherhood and their marriage to do so. Naila trembled, fear lacing her words, *I can't be an Ecstatic*. Ahilya had said she would protect her, she had said she would speak for her, and she thought of the carvings in the cave within the habitat, Maiya's drooling face within the sanctum, Bharavi strangled by the spiralweed.

Chaiyya opened her mouth to answer, but Ahilya cut across her. "With respect, councilor," she said coldly, ignoring Chaiyya's grip. "I did not think we were collected here to discuss *power*. We are here to discuss survival. A moment ago, you were concerned about the battery enslaving normal architects, yet you have no qualms about using Ecstatics without their consent and enslaving *them*?"

THE UNRELENTING EARTH · 137

Senior Architect Basav's head swiveled to her, shock plain on his face at her audacity.

"How dare you equate us to Ecstatics, girl?" he hissed. "The Seven Northern Sisters excise any architect within our ranks that even *dreams* of Ecstasy. We have been the ones to keep to the truest, oldest ways. We don't wait until Ecstatics destroy our ashrams, we take them out immediately. You would do well to remember who you are speaking to."

Nods and mutters broke out among the others. Outraged whispers filled the chamber, angry glares directed at Ahilya. Chaiyya breathed out in exasperation and let go of her arm.

Pain flooded in at the release, but Ahilya barely noticed.

What did Basav mean? Nakshar had done away with the Examination only recently—there was no need to have one, not with Dhruv's invention of the radarx that detected Ecstasy. But the other ashrams did not have that technology. The council had not yet shared that.

Airav nodded at her, the slightest of movements. He leaned closer and his voice was a murmur. "Chaiyya did warn you about traditionalist architects, Ahilya-ve. This is not as simple as architects against non-architects, unfortunately. The balance of power has always been delicate. They care very much about the *right* kind of architects."

She stared at him in disbelief as understanding flooded into her.

These other ashrams, they *had* no Examination. Likely, every architect was excised at the slightest indication of breaking the three conditions of Ecstasy. Iravan had rebelled against the rules of Nakshar, but Ahilya could see now how lenient those were compared to the bone-hard grip of the Seven Northern Sisters. What kind of man would her husband have become had he lived there? What would their marriage have been like—if they had been allowed to marry each other at all?

Chaiyya had interjected, trying to smooth over Ahilya's interruption, but Ahilya could not focus on the words. Horror and nausea arose in her, churning within her belly.

What a child she had been. The council seats were always about fit, and that differed from ashram to ashram. What would these people make of the truth of the cosmic beings? They were consumed in their arrogance and identities as architects, the *right* kind of architects, and clearly Ecstatics did not fall within that definition. With an instrument like the radarx, they would excise innocent architects at the first whiff of Ecstatic energy.

"It is not merely about an Ecstatic's opinion," Chaiyya was saying. "But just as regular sungineering devices cannot be used without an architect trajecting, the energex cannot be used without an Ecstatic architect maintaining their hold in the realm we call the Deepness."

"Ecstatics famously have no control," Weira said. "Sooner or later, they will erupt with power, and we can use that with this energex. Why is Nakshar wasting time with building an Ecstatic battery at all?"

Chaiyya paused and her eyes caught Ahilya's gaze.

Terror like she had never felt before seized Ahilya.

She herself had agreed to say nothing about her revelations at the council, but how far did Chaiyya's own promise go? The Senior Architect had allowed Ahilya to deal with Iravan, but she had not agreed to protecting him or the other Ecstatics. She had been most vocal about retaining the current status quo. She had wanted to use the energex on the Ecstatics already, and had only stayed her hand because of Ahilya's revelation of the events in the jungle to all of Nakshar. Chaiyya had been counting on Katresh's aversion

to Ecstasy to achieve approval for the use of Ecstatic energy—
something she had wanted from the start.

Yet she had trusted Iravan with the Conclave's construction in
her time of need. She had declared he was still a part of the ashram.
She had listened carefully to Ahilya when she had outlined her plan.
The details would have to be worked out, but Ahilya had convinced
Chaiyya, hadn't she?

Please, Ahilya thought, her gaze locked on the Senior Architect.
You need to give us a chance.

Chaiyya was silent for an interminable instant, studying Ahilya.
Then she blinked and turned back to the Conclave.

"We intend to use Ecstasy with the energex," Chaiyya said, her
voice measured. "Whether we can store it or not. But perhaps we
don't need to simply *take* the energy from Ecstatics. Nakshar believes
that Ecstatic architects can hold onto material reality while
being in Ecstasy. Two Senior Architects studied the possibility
for years—"

"Madness—" Basav began, eyes narrowing.

"We intend to present an architect to you who has achieved this,"
Chaiyya went on. "One who has gained control of his Ecstasy."

The theater broke out in agitated shouts. Basav rose to his feet,
his dark face outraged, along with the rest of the councilors from
the Seven Northern Sisters. Garima of Yeikshar looked stunned, her
hand on her chest, eyes bulging. Other councilors banged on the
tables, their voices raised in a dozen questions.

"How do you know he is safe—"

"Does this have to do with that bird creature we saw from our
lenses—"

"Are you implying you have unexcised architects freely roaming
around Nakshar—"

"Is this why you changed the construction of the Conclave—"

Wind rushed through the theater, mingling with the shouts. Basav raised his hand until a reluctant, uneasy calm grew. Several people were still on their feet, but many others sat down, their faces worried, their fingers twitching to their beads.

Basav's eyes glinted and he leaned forward, looming over the table. "You will answer for this, councilor. Yourself and all of Nakshar. Your ashram has jeopardized the safety and construction of the Conclave by allowing freedom to an Ecstatic architect."

"We have means to stop him from trajecting Ecstatically, councilors," Chaiyya began. "We are not trusting everything simply to his word."

But Basav did not seem to be listening. "You are aiming to create a world which breaks our oldest traditions. We were willing to overlook your most egregious mistake in light of your desperation, but your selection of the non-architect councilor, your embedding of sungineering, and now your freedom and allyship for the Ecstatics is far too much to countenance. We seem to be judging not just your Ecstatic's sanity but all of Nakshar's."

"Councilors, please," Chaiyya said quietly. "There is no need for this. Nakshar believes that survival of our traditions is paramount. Our technology is yours, if you wish it. The sungineering devices we have embedded into our ashram do not allow Ecstatics to walk freely, but inhibit them. If you do not agree to our Ecstatic's sanity, we can decide together whether we must excise him or use his power, regardless of whether we can store it or not. Nakshar merely wishes to take action with all of your concurrence. This is why we ask for permission to present him to you, just as we ask time for perfecting the Ecstatic battery."

Ahilya's heart hammered in time to the rain. Mutters broke out over the theater. Basav, Weira, and the councilors from the other Seven Sisters put their heads together, conferring.

The implications of Chaiyya's words were clear. In matters of the battery, the Ecstatics' freedom, even—it appeared—Ahilya's own participation in the council, Chaiyya was giving away all of Nakshar's power to the combined will of the Conclave.

Ahilya turned to Airav, disbelief in her face. "Why would Chaiyya do this? What about Nakshar's sovereignty?"

Airav sighed, a deep resigned sound. "Our sovereignty is only what is allowed by the sister ashrams, Ahilya-ve. There are some rules that all ashrams are bound by. Age-old contracts that tie us together. If we break those, the others can choose not to recognize Nakshar as an ashram at all. They can refuse to trade with us, or to share intelligence and technology. Nakshar would become an outcast, and even Reikshar would not support us through that. It would detach itself and leave us to fall below to the earthrage. And that is the best-case scenario."

Ahilya's forehead crinkled. "There is something worse than the total annihilation of our ashram?"

"Can you really not imagine it?" he asked gently. "You who have suffered so much? Whose identity has been erased over and over again? Who fought to be acknowledged even if it meant going against survival, our entire culture, even your own husband?"

She stared at him. In her mind's eye, she saw not herself but the cosmic creature as she had seen it in the vortex within the jungle. *I've been so lost, Ahilya,* Iravan said. *It is harrowing.* And her sad reply, *I've been erased, my love. It is harrowing too.*

She stared at Airav. "What are you implying? What is the worst the ashrams can do to us?"

"They can subsume us," Airav said quietly. "The combined power of their core trees could destroy Nakshar's own rudra, even if we weren't so weak. It has happened before to other ashrams. Surely, you did not think that only five hundred ashrams have been flying in the sky for thousands of years, did you? You told us about the carvings yourself, you said you saw thousands of core trees taking to the skies."

"I... I..." Ahilya took a deep breath. Her mind reeled with what he was saying. Had she believed the right kind of survival took precedence over simply surviving itself? Did she think even now that erasure was a worse destiny than death? Surely not. "I saw some of the ashrams crash into the earthrage," she choked out. "Not all the core trees that flew survived. I assumed that contributed to our numbers."

"Some of them crashed, undoubtedly," Airav admitted. "But others were overtaken by the rest of the ashrams, divided into parts, their citizens scattered. It is always a desperate tactic, but once there were a thousand ashrams in the sky, more, and now there are only five hundred. Cities once fought one another in terrible wars, because they were unable to accept each other's decisions on how to live. Once those wars endangered our species altogether. This is the reason altitude bands were created, why sister ashrams came into being in the first place. Each band contained ashrams that agreed on a common code of laws. Cities like Inkrist, Karran, Erast are sisters to each other. They exist at a different height, and Nakshar ceased interacting with them long ago except during times of great duress—as soon as we made a treaty with *our* sisters, in fact. But once upon a time, even our Conclave contained more cities—until those were subsumed to ultimately become the fifty you know. History was rewritten for all our transgressing sisters, so that their names were forgotten, their crimes cast into oblivion so they may never be repeated."

"Crimes," Ahilya whispered. "You're saying they were subsumed because of crimes, but Nakshar has not broken any rules. Why would subsummation be a threat to us today?" She caught his eye and her breath hitched in her throat. "Surely Basav and the others don't truly think the skyrage is our fault?"

"No. Without proof, they can't cast us out, though the skyrage has undoubtedly contributed to this situation. It is not our advocacy for the Ecstatics either. Once we demonstrate the deathmazes, they will know we have acted with caution."

"Then what? Is it the fact that I am on the council? That sungineers have slightly more power than they did before? What is our egregious mistake?"

"I am," Airav said quietly. "Nakshar experimented on a fully functioning Senior Architect. That cannot be countenanced and encouraged."

Ahilya stared at him, but all she saw was him in a healbranch chair, bucking in pain while she used his energy on a battery that would take her to Iravan. The sound of the wind, the storm outside, it reminded her of that fateful day.

"You were once a citizen of Katresh," she breathed.

"Yes," Airav admitted, the ghost of a grimace upon his face. "The Seven Northern Sisters do not easily let go of their architects, Ahilya-ve. I may be a citizen of Nakshar now, but I am a son of Katresh, and if they allowed Nakshar's experimentation on me to go unanswered, they would be allowing experimentation on other architects they transferred to our sister ashrams. Consciousness is sacred, you see, and to them, an architect's consciousness most of all. Allowing us to get away with what happened... especially now, when I cannot traject... It will send the wrong message. This they cannot abide."

"You knew this," she said, drawing back. "When you volunteered to test the battery, when you volunteered to help me find Iravan. Chaiyya tried to stop you, but you knew."

Airav held up a hand. "Yes, I knew. But my actions were not dictated by this. I could not have allowed any other architect to take a risk I was unwilling to take myself. But you're right, this is why Chaiyya tried to stop me. Did you not wonder why we vacillated so much on attempting the battery, even while death looked Nakshar in the face? Experimentation on architects is strictly prohibited by the code that binds all the ashrams. When you asked to chase after Iravan, it forced our hand, and so we decided. But it was always dangerous."

Shock seized Ahilya, cramping her stomach. She felt as though knives had pierced her from within. The choices she had made, the events she had put them all through—this here was their fruition. Iravan against the world. That had been her choice, and she was paying for it. They were *all* paying for it.

Airav was still watching her, exhaustion in his face. "You must understand something, Ahilya-ve," he said. "Chaiyya did not want you to speak about the cosmic beings, but it was not because she wanted to protect traditionalist architect sensibilities. Revealing such a truth would break a core tenet of sisterhood with the ashrams. It would indicate how Nakshar no longer reveres architects—something that would only make matters worse after the use of the battery on me. All ashrams are embedded with permissions to protect architects, first. That is encoded within our core trees. There was indeed a time, long ago, when non-architect citizens rebelled against this—it led to the downfall of many ashrams—and architects soon learned that a citizen's desire was necessary to sustain active trajection. That allowed for several changes in the ashrams. Nakshar opened its council to sungineers, and now you sit on it, an ordinary citizen, but these changes, they were not easy, and they were not well received. If you had spoken your news, it would have indicated to the others just how far from the traditions we have gone, how much we have broken the bonds of sisterhood. As it is, they are close to punishing us. They are not ready to hear the news about the cosmic beings."

Ahilya's voice was a whisper. "Why was I not told all of this earlier? I am a councilor."

"Yes, but you are not an architect. These are part of secret architect histories."

"Yet you are telling me now."

"What makes you think I don't have my reasons?" Airav asked, raising an eyebrow.

Ahilya stared at him. She knew so little of him. The man had been Iravan's friend, not hers. He had been the leader of Nakshar before Chaiyya had taken over; he was practiced in the art of manipulation, far more than Ahilya could know. Yet he had supported her desire to speak at the Conclave before Ahilya had made the bargain with Chaiyya. He had volunteered himself for the battery not for the architects, but for all of Nakshar. He was not a man to shy away from hard decisions—after all, he had voted for Iravan's Exam of Ecstasy, excised his own friends when matters called for it, and voted against Chaiyya, when his mind had been changed.

A chill ran through Ahilya as in the Conclave around them, councilors continued to confer.

As varied as Airav's actions had been, the Senior Architect had always been consistent. His actions had always somehow been to the benefit of Nakshar, and he told her all this now, she realized, because he intended to give her methods a fighting chance.

If she and Iravan failed in their attempt at swaying the Conclave, if the sungineers with their Ecstatic battery failed, then Airav—like Chaiyya—would allow the excision and draining of Ecstatics. If that were the only way to keep Nakshar and its citizens safe, the only way to prevent other ashrams from subsuming the rudra tree and erasing Nakshar from the histories, Airav would stand by and let the atrocities happen, and he would sacrifice Ahilya too. Without his support, she would be dismissed from the council. Her life in Nakshar would be over. Likely, she would be exiled to another ashram for all her failures, returned to a life where the architect histories were the only ones that mattered, and now—knowing everything that she did, after all the promises she had made—that life would kill her, slowly but surely, even as all of them inexorably came closer to destruction in the face of the earthrages.

Senior Architect Basav banged on his table again, and Ahilya looked away from Airav to the Conclave. Everyone was staring at Basav, though quite a few councilors darted furtive looks at Chaiyya, and at Ahilya herself.

"The Seven Northern Sisters have decided," Basav said into the silence, "that you will present your Ecstatic architect tonight, Chaiyya."

Chaiyya frowned. "That is hardly enough time, councilors, and we have other matters we should attend."

"No matter is as important as this," Weira said coldly. "The construction of the Conclave is fragile, and our citizens are in danger until we deem this architect safe. Prove his control, Chaiyya. We will have an answer to the problem of Ecstasy one way or another."

A muscle in Chaiyya's temple twitched. "Very well. Nakshar accepts this."

Ahilya said nothing, but her palms began to sweat.

Iravan was not ready to be presented to the Conclave, she knew this much. Besides, could *anyone* ever be ready for an interrogation to prove their control over themselves? Iravan had always done what he had thought was right; he had always played by his own rules. She needed to prepare him.

Basav leaned forward. "You will also immediately share the technology to detect and use Ecstasy with us. You will show our sungineers how you have trapped your Ecstatics."

Chaiyya exchanged a glance with Kiana, who nodded. "We have several radarx and energex devices already made to distribute to you. Our people will help you embed deathmazes within your ashrams if you wish. It is not a time-consuming process."

Basav did not expect much from Iravan's presentation, clearly. He was readying to use the devices on his ashram's Ecstatics. If Iravan succeeded in his trial, perhaps the other ashrams would stay their hand, but if her husband failed... It would result in the instant enslavement of architects all around the Conclave—those who were yet undetected as Ecstatics. Nakshar would likely have to use the energex on its own Ecstatics first, to appease the Seven Northern Sisters.

Ahilya made to speak to Chaiyya, but the Senior Architect stood up, calling for a brief break. Immediately councilors of all ashrams rose from their seats, crossing the chambers to discuss the events of the morning. Kiana and Laksiya made their way to their colleagues. Airav slowly wheeled his chair away, and Maze Architects of Nakshar in their brown kurtas poured into the theater, carrying refreshments. Senior Sungineers tapped on their beads, immediately surrounded by holograms, no doubt checking on their ashrams.

Ahilya sat where she was, reeling from everything that had happened. Vaguely, she noticed a Maze Architect wheeling in Chaiyya's infant twins, while the Senior Architect settled herself in a quiet corner to nurse them. A twinge of sadness prickled through Ahilya; it felt like loss, like grief, but she couldn't begin to analyze it.

Instead, she connected her communication bracelet to Naila, her fingers shaking. The Maze Architect responded at once, clearly waiting to hear what had occurred in the Conclave. Her image hovered over Ahilya's palm.

"Naila," Ahilya said, her voice low. "It's happening faster than I could imagine. They want to see him tonight."

The Maze Architect glanced around her. Her image moved—she seemed to be walking, perhaps away to a place of relative privacy. Ahilya had charged her with watching over Iravan, but that meant Naila was surrounded by other Maze Architects, those who were loyal to Chaiyya.

"Is something wrong?" Ahilya asked. "How is his training of the Ecstatics going? And the sungineers—are they making progress with the Ecstatic battery?"

"Um…" Naila demurred. "It has stalled, Ahilya-ve. We detected a weak Ecstatic signature coming from the sanctum."

"Why is that a problem? Isn't that where the training is occurring?"

"Uh, yes," Naila said. She shot another glance behind her. "But I meant the sanctum proper."

For an instant, Ahilya did not understand.

Then her eyes grew wide.

"Do you mean to say that you're detecting an Ecstatic signature from the excised architects? From Maiya and Manav and the others?"

"Yes—think," Naila's voice crackled as she walked.

"How?" Ahilya asked. "Iravan said excision cut them away from their yakshas and the Deepness."

"I'm—not—" The image flickered. "But—happening—excised—"

Her voice cut out, and the image blinked away. Frustrated cries grew over the theater, and Ahilya noticed holograms everywhere flicker and die. Chaiyya's head snapped up, mid-nursing. Ahilya tried reconnecting the rudra bead to Naila but all she received was static. The sungineers in the chamber were frowning, calling out to each other, even as the glowglobes darkened. Rain thundered down, rattling the glass dome.

11

IRAVAN

The Ecstatic architects in the deathcage stared at Iravan, terror and hope in their eyes.

He stood in front of them as though on display. Beyond the cage and the glimmering forcefields, Maze Architects clustered, dressed in their green uniforms, alert and guarded, Naila among them. Sungineers gathered to one side, fiddling with optical wires and glassy solarnotes, muttering among themselves. Wind roared like a creature in pain and rain thundered down, audible despite the bark roof. Iravan tried to ignore it all.

He focused on the bedraggled bunch in front of him. There were four of them, still in the clothes they had been trapped in. So many, so quickly, when Ecstasy had once been a rare event. It was all a bad sign.

Two of them had been Maze Architects: a young woman named Trisha, with short-cropped brown hair and watchful eyes, and a man half Iravan's age, who had introduced himself in a gruff voice as Pranav. Iravan knew the both of them from his own time as a Senior Architect, though only in name. They must surely have known of him. It was obvious from their faces, awash with barely hidden awe and wariness.

The other two were even younger. Darsh was a sullen-looking Junior Architect, no older than fifteen. Reyla was nine, dressed in her gray kurta, clearly a beginner architect. She, among them all, studied him with avid curiosity unobstructed by fear. Iravan took a few deep breaths, trying to contain his surging anger at seeing them trapped in this way.

It was their combined fury, he knew, his and the falcon's.

The yaksha had not fully recuperated, though he sensed the silence in the back of his mind stirring, a beast awaking from a deep drugged slumber. For two days, Iravan had watched over it, unsure of how to heal the creature except for covering it with the firemint moss he had grown out of the jungle seeds, before throwing them away at the council's insistence. The silence had grown and ebbed through those two days, as had the anger, but Iravan had not found the Resonance in the pocket Moment or the pocket Deepness he had been trapped in. The falcon had not trajected since their fall from the sky.

It was not trajecting now either, although Iravan supposed he would not have been able to tell, even if it had been. This morning, he had left the deathcage within the courtyard and made his way in the rain to the sanctum, escorted by a contingent of Maze Architects. He and the falcon were trapped now within separate glass cages and deathmazes. The pocket Moments, shard Moments and pocket Deepnesses each of them could access would not be able to interact with each other.

Iravan had asked his escort of Maze Architects how the deathmazes worked, but they had warned him not to traject, instructed him to walk on the patch of red grass they created, and offered no more.

He hadn't truly needed them to answer. He understood enough.

Each deathmaze had a different pattern, he guessed, a different arrangement of the glass columns, tiny though those columns undoubtedly were now that they were embedded within the ashram. The red grass, which the architects called perileaf, covered the area of underlying deathmazes, and with every step Iravan had taken toward the sanctum, he had separated from his yaksha even more.

The falcon would have to wait. He could not help it now. That was the deal he had made.

Iravan cleared his throat, cleared his head, and studied the four Ecstatics in the cage with him. These children would form his army that would beat back the cosmic creatures. Their fear seeped at him, reflected through the blinking glowglobes of the dim sanctum.

"You've been taught all your life that Ecstasy is dangerous," he began slowly. "That it can destroy ashrams. That it can harm the people you love, because it is unadulterated power. All that is true. There is only one thing that they got wrong. Ecstasy is not evil. It is your natural state. I am going to teach you how to control it."

The four Ecstatic architects exchanged nervous glances. Darsh coughed, a sound of disbelief, and Trisha studied the red grass they stood on, frowning.

A few months ago, Iravan had been as mistrustful as them. His own ascent had been fast, too fast, a matter of mere weeks. What would have happened had the falcon not carried him away to the jungle? Fury throbbed through him. Iravan took another deep breath, trying to contain it, wary of being away from the creature.

"The Ecstatic architect has only one purpose," he said. "It is to make amends to the complete beings—the non-architects. It is to end the earthrages. Before you do that, you need to unite with each of your yakshas. And before that you need to understand the Deepness. That is where we will begin."

He entered the pocket Deepness and his visions split into two. His dark skin lit up. The others focused, their faces strained, but none of their skins glowed.

"We don't know *how* to enter the Deepness," Pranav growled. "It doesn't happen when we want to."

Iravan nodded. He had expected this. The first few times he had entered the Deepness, it had been accidental. He had not understood it either.

"Then enter the Moment," he instructed. He slid from the pocket Deepness into the pocket Moment. Immediately, he was surrounded by a dozen stars, the possibilities of the green plants within the deathcage. Trisha, Darsh, and Pranav glowed alongside him, and he saw their dust motes. But the youngest of them did not light up.

"Reyla?" he asked.

"I... I don't know how," she muttered.

Iravan frowned. "How long were you in the Academy?"

Reyla looked away. "Six months, sir."

"But you haven't been trained in the Moment?"

"I... I could never find it."

"Yet you found the Deepness."

"Once," the girl whispered. "A few weeks ago. I... I thought it was the Moment. I trajected then, a jet of light, but they brought me here instead."

Iravan nodded again, this time more slowly. With the truth about Ecstasy now known, it was only a matter of time before beginner architects bypassed trajection altogether and discovered Ecstasy directly. A day would come when they would unite with their yakshas as effortlessly as though there had been no obstacle of trajection at all. Reyla was the start of a new generation—a pure Ecstatic who would never need to unlearn the limits of trajection.

Had that happened before, too? It was impossible to separate trajection and supertrajection in one's first vision. Beginner architects were trained to find the Moment, to dwell in it before they truly trajected, but that was not always an easy lesson. Their sight was not always clear. Perhaps architects from the beginning of time had always found their natural state with Ecstasy before they had been forced into trajection. Perhaps Iravan himself had done that. He could not remember it. His own days of youth and innocence had melted away; it had been so long ago.

"There is a tunnel between the Moment and the Deepness," he said to all of them. "A... a *Conduit*. The Moment and the Deepness are like two caverns, and the Conduit connects them. Try to find it."

All except Reyla focused their minds, their eyes screwing shut, their faces contorting in determination. In his second vision, they darted around the pocket Moment trying to find the Conduit. Sweat beaded their brows, and Trisha began to tremble. Darsh looked close to tears. He sniffled, then wiped a sleeve across his nose.

Iravan called a halt.

Pranav turned away and took a seat in the corner, his head in his hands. Trisha followed him, and shook his shoulder, muttering, but the two younger ones stared at Iravan, worry in their faces. Mutterings of the Maze Architects and sungineers echoed beyond the glass cage. The rain patterned through the foliage. Shadows moved at the edge of Iravan's vision, formed by the several glowglobes embedded into the earth.

He was missing a step. He had thought the Conduit an easy thing for them to find, but had it been easy for him? He could not remember—and besides, he was—he had been a Senior Architect. Perhaps that made a difference. After all, the last three Ecstatics of Nakshar had been Senior Architects, skilled in the ways of trajection: Manav, Bharavi, and Iravan himself.

"What are they going to do to us?" Pranav asked in a low voice, his head still in his hands. "Will we be excised?"

The man's question carried beyond the deathcage.

Iravan felt more than saw the Maze Architects quieten, awaiting his answer too. There were those here like Naila who seemed loyal to Ahilya, if their slight bows to him were any indication, but there were others too, architects loyal to Chaiyya, and sungineers whose allegiance was surely to Kiana and Laksiya. They had watched him with fear and suspicion. How must he appear to them? Iravan had studied himself in the mirror that had been in the satchel. The fury had become a part of him, he had seen it in his eyes: a darkening, a coldness. The silence in his mind deepened. He imagined the falcon ruffling its feathers, rousing.

"If the council or the Conclave wished to excise us," he said carefully, "they would have done so already."

"But if we don't find control," Pranav insisted. "What then?"

Then they would be harvested for their Ecstasy whether they liked it or not, but Iravan did not say that.

There was tension brewing within the council, more than he had ever seen in his time as a Senior Architect. What had it been like for the ashram to be so close to extinction all those weeks where Iravan had been ensconced in his strange sleep while within the habitat? Fear dripped through the plants here, soaked into the construction, and if it was not controlled, it would devastate them all.

He did not answer Pranav. There was nothing to be gained from terrifying these four. For a second, the falcon flickered in the Etherium, the image dull and colorless. The creature flew in the skies, hunting for him, then it crashed into Nakshar, in pursuit of him, until the Etherium dissolved.

"Did any of you ever find anything else in the Deepness?" he asked. "A resonance... or another awareness?"

They shook their heads.

Iravan hadn't expected them to. If they had been trapped inside deathcages and deathmazes since their first Ecstatic trajection, they were as surely cut off from their yakshas as he was now from his. They would not have had the time to explore the infinite darkness of the Deepness, to understand it and notice their own counterparts.

Trisha seemed to be following his train of thought. She frowned, still crouched by Pranav, and said, "Have you seen our yakshas? Do you know what they look like? Are they falcons too?"

Iravan tilted his head. "Have you seen a yaksha before?"

All except Pranav shook his head. "I accompanied your wife once on her expedition," he muttered. "We tagged a bear-yaksha. It was gargantuan."

Corporeal yakshas were massive—and Iravan himself hadn't seen one since his own union with the falcon. Non-corporeal yakshas were probably amorphous. He and Ahilya had theorized about the forms those could take, and had come to no conclusion. Still, the others' responses gave him an idea.

He turned away from the Ecstatics, knocked on a pane of glass, and waited until a Maze Architect let him out. The cage closed behind Iravan again. He walked a few feet away from it and the glimmering golden forcefields of the deathcage, leaving the Ecstatics within.

At once, the sounds of the pouring rain became sharper. Under him, thick red perileaf grass moved lightly, an indication of his still being trapped by the deathmaze, but despite knowing that the Deepness was limited to him, the ten or so Maze Architects appeared uneasy. Perhaps they remembered that he had as much access to the full Moment as they did now that he was outside the deathcage. Even if he could not supertraject, he could traject just as easily, *better*, than any of them.

"I need you to bring us to my falcon," he said.

The Maze Architects exchanged glances, then Viana stepped forward. She was as tall as Iravan himself, and she gazed at him critically.

"Why?" she challenged. "Your task today is to train these… these people. That is all."

"Every architect has a counterpart out there in the jungle," Iravan said, waving his hand. "Ecstatic architects seek unity with theirs, it helps control their Ecstasy. Perhaps my yaksha will help them see the Deepness."

"This was not agreed—" Viana began, but Naila pushed through the group and strode up to them.

"Give up, Viana," she growled. "You asked him a question and he gave you an answer."

"We cannot simply do what he asks," Viana snapped. "He is an Ecstatic. He shouldn't even be walking so freely."

"He has Ahilya-ve's backing," Naila retorted. "Are you going to disobey Nakshar's councilor now?"

"Your precious citizen is not the only councilor. Chaiyya-ve is doing this under duress."

Iravan's fury spiked at this casual dismissal of Ahilya, but before he could do more than clench his fists, Naila stepped closer to the taller woman, her eyes narrowing in displeasure.

"My precious citizen is trying to do what is best for the ashram," she snarled. "Without their training, the Ecstatics cannot participate in the battery. Without that battery, we cannot store Ecstatic energy. Without that energy to sustain us, we will all crash into the earthrage. Think on whether a single councilor has your loyalties, Viana, or the entire city of Nakshar. And you call yourself a Maze Architect."

Naila practically spat the last sentence out. Iravan glanced from her to Viana. Viana glared, but did not reply.

Naila's words were characteristic of her. Iravan had trained her for years, after all, coaching the same sensibilities toward Nakshar, though he had not expected such reverence toward Ahilya. Something had happened between the two women that he did not know, but if she supported Ahilya then it was for the best.

The Maze Architects glared at each other for a few seconds longer, then Viana grunted and called out to the sungineers. Two of them disengaged from the group and trotted toward them. The Maze Architects and the sungineers walked a few feet away and put their heads together, clearly discussing how best to entertain Iravan's request.

Naila sidled closer to Iravan, watching them with a frown on her face. "This better work, Sir."

"In truth," he admitted softly, "I don't know if it will."

Naila bit her lip in worry.

Rain pattered down over the bark roof, and though it did not touch them, Iravan felt the coldness of the wind. The architecture could do nothing to stop it, sluicing past the gaps in the bark.

He had asked for the falcon partly for himself and for the benefit of the Ecstatics in the cage, but in truth it was for Nakshar's own safety. He could not see the falcon but he could sense it, and the creature was nearly awake. It would not be pleased to find him gone or to be trapped again. Iravan had to be there, to tamp down its fury, before it did something reckless.

Still, asking for the falcon might help the Ecstatics anyway. When Iravan had first discovered Ecstasy, no one had detected the Resonance in the Moment except for him, but the Moment was not the yaksha's natural realm. Maybe they would be able to sense it in the Deepness? Maybe the falcon could guide them through the Conduit like it had guided him? Before he had truly understood

Ecstasy, Iravan had touched the Resonance and found himself carried from one realm into another, riding the wave into the Deepness. When he had been Askavetra in a previous life, she had felt an affinity with the tiger-yaksha even though it had not been hers. If nothing else, the four Ecstatics might feel a similar affinity with his falcon now.

Viana and the others stopped their muttering and approached the two of them.

"Fine," the tall Maze Architect said. "We will bring your falcon here."

Iravan stirred. "It would be better if *we* went to the courtyard, instead."

"You don't give the orders here, Ecstatic. This is where the sungineers have set up the battery, and we're bringing it here."

A spike of alarm went through Iravan. "This isn't safe. You will only be putting yourself in danger if you attempt to bring it here without me."

"We can take care of ourselves," Viana retorted and gestured to her team of Maze Architects, who began filing out of the sanctum behind her.

Two sungineers followed, undoubtedly to control the deathmazes beneath the falcon's cage, and Iravan caught the arm of the closest one.

The man jumped, his eyes wary.

"Be careful," Iravan urged. "Whatever you do, keep everyone outside of this red grass and the deathmaze itself. If you are within it, you are in danger. Do you understand what I mean?"

He did not add that the falcon could traject everyone who was within the deathmaze with it through the shard Moment, but it seemed the man understood regardless. The sungineer's eyes grew wide. He gulped and nodded, and Iravan released him. The man darted a glance at the other Ecstatics within the cage, then hurried behind Viana and her group.

Naila turned to Iravan. "If it won't work, why risk it, sir?"

"*All* of this is a risk," Iravan said darkly. "Even if the Ecstatics enter the pocket Deepness and sense the Resonance, they are never going to be able to control their Ecstasy until they unite with their own yakshas. That's what makes Ecstasy dangerous."

It was what had resulted in Bharavi destroying the ashram, in Manav attempting to traject the rudra tree. Iravan himself had only found some measure of control of the Deepness after uniting with the falcon in the vortex.

"The Ecstatics need to learn fast," he said grimly.

"You might have more success if you comfort them first, sir," Naila murmured.

It was so much like something Ahilya would have said that Iravan was momentarily robbed of speech. In the Etherium, his wife gave birth while he held her hand. The image was colorless, yet for an instant, his breath caught in his chest. Here it was. Fatherhood.

The image was replaced by the screaming of the cosmic creatures, sharp and urgent. They appeared like wisps of air and a raging mouth of lightning. Skyrage.

"I need to take them away," he said at last, more to himself than to Naila. "That must come first."

"The battery will *help* you take them away," the Maze Architect replied, though her voice was worried. "Without it, the council might be compelled to use the energex on the Ecstatics."

Iravan clenched his fists. The energex. He had learned about it in the past two days. The sungineering device had been adapted from Dhruv's invention of the tracker locket that had once been used to tag yakshas for Ahilya's expedition. The energex could use Ecstatic energy, with or without the battery. It could drain the architects, whether they found control or not.

The Maze Architect was right. If Iravan and Ahilya played their cards right, the battery would create a tighter bond between the sungineers and the Ecstatics, giving a relevance to both groups that could evolve society itself—something that Kiana probably wanted.

Yet unless they united with their yakshas, the Ecstatics would be unable to sustain a battery willingly. And without first charging the battery, the council would not allow them to leave for the jungle to *find* their yakshas. He and the council were going around in circles.

Iravan turned his gaze to the sungineers fiddling with a bone-white device in the distance. A tall bespectacled man led the group. Dhruv had exchanged glances with Iravan when he had entered the sanctum a few hours ago, but had not returned Iravan's nod. The sungineer had disliked Iravan even before he had become an Ecstatic. Still, if there was anyone here who could give Iravan information on the battery and on Kiana's plans with it, it was Dhruv.

"Can you take me there?" Iravan asked, gesturing to the assembled sungineers.

Naila nodded. Her skin lit up. She entered the Moment and trajected the red grass; it began to ripple forward, and the two followed it toward the sungineers. With her rudra beads, she activated the deathmaze under the perileaf, keeping Iravan in the pocket Deepness.

Dhruv froze as he noticed them approach, then detached himself from the group he had been supervising. He walked away to an edge of the sanctum courtyard, next to an empty deathcage, and began fiddling with optical wires and cords. Glowglobes carved out his shadow, throwing him into sharp relief.

Iravan walked slowly next to Naila, calculating his approach.

So much had changed in the last few months. Once, the sanctum had been sacred, a part of the inner chambers of Nakshar. Now it was on the outskirts, where presumably they could eject Ecstatics into the earthrage should the need arise. There was a time no non-architect would have been allowed in the sanctum, though Iravan himself had broken the rule by inviting Ahilya in and telling her about excision. He had done it, embracing the possibility of being removed from office, yet here were sungineers moving about this space fully sanctioned now, their presence a clear sign of their elevation.

If the ashrams were already making a move toward reducing reliance on architects, if the sungineers were finally coming into their own, Iravan could use that. Despite what he had told Ahilya— and the listening ears perched over her shoulder—trajection had to end someday. As long as that power was used, architects would be necessary. And as long as architects were necessary, there would be no real end to the earthrages.

What they needed—what the world needed—was a planet without trajection altogether. A planet where each architect was united with their yaksha, where they were free to become Ecstatic in what would become their final life, and where ultimately the line of trajectors and earthrages came to a complete and irrevocable end.

That, in the end, was where civilization needed to go.

Sungineering would fill the gap left by trajection.

Iravan and Naila stopped by the empty glass cage near Dhruv. Naila nodded to Iravan, then drifted a few feet away, distracted, her eyes focused on her rudra bead bracelet, awaiting something.

Iravan leaned on the glass cage, gazing back toward the Ecstatics. To find the complete infinite darkness of the Deepness would be as simple as stepping outside the ring of perileaf, one mere step closer toward Dhruv, but when the council seemed intent to judge him for his cooperation, he could hardly afford to be reported for rule-breaking, even to Ahilya. It was why he hadn't entered the Moment either, though it was available fully to him now.

For a while, he and the sungineer simply ignored each other.

Rain thundered above, blocked by the bark roof. Golden light from the glowglobes spilled dimly along the courtyard, illuminating a reflection here, a blade of grass there.

Then Dhruv looked up. "Whatever you want, the answer is no."

"I just want to talk," Iravan said.

Dhruv grunted. His scowl grew deeper.

Iravan decided to begin with his only common link to the man. "Ahilya," he said. "What do you make of her as a councilor?"

"Why ask me?" Dhruv muttered. "We haven't spoken in months."

Iravan raised his eyebrows. This was yet another change. His wife and Dhruv had been inseparable before. They had once helped each other to try and fill the council's vacant seat.

"Then your loyalties are not to her? I'm shocked, Dhruv."

"Not that it's your business, but I have always been loyal to the sungineers."

"Kiana and Laksiya, you mean."

"No," Dhruv snapped. "I mean the sungineers."

Surprised, Iravan glanced at him, but Dhruv did not look up. Instead, he pushed his glasses back up his nose, his mouth drawn into a deeper scowl. His hands worked deftly, detaching and reattaching parts of the device he was fiddling with.

Fury grew in Iravan at the need for this dance. This was hardly a good beginning, but he had not become a Senior Architect without learning patience. He waited, a muscle twitching in his jaw, his gaze away from the sungineer.

"Your falcon killed them," Dhruv said at last.

Iravan turned to the sungineer but said nothing.

The quiet between them stretched. The pace of Dhruv's work became faster. Iravan turned back to the sanctum courtyard, his heart thudding in his chest.

When Dhruv spoke at last, his voice shook with emotion. "Your falcon attacked Nakshar. It destroyed the solar lab. So many sungineers died. My friends. My brothers and sisters. They were some of the most brilliant people I knew."

Iravan closed his eyes in a long slow blink. What could he say? The falcon was out of his control at the best of times, and when it had attacked Nakshar, their unity had not yet occurred. Even now, the creature terrified Iravan. He remembered how it had tried to strangle him. He remembered how it had trajected the Maze Architects. Were the architects who had gone to fetch it all right? Had the yaksha awoken and wreaked havoc yet? Should he have been clearer with his warning? Surely, if they had kept outside its deathmaze, it could do little to them, and the sungineer he had spoken to had seemed to understand. The man would do his duty and inform others of his team about the limitations of the deathmaze.

"I'm sorry," Iravan said quietly.

The sungineer shot him a dirty look. "Save your apologies. That's not why I'm telling you this."

They fell silent again. In the Etherium, the images flashed, dull, colorless, constant. Bharavi with her children. Nakshar floating in the sky. Ahilya giving birth. Iravan's parents holding each other. For the last two days, the images had haunted him, just as they had in the habitat within the jungle. The only sharp images were those of the cosmic creatures screaming, but beyond that the Etherium seemed to have abandoned him.

More to escape those images than to continue the conversation, Iravan spoke again.

"Is that why you invented all this? To get revenge on the architects? On me and the falcon?"

Dhruv cursed under his breath. "You really don't understand anything at all, do you? Sungineering was created to replace trajection and a need for dependence on the architects. *All* architects—Ecstatic or otherwise. You think I like any of this? These mutilations of my inventions, the radarx and the energex and this... this *battery*? Sungineers are well on their way to becoming slavers. Yes, we are becoming more powerful. In a few years, we will be as indispensable as an architect—but this is not any better than where we were."

"I'm surprised you feel this way. You seemed to hate the architects. I'd think you'd rejoice at our downfall."

"You don't know me," Dhruv retorted. "It was *your* idea to make a battery, not mine. I never wanted to because I knew where it would lead us. I was pushed to it, and here we are, becoming the worst version of ourselves and what we could be, thanks to you."

That is not what I wanted either, Iravan thought, but he did not utter the words. The silence in his mind roared, filled with a latent anger: anger at Dhruv for saying these things that were true, anger at his past self at the blunders he had made, and anger now, which was not his own, but the yaksha's, bleeding into him, undifferentiated, unforgiving, ever-present.

Dhruv took a deep breath and seemed to master himself. "Kiana assures me she won't let it get to anyone's enslavement. She says the radarx has already helped the ashram—even the architects." He nodded at the slim glass device he was tinkering with, then bent toward it once again.

"The radarx," Iravan repeated. "You extracted the technology from the yaksha trackers you had built for Ahilya, like you did for the energex."

"Caught on, have you? The work I did with those trackers has advanced sungineering in ways I'm sure *you* never expected. The radarx runs on trajection but it detects Ecstasy. We use it in the Academy and the Architects' Disc and all other places architects frequent."

"And now you have a complete way to bind the architects. Well done, Dhruv."

"Detecting Ecstatics has saved the city from the kind of damage Bharavi and others like her wrought. The radarx has already saved our lives."

"By imprisoning little children?" Iravan said, nodding to the cage where Reyla was peering at him.

"By preventing damage before it can happen," Dhruv said, though his gaze went to the cage as well and a frown drew down his face. "Kiana says it isn't a tool of imprisonment, but a tool of freedom for the architects. They've done away with the Examination of Ecstasy since I created it, did you know that? Now, architects needn't be forced to marry or have children if they don't want to. They don't need to keep vigilance to check each other for breaking arbitrary limits of trajection. The safety of the ashram is guaranteed, as long as architects don't emit an Ecstatic signature. My device has changed our culture already for the better."

"Your device presumes guilt before any kind of crime has occurred," Iravan said, then paused to shake his head in disgust.

Crime. How easily he had fallen back into their vocabulary.

Ecstasy wasn't a crime, it was his natural state. *I need to leave here*, he thought suddenly. *They are turning me back into one of them.*

Dhruv was right about the radarx removing the need for the Examination of Ecstasy. Iravan had never liked the exam, and the memory of it still haunted him. In the last few months, he had awoken from restless nightmares, screaming out loud, reliving the torture of his examination, the images still clear from the veristem stars. He had seen himself in them, ugly and power-hungry, a selfish petty man, who had cared for nothing but his own ambition. He had let go of Oam. He had nearly killed Ahilya and Dhruv. Iravan pressed a hand to his head, shuddering, the images still fresh, as though he had only just stumbled out of the veristem chamber.

The exam had left its scar on him, but at least an exam was called in Nakshar under great duress. An architect had to exhibit several disturbing behaviours before being summoned to it. If it were still in place, Reyla would never have been trapped in a deathcage.

He released his hand to find Dhruv watching him.

The sungineer met his gaze evenly. "As it happens," he said, "I agree with you."

Iravan straightened. "You do?"

"Yes. I am smart enough to see sense even if the man speaking it is an arrogant idiot." Dhruv turned back to the radarx, screwing bolts in to close it.

Iravan studied the man, but said nothing. Perhaps he had misjudged Dhruv. After all, the sungineer had given the Ecstatic tracker to Iravan when he'd asked for it a few months ago. He hadn't liked the implications of his technology when they'd collected in Ahilya's house to discuss why trajection was becoming harder. He had agreed to keep the technology secret, even from his own superiors.

Dhruv frowned then spoke again, seeming to follow the same thought. "Kiana thinks the sungineers will never truly become slavers. But if that's the case, why is she so intent on making an Ecstatic battery? As long as there is a supply of Energy X, devices like the energex will work. I haven't yet figured out how to stop a battery from draining an architect, but if I don't, someone else will soon enough. But even a perfectly working battery could be used all too easily to create a future of uncontrolled Ecstatics just to harvest them for their energy. They wouldn't *need* to learn control. In some ways, if Ecstatics never learned control, it would be better for the battery—the ashrams would have a constant supply of Energy X without needing the consent of an Ecstatic. We could have a world where Ecstatics could be imprisoned and strapped to the battery to constantly power sungineering devices—freedom from worrying about survival for everyone except the Ecstatics, who would just become energy sources."

It was what Iravan himself had feared, even though Ahilya had dreamed of a different future. It was what devices like energex could do as well. He studied Dhruv. "You think that's what Kiana wants? A world where sungineers are more powerful than architects—Ecstatic or otherwise?"

"No," Dhruv replied, still scowling. "Kiana's plan is more subtle than that, and I don't know it yet. She is playing the long game. She has given support to Ahilya in the council because Ahilya intends to give Ecstatics an identity—something Kiana agrees with."

"But?" Iravan asked, sensing the question.

"But Kiana also supports Chaiyya, who wants to retain the status normal architects have had, and who doesn't seem to care much for the Ecstatics at all. I think Kiana is waiting to see where the chips fall. Waiting to see who between Ahilya or Chaiyya wins within the council." Dhruv gave Iravan a long look. "You asked what I made of Ahilya as a councilor—well, I think she is in over her head. Chaiyya will eat her alive, and Kiana will side with Chaiyya, and sungineers will descend into becoming the worst kind of monsters. So don't accuse me of binding people, Iravan. Think of what your own wife is doing, and where she will take both sungineers and architects in her juvenile desire to be everyone's favorite councilor."

Iravan's mind churned with the implications.

Ahilya was trying to do right by everyone. He wasn't about to underestimate his wife—he knew her too well for that, she had changed the world already by the sheer power of her desire—but Chaiyya *was* a seasoned politician. In a perverse way, Iravan could understand why the Senior Architect wanted to keep to the old traditions of the architects; she owed it to Nakshar's safety, and the Conclave would be hard to convince. The more Chaiyya tried to wrest power away from the architects, the more the Conclave would make Nakshar suffer.

But Kiana? Her agenda was still hidden. She had been the first non-architect councilor of Nakshar, and she had not come to that position idly. Kiana was smart—*very* smart. She had held her own in Nakshar's council against six Senior Architects, and when a position had become vacant, she had convinced the others to bring on a second sungineer instead of another architect. She had done it by maneuvering architects—*architects*—to make them believe that it would be for their own good, and in the process she had grown Nakshar's solar lab.

She had created a culture where sungineers had become indispensable, so much so that Iravan himself had asked for a sungineering battery during his own tenure. What would she do now when times were changing so much that architects fought between themselves? Kiana's motivations were unclear, even to him, but one thing was certain—whatever she was doing was to ensure sungineers did not lose their relevance, whether the world fell to Ahilya's wishes or Chaiyya's. Perhaps to her the kind of world she created was secondary to the fact that she and other sungineers remained in it, in some position of power. Worry grew in his chest at the agreement he had made with Ahilya.

"I need to test something," Dhruv said. "You will need to stop supertrajecting."

"I'm not," Iravan replied, cautiously. "Besides, I'm still within the deathmaze. Wouldn't you have to be inside it, too, to detect my Ecstatic signature?"

The sungineer didn't reply, though his frown was answer enough.

Iravan straightened, his heart beating fast. Here was another bit of information to piece together his understanding of the deathmazes. Just like normal sungineering devices could only work inside deathchambers and cages if sustained by active trajection, Ecstatic devices like the energex worked within the deathmaze only if sustained by active supertrajection.

A device like the radarx, though, that worked on trajection but detected Ecstasy, could be charged anywhere trajection was occurring. But it could detect Ecstasy only if supertrajection were occurring in the pocket it was in.

The sungineer frowned at the red grass by Iravan's feet, perhaps making the same assessment. His gaze traveled from the radarx to the other Ecstatic architects in the deathcage, a few feet over.

"It can't be them, either," Iravan said, mind racing. "Same reason."

"Well, if it's not you and it's not them, who is it? Someone is clearly supertrajecting."

Their eyes met, and Iravan saw his own alarm on the sungineer's face. Dhruv must have suspected another architect in Ecstasy, somewhere beyond the bounds of all the active deathmazes in the ashram, but Iravan felt the silence in his mind sharpen into something like impatience.

The yaksha was awake, quite likely fully.

The Maze Architects were bringing it here.

Had the creature begun Ecstatically trajecting them? If they had entered its shard Moment, it could have done so easily. He wouldn't know, not from this patch of the grass he was on. They were both in separate pocket Deepnesses.

But no, that wasn't completely right. Even if Iravan had stepped out of his own circle, and entered the true Deepness, he would not know about the falcon. The falcon would still be cut off. As long as at least one of them was within a deathmaze, they were separated, as surely as if they had never found each other in the first place.

Iravan blinked, adjusting his understanding of the technology.

Dhruv tapped some dials on the radarx, and looked behind him, into the dim chambers of the sanctum. "It's coming from here," he muttered, and walked away.

"Naila!" Iravan called, and waved at her. The Maze Architect frowned then jogged over, and at Iravan's gesture to follow Dhruv, tapped at her rudra bead bracelet.

The two of them followed the sungineer into the dimness, their path lit by intermittent glowglobes, Iravan careful to step only on the red grass that Naila trajected.

Dhruv had come to a standstill in front of a glass chamber. The sungineer's eyes had gone wide behind his spectacles as he stared at the person within the chamber, a short dark-skinned man, his face waxen, and his hair prematurely gone gray.

Manav had been a Senior Architect once. Iravan had excised him personally. Dhruv threw a confused look from his radarx to Manav in the glass cage, then back at Iravan.

"How is this possible?" Naila gasped.

"What exactly *is* excision?" Dhruv asked at the same time.

Iravan stared at Manav. Shame and anger bubbled within him. *He* had done this. This is what could happen to all the Ecstatic architects if he and Ahilya did not win at the Conclave. He blinked and answered the question that he could.

"Excision cuts away an architect from their trajection. It cuts them away from entering the Moment."

Dhruv's gaze went back to the cage. "Perhaps Excision doesn't cut them away from their supertrajection. After all, Ecstasy and trajection are different energy signatures. Maybe it cuts them away from the Moment but not the Deepness."

"But no excised architect has ever entered the Deepness," Naila said.

"They might have done," Dhruv said, shrugging. "We don't know. Up until two months ago, we didn't even know the Deepness existed."

"No," Iravan said softly. "I think Naila is right. As different as trajection and Ecstasy are, they share similarities. Whether an architect enters the Deepness or the Moment, their skins begin to glow. When they traject in either realm, tattoos articulate themselves on their skin. Yet nothing like that has happened before with these excised architects."

"It's not happening now," Naila said, pointing at Manav, whose skin remained dark.

"Yet," Dhruv said dryly, "the radarx detects Ecstasy from him."

"Maybe your device doesn't work properly," Naila said.

"It works fine."

"I'm just saying, it wouldn't be the first time."

"Last time, I worked on my devices alone, in secret. This time I had help, and all of the remaining solar lab's backing."

"Then why is the signal working only now?" Naila asked.

"I tuned it to a more sensitive frequency," Dhruv said, exasperated. "It's detecting a weak Ecstatic signature."

Iravan tuned out their squabbling.

Manav. He had once been a councilor of Nakshar. He had been a poet-scholar studying Ecstasy for years. He and Iravan had been Senior Architects together for only a few months, the last time Nakshar had a full council. It had ended with Iravan's discovery of Manav's Ecstasy and the man's subsequent excision. Over the last few days, Iravan had studied Bharavi's notes, reading her interpretations of Manav's poetry. With a jerk, he realized it had been here, this very sanctum—though it looked nothing like it had then—where Bharavi had asked him to embrace Ecstasy for the first time. She had brought him to study Manav and learn from him. She had recited Manav's poetry, hoping to find a clue in his flashes of lucidity. *Two roads in sleep, and yet I rouse to many.*

Two roads.

Bharavi had fixated on that. Pages and pages of notes had covered her notebook in an attempt to understand it. She had thought the two roads meant the Two Visions, but what if they meant the Moment and the Deepness? Manav had confirmed that he had been able to balance his material bonds with Ecstasy for a brief time. But that was only possible after unity with a counterpart yaksha. Had Iravan excised Manav *after* his unity?

Iravan approached closer to the glass, his hand reaching out slowly.

At the edge of awareness, he heard Ahilya's voice. Naila seemed to be speaking to his wife, her gaze on her rudra beads. *Two roads in sleep,* Iravan considered abstractedly. *Yet I rouse to many.* The silence in his mind grew bolder, an impatient rustling of wings.

He thought of the Moment and the Deepness.

He thought of the yaksha and himself.

And he thought of the combined webbing of their trajection shooting into the darkness of the Deepness, away from the Moment.

The Etherium flared, so sharp, so bright, that Iravan cried out. He saw, then, the cosmic beings, their shape, their home, their form—not in the manner he had seen before, as wisps of air, but their *true* identity, like a vibration that screamed through his heart, that seared his vision so he stood there, blind tears falling down his cheeks, unable to articulate it.

Manav began to writhe. The man's eyes rolled back into his head and he shook even while on his feet. Naila shrieked, and Iravan turned to see her rudra beads sizzle as though on fire. Glowglobes along the path flickered over and over again, malfunctioning.

Dhruv exchanged a startled glance with Iravan, and began to tap at his solarnote, presumably to call for help, but the tablet flickered and died away.

"What's happening?" Iravan asked.

"It's dead," Dhruv said hoarsely. "Sungineering is dead."

Thin cracks appeared in the ground, the plates beneath them shifting. Overhead, bark broke away completely, letting in the rush of rain. The three of them stumbled against each other as the sanctum plunged into storm and darkness.

12

AHILYA

Shadows shifted within the Conclave theater.

Ahilya had risen to her feet as soon as everything had gone dark, her palms clutching the table. Around her, several Senior Architects had begun to glow, clearly having entered the Moment. Blue-green light glimmered in the darkness replacing the dying golden rays of sungineering devices. Voices grew hushed, even as the councilors of all the ashrams tensed, their gazes flicking between one another.

Ahilya hurried through the throng toward Chaiyya. The Senior Architect still nursed her infant girls, but as she noticed Ahilya, she handed her wailing daughters back to the Maze Architect who had brought them and excused herself. Kiana completed their group of three, though both Airav and Laksiya were treating with counselors, surely in the middle of giving Nakshar's reassurances.

"Skyrage?" Ahilya whispered, her stomach turning.

Chaiyya glanced up at the glass dome where heavy rain hammered down. "I don't think so," she said, her voice equally quiet. "The Moment is still, it is not vibrating. Besides, the last time, several Maze Architects burned with crimson light."

"I think trajection is failing," Kiana said. Her glasses reflected the blue-green light around them.

Ahilya and Chaiyya exchanged a glance. The council had anticipated this—with trajection becoming harder, and fewer Maze Architects showing up for duty, this had always been a risk. It was why the council had created an emergency protocol around the eventuality. It was why sungineering had been embedded into Nakshar so deeply.

Kiana tapped at her rudra beads. A hologram arose over her hand, a map of Nakshar and the Conclave. Ahilya heard her own breath of relief echoed by Chaiyya. If Kiana's sungineering beads were working, then the rest of Nakshar's councilors had retained their permissions within the beads too. Naila's beads had cut out because she was no councilor. Soon all would be restored, this was a mere flicker, the emergency protocol would kick in, and—

"We have a problem," Kiana said.

Ahilya's head jerked back to her.

"The emergency protocol can't kick in," Kiana said. "We've been working *off* emergency protocol for the last two days."

"What do you mean?" Ahilya asked, her stomach clenching.

Kiana removed her glasses and wiped them with the edge of her kurta. Her hands trembled as she explained.

All sungineering worked on trajection, everything except the few devices like the energex that worked on Ecstasy, but without active trajection, sungineering failed. The emergency protocol had been designed from the last of the original battery that had once drained Airav. If anything occurred to the design of the ashram, then the emergency permissions kicked in. The protocol was that if damage occurred to Nakshar, sungineering would take over. Glass would expand to replace and bolster the foliage, taking the weight off weak constellation lines and helping to maintain architecture and permissions.

"But that is only meant to be a temporary, one-time operation," Kiana said, replacing her glasses. "It was only meant to be used in case of dire need, and it was only supposed to last until architects could bring us back to status quo. Sungineering cannot power the entire ashram for long—it's not equipped for it. Except that's exactly what has been happening. We've been running on Airav's remaining power ever since you changed the construction of the Conclave, Chaiyya. Now we're on the last drops of it. We have nothing remaining for a true emergency."

Ahilya's own understanding reflected in Chaiyya's eyes. Apparently, status quo had not been achieved since the change to the Conclave's construction. When Iravan had changed the construction from the original agreed design, sungineering had recognized it as an anomaly, and the emergency permissions had kicked in. That was normal, that was what was supposed to occur. The protocol had to manually be changed back from emergency power when safety was achieved.

"How could you overlook this?" Chaiyya hissed at the Senior Sungineer.

"I—I didn't think I had," Kiana stuttered. Ahilya had never seen the woman so unsettled. "I expected the Conclave's redesign to trigger the protocol, but Laksiya manually changed it right after—I watched her do it. Something must have triggered it again, soon after her manual reset."

"And no one from the lab was equipped to catch an error like this?"

"They—they should have. And they should have told us—told me—"

"What does this mean?" Ahilya interrupted, more interested in the implications.

"It means we're fucked," Kiana said, her voice shaking.

Ahilya felt a chill go through her.

"The emergency protocol has been working extra hard to sustain Nakshar, and by extension the rest of the Conclave," Kiana said, her words fast. "Everything has been running on emergency power when it shouldn't have been, all the deathmazes, all the glowglobes, all the rudra beads—sustained by Airav's remaining battery. But the protocol is now on its last beat. First, low-priority sungineering cuts out, glowglobes and citizen rings and non-Nakshar devices." Kiana waved a hand around at the dimness. "Next, it will be high-priority experimental devices like the deathmazes. Then, the councilor beads. Soon, all of Nakshar's construction will collapse, beginning from the least important places. In a matter of minutes."

"Won't active trajection pick back up and replace the emergency power?" Ahilya asked, frowning.

"Yes, but Maze Architects will have to recreate the lines, immediately. Even so, I will have to manually end the emergency protocol like Laksiya did before, or the new trajection of the architects will fight Airav's remaining energy from the battery. The ashram exists on a balance between sungineering and trajection right now, and one can easily damage the other. Unless active trajection steps in at the same moment as sungineering ceases, it could ruin all of sungineering in the ashram permanently."

Ahilya's stomach roiled. The dome above them collapsing. The glass cages of the Ecstatics shattering, along with any attempt at an Ecstatic battery…

"We have to tell the Conclave," she rasped. "The other ashrams can help us."

"Have you lost your mind?" Chaiyya snapped, and Kiana shook her head furiously. "If we tell them, it would be another mark against us. We will simply move one step closer to being subsumed by the rest of the cities."

"You can't keep this a secret," Ahilya replied, aghast. "They will see our constellation lines breaking in the Moment, not to mention any physical devastation that happens. If they can disconnect from us to save themselves and help us, is that not worth the risk?"

"Those are opportunities we can spin to our advantage. We're all collected here because trajection is getting harder and we are all vulnerable. We can use this accident as a reminder of that. Is that not what you want, Ahilya? For them to come to fast solutions and actually give Iravan a chance?"

Ahilya opened her mouth, then closed it, confused. *They can subsume us*, Airav said in her mind, and she thought in response to Airav, *These are the choices then. Iravan or the world. Nakshar or the Conclave. We save ourselves and let the others die.* Dhruv gazed at her. *You two deserve each other.* Revulsion and nausea filled her, in acceptance of what Chaiyya was saying, in the sheer selfishness of her circumstance.

Chaiyya's voice became grim. "All right. Airav can stay here entertaining the Conclave. Kiana, go to the solar lab. Prepare to surrender emergency protocols back to active trajection. I'm going to find a private alcove to communicate with the Architects' Disc and begin recreating constellation lines to replace the old ones. With luck, short of a few breakages, the construction will remain the same."

"What about me?" Ahilya asked. The other two exchanged a glance. She detected something on both their faces, consideration, solemnity and an evaluation of Ahilya and her skills.

Chaiyya finally nodded. "You heard Kiana. My takeover of the constellation lines and Kiana's surrender of the emergency protocol must align. But if our rudra bead permissions fail during that, we won't be able to communicate with each other."

Ahilya understood. Those permissions could only be restored from the council chambers.

"I'll go," she said.

"Not so fast," the Senior Architect said. "Your condition…"

"I'm pregnant, Chaiyya, not dying."

Chaiyya and Kiana exchanged another glance. "We don't really have a choice," Kiana said. "Unless you want to send Laksiya, instead."

The Senior Architect gazed back into the crowd, but Laksiya had drifted far away, in the middle of the other sungineers, clearly trying to calm them down. Nakshar's other Senior Sungineer might not know what had occurred, but she knew enough not to raise panic.

"Very well." Chaiyya detached a rudra bead from one of her necklaces. "You'll need this."

Ahilya accepted the bead, but instead of letting go, Chaiyya's hand covered her own. The Senior Architect's skin lit up blue-green, vines crisscrossing over her hands. "This is a key," she said. "I'm simplifying it and transferring it to you. You'll have to focus all of your desire to build the circuit when the councilors' log becomes visible."

For a second, an image flashed behind Ahilya's eyes, of Iravan's dark hand closing over Naila's as Ahilya and Oam prepared for that fateful expedition into the jungle. She had stood against the cosmic creatures as they ripped into her. The only thing that had kept her whole was her unfailing desire to exist. How much harder could this be?

"I can do it," she said, nodding.

Chaiyya met Ahilya's eyes. "It will be dangerous. Outside of the Conclave theater, things are likely beginning to shake already."

"I'll be careful."

"And I'll clear you a path. Now, let's move."

13

IRAVAN

The ashram rumbled in the darkness.

Iravan felt a hand steadying him—Dhruv, he realized—but he shook the sungineer off and straightened, trying to capture again what he had seen in the Etherium. It had been so *fast*, just a glimmer, but he was certain he had seen the cosmic creatures in their true form.

He pressed a hand to his forehead, trying to remember what they had looked like, but the image eluded him, as surely as a whisper in the storm. Thick rain cascaded from the now non-existent ceiling, soaking him and the others. Beyond it, wind howled, and he glimpsed a furious sky replete with angry thunderclouds.

What had the Etherium shown him? Was this another skyrage?

But no, Naila glowed blue-green instead of red, and though she looked as anxious as he felt, she was not reacting to an unnatural thrumming of the Moment.

Besides, the skyrage before had been a twisting of the weather, lightning and rain appearing in a cloudless sky. Now, the elements roared at them, striking somewhere far above, illuminating the broken ceiling and the faces of Dhruv and Naila. Over the last couple of days, the weather had become worse. A balance, Iravan had thought, to what had been mutilated by the cosmic creatures in the sky.

"What in rages is going on?" Dhruv yelled, his voice carried away by the wind. The ground shifted under them again and they rocked, trying to keep their balance.

"I don't know," Naila replied, her voice terse. "The constellation lines in the Moment are holding, though they appear weaker. I think this is only affecting sungineering, and those parts of the ashram where sungineering is embedded."

"Sungineering is embedded in *all* parts of the ashram," Dhruv said, alarmed. Slashed by the torrent of rain, his glasses reflected Naila's blue-green light. They were huddled close, but despite that Iravan barely caught the edge of Dhruv's shout.

He glanced back toward Manav. The excised architect still writhed in his cage, vibrating while upright. A chill went through Iravan. The silence in his mind burgeoned, a spike in his brain. The falcon was awake. It was impatient.

"Whatever this is," Iravan said, "we can't let the ashram collapse."

"The councilors must be trying to fix it," Naila replied. "We have to trust them."

The order formed on his lips, to command Naila's obedience, but with a start, Iravan realized that the Maze Architect outranked him now.

The sungineer must have noticed the same thing. Dhruv bent lower to the Maze Architect. "So, we just wait?" he shouted, incredulous. "Naila, sungineering is likely failing all around the ashram. Citizens—*sungineers*—could be getting hurt."

The silence in Iravan's mind grew heavier, a weighty intentionality. The yaksha was preparing to do something. Viana and the other architects flashed in his mind's eye. Where were they? Had they been interrupted on their way to the sanctum while bringing the yaksha to him?

"I don't like it either," Dhruv was saying. "But he is right. We have to do *something*."

"There is an emergency protocol around this," Naila said stubbornly. "We have to—"

Thunder cracked loudly, taking away the rest of her words. The sound rolled on and on, and Iravan felt Nakshar's answer in the rumble beneath his feet. He blinked, but rain poured down his cheeks like tears, it plastered his hair to his scalp. In the back of his mind, the silence growled. He could almost see the falcon thrashing in its cage.

"If sungineering is failing," he said, as soon as the last of the thunder subsided, "does this mean the deathmazes don't work?"

Dhruv and Naila exchanged a glance. It was all the answer he needed.

"The Deepness," Naila breathed.

"The Ecstatics," Dhruv said, eyes wide.

The falcon, Iravan thought grimly. He didn't wait anymore; he entered the Deepness and summoned the Moment.

Immediately, his visions split, and this time the infinite velvety darkness of the full Deepness stretched in all directions, a familiar fatal friend. It was accessible to him once again, and—his heart skipped a beat—it was accessible to the Resonance, too.

The silvery-molten particle pulsed right next to him, a jet of light beginning to form in its depths.

No, Iravan thought, streaking toward it. The falcon was conscious, the deathmazes had stopped working, and it was preparing to traject Ecstatically. What had it already done? Iravan could not trust it. The falcon could destroy the entire Conclave in its disregard.

The Resonance paused.

It fluttered closer, curious. The silence built in the back of Iravan's mind, and the creature's eyes glinted with grim purpose.

Iravan took a deep breath, preparing to knock into it to stop it from trajecting, to fight it if he must—but Naila clutched at his sleeve in the darkness.

"You're not supposed to," she said, terrified. "You could ruin everything Ahilya-ve is trying in the Conclave."

"She'll only know if you tell her," he answered darkly. "Are you going to tell her, Naila?"

The Maze Architect hesitated.

The Resonance reared back, preparing to traject.

Then Dhruv pulled Naila away. "Don't be foolish. He knows what he is doing."

For a second, Iravan wondered why Dhruv was helping him, but then the thought passed. The sungineer had already proved his personal likes mattered little to what he thought was right.

The Maze Architect threw her hands up. "Oh, all right. But please be careful, sir." She gestured to Dhruv, and the two of them hurried out of the dark corridor into the main courtyard.

Iravan did not follow. He could already tell that, despite the fall of the deathmazes, the other four Ecstatics were not in the Deepness, least of all in the part surrounding the Moment.

They were not the danger.

He was.

Standing within the darkness of the sanctum corridor, Iravan turned his entire attention to the Resonance.

A bar of pure silver light shot toward him.

14

AHILYA

She hurtled through the ashram, rushing toward the rudra tree. Ahilya left the Conclave on Chaiyya's instruction and entered a shaking corridor. The Senior Architect had assured her it was the fastest way, but the ground was cracking even as Ahilya ran and the ceiling split open, rain and wind stabbing her like a hundred knives.

She raced through the corridor, slipping and sliding over wet grass. The earth moved, and she could still hear Kiana and Chaiyya. Vaguely, she registered that the sungineer had reached the solar lab, and was preparing to transfer the permissions.

Ahead, the ground fractured.

There was no time to stop, no time to plan, no time to think.

A yawning crevasse grew, bottomless, a black mouth gaping.

Ahilya ran full tilt at the chasm and kicked her legs, leaping into the air. She didn't feel panic. She felt a deep sense of excitement as the earth on the other side came closer to meet her, as she landed with a thump. She had made it. She had *made* it.

She was far ahead of the chasm. She did not know she had risen and begun running again, skidding in the rain and mud, her hair dripping, her body shivering, but her destination was close, the wall in the distance where the council chambers were.

A sound like an explosion, and Ahilya found herself on all fours. Her cheek scraped against rock, and though she saw red, she didn't feel the blood. She scrambled up, not bothering to understand the sound, and dashed over the trembling earth. In her mind, she was in the jungle again, pursuing a yaksha on an expedition, tracking ahead of the architects. It had been her jungle, just as this was *her* ashram.

Ahilya skidded to a halt in front of the council chambers.

Behind her, the corridor had split open. The ceiling ripped apart fully, letting in a flood of rain and wind, pushing her against the wooden wall. The chasm had grown. It was racing toward her. That's what the explosive sound had been.

She reached for her rudra beads, and tapped, centering all her desire on opening the wall.

The bead didn't react.

It took a second for the meaning of that to pierce through her elation. The floor behind her was falling into nothingness, she was standing on the last square of earth, and the bead didn't react. She couldn't get to safety.

Ahilya pounded on the wood in frustration. She was alone here, no architect to traject her path though she could still hear Chaiyya's voice over her communication bracelet. Why wouldn't the door open? She was a councilor, and if she could still hear the Senior Architect, it meant the damage hadn't reached the councilors' rudra beads yet, then why—

Of course. When the ashram was in danger, each rudra bead reverted to its original permissions instead of sharing between each other in order to conserve energy. She needed to find the right one.

A crash sounded behind her, loud enough to cut through the torrential rain. Ahilya didn't turn to look. Her feet slid precariously, she could hear Chaiyya's urgent voice, staticky. She pulled out her many rudra bead necklaces, her fingers cold and trembling, fighting panic, trying to find the right one, the one bead that would open this damned door.

Chaiyya's voice cut out.

The static was worse than any other sound. Illogically, Ahilya thought of Oam diving for her satchel. *It always comes down to something small,* she thought. *Like not finding the right bead. Like stopping to look for a fucking satchel.*

Her feet were starting to lose purchase. She slid to her knees, her back to the wall, and stared into the cavernous darkness of the growing chasm. She couldn't believe that after everything this was how it would end, and now she was sliding, the beginnings of a scream forming in her throat—

The wall behind her groaned open.

Ahilya pulled herself backward, pushing against the opening wall until she had dragged herself into the council chamber. She caught a last glimpse of the earth tearing, a deep blackness through the cascading rain.

The wall slid shut.

All she could hear was her own breath, reverberating in her ears.

Ahilya stayed unmoving, the stitch in her side painful, the cramps in her stomach building, the dark chasm still in her mind's eye. It had been so close.

Still in shock, she stood up slowly, supporting herself on the wall.

She tried reconnecting her communication bead to Chaiyya and Kiana but received nothing. Her councilor beads were no longer working. This was why she had been able to enter the chambers without the right permissions. First inessential sungineering stopped, Kiana had said. Then experimental devices like the deathmazes. Then, the councilor beads—including any permissions to enter the council chambers at all. The failure of the councilor beads had allowed her entry into the chambers, but she only had minutes before all of trajection failed in the ashram, minutes to restore the communication between Chaiyya and Kiana to ensure Nakshar's safety. The devastation from the corridor could already be replicating itself across the ashram, for all she knew.

The council chambers glittered, holograms erratically blinking, the canopy susurrating, birds squawking in alarm.

Ahilya stumbled into chaos.

15

IRAVAN

Iravan and the Resonance crashed into each other, with the fury of self-condemnation.

In his first vision Iravan braced himself against the darkness of the sanctum hallway. Manav was still in the glass cage, writhing next to him. He could imagine the falcon in its own cage, thrashing against its bindings, the Maze Architects around it screaming.

The rain grew worse, falling so thickly that Iravan could barely see two feet ahead of him despite the blue-green light of his own body. The Resonance smashed into him again and again in the Deepness. It trajected a bar of pure silver light, aimed once again for him, but Iravan dodged it, and cut his own golden light against the Resonance, slashing its light into two, before zipping through the darkness, always a moving target.

In the back of his mind, he tried frantically to understand what the Resonance was attempting. Iravan had seen it do many things, but in the end, Ecstasy was pure power directed *into* the Moment. *That* was its form. Both he and the falcon had Ecstatically trajected their rays of light into the stars of the globule to affect their environment. Never before had the Resonance shot its jet of light *at* him. What was it trying to achieve?

The Resonance reared back, and aimed at Iravan again. He dodged, but it released a jet of silvery light toward the Moment instead, and Iravan cut it again with his own golden ray.

In his mind, the silence grew keen, a rush of cold anger. Iravan knew he could not keep this up. He was weaker than the Resonance here. Sooner or later, he would tire, and then there would be nothing standing between the falcon and its destruction of the ashram. There would be nothing to stop whatever the falcon was attempting by shooting its ray of light at him.

A rushing wind gusted through the hallway, rattling the glass cages. The earth rolled, and Iravan stumbled to his knees. Lightning flashed, and he blinked at the courtyard. For an instant, he did not understand what he was seeing in his first vision, but it seemed—

The hallway was *gone*.

One second the corridor was a set of walls, the next the walls had disappeared.

Trajection was failing—it had failed already—and the sanctum had become the courtyard, all walls and framing disappeared. Dust swirled everywhere, and Iravan coughed, the moistness entering his nose, the back of his throat. He stood in the extended courtyard, glass chambers all around him. Ahead, the forms of Dhruv, Naila, and the other sungineers waved their hands, shouting in the downpour.

In the Deepness, the Resonance swung back toward Iravan, with renewed purpose.

He faltered forward in the sanctum, unsure of the commotion, watching as blue-green light flashed among the Ecstatic architects. Golden forcefields still glimmered around the deathcage, but little Reyla's skin had lit up blue-green. Her mouth fell open, and she stared at Iravan through her glass cage across the stormy courtyard, a hand reaching forward.

Reyla had lit up not because she had entered the pocket Moment of the deathcage, but because she had found the Deepness, now, accidentally, when it was so dangerous.

Iravan swung in the velvety darkness and saw her, a tiny little dust mote, barely visible, darting in fear and confusion.

The Resonance saw her too.

It shifted, and a thin bar of silver light shot out toward her instead of toward Iravan.

NO, he screamed, and he struck his own golden light to intercept it, crashing into it at the same time. His light slashed the Resonance's into two, splitting across Reyla.

Iravan whirled in the Deepness, trying to arrest the momentum from his crash.

He had seen something in the collision.

The Resonance had not been trajecting a simple bar of silver light at him. No, the trajection was more subtle than that—the pattern had been complex, tiny filaments of light weaving in and out of each other like links in a chain. What would such a linked trajection do?

He could still see Reyla, staring at him through the glass in his first vision. The silence in his mind built to a furious roar at denying the falcon whatever it was attempting. The Resonance reared itself, its fluttery wings expanding, reflecting Iravan's own fury. It was going to shoot power at the girl again, an Ecstatic action Iravan still did not understand, but he knew he could not let it succeed. Iravan raced through the darkness, preparing his own trajection in imitation of what the Resonance had done, complex thin tendrils of light weaving in and out of each other like branches, like links—

The Resonance shot a linked jet toward Reyla—and with no time for elegance, so did Iravan. The child panicked, backing away, unable to leave the Deepness now that she'd accidentally found it, even as two rays of light approached her.

Iravan pushed, screaming, his golden links racing the falcon's.

He was going to fail. The falcon would get there first—

His trajectory reached Reyla an instant before the Resonance's did.

The second his linked light hit Reyla, a jolt of renewed energy ran through Iravan like a current.

Reyla's dust mote soared through the Deepness and bound itself to him.

A roar of anger sounded in Iravan's mind. In the deathcage, the girl smiled, a flash of white teeth visible in the lightning. *Stay with me*, Iravan thought grimly. *I'll keep you safe.*

He suddenly understood what the falcon had been attempting. Iravan had fastened the girl to himself. Her untrained Ecstatic energy was out of her control, but it had tethered to *him*, to do with as he wished. The falcon had wanted control of Iravan's Ecstasy. Perhaps to destroy the architects. Perhaps to free itself from its cage.

He and Reyla spun together in the Deepness, facing the Resonance.

The silence in Iravan's mind was deafening. He could nearly see the falcon rattling against its deathcage, smashing into the walls. Iravan prepared to traject, careful not to draw on Reyla's power too much lest it weaken her.

The next instant, Pranav, Darsh, and Trisha lit up blue-green right next to Reyla in the cage. They appeared in the Deepness, three more startled dust motes, then five, no ten, another twenty or so Ecstatics, far more than were stood in the courtyard, Ecstatics triggered from beyond the sanctum.

Terror gripped Iravan, seizing his throat, drenching him in a cold sweat. How had they found the Deepness? Why *now*?

Out of control, the Ecstatics would destroy the Moment.

They would be destroyed by the Resonance.

He did the only thing he could.

Before the rogue Ecstatics could react, Iravan spun out a dozen hair-thin filaments of golden light into the Deepness, tiny links that caught them before they hovered away. He bound them to him as he had Reyla. Trickles of their power filled him. They spun together in the infinite darkness, over and over again, the Moment and the darkness whirling in and out of their second vision, before they came to a sudden stop.

In the deathcage, fifteen-year-old Darsh fell to his knees, retching. Reyla trembled, and both the older Ecstatics stopped short, terror in their eyes, their faces stark in the lightning. From his position in the courtyard, Iravan saw it all, the Ecstatics in the deathcage, Dhruv and Naila and the sungineers yelling, Manav next to him, still writhing, the relentless storm.

Lightning cracked, and the cosmic creatures screamed in the Etherium, a sound of jubilation as they made to escape their webbing.

The Resonance fluttered, and Iravan detected a grim finality. A thrill of horror swept through him.

Gasping, he turned in the Deepness. Linked to him, the Ecstatics turned too, a battalion in the darkness, raw untrained power with him at its head. What must it be for them, this first experience of the Deepness?

Iravan moved, he thought to move, but light *burst* from the Resonance, so much, so fast, that he cried out and shielded his eyes, despite knowing the futility of the action.

In his second vision, the Resonance spun a trajectory of massive proportions around itself. Razor-thin threads extended to the particle's sides, growing *enormous*, so that for a second the Resonance looked like a gigantic silvery falcon, filling the dark of the Deepness. The Resonance-falcon of silvery light *roared*, its wings sucking in Iravan and his battalion.

Iravan drew in a deep breath, gathered the fledgling power of the bound Ecstatics to him, and prepared to meet himself.

16

AHILYA

The council chambers were eerily silent.

Golden holograms flickered over every surface, on the bark, the window-like bio-nodes, the rudra tree's black trunk. Ahilya leaned over a screen, her hands moving fast to sift through the several images. With a wave, she raised Nakshar's map at the center of the circular chamber, where it grew larger. So many areas were flashing red. Sungineering was inactive in those parts. Trajection would soon collapse too.

She had to restore Chaiyya and Kiana's permissions—but even as she pulled up the hologram of the councilor log and withdrew Chaiyya's borrowed bead from her pocket, the council chamber shuddered. Instruments whirred. Static crackled. Glowglobes sputtered over and over again. The rudra tree shook as though in a gale, and in her mind's eye, Ahilya heard it *scream*, a memory from when Bharavi had Ecstatically trajected it.

Her fingers moved over the screen, and she cleared all the other images, until only the five councilors of Nakshar remained.

Ahilya tapped at Chaiyya's bead.

It grew warm in her hand. This was no ordinary councilor's bead, it was Chaiyya's, the leader of Nakshar, at the highest priority level possible, and Ahilya remembered the Senior Architect saying, *You'll have to focus all of your desire to build the circuit.*

Ahilya consolidated her desire, and focused all of her being on restoring the permissions of the councilors.

Blue-green lights grew between the hovering images of all four councilors.

The light formed like branches growing, crisscrossing the air, erupting from Ahilya's image toward those of Kiana, Chaiyya, Laksiya, and Airav in an intricate network. Her own rudra beads grew warm over her chest and her wrists, the heat seeping through her wet clothes, tingling her skin. It was working, rages, it was *working.* Soon all the permissions would be restored. The ashram would be back to normal.

The network grew more complex, connecting from one councilor to another. The images started to flash, throwing reflections all around the circular council chamber. Ahilya kept her focus strong, her desire complete. A few more seconds, and Chaiyya and Kiana would be able to rebuild from the failure of the emergency protocol.

Something moved, at the edge of her vision.

Ahilya turned slightly. Red flickered on the map of Nakshar that floated on the floor.

Then a part of the map turned completely black.

Horror seized Ahilya, a spasm in her chest.

Instantly, she knew. The parts of the city that had darkened—those were citizen spaces—the homes, the infirmary, the schools. Naila's voice reverberated in her head, *They are not recognized as a part of the ashram at all.* Kiana said, *Soon, all of Nakshar's construction will collapse, beginning from the least important places.* The citizen spaces were the least important places. The architecture was breaking already.

She looked back to the councilor log, to the last permission that would complete the networked circuit to revive the councilor beads. Her desire wavered, and so did the circuit networking the councilors.

A dozen thoughts rushed into her mind.

She needed to strengthen her desire for the circuit to complete for Kiana and Chaiyya to begin communicating. That would allow the Disc to immediately recreate constellation lines to repair the ashram. But the citizen spaces had already darkened. Likely, trees were cracking, branches breaking, homes collapsing to trap citizens inside them. Would Chaiyya and the Disc Architects resurrect those before they powered the architect spaces? Could Ahilya gamble her sister's life on Chaiyya's unearned faith? Arth and Kush's life?

In her mind's eye, her sister smiled, beautiful and radiant, holding Bharavi and their two sons; Tariya wept at her wife's funeral, Kush standing next to her, silent tears flowing down his young face. Precious seconds ticked by. The Conclave or her sister? Iravan or the world? Such had always been her lot.

Not this time, Ahilya thought grimly.

She moved without knowing, and now her hands abandoned the half-built councilor permissions. Instead, she strode over to Chaiyya's terminal where the architect spaces still blinked at full power.

Ahilya's fingers hovered over the glassy screen, over the Architects' Academy, the architect homes, the sanctum, all places with their sungineering still functioning, though down to the dregs. That power was what the citizen spaces needed to be safe until Chaiyya and the Disc could rebuild them. The architects would be protected by the rudra tree. Those permissions had been embedded into Nakshar from the ashram's inception hundreds of years before.

Ahilya tapped at Chaiyya's borrowed bead, and individual architect spaces immediately flashed on the Senior Architect's screen. Her fingers danced frantically over the screen, like she were playing an instrument. If this didn't work, she would condemn Nakshar and the rest of the Conclave to destruction. Even if it worked, intruding into the architecture was a crime. She would be dismissed from the council on discovery, perhaps even exiled, but there was no time to think of that. If she didn't do this, she would betray everything she was.

The rudra tree shook, showering Ahilya with leaves and drops of rain, as though warning her of how little time she had, but with a final tap at Chaiyya's screen, Ahilya picked a tiny hologram and flung it toward the map of Nakshar on the floor, hoping, wishing, *desiring*.

The citizen spaces lit up.

The sanctum darkened.

For a thrilling second, Ahilya couldn't believe what she had done, that it had worked.

Then, she darted back to the floating circuit of the councilor network and impressed her desire to restore communications while pressing Chaiyya's rudra bead. She watched the circuitry complete.

Around her, lights stopped flashing. The ceiling reknitted itself with thick canopy.

Chaiyya and Kiana burst back on Ahilya's communications bracelet.

"—just in time," Kiana said, and Ahilya saw her make a series of waving gestures.

Chaiyya's dark skin was riddled with a thousand vines, like green fractures in the soil. Nakshar's map grew sharper, the architecture became brighter, blue-green light flaring before subsiding. Chaiyya had already begun to coordinate the Disc Architects. The emergency protocol was giving way to active trajection that would power sungineering again, allowing sungineering to power trajection back, keeping the ashram and the Conclave safe and in flight.

Ahilya sat back on the closest chair, her chest heaving. With each breath, the stitch in her side grew sharper, but she couldn't allow herself to feel the pain, not quite yet.

Her eyes drew to the citizen spaces then back to the sanctum, which had returned to blue-green.

There had been only one way to save the citizen spaces. Ahilya had transferred sungineering from the sanctum to the homes of the citizens. She had chosen the sanctum instead of any other architect space because it had been the safest option. Undoubtedly, the forcefields around the deathcages there had dropped, suddenly allowing four surprised Ecstatic architects access to the full Moment, but the cages were physically up— the Ecstatics would not be able to walk out of them. Surely, Ahilya had not endangered anything? Besides, with all the experimentation happening there, perhaps Chaiyya would not detect what Ahilya had done.

"Thank rages," the Senior Architect said. "Good work, the both of you."

Ahilya straightened. "In light of this, perhaps we can ask for Iravan's presentation to be delayed?"

Chaiyya shook her head over the hologram. "We're not asking them for anything that will anger them. The fact that this accident occurred at all is a catastrophe, and if you were right earlier, they've probably noticed some of the damage. I'm going to have to provide explanations during the afternoon session—try and get them to think about the importance of coming to a resolution. You two will have to corroborate what I'm saying."

"I must stay at the solar lab," Kiana interrupted, her voice guarded. "I've checked, and the accident with the emergency protocol wasn't an oversight. Something happened in the solar lab that I must investigate. Besides, we need to begin the distribution of the radarx and energex to the other ashrams. I want them to have it before the evening session starts."

The Senior Architect frowned. "I will allow it, but I want a full report on the lab, Kiana. If you cannot handle your own sungineers, we have a problem. As for you, Ahilya—"

"I'm a mess," Ahilya said, drawing back. "I can't come to the Conclave, not with my clothes muddy and torn. Besides, if the Conclave is discussing why trajection is getting harder, surely you don't want me there. Not with my news of the cosmic creatures and the origins of an architect and earthrages."

This time Chaiyya's silence was longer. How long before she thought to pull up a log of councilor activities? Eventually, she would want to examine what had happened with the failure of the emergency protocol herself. If so, the longer Ahilya could delay returning Chaiyya's bead, the better.

Finally, the Senior Architect relented. "Clean up, both of you, but I will need you here for Iravan's defense tonight. Make your preparations."

The images over Ahilya's communications bracelet blinked out.

She collapsed all the hovering holograms around the council chamber. Mechanically, she looked to her own screen, where dots had returned, showing the location of every citizen of Nakshar. Naila was still at the sanctum, along with Dhruv and a dozen other sungineers and architects. She thought of sending a message to her to ask how the sanctum had fared, and if Ahilya's manipulation of the energy had been noticed, but that was not a conversation to have over rudra beads. She would have to wait until she saw Naila. Until then, the Maze Architect would have to manage.

There were so many things that Ahilya needed to do. Prepare Iravan, plan for the night's Conclave session, check on her sister and the damage that had occurred to the citizen spaces of Nakshar. But she sat still, her mind racing.

The emergency protocol had failed, even down to councilor beads. Even so, Chaiyya's rudra bead had worked. The Senior Architect hadn't wanted to give Ahilya her bead. She'd gone so far as to bring Ahilya's pregnancy up as an excuse, and ultimately had only relented under duress. Why? The little black bead that Ahilya now rolled between her fingers had allowed her to transfer energy from the sanctum to the citizen spaces. This was no ordinary rudra bead, it contained several thousand permissions, packed tightly atop each other. As Chaiyya's bead, it was at the highest possible level of clearance, superseding every other in the ashram. Which meant that, short of Chaiyya, Ahilya held more power now than anyone else in Nakshar.

What would Dhruv give for such a bead? In another time, Iravan had gifted his rudra bead to Ahilya and the sungineer had wanted to use it for his own benefit. Ahilya had denied her friend then, unwilling to break a rule, but now? Chaiyya's bead held far more permissions than Iravan's ever had. Ahilya would never have an opportunity like this again, alone in the council chamber with a key from Senior Architect Chaiyya herself.

Ahilya's eyes went back to the map that still floated in the center of the chamber. Light glowed in the citizen spaces, light that *she* had allowed there.

Airav had assured her that the architecture would return to some sort of normalcy after the merging with the Conclave, but she had seen first-hand now what that *normalcy* meant. Non-architects were not recognized as a part of the ashram at all. That was the council's thinking, the pattern of their behavior. The child Ahilya had seen hidden in the rudra tree, the mother who had moved away in the darkness, flashed once more in her mind.

Airav's normalcy had returned the citizens as a part of the ashram, but put them at the lowest priority level. What would happen to those areas if there was another Ecstatic outbreak? Another skyrage? Especially now that the one-time emergency protocol had been drained?

Next time, those people would not have minutes.

Next time, Ahilya would not be here to protect them.

To save the rest of the ashram, the architects would sacrifice the people of Nakshar. They would let them fall to the earthrage.

You two deserve each other, Dhruv had said when she had chosen to rescue Iravan at the cost of the entire ashram. *What exactly is your status?* Basav had asked her, jeering. *I am a citizen of Nakshar,* Ahilya had said proudly, shamefully, but was she? For so long, she had forgotten about the non-architects. In an attempt to save the Ecstatics, she had released the truth about excision, but that had angered Chaiyya so *all* citizen permissions were now rescinded. The non-architects lived in darkness, the structures around them weak, dangerous, while Ahilya herself lived in luxurious councilor quarters.

Was this what Chaiyya had hoped for, while selecting her as a councilor? An attempt to seduce and change Ahilya with her new powers and sudden comfort? So that her fall might be greater? So she would become hated among her own kind? How easily she had fallen for it. The council had changed Iravan once too. This is how it began. She had been trying to protect the Ecstatics and the citizens of Nakshar equally, but in helping one, she had failed the other.

Anger flared in Ahilya, for being put in this position. Her eyes burned with shame and resentment. When would it end? Was her hope to save everyone simply naivety? Would it have been different if she'd been more prepared from the start?

She had no real allies for what she wanted to do. Even Iravan had only agreed reluctantly. She wanted to ask him for his opinion, confer and counsel with him—but how could she, right now, when he was caught in so many traps, unsure of his own balance with his yaksha? He had not told her of his problems with the falcon, but they had been married over eleven years. She knew her husband, and right now she could not afford for him to lose control. She had to watch for his reactions and consider the impact of her actions on him—and she had to do it now, when the child growing within her womb… it was… it was…

Tears blinded her vision, and Ahilya swept them away angrily. Her anxieties about her pregnancy loomed in her mind, but she couldn't look at it, she couldn't accept it, not truly. A part of her wished she could share at least this burden with someone—but now when material bonds were being questioned, and when *she* herself was at the heart of that argument… When her own path to motherhood had been so thorny, with her arguments with Iravan and her challenges to the architects… What would anyone else make of this—this pain she felt, this fear of the collapse of her own pregnancy?

The truth was that she was alone in every way. Iravan had asked, but he did not have the strength to accept what was happening— either to her or the child inside her. *She* barely did. *Nothing is more important*, he had said, and yet the two of them had prioritized the training of the Ecstatics, the welfare of the citizens, their plan to save the world, again and again and again.

There was so much to sort out between them. Oam's death, Bharavi's murder, their near-divorce, Iravan's absence for *seven fucking months* when he had chosen to stay in Nakshar's temple instead of visiting her. There had been reasons behind all of those actions, but each revelation and secret had only eaten away at the solidity of their marriage, and now when they were pressed for time, for space… She understood the rationales, but anger, resentment, guilt, and helplessness circled one another in her head, paralyzing her. Her choices had led her again to this moment, to decide who was important, who *needed* to be important, which group within their world took precedence, which of her family and friends meant more, or if the things happening to her own body mattered, as though she could put all of these on a scale against each other, as though she *should*...

Ahilya took a deep breath, then another. The chaos built in her, rising and fading, rising and fading.

Eventually, her breathing slowed. Her fists stretched open. There was nothing she could do about her pregnancy or Iravan— no more than she was already doing. But here and now, she could gain another victory. She was neither an architect nor a sungineer, but she had learned enough in the last few years. She had gathered enough power.

Brushing a fist across her wet eyes, Ahilya leaned forward at her bio-node and began to rearrange the permissions of the ashram.

17

IRAVAN

Iravan weakened.

The rain pounded at him, and he sank to the wet mud. Across the courtyard, the Ecstatic architects stumbled in their cage, nearly all of them on their knees, palms against the glass. Darsh had grown pale, the blood leaving his face. Trisha was whimpering. She and Pranav held each other, collapsed on the floor of the cage. All of their bodies glowed blue-green with Ecstasy.

Only little Reyla stood upright. She continued to stare at Iravan in the rain, curious and fascinated. In the Deepness, he discerned her Ecstatic power, continuing to supply him with power.

Iravan eyed the Resonance across the infinite velvety darkness. The mercurial silvery particle shook itself. It looked so much like a falcon now, its pulsating shape gigantic in the Deepness, light made into wings. He could almost see its eyes glinting, its head cocking, as it considered him. They had thrashed and dodged each other, shooting and splitting beams of light—for how long? Iravan could not say.

He could still feel the laughter of the cosmic creatures. Iravan knew they laughed because the webbing was weakening. They were going to escape to form another skyrage, but there was nothing he could do about it right now. His muscles had grown weak. He had drawn too much on the other Ecstatic architects. Despite their Ecstasy, they were none of them a match for the falcon. They were untrained, their power latent—even all of it combined could do little against the yaksha.

The silence in his mind rose to an angry crescendo. *So this is how it ends*, Iravan thought abstractedly. He had lost against himself again. At the close, *this* was his destiny.

He severed his links to the other architects, unbinding them from himself.

At once, their dust motes soared away.

In his first vision, Darsh, Trisha, and Pranav staggered up to their feet, and joined Reyla at the glass to stare at him through the rain. *Go*, he thought tiredly. *Leave the Deepness. Go.*

But the dust motes returned immediately. They hovered around him, not just the four Ecstatics in the cage, but the dozen others he had released, Ecstatic architects he did not even know the names of, who were even now somewhere in the Conclave. They formed a slim defense in front of him, determination in their movements.

Iravan laughed out loud.

What could these children do? They could not protect him from himself. The falcon was a part of him; it owned him as much as he owned it. He pushed against the wet ground as he thrummed in the Deepness, trying to rouse himself.

He stared past the dust motes at the Resonance, at its fiery winged glory. He watched it prepare the complex linking trajectory. If that linking hit any of them, not only would their control of

Ecstasy transfer to the falcon, the Resonance would squeeze them dry, draining them of their power.

Is this what you want? he thought angrily at the Resonance. *For me to succumb to your desolation? To take me over completely?* With a burst of sudden energy, Iravan exploded forward, startling the dust motes. He closed in on the Resonance. *Take me*, he thought, enraged. *And when I am subsumed, I will take you.*

The silence in his mind laughed at him. He remembered, for an instant, how he had once fought the magnaroot. His Two Visions had merged then. He had become something else, something that had tried to kill his own self.

He had barely won then, and only because of the Resonance.

He would not win now.

Next to him, Manav continued to writhe. Iravan smelled the scents of rain. In the Etherium, the cosmic creatures strained against their leash.

The Resonance grew brighter. It flapped its wings, and the gesture was cold. It would make nothing of completely engulfing Iravan.

Iravan gathered the last of his energy, a final hope of deflecting his yaksha.

The Resonance shot out a razor-thin beam of linked light, so intricately woven with a thousand patterns that, for a second, all Iravan felt was wonder. What would it feel like when he linked with the yaksha? Would it be like his Two Visions merging? Would it be painful? Would he remember his name?

The silvery light reached him, and he shot out a final faltering golden beam to slice it, evade it.

A new presence burst in front of him, shielding him, cutting through the falcon's trajection.

Iravan staggered back. In his second vision, he froze, unable to understand. Beyond this new entity, the Resonance paused.

A recognition formed on its mirrored surface, and the silence in Iravan's mind grew distracted, surprised.

The new presence floated forward, but Iravan could still not tell its shape clearly. It seemed amorphous, like a dust cloud, simply weaving in and out of any true form. Yet there was a familiarity to it that reminded him of the Resonance itself. It felt like a jewel pulsing, its surface opaque and shiny, even as it moved sinuously.

With a start, Iravan realized that this new presence was another yaksha, perhaps a non-corporeal one. Where had it come from? Did it belong to one of the Ecstatic architects?

He raced back to the waiting dust motes of the Ecstatics in the Deepness, then swung around to see the new yaksha float up to the falcon, reverberations in its movements.

The Resonance shifted. The silence in Iravan's mind grew resigned, accepting, a feeling he had never truly felt from the falcon.

The Resonance shot out its silvery jet link at the new yaksha. The amorphous particle soared to the Resonance. Iravan and the Ecstatic architects watched as a complex web of trajection wove itself, directed by the Resonance and the new entity—the same web Iravan had seen the falcon use first in the jungle when it had held back the earthrage, and then in the sky to delay the cosmic creatures. The Resonance directed the web into the infinite darkness of the Deepness, a trajection of unrestrained power, so bright and sharp that Iravan squinted in his first vision.

The Etherium screamed, the joy of the cosmic creatures turning to despair.

The two yakshas pushed their combined trajection.

And then it was done.

Iravan blinked, and both the Resonance and the other entity were gone.

He and the other Ecstatic architects hovered alone in the infinite darkness.

Iravan lurched to his feet in the rain. He watched as, one by one, the dust motes blinked out of the Deepness. In his first vision, the Ecstatic architects leapt forward as though no longer inhibited by glass, making to run toward him, even as Naila, Dhruv, and the other sungineers blocked their way, hands open, voices raised in agitation. Manav had stilled in his own cage and sunk to the floor, his head thunking against the glass, but Iravan could do little for the excised architect. There was so much still that he didn't understand.

For a long instant, he stood there, his knees shaking.

It took him some time to realize that the rain had stopped—but no. Iravan glanced up and noticed the ceiling had grown again, all over the courtyard. The walls were returning, growing in front of his eyes, the bark curling and hardening. Active trajection had returned to the ashram. The councilors of Nakshar had regained control.

Iravan stumbled forward on weak legs toward the four Ecstatics in the cage. Shattered glass crunched under his feet, and it finally registered—the Ecstatics were no longer in a deathcage. Had Dhruv and Naila released the Ecstatics. No, they were trying to stop the four from leaving the courtyard. Even as Iravan approached, pushing his wet hair out of his eyes, he could tell the four Ecstatics were ready to bolt, their faces terrified.

"What in rages is going on?" he rasped, and the assembled sungineers shrank away from him.

Only Dhruv did not step back. He squinted at Iravan from behind his wet glasses, and jerked his head in warning.

Several Maze Architects surrounded the Ecstatics. Chaiyya's crew had returned. Viana, Brinda, and Savar were lit up with trajection, their fists curled by their sides, their clothes still dripping despite the cover of the roof.

Naila stood between the Maze Architects and the Ecstatics, her arms outstretched as though to keep them apart. She turned as Iravan drew closer, the worry heavy in her eyes.

"The deathcage," she said. "The Ecstatics broke it. The forcefields came down, failed sungineering perhaps—but they were able to enter the Moment, and they *broke* the deathcage." She tapped at her rudra beads, and a hologram blossomed over her palm. "Sungineering is back now, and I can raise new cages and forcefields. But these architects…" She swung back to face the four. "You must return to the deathcages. Please, it's for your own good."

"So you can imprison us again?" Pranav demanded. He had been leaning on Trisha, but now he glared and drew himself to his full height. "I am not going back in there."

"You can't keep us here," Trisha added, her voice loud. "We didn't do anything wrong."

Iravan's eyes widened. Only a few seconds ago, the Ecstatics had been in the Deepness with him. He had watched them leave the velvety darkness, and had thought they too had collapsed their Two Visions like he had, but it seemed they had instead found the Conduit, and returned to the Moment. In that time of crisis, they had learned what he'd been trying to teach them, but how had they broken *glass*? Glass was one of the strongest materials in the ashram. Iravan himself had been unable to break the deathcage he and the falcon had landed in, and he had used Ecstasy. He'd only had a few minutes before deathmazes had been raised, he hadn't had time to prepare truly—

Iravan paused.

He hadn't had time to prepare.

But the four Ecstatics had.

They had likely known sungineering was embedded into the ashram. They must have been strategizing some sort of desperate escape ever since they'd been found to be Ecstatics. Darsh and Reyla were children, but Pranav and Trisha had been *Maze* Architects. They would have planned, they would have discussed between themselves a drastic type of jailbreak. Shards of glass were littered around the courtyard, veined with thin green vines. Pranav and Trisha had done a subtle trajection, creating constellation lines through the Moment as it became available to them, threading sharp vines through the cages to shatter the glass from within. They had used the fact that sungineering was embedded within the city to their own advantage, doing what he himself would not have thought possible.

They were teetering on the edge.

"Let us leave," Pranav said again. "We will—we will go away." But even as he spoke, the man's face fell.

Iravan understood. Where could an Ecstatic architect go? There was no place for them, no ashram that would take them.

Viana and the others broke into shouts, the patterns on their skins growing fiercer. They were trajecting in the Moment, perhaps to bind the Ecstatics forcefully, but even as they pushed back their sleeves, patterns grew on Pranav and Trisha as well. After a second's hesitation, fifteen-year-old Darsh's skin began glowing too, though Reyla—who did not know how to find the Moment—remained dark.

"Please," Naila said again to the Ecstatics. Her skin remained dark too. It seemed she was afraid to enter the Moment, now there was an imminent standoff between Chaiyya's architects and the Ecstatics. "Please, you have to trust Ahilya-ve. She will help secure your freedom. But for now, you must return to the cage."

Iravan felt the gaze of the four Ecstatic architects on him, their faces masks of questions and fear. He knew what they were waiting for—his command. He had led them in the Deepness, and they looked to him now to lead them again in the Moment.

He studied them, the two older ones who were still half his age, Reyla who had been so strong in the Deepness, and Darsh who stared at him, with fear and awe.

I trust you, Iravan had said to Ahilya. They had both earned it with each other—but what about these four Ecstatics, and the others who had supported him in the Deepness, lending him their strength, fighting beside him, refusing to abandon him even when he had set them free?

They looked so confused, ready to fight or bolt, even though there was no place to go. What must it have been like for them, to experience the Deepness with such turbulence? To be taken into a fight with himself, his own yaksha, when they could not have made sense of what they were seeing? They were his responsibility now, and he could not allow them to go back into a deathcage, not when he walked free.

Iravan strode forward. He placed a hand on Darsh's shoulder and faced the Maze Architects. "They are my charges," he said. "You will not touch them."

Viana's eyes narrowed, and she took a threatening step. "You have no authority here," she snarled. "They belong back in the cages."

Fury built in Iravan. All of them stood on red perileaf grass. Certainly, the deathmazes had begun working again if sungineering were back. But like the Ecstatics, he could access the whole of the Moment again, unrestrained, even if they stood now in a pocket Deepness. He would show these Maze Architects who they were truly dealing with, how much *authority* he had. Iravan almost entered the Moment too—but a hand clutched his sleeve and he looked down to see Naila shake her head.

"No, please, sir," she breathed. "You can't. You need to be at the Conclave in a few hours, and you can't, please. This—this would ruin everything."

He heard her, and the words registered, but Iravan did not move. He stared at Naila, but it was not her he saw. Instead, Ahilya reflected to him, and for a second, intense fury consumed him, for this performance he still had to do, for this *farce*, when the falcon had nearly overtaken his senses, when the cosmic creatures had delighted in their near escape, convinced of their victory. It would be so easy for him to break away now, to traject in the Moment and constrain Chaiyya's Maze Architects. So easy to go find his yaksha and release it somehow, and fly away back to the Garden in the habitat.

I trust you, he had said to Ahilya, but that had been before the Ecstatics lent him their power in the Deepness. That had been before his battle with his own self. Ahilya was caught playing the council's games. The politics of it would not end well—he knew that, he had played those games once too. The battery, the training, the deal he had made with her—all of that was pointless, and Dhruv was right. *All* of them would fall in an attempt to save everyone. Iravan needed to take risks. He needed to save what he could.

Do it, he thought to himself. *Do it, break them, take them, it is your purpose to end the rages, this is the only life you have, this is the choice you made—*

With a start, Iravan realized that the thought was not his own, not truly.

Shock unlike anything ever before filled Iravan.

His hand dropped from Darsh's shoulder.

He took a horrified step back, away from them all.

Naila's face grew concerned, and the Ecstatics around him looked confused too. Iravan took a shaky breath, for the first time truly afraid of his own self.

"Please," Naila said again to him. "We're so close. This can be settled at the Conclave. We can all win."

"What do we do?" Darsh asked Iravan quietly.

What *could* they do? They did not really have a choice.

Iravan took another slow rattling breath.

He gazed at them, the group that surrounded him and the Ecstatic architects, Naila still holding her arms outstretched, Viana and the others filled with the threatening light of trajection, and beyond them, Dhruv with the other sungineers waiting to see what would happen.

He could overwhelm them all, he knew. But to what purpose? It would only convince them that Ecstatics were dangerous and needed to be confined. Ahilya's pretty dream—no matter how unrealistic—would die before it had any chance of success. *His* dream would die, of a life with her in a world that was equal, of children and family, and peace, finally peace. Iravan would never be allowed to take the Ecstatics away to the habitat, and even if he escaped with these four, the other Ecstatics in the ashrams those who had helped him—would be trapped, used for their Ecstasy or excised forever like Manav had been.

In the Etherium, he heard the cosmic creatures wail. They would break through again. Whatever webbing the Resonance and that other entity had created would not last forever. *I'm trying to find the best way for all of us to win*, Ahilya said in his mind, and Iravan thought, *Is it possible, my love? Soon, we will need to make a choice.*

Iravan dropped his shoulders. "Stand down," he said to his unit of four.

The Ecstatic architects exchanged glances.

Slowly, reluctantly, the light of trajection died down from Pranav, Trisha, and Darsh. Reyla sank to her feet, as though all of this had been too much, and Iravan was struck again by how small she was, just a child.

"If anything happens to them…" he began, his eyes narrowed.

"It won't," Naila said at once. "You will stop it in the Conclave. But please—they must return to the deathcages now. And, sir, you must prepare."

Iravan nodded. He turned his attention to the Ecstatics. "I will be back," he said quietly. "I promise. Just… hold on, for a little while longer. I won't let them hurt you."

One by one, the four of them nodded. He watched as Viana and the other Maze Architects led them away, constructing new deathcages using their rudra beads. He watched as each of his four Ecstatics entered a separate cage. Darsh turned his back to Iravan, sullenness to his posture. Pranav sank to the floor and put his head in his hands. But both Reyla and Trisha stared at Iravan. He could see the assessment in Trisha's eyes. She did not trust him, not yet. *I will earn it*, he thought. *You are mine to protect, now.*

Iravan transferred his gaze to Naila. The sungineers had dispersed again, all except for Dhruv who strode forward as though wanting to discuss all the events that had happened.

Iravan ignored him. "Where is my falcon?" he asked instead.

"Still in its deathcage," Naila replied. She had clearly been anticipating the question. "The forcefields around the deathcages dropped only in the sanctum, for some reason, allowing Pranav and Trisha to destroy them."

"I want to see the yaksha. Immediately."

"I—uh—" Naila wrung her hands together. "Iravan-ve. That will waste precious time. The training is at an end for now. You must prepare for the Conclave. You will have to present yourself in only a few hours."

Iravan's eyes met Dhruv's. The sungineer shrugged, but there was a world of meaning in the gesture. What would seeing the falcon achieve? It would only thrash, perhaps still furious at Iravan. Iravan thought—he was *convinced*—that the falcon could see him contemplate their meeting again. Laughter bubbled, wicked and vicious, and he knew it was not his own humor but that of the yaksha. *You bastard,* Iravan thought to the falcon. *Don't think I will forget what you tried to do.*

"Sir?" Naila prompted.

Iravan closed his eyes and sighed. "All right, Naila. We'll do it Ahilya's way."

Relief relaxed the Maze Architect's features. "First, a change of clothes, I think," she said briskly. "Then, I will relate to you the things Ahilya-ve has asked for you to remember."

Iravan glanced back at the deathcages, but none of the Ecstatics were looking at him. His heart heavy, Iravan turned and followed Naila out of the sanctum.

18

AHILYA

Ahilya trod carefully over darkness and broken earth.

Water squelched under her boots, and rain dripped on her shoulders as she entered the citizen quarters of Nakshar. She squinted, trying to see, but despite her manipulations at the council chambers, there was hardly any light here. Slabs of wood and pools of stagnant water quivered where she walked.

She had returned home after the council chambers to change into another set of kurta and trousers, both black, just like she had told Chaiyya she needed to, but she had chosen not to return to the Conclave yet. Instead, Ahilya had draped a raincloak over her shoulders, changed into heavier boots, and decided to see for herself what fruit her changes had borne. She had walked all the way from her home to the citizen spaces, where the muddy earth absorbed chunks of broken wall, creepers and roots curling even as the floor knit itself together.

Yet the further she had travelled from the Architects' Disc, the fewer the repairs had been. It was as though the archival memory of Nakshar was attempting to erase evidence of the damage, but could not contend with the Disc's selective return to *normal*.

The scent of moist earth climbed up her nose, but there was something else here, too, in the citizen quarters, a despair that hung heavy in the foliage. Ahilya had not dared to alter too much of the architecture. Chaiyya would have noticed immediately, and besides, Ahilya was no architect—she could not *build*. She had transferred more sungineering light to the citizens, increased their priority level so the damage would not be as severe the next time, and hidden her doings within layers of other commands. Even that much was a risk, for the Maze Architects were exhausted. Already two shift rotations had occurred since the error with the emergency protocol, where none would have a few months before. Ahilya had done what she could for the people of the ashram, even if she was acutely aware it was not enough.

She emerged onto a small square compound. Glowglobes and phosphorescence glimmered here and there, their rays dissected by the relentless rain. Tall wooden buildings grew around the quadrangle—apartments, Ahilya knew, one for each citizen family. The structure was unsound even at the best of times, but now, when Nakshar was so fragile, these high-rise towers would collapse with the merest shake. Her own independent home was lavish in comparison. Everything in the citizen spaces appeared abandoned and desolate— so different from its expansive layout during the landing.

A lone straggly tree waved in the dim hazy light at one corner of the compound. Shadows moved in the darkness under it—citizens, Ahilya realized, congregated under the poor shelter of the canopy. Voices drifted from the crowd, raised in agitation. Ahilya approached closer, searching the crowd for her sister, but Tariya was nowhere to be seen.

"—shown us how we are treated," a voice was saying. It belonged to a young man, no taller than Ahilya herself, a glowglobe clutched in his hand as though an orb of power. He looked to be about Oam's age—and for a moment, Ahilya's heart seized as she thought of her apprentice. Her profession as an archeologist had become important recently in the pursuit of yakshas, but once, Oam had been the only one to believe in her and her expeditions.

"They did tell us the architects are overworked, Umang," someone said from the crowd, though they sounded doubtful.

The young man shook the glowglobe. The light shone off his glasses, and for a second they appeared opaque. "The architects *owe* us," Umang said, his voice carrying. Around Ahilya, several people began to nod. "Think of your daughter, Hari, as she lies sick in the infirmary. She has not risen since the ashram returned to flight. For too long, the architects have lied to us, they have denied us a voice. Now they deny us basic comfort and information, too."

"Yes, but we cannot *seize* power."

"Not in the skies, but the jungle is another matter." Umang pushed up his glasses. "We know we can end the rages, and we must think of a new life, and *she* said she had found such a place, a habitat."

"We don't *want* to go to the jungle. Our lives are here."

"Change is upon us," Umang said. "We must control it, and in the jungle we might—" He broke off as his roving gaze landed on Ahilya. His eyes grew wide behind his glasses.

"Councilor," he breathed, and the crowd shifted, every head turning to Ahilya, every eye examining her.

She took a step back, faltering under the attention. Rain dripped from the hood of her cloak down her neck.

"What news do you bring?" a man's harsh voice said from somewhere within the crowd.

"Where is the healbranch?" another woman said. "Why did the construction fail?"

"Are we safe here? Have the architects given up on us?"

"Do you speak for us? Are you loyal to us?"

Ahilya stumbled back. The crowd surrounded her, anger thrumming through them, each question hurled one after another before she could respond. She held up her hands in a calming gesture, but it seemed more like defense, even as the people closed in on her.

"Give her space," Umang said sharply, pushing through the people. He approached her from under the canopy, pulling the hood of his own cloak over his head. The glowglobe shimmered in his hand, but up close, Ahilya noticed what she hadn't before. The glowglobe radiated purplish-black light instead of its usual golden. Had the citizens done something to it? She was certain it wasn't Kiana-approved.

Umang neared her and paused. "We are glad to see you, councilor," he said formally, and bowed. The others grew quiet around him. "We have heard nothing since Nakshar took to the skies again." His gaze went around the compound to the rising buildings. "We have no food-bearing plants, no healbranch, no room to move, no occupation or markets. A thousand of us live here, waiting for the architects every day. They bring us grain but we cannot mold the architecture to our desires anymore. We are utterly dependent on them. The architecture failed us a few hours ago, councilor— people were *injured*. Tell us you bring good news."

"News," Ahilya repeated, nodding. She had wondered if she had allies among the citizens; this young man seemed to support her, but nervousness filled her now. Her gaze took in the congregation. "Yes, I bring news, but only of a kind. The Conclave has assembled. I will be bringing your concerns to it. The architects—" She paused. The Maze Architects were exhausted, but that would not go well with this crowd. Besides, Umang had a point. The citizens were too dependent on the architects. They had always been. It was why she had wanted life to return to the jungle, even before she had become a councilor. "We are attempting better construction in the ashram," she said awkwardly, unable to give voice to these thoughts.

"What about freedom?" someone said.

"What about healbranch?" Umang asked, over this. "Ahilya-ve, I work in the infirmary, such as it is." He waved his hand toward one of the buildings. "We need healbranch to make our medicines, to help the ones who were hurt during the collapse."

Technically, healbranch had returned to the citizen spaces, but the plant itself had not grown as much as expected over the last few months. There was a terrible shortage, and all of it was being used in architect spaces to give Maze Architects a respite from trajection.

"I will speak to the Senior Architects," Ahilya said, hearing the hopelessness in her own voice. "I promise I have not forgotten."

The crowd surged and muttered. Umang stared at her, frowning. Ahilya took another step back. She could feel their distress and anger, bubbling over. It would erupt. Umang had barely held it back, and she had given him no reason to believe her. Chaiyya's face sparked in her head and the Senior Architect said, *Do you accept?* Chaiyya had offered her the council seat *because* she was a normal citizen, albeit one who was associated with the sungineers and the architects. Ahilya had wanted to be on Nakshar's council to represent the non-architects. She had begun on this journey to watch out for those who, like her, had no power—but somewhere along the way, *all* of the citizens had become her responsibility.

Was this evolution? Or was this corruption of her purpose? Had Ahilya allowed herself to become an easy scapegoat? It was tearing her apart inside, this need for balance between all of them. She had forgotten the citizens in all her other priorities—and what could she say now? Professing anger at the architects would assuage the crowd's own anger at her while inflaming it toward the architects, but she could hardly incite rebellion, not when their position in the skies was so tenuous. The architecture would respond to the citizens' fear and terror. They would all crash into the earthrage. She staggered as the people around her closed in, questions flung at her.

A smaller shape appeared by her side, tugging at her sleeve. Ahilya glanced down to see her nephew Kush, gazing at her. "You better come with me, pinni," he muttered.

Ahilya raised both hands to the congregation. "I have heard your questions. I promise I will bring it up with the others. Please, for now, await communication on your citizen rings. You will have more news soon."

Mutters grew, but she clutched Kush's shoulder and allowed him to lead her out of the press of citizens. The two hurried away into the drizzle, and Kush made his way toward a tall row of apartments that formed the perimeter of the compound.

When Ahilya looked back, none of the people were visible through the darkness and the incessant rain, though she felt the stabs of eyes, prickling her. Guilt and shame roiled in her belly. She knew she had done the right thing. Then, why did she feel dirty? Was this what Iravan had fought against, too? Her hand trembled on Kush's shoulder.

The boy walked silently next to her, his young face shut and brooding. A shock of black hair fell on his forehead, dripping with the rain. Ahilya pushed it back gently, and Kush met her gaze with uncertain eyes.

How old was he now? Eleven? Twelve? So serious for one so young. He had been part of the citizen group under the tree—the group that had attempted to find out what was occurring in the ashram, because all citizens had been kept in the dark, quite literally, ever since flight. Ahilya should have taken away their fear, offered some comfort, but her non-answers had aggravated them further. She had deepened the insecurity in her nephew's eyes.

"Kush," she said softly. "What happened here?"

"It was scary," he said, his voice just as soft. "The buildings shook... *before*. All of them. We hid under the table in our home, but we could hear the wood groaning, and the storm outside. I thought... I thought the buildings would break. They *did* break, in parts of the congregation hall and the infirmary."

Ahilya slowed down. "Are you three all right?"

"Arth is fine," Kush answered. "He was asleep when I came down here. I've been taking care of him."

"And Tariya?"

Kush blinked at her, then looked away. "Amma is... the same. I make sure she is taking her medicines."

A coldness swept over Ahilya that had nothing to do with the sudden burst of breeze. She'd spent as much time with her sister as her work had allowed in the last two months. Tariya had been on the mend, still prone to bouts of sudden crying, but with a will to recover—until Ahilya had exposed the secret of Ecstasy and the true consequences of excision. Tariya had refused to see Ahilya since then.

Kush seemed to be following the same train of thought. "Is it true?" he asked. The wet hair had fallen onto his forehead again. "What you said about Ecstasy and excision?"

"Yes. I'm afraid so."

The boy nodded and swallowed. "The architects came to us during the landing. They think Arth will one day be able to traject."

Ahilya closed her eyes, trying to contain her sudden sorrow. Kush's baby brother had been born a year ago, a delivery her sister had made, while Kush himself had been born of Bharavi. Tariya had wanted her children to become architects, to contribute to the ashram like Bharavi, but now? When the status of architects was being questioned? For every Umang, there was a citizen like that woman who had stared at Ahilya from the rudra tree during flight.

She looked up to see Kush watching her. "If you had known about Ecstasy before," he whispered, his voice trembling, "would Ma still be alive?"

Ma.

Bharavi.

Tears blurred Ahilya's vision, and Kush rubbed his eyes with his fist. She crouched to her knees and crushed the boy to her. His thin body trembled in her arms, and he hugged her back, stifling his sobs.

Ahilya patted his back, choking on her own tears. Kush deserved the truth, or at least some measure of it—but every explanation seemed hollow and incomplete, an excuse that attempted to justify his loss. She couldn't explain that his mother had died because history had been against her. She couldn't explain that there were people like Basav of Katresh who would never have allowed Bharavi to be Ecstatic, or that Bharavi had been the first, even before Iravan, to truly embrace the idea of Ecstasy. What difference would any of that make to Kush? His mother was dead. She had been killed for wanting to be who she really was.

Kush sniffled, then extricated himself from Ahilya's arms. He wiped his eyes, then started up the ramp toward one of the tall apartments. Ahilya's heart felt heavy, each step as though pulling herself through quicksand.

The ramp narrowed through the building. Ahilya's hand found Kush's shoulder again as he led her through the darkness, the both of them walking in a single file. They were out of the rain, but no glowglobes appeared here, despite Ahilya's manipulation of the architecture. Damp wood reeked on either side. Was this how the citizens lived now, ever since the ashram had taken flight? Each of them packed behind the wooden walls? Her stomach clenched in anger, and for a second, she remembered the tiny room she had woken in when she had broken her arm because of the falcon's attack on Nakshar. It had been little more than a stall, just as these homes undoubtedly were.

Kush paused in the darkness. Ahilya felt his shoulder move as he tapped on his citizen ring and waved his arm. The wall in front of them unfurled into a small doorway. Ahilya ducked behind Kush and entered her sister's house.

The room was small and rectangular. Its walls gleamed with blue-green phosphorescence, but instead of giving light, the plant only seemed to illuminate how dim everything was. A long bench lined one side of the wall, and a table had been grown to another side. Ahilya guessed that perhaps a window opened somewhere inside out of sight, but even as the thought occurred to her, she knew there were no windows in this apartment. Permissions of windows consumed both trajection and sungineering power; those would hardly be used here.

This was yet another consequence of telling everyone that an architect became insensate after they were cut off from trajection. If Ahilya had not said anything, then Tariya would have had leverage over the council. Her sister would have been afforded luxurious apartments by the council, if only to keep her quiet about what she knew. Perhaps during Nakshar's takeoff, she would have been in the highest, safest tier of the rudra tree along with other citizens who were married to architects.

But now there was no need for such concessions. Ahilya had seen to that.

She took a deep breath, and removed her cloak, leaving it at the threshold.

Footsteps resounded on the cold hard floor. "Kush?" a soft voice called out from the doorway. "Is that you?"

Tariya stopped. She stared from the darkness at Ahilya.

The last few months had been unkind to Ahilya's older sister. Despite the dimness of the apartment, tear tracks stood stark on her face. Tariya had lost weight since Bharavi's death, her lustrous hair dull and limp, her usually radiant skin now waxen, etched with permanent grief lines.

Ahilya's stomach lurched. She remembered how beautiful Tariya had looked when the ashram had landed—when, consumed in her Ecstasy, *Bharavi* had landed the ashram, several months before. Tears formed in her eyes to see her sister so. She had hoped Tariya's grief would heal with being back in the skies, an environment Tariya was used to, but Tariya seemed no better than the last time Ahilya had seen her. Ahilya reached forward and hugged her sister, wrapping her arms around her slight body.

Tariya did not return the embrace. She remained stiff and frozen, but when Ahilya reached to take Arth away from her, she did not protest. Instead, Tariya sat down on the bench, still staring at Ahilya, her face withdrawn.

"I'll bring us something to eat," Kush muttered, disappearing the way his mother had come.

The both of them watched him go, then Tariya turned back to Ahilya. "What are you doing here?" she asked, her voice hollow. "Shouldn't you be at the Conclave?"

The evening's session was scheduled to begin in a few hours, and Ahilya needed to prepare Iravan, needed to speak to the sungineers, needed to enlist the support of the councilors of Reikshar, Kinshar, and Yeikshar. Yet she had chosen to make her way here, to her sister.

She could not shake the terror in her throat. With the blunder of the emergency protocol, she had come so close to losing Tariya and the boys. All it would have taken was one more minute, a delay in the reaction of the architects, a delay in Ahilya's own decision-making. She stared at Tariya, her heart heavy. She could not tell her sister any of this. Even if the secrecy of a councilor hadn't forbidden her from sharing the information, her sister was in no position to bear the burden of this news, not right now.

"Amma and Appa asked to return to Nakshar," Ahilya said, at last. "I have their papers in the council."

She had never been close to her architect parents who had retired several years ago to live in Kinshar, but Tariya had loved them dearly. Their leaving Nakshar had affected her, an abandonment as Tariya understood it, provoking a deep, recurring despair. Ahilya looked away toward Arth, who burbled in her arms, waving a chubby fist.

Her sister didn't say a word, waiting, and Ahilya took a deep breath before continuing. "I'm afraid the councils are not allowing citizens to cross into each other's ashrams yet. The construction—"

Ahilya cut herself off, and pressed a hand to her belly where a tightness had built.

How much could she tell her sister? There were formalities to visitors, ones that all councils had to fulfil before allowing travel between ashrams. Establishing borders alone had taken so long, and the effects of the modified construction were still being debated. Each ashram had to resolve their own constructions to align with Iravan's modified version. They would then have to provide immunity bracelets to visiting citizens so they remained unharmed by foreign plants. Ahilya had tried to expedite her parents' request, just as she had for Iravan's parents, but it was still too soon. The Conclave had formed only two days ago, in all of its risk and abnormality. None of this information would help Tariya now.

"I'm hoping Amma and Appa can visit soon," Ahilya said evasively, instead.

Tariya remained silent, her face still. Arth cooed to himself, then grabbed a lock of Ahilya's hair in his fist and yanked. She extricated it gently, and nuzzled her nephew's nose, giving herself time to think on how to approach her sister with her real reason for being here.

One glance at Tariya, and Ahilya knew there would be no point to subterfuge.

She took another deep breath. "Tariya," she began softly. "I want you to come and live with me—"

"No," Tariya replied, her voice quivering.

Ahilya flinched. Tariya knew why she was here. Of course she did. Ahilya had asked her this before, many times in the last two months when the ashram had still been in the jungle, when the ashram had been *different*, but she had always received the same response. Yet Tariya's stubbornness could not be indulged anymore.

"Please," she said, still cradling Arth. "It's safer with me. Safer in my home."

"No," Tariya said again, this time louder. Angry tears spilled onto her thin cheeks. "It is *not* safer. Do you think I need a reminder of you and Iravan, of the fact that he killed Bharavi?" Her sister's voice caught on the last word. She brought the edge of her sari to her eyes and began weeping quietly. "It's not fair. It's not fair that he is alive, that *all* the other Ecstatics are alive when Bharavi is gone."

Ahilya didn't realize she had moved, but in two strides, she was sitting next to her sister, holding her shaking shoulders while Arth warbled, still cradled within one arm.

There were no reminders of Iravan in her home. Everything Ahilya owned had been destroyed in the falcon's attack on Nakshar. Yet, how much more fragile everything had become since then. The same falcon was now captured in a deathcage. Several Ecstatics had formed, their energy dangerous and unknown. The Conclave had assembled only to risk collapse at any minute. Their entire existence in the skies could unravel with one mistake.

"Tariya, listen to me," Ahilya said to her weeping sister. She squeezed her shoulder tighter, and struggled to keep her own tears from falling. "You have to trust me."

"Trust *you*?" Tariya sobbed harder. "You l-left us to go rescue Iravan. But you did nothing to rescue Bh-Bharavi. You could have saved her. You could have told us what you knew about Ecstasy before Iravan m-murdered her."

"I—I didn't know then, Ta," Ahilya replied, tears in her eyes, her anguish prompting her to use a name for her sister she had not used since they were children. "Ta, I didn't know. If I could change it—"

But this was fruitless, and Tariya only sobbed harder. In her mind, Iravan flicked open Bharavi's deathcage. Spiralweed strangled Bharavi—spiralweed that *Ahilya* had smuggled into the ashram. She had watched it happen.

Tariya was right. She had done nothing to stop it.

Ahilya trembled against her sister. "Please, Ta, please. This is not safe for you anymore. But I can save you—you and the citizens. I just—Tariya—I need some time, and if you're with me, I can stop worrying about you."

Tariya straightened at that and shook Ahilya's arm off herself. She wiped at the edge of her nose with her sari and her eyes glittered in anger. "You needn't worry about me. I'm fine."

"I can make it better—"

"How?" Tariya asked. "Because suddenly you are a councilor? Because you took Bharavi's place?" Tariya stood up. "Your arrogance has no bounds, little sister."

The statement was so cruel, so unfair, that for a second Ahilya was robbed completely of speech. She stared at Tariya, and everything she had been repressing for the last few months—all the fear and loneliness with Iravan gone, all the sorrow of Bharavi's and Oam's deaths, the immense impossibility of everything she was trying to achieve with the Conclave in attempting to save the citizens, the sungineers, the Ecstatics, the very ashrams themselves, while the cosmic beings raged in an unknown dimension, intent on destroying them—all of it rose to the surface, crushing her.

She had lost Dhruv already. Iravan was as good as absent from her life. Now her sister wanted to take herself away too? Fury, hurt, and terror coursed through Ahilya, blurring her vision, and she held Arth close, even as the stabbing pain in her stomach attacked her again—the same pain she had been ignoring for *days*, one she was too terrified to examine closely because of the horror that clutched her each time she thought of what it could mean.

She had lost so much already. She would be damned if she lost any more.

Ahilya stood up, gripped Tariya's arm tightly, and shook it. "Bharavi is dead," she spat. "Would you have Arth and Kush die too? Is that what you want?"

Her sister stared at her, hair in disarray. Shock and fury mingled on her tear-stained face. Ahilya noticed Kush stagger forward, a small bowl of nuts in his hands. His wide eyes went from his mother to Ahilya. How much had he heard? How long had he been standing there?

Ahilya tried to calm herself. "You're stronger than this. I need you to—"

But Tariya had snatched Arth from Ahilya's arms. He began to wail.

Her sister pushed Kush back as though protecting him from Ahilya. Tariya backed away several steps, and wood creaked loudly. The sounds of the downpour rushed along with the cold rainy breeze into the house. Protests and apologies formed on Ahilya's lips, but before she could open her mouth, Tariya flung an accusatory finger toward the doorway.

"Get out," she whispered. "Get out of my house."

"No," Ahilya said. "Not without all of you."

She made to move, to close the distance between them, but so strong was Tariya's desire that the walls began to shrink, fighting against the fixed trajection of the Disc Architects.

"Tariya—" Ahilya began, but the ground shook under her feet. Vines curled around her ankle growing from the bare earth below, inhibiting her movements. She reached a hand, but the vines pulled her back, wrapping around her wrists, pulling her away from Tariya and the boys. She strained, but Tariya's desire was too strong. It was unadulterated, too fierce in this instant, so that even the Disc Architects and their combined trajection could not stop her.

Ahilya found herself dragged back, standing on the threshold of her sister's home.

"Wait," she gasped. "Please. I'm sorry."

Tears fell down Tariya's cheeks, mirroring Ahilya's own, but her sister said nothing, holding her children. The vines released Ahilya even as the doorway began to close just past her still-wet cloak. Ahilya leapt forward, but the walls were already creaking shut. Her last view was of Arth wailing in her sister's arms, Kush standing next to them worried and confused.

Sobbing, Ahilya pounded on the wood, crying out Tariya's name.

19

IRAVAN

Iravan rolled up the sleeves of his kurta, straightened them, then pushed them back again. He resisted the urge to pace within his deathcage, but it took all his willpower, and he had little of that left now.

The battle in the Deepness had exhausted him. He could not rid himself of Darsh's eyes; how Reyla and Trisha had looked at him; the defeated way Pranav had sunk to the floor. It was why he had entered a deathcage *willingly* of all things. He was minutes away from being taken to the three hundred councilors. He had made the decision to trust the Conclave, trust Ahilya, instead of taking the Ecstatics away to the jungle immediately, but what would that cost him?

Naila had impressed upon him that everything about the Ecstatics and the battery would be decided tonight at his presentation, yet Iravan knew the games of the Conclave. He understood the politics. A dull fury burned in him at the need for this formality. He leaned his forehead against the cool glass of the cage, closed his eyes, and took a deep breath.

A dozen thoughts circled his mind. In the Etherium, the cosmic creatures laughed and raged in turn. The silence pressed in the back of his head, and the yaksha ruffled its feathers. The creature cocked its head, as though aware of his scrutiny, and uttered a low yarp of greeting. Of all those things, the falcon scared Iravan the most.

Whether through the falcon's constant trajection of him, or the maturation of their unity, Iravan could now see the yaksha in his mind, as though the silence had become a window into the creature's whereabouts. *I am coming for you*, he thought in dull anger at the falcon. *And we'll settle it once and for all, rage you.* The creature laughed in his head.

Voices sounded in the narrow corridor, and Iravan immediately pulled away from the glass. He rolled his sleeves back one more time in a gesture of finality, and stared into the darkness in front of him.

His deathcage was in a tiny alcove just beyond the main Conclave theater. Iravan had been led here by Naila several minutes ago, and although he could not hear any discussions from the assembly proper, every now and then he'd discerned agitated shouts.

It did not bode well.

Conclaves were called in emergencies, but they always maintained decorum: they *had* to. Extreme emotion could feed into the plants, debilitating the architecture. It was one reason no Conclave lasted long. Any more than a week and the construction grew fragile.

If the councilors were already so divisive, if the architecture was already failing, Iravan had only one chance to convince them of the true nature of Ecstasy. What he said tonight—how they perceived him—would shape the future of all architects within the ashrams. It would shape who the sungineers supported.

Shadows moved in the darkness. Footsteps hurried toward him. He squinted, trying to see, then suddenly glowglobes blinked on, and Ahilya was there, coming to a halt right in front of him. She wore the same black as he did, though she had no feather cloak draped around her shoulders. His wife tapped at several of her rudra beads in succession, waited for the glass pane to whisk up, then entered the deathcage.

He didn't wait for her to come to him.

Iravan took two steps forward and enveloped her in his arms.

Ahilya was still for a long second, but he did not let go and he didn't move away. She shuddered once, then relaxed against his chest.

"You're all right," Iravan murmured.

"I'm all right," she echoed, quietly.

Naila had assured him that Ahilya was unhurt, despite the failure of trajection in Nakshar, but it was not until now that Iravan realized how worried he'd been. He breathed Ahilya in, as though trying to capture her scent and carry it with him. The silence in his mind moved; the falcon tapped its talons on the grass and shook its head. There was weary amusement in the gesture.

"Are you ready?" Ahilya whispered.

Iravan shrugged. He had listened to Naila's instructions, but all the Maze Architect had given him was an introduction to the councilors of the ashrams and where each of them stood on the matter of Ecstasy, something Iravan already knew from his own days as a Senior Architect. The young woman had warned him not to speak of the cosmic creatures, directed him to keep his answers in the presentation constrained, and reminded him that his only purpose was to indicate he was in control of himself. Iravan had prepared better through reading Bharavi's notes than anything the Maze Architect had said. He trembled slightly, the thought of Bharavi a stab through his heart.

In reality, the performance with the Conclave was just another kind of Examination of Ecstasy. At least in this one, he had Ahilya's support. He crushed her to him and bent to kiss her, but she pulled away before he could.

Ahilya's hand went to her stomach, and she grimaced, but as she caught his eye, her hand dropped. In the dim light of the sparkling glowglobes, her eyes were bloodshot. She'd been crying, he realized with a jolt.

"Ahilya—" he began.

"It won't be as easy as you think," she blurted out.

Iravan's eyebrows drew together in confusion. Then he realized she was speaking of the Conclave.

He pressed his eyes closed with a forefinger and thumb. "I'm prepared, my love, but believe me. I don't expect it to be easy."

Ahilya shook her head. "You don't understand. Chaiyya is planning something, she and Airav and the other councilors of Nakshar. I think I still might have Kiana's support—she certainly wants the Ecstatic battery to work—but radarx has already been distributed to the other ashrams, and they're likely already checking their architects for Ecstasy—either to excise them or to use the energex on them. Iravan, we are not going to change the minds of the Conclave tonight. But we might be able to push a decision until later. Our goal is to make them question their existing beliefs—that is all. Wield your charm, be polite, and do not antagonize them."

Iravan nodded slowly. He knew his way around the Conclave, but he'd be a fool not to heed Ahilya's words.

"They're going to push you, Iravan," she said quietly.

He scratched at his beard. "Push me how?"

"I'm not sure. There is no precedent for something like this. I missed the afternoon session, but the Conclave's councilors have selected a tribunal from among themselves. Basav of Katresh heads it, and Garima of your own ashram is on it too. More than anything else, they will question your material bonds—to see if you are indeed balancing those with your Ecstasy. That is where it begins for them."

Iravan knew of Basav of the Katresh ashram, a man so steeped in traditionalism that Iravan was grateful he'd never had occasion to meet him. But Garima, who headed Yeikshar, was the most forward-thinking architect of Iravan's own native ashram. She had been the one to approve his transfer to Nakshar when he'd been a Junior Architect. She'd expected him to become a Senior Architect in his own right and had been the first to send her congratulations when he'd achieved it. Surely, he could count on her support now?

"Chaiyya will speak for Nakshar," Ahilya went on. "She will help you for Nakshar's sake, but be prepared for anything, speak only when you're spoken to, and watch your words. Veristem has been grown all over the theater. Its use is already debated in the Conclave, and a single accidental lie, an innocent exaggeration— those could ruin everything. Basav will try to trick you into saying something you don't want, so the less time you remain on the stand the bett—"

Ahilya broke off with a gasp and clutched her stomach.

Iravan's heart skipped a beat. He drew closer immediately. "You're in pain," he said sharply.

"I—"

"Ahilya," he said, and he could hear the alarm in his own voice. "Something is wrong, isn't it? What aren't you telling me?"

"It's nothing—"

"It's *not* nothing," he rasped, and he put his hands on her shoulders, pulling her to him. In her eyes, he saw his own terror reflected. "Your pregnancy. Is something the matter with it?"

Ahilya pushed him away and stepped back. "You want to talk about this *now*?"

Iravan closed the distance between them again. "Why not now? You've refused to speak of it so far, and I need to know. It's my child, too, Ahilya."

"What would it achieve, Iravan?" she snapped, sudden bitterness lacing her voice. "Whether we win at the Conclave tonight or not, you won't be here anyway, not during the pregnancy nor the birth. Not when our child is growing up. Do you want to know simply so you can assuage your guilt?"

Iravan recoiled.

A silence grew between them, harsh and thorny.

Ahilya shuddered, and Iravan knew she was holding back tears, that she was frightened, just as he was, and tears filled his own eyes. He could not bear it if something happened to her or their child.

"I'm sorry," Ahilya said, and her voice quivered. "That was unfair."

"No," Iravan said quietly. "It was not. Ahilya, you're *pregnant*, you have the right to all your anger, to whatever you're feeling—and I—this—" He turned away, running his hands through his hair, clenching his fists and releasing them by turn. "This is not how things were supposed to be. This is not where I thought we would be."

There was so much he wanted to say, so much he could not articulate. The silence reared in his mind, the falcon beating its wings against the cage as it sensed his anguish. He and Ahilya had so little time, each of them being pulled in different directions, the things they had to do to save their world, to save their people. Could all of that justify this? In the end, no matter what he did, he hurt her—always he hurt *her*. The shame and agony of it dug deeper in him, a corrosive hatred of the cosmic beings who had set him down this path because of their *existence*, and Iravan turned to see Ahilya's face, and knew she could see his emotions.

She touched his shoulder and reached up to kiss him, and he kissed her back, tasting his own tears and pain on her, tasting his own heartbreak. When they pulled apart, he rested his forehead on hers and took a deep, shaking breath. In the Etherium, the cosmic creatures roared, their fury pushing against his own.

"If I know anything," he said, "it is that I love you. You must know that. You must believe it."

"I love you too," she whispered, an assurance, but not the one he needed.

He opened his mouth to speak, but she was pulling back again.

This time, Iravan stepped back too, for he could hear it as well— footsteps coming ever closer in the darkness.

Ahilya brushed at her eyes and cleared her throat. Her hand went to her stomach and she spasmed, a quick shudder, but immediately straightened, as though forcibly willing away her agony.

Iravan braced himself. He had thought himself prepared, but now his palms were growing clammy, and a cold unreality was descending over him—not for the trial, he knew, but the unsaid things between him and Ahilya. They were supposed to be at the Conclave, but he couldn't focus, not right now, not when Ahilya needed him. Not when she was so clearly in pain.

The footsteps resolved into a shape, and then Senior Sungineer Kiana was there, her gray gaze resting on them both, standing just outside the red grass of the deathmaze, supporting herself with a cane. "It's time," she said quietly.

Ahilya produced a watery smile. She squeezed Iravan's hand one last time, whispered *good luck*, and then she left the deathcage and followed the sungineer back the way they had come.

Bereft of her, now entirely alone, Iravan tried to center himself.

He saw Ahilya leap after him in the vortex. He saw himself turn away from her after their fight about making a child. He had thought he had grown since then. He had become better, but would it never end? Was this who he was forever condemned to be? The man who hurt her? A deep desire seized him to return to the Moment, to find the peace within the infinite stars, to escape the anguish that was too much to bear, but Iravan tried to still himself. If this was his lot, he would bear it too. In his mind, Bharavi whispered, *We need to start anew. Isn't that what you want?* And he thought in answer, *I'm trying, Bha. Rages help me, I'm trying.*

The wall next to him creaked open toward the Conclave theatre. A hundred glowglobes glimmered from the benches and the foliage. Above, a glass dome reflected the night sky, stormy clouds pounding rain. The deathcage moved forward as though on wheels.

Iravan took a shivery breath, braced himself, and prepared to meet the Conclave.

20

AHILYA

From her place among Nakshar's councilors, Ahilya watched the deathcage roll forward.

It advanced slowly, a circle of red perileaf grass rippling in front of it, Iravan's shadow casting a dark shape before the cage fully emerged. He stood at its center, back erect, head high, his feather cloak swishing low behind him. Despite his exquisite black kurta and narrow trousers, there was no disguising his barely restrained wildness.

Sickness grew deep in Ahilya's stomach. She knew her husband well enough to read the signs of his tension—the cold gaze, the tightening of his jaw, the fists that clenched and unclenched—but the others would not read subservience in Iravan's posture. To them, he'd appear imposing, an entirely wrong attitude to bring to his trial as an Ecstatic. She knew his nervousness came from being locked inside the glass cage. It set the wrong expectation, and Ahilya had argued against it, but Chaiyya had point-blank refused to allow an Ecstatic within the Conclave without adequate protection for the councilors.

Ahilya glanced around now, sweat coating her upper lip. The theater looked much the same as it had in the morning, with rows of benches circling the chamber, and incessant rain pounding on the glass dome. Yet now, a space had been cleared in one section, and velvety black veristem flowers grew in patches all over the ground. She sat with Nakshar's other councilors, looking out at the semicircle of three hundred people, the tribunal just opposite her.

Chaiyya had already told her how angry the Conclave had been with Nakshar's near collapse. She had barely kept them from leaving the assembly and detaching from Nakshar altogether. Yet that was only a part of what had nearly befallen all of them.

The failure of the emergency protocol had been terrible in itself, but Naila had informed Ahilya of how the Ecstatics in the sanctum had broken their cages the instant sungineering forcefields had dropped. Iravan had talked them down from bolting, and had her husband not been present among the Ecstatics, Ahilya's transfer of critical energy to the citizen spaces could have resulted in another catastrophe—one neither Nakshar nor the Conclave could have healed from, one that would have ruined all her plans.

As it was, there was no telling when another Ecstatic outbreak could occur, or when trajection or sungineering would fail again. They needed to manage the trial swiftly and without incident. The freedom of the Ecstatics, the ending of the earthrages, the subsummation of the ashram—all of it pivoted on this event. This was as much a trial of Nakshar as it was of Iravan. Dread tightened Ahilya's throat. She tapped her feet restlessly over the soundless moss.

Directly opposite her, the councilors of the tribunal shifted on their benches, watching Iravan's deathcage. Basav and Garima spoke in soft voices to each other, but the other two, Jyothika of the Three Southern Sisters and Dheeraj of Reikshar, studied the papers in front of them, glancing every now and then at Iravan. Those papers contained a dossier on her husband. She and Iravan would both be on display in front of these people. How would Iravan handle it?

In the best of times, he was an intensely private man, and here he was the enemy. Garima caught her look and gave a slight nod, but the gesture did nothing to comfort Ahilya.

Iravan's cage came to a halt in the space between the tribunal and Nakshar's council.

The murmurs in the Conclave quietened.

Basav leaned forward, and every eye turned to him.

"Citizen Iravan of Nakshar ashram, born of Yeikshar, and member of the fifty sister ashrams," he said, his voice wry. "You are here because you wish to address the 785th Conclave to present your petition to allow Ecstasy to be unchecked by excision. Is that correct?"

Iravan gave a tight nod. His hands clenched into fists, then released. Laid out in such stark terms, Ahilya sensed the audacity of Iravan's request. Disbelief rifled through the councilors, mutters susurrating in the theater.

"Do you agree to lay bare your activities regarding Ecstasy to the Conclave?" Basav went on, his gaze on Iravan.

In the deathcage, her husband gave another curt nod.

Next to Ahilya, Chaiyya stood up. The bead she had given to Ahilya now chinked against one of her many bracelets. She had taken it back as soon as she had seen Ahilya. "As a citizen of Nakshar," she said, "Iravan is protected under our laws. I speak on behalf of our council and the decisions we made."

"The tribunal consents," Basav said. "Iravan, do you agree?"

"I agree," Iravan said quietly. "Know that there is nothing to fear from Ecstasy, councilors. I stand here as proof of my statements."

Basav glanced at the others in the tribunal, and they nodded one by one.

Ahilya leaned forward as the proceedings began.

21

IRAVAN

He had feigned confidence with both Naila and Ahilya, but in a corner of his mind, Iravan could not contain his incredulity that he was in a Conclave for the first time, not as a Senior Architect like he'd hoped all his life, but as an Ecstatic.

The realization was so absurd, so ludicrous, that his lips almost turned into a grin of hysteria—but he bit the inside of his cheeks to control himself. It would not do to display any levity, not now, when each of the three hundred councilors except Ahilya stared at him with a mixture of terror and wariness.

Still, it was hard to remember that when Garima stood up to speak, the same woman who had taken such an interest in his career when Iravan had been a fresh-faced Junior Architect in Yeikshar. Her words swept over him now as she addressed the Conclave, "…one of Yeikshar's most gifted … destined for greatness … entered the Moment at the age of five without training."

Past the ruffling feathers of the falcon within the silence, and the colorless images hovering in the Etherium, Iravan thought not of what Garima was saying, but the last time he had seen her. It had been more than fifteen years ago, when he'd left for Nakshar. Senior Architect Garima had called him to her office within Yeikshar's council chambers, and he'd stood at attention in front of her desk.

"You will change things, my boy," she'd said, her face broken by a rare smile. "Remember where you come from, for Nakshar will need guidance. It is an ashram that only dips its toes into the future, afraid to do any more. You are being sent there to usher it further into prosperity. Becoming a Maze Architect is not the end of your journey."

Neither of them had known the truth of that statement.

"He comes from a close family of three parents," Garima concluded now, reading out from her papers. "He is an only child, and Iravan himself has shown nothing but affection toward his family. No records of breaches exist with regard to his material bonds from his time as a beginner and Junior Architect in Yeikshar."

Mutters and whispers filled the council chambers, eyes darting from Garima to Iravan. In the silence, the falcon cocked its head, looking at something beyond its deathcage.

It had been so long since he'd thought of his fathers and mother. Did they know what had happened to him…who he was now? Haren-da had been an architect too. What would he make of Iravan's power? They were all certainly in the Conclave within Yeikshar. His parents' fate was tied to this trial as much as anyone's else. The notion was so unnerving, Iravan nearly lost the calm he was holding onto.

Within the theater, Garima sat back down and settled her notes. Next to her, Basav scowled, evidently unimpressed with her debrief.

The man from Katresh waved a dismissive hand. "It hardly matters if his material bonds held tight while he was a youth in Yeikshar, Garima. All it tells us is that Nakshar ruined him, edging him to the brink of Ecstasy, a poor commentary on our sister ashram and her independent future."

Chaiyya bowed slightly in the direction of the tribunal. To Iravan, it appeared like glass bending, a painful action coated with humiliation.

"Nakshar will abide by the final directives of the tribunal regarding Iravan, councilors," she said. "But rest assured that Iravan's material bonds remained strong even as he became a citizen of our ashram. Nakshar is not to blame, and we hope to show you that any mistakes, if they occurred, occurred out of ignorance, not malintent."

Iravan frowned. Chaiyya was being too submissive—an approach he could not agree to, not in front of these people. What would Bharavi have said had she been here? She had taught Iravan to answer strength with strength. If you gave an inch to the councilors, you gave a mile—and a mile with the Conclave would create a noose around Nakshar's own neck, opening it to subsummation. What was Chaiyya playing at?

Evidently, Basav agreed. He leaned forward and snorted. "Not malintent, you say. Then perhaps you will explain this to me, Chaiyya. He has been married for nearly eleven years—to Ahilya of Nakshar, apparently—and yet he has no children to speak of. How did Nakshar allow him to rise to the position of Senior Architect?"

Iravan had expected the question, but his heart sank as he glanced at Ahilya and saw her hand wrap over her stomach. His wife did not meet his gaze. Her eyes remained fixed on Basav, whose lip curled contemptuously. In the silence, the falcon ruffled its feathers and uttered an indignant cry.

Chaiyya cleared her throat. "He was an exceptional Maze Architect. His study of consciousness directly impacted our methods in the Moment—"

"He is an architect," Basav interrupted, "who broke the limits of trajectory. You have proof here, in your own records. Iravan's Examination of Ecstasy indicated that he was flirting with danger, and yet he stands here unexcised."

"Nakshar adhered to *all* conditions of Ecstasy during the Exam, councilor."

"Look where that has brought you. The last three Senior Architects of your ashram succumbed to Ecstasy one after another. With every action, Nakshar shows it is not fit for independent existence, and your defense of this Ecstatic further convinces the tribunal of your intentions."

Chaiyya said nothing, but a bead of sweat dripped down her forehead.

Iravan's hands clenched into fists. *Speak when you're spoken to*, Ahilya had said, but it was him who was on trial. This was no way to win freedom for the Ecstatics, no way to end the rages, not with the cosmic creatures ready to unleash another skyrage any instant.

Iravan took a step forward and folded his arms over his chest. "It is true that my wife and I have borne no children yet," he said coldly. "But it was not for lack of trying, councilors."

His words echoed in the dim theater. Every head snapped to him. Basav's eyes narrowed. Ahilya's gaze darted to the black veristem flowers that grew in front of Iravan's deathmaze.

He could tell what she was thinking. Speaking was a risk, and to speak this—words that were the truth, but barely—opened a line of questioning that could derail the entire trial, but there was no other way except forward, so he maintained his stance and met Basav's disdainful gaze with his own. The falcon ruffled its gigantic feathers, pushing against its glass cage.

"Surely you understand," Iravan said to the Conclave, "that sometimes making children takes time. It is not under anyone's control, no matter how many herbs and healers one consults."

Garima's face grew considering, and the other two councilors muttered to each other, but Basav's eyes grew hard.

In the corner of Iravan's vision, Ahilya froze.

She knew, as he did, that a physical irregularity was not the reason they had no children. Iravan could remember every fight between him and his wife, when he had tried to argue for children and she had refused. He wanted very much to look at her now, to tell her that he did not hold her decision against her, that he understood, that he *agreed*, but he didn't dare. If the growing whispers in the Conclave were any indication, he had gained the upper hand with his statement. With the implication of his words, he had bought their sympathy instead of their censure. He could not lose it now.

Basav looked like he knew exactly what Iravan was thinking.

The Senior Architect waited until the mutters had died down, then lifted a paper from the bench, fingering it carefully. "A record from your ashram shows that Senior Architect Bharavi noted you and your wife were having troubles in your marriage."

Iravan froze. A stab of betrayal ran through him, and he thought, *What the fuck did you do, Bha?* She had threatened him often enough with making an official report, but he'd never thought she'd actually done it. In the silence, the falcon bristled, flapping over and over again, looking to the rainy sky. Iravan stilled himself with effort and took a deep breath.

"I passed that question during the Examination of Ecstasy," he said through gritted teeth. "As I did the condition about my commitment to the safety of the ashram. Question me about the limits of trajection, if you must, councilors, and I will vouch before the veristem just how arbitrary those are, but rehashing what has already been proven makes a mockery of this trial."

"Oh, we'll come to that," Basav promised dryly. "For now, perhaps it's fine with you, an Ecstatic Architect, that the tribunal selected by the three hundred councilors of the sister ashrams just asks you its questions?"

Iravan's jaw tightened. Mutters filled the theater. Chaiyya pursed her lips, but he read her tension in the way she held her breath.

"I am at the Conclave's service," he said, tilting his head with forced grace. The yaksha screamed, a blood-curdling sound that reverberated through Iravan, though he knew he hadn't heard it, not really. In the Etherium, the cosmic creatures pushed against their bonds.

"Good, good," Basav said, smiling. "So. No children to date, historical problems in your marriage, and now you're an Ecstatic who claims to still be tethered by material bonds." Basav looked up from his papers and his voice hardened, cutting across like a whip. "Tell us, Ecstatic. When did you and your wife last lay together?"

Iravan's eyes grew wide.

The shock of the question momentarily wiped every other thought from his head.

He stared at Basav, even as whispers erupted around the theater from the watching councilors.

"You go too far," he began at last, the falcon's fury pushing against his own.

"This is highly improper, councilor," Chaiyya said at the same time.

Basav's eyes narrowed at the Senior Architect. "Everything about these proceedings is *improper*, Chaiyya. You will allow this question."

"Intimate relations are no indication of material bonds," Chaiyya argued.

"We are judging a proven *Ecstatic's* material bonds, an absurdity if there ever was one. This man has no rights. His presence here is because of the magnanimity of the Conclave. Each of our lives is put in peril by the mere fact that he exists, let alone stands in front of us, unexcised." Basav stared at Chaiyya unflinchingly. "Are you saying that this question and his dignity now are worth more than the safety of the Conclave? The safety of the sister ashrams and humanity itself?"

Chaiyya's eyes flickered to Ahilya, and Iravan read his own humiliation on his wife's face—but it was as though Ahilya refused to be shamed. She watched Basav with a mixture of calculation and wrath, even as every eye in the theater dashed between her and Iravan. She nodded once, curtly.

Senior Architect Chaiyya cleared her throat. "Very well," she said, her tone clipped. "Iravan, the last time you and Ahilya lay together, if you please."

Iravan clenched his fists. "Two months ago," he bit out. "Within my home in the jungle."

He could remember it clearly, the feel of Ahilya's skin, the unreality of seeing her in the habitat on opening his eyes, the way their bodies had melded together. *They're going to push you*, he heard Ahilya say. Fury built in him like an earthrage erupting, and Basav smiled thinly, knowing it, seeing it. The yaksha screamed, an unearthly howl. The memory of the intimacy he and Ahilya had shared grew tainted, sullied.

In that instant, Iravan knew that he could kill Basav.

He would not even need to traject.

Basav held his gaze for a long second, still smiling. Then the Senior Architect looked away to flick through his notes again.

"The jungle was not always your home, however, was it? You lived in Nakshar, and during a recent flight, you did not leave the temple premises at all. For *seven* months, if these records are to be believed." The Senior Architect of Katresh looked up at Iravan, an eyebrow raised. "Tell us, Ecstatic, what was so terribly important that not only did you ignore your material bonds, but also the rules of vigilance and shift duty? One that your own council decreed?"

The silence of the falcon receded. In his mind's eye, Iravan walked away from Ahilya after their fight about becoming parents. He heard her say, *You won't be here anyway, not during the pregnancy or the birth.* A flush crept over his cheeks, of humiliation and self-loathing.

Basav was not a fool; he could sense Iravan's discomfort. The Senior Architect leaned forward, pressing his advantage.

"Tell us, Ecstatic," he said softly. "If you could return to Nakshar from the jungle anytime, why did you not return to your wife sooner? She is with child now, finally, is she not? After all your... *trying?*"

Iravan's eyes snapped to Ahilya.

He watched her throw his rudra bead bracelet at him. *Your secrets and your games made me appreciate you're a terrible husband and will make an even worse father.* Sorrow replaced the fury in his heart. His arms fell to his side. His chin trembled. He knew he was being manipulated by Basav, his emotions being hurled deliberately from one direction to another to unhinge him, but did that make any of it untrue?

Iravan had chosen himself and his yaksha over returning to Nakshar. All of his considerations about Ecstasy were, in the end, excuses. He had delayed his return to his wife because learning of Ecstasy and understanding the falcon had taken precedence. Ahilya, her pregnancy, their child, had all taken second place. Guilt washed over him like a wave, threatening to drown him. In the silence, the falcon screamed and thrashed against its deathcage.

"Tell us, Ecstatic," Basav said quietly. "Do you truly care so little for your wife and your child?"

Iravan flinched as though slapped.

Ahilya stood up.

Her face was furious and tears glinted in her eyes like little jewels. She opened her mouth, even as Kiana grabbed her arm, and Iravan knew that anything his wife said now would only ruin the proceedings. She was a citizen-councilor, already an anomaly. Basav would hold that against her and the council. He'd consider it a lack of control from Nakshar. Everything Ahilya had worked for, freedom for the Ecstatics, the end of the rages, a way for everyone to win, all of it would disintegrate.

Iravan could not allow that.

It stirred him into speech.

"Please," he said, and raised his hand in quiet entreaty.

Ahilya turned to him. He could hear the plea in his voice, and he didn't know who it was for—Basav, the tribunal, the Conclave, or Ahilya. His eyes met hers, and for a long second, they stared at each other, their pain reflected in each other's faces.

Iravan drew in a deep shaky breath. In the silence, the yaksha thrashed within its deathcage, and Iravan felt his own imprisonment in its movements. He wanted to go to Ahilya, to hold her and protect her from this shame and humiliation that was his to own but not hers to witness, not when it only brought her pain. *I love you*, he thought. *You know this.*

Ahilya blinked. Her chest rose and fell in a quiet spasm.

Slowly, she allowed Kiana to pull her back into her seat, and Iravan closed his eyes briefly, grateful for the sungineer's intervention. He could not maintain this much longer, he knew. It felt as though his heart were truly breaking. The cosmic creatures pushed against the webbing; the silence roared with the yaksha's impatience. This trial had already gone on too long, too far, in a direction he had not steered. He had overestimated his abilities to withstand this interrogation. He needed to seize control, before matters grew further awry.

"Please," he said again, and turned to the tribunal, his voice quiet. "We are here to assess whether it is possible to hold material bonds during Ecstasy, and I can assure you they are. You have my word, and the unbloomed veristem proves it. There is no need for this exhibition."

Chaiyya cleared her throat. "Councilors, listen to him. Nakshar has long believed that veristem goes beyond intent and perception down to *facts*. He is fulfilling a condition that we use for the Examination of Ecstasy. His bonds to Ahilya and the ashram are not in question."

Basav's eyes glinted. "How do we know he did not change the nature of the veristem by Ecstatically trajecting it?"

"The deathmaze is constructed to prevent exactly that," Chaiyya responded. "The boundaries of the deathmaze are shown by the red grass. That is all he can affect through the pocket Deepness."

Iravan took another step forward. This time he looked away from Basav and into the rest of the Conclave, his gaze meeting as many eyes as he could.

"Senior Architect Basav asked why I did not return to my wife," he said, voice carrying. "I can tell you that my absence had to do with Ecstasy, a confirmation of my priorities that he would like, I'm sure. But we aren't here to debate the conditions of Ecstasy—we are here to understand it: whether it can be controlled, whether it should be encouraged, whether it is *natural*. Senior Architect Basav wishes to uproot me with his questions, but everything the tribunal has asked so far has been nothing more than a distraction."

Garima stirred, watching him, and Iravan knew he was pushing his luck with the beginnings of a speech. He expected Basav to chastise him, but the man held up a hand to quieten Garima. He watched Iravan and did not interrupt.

Iravan drew in another breath. "You sit here, councilors of the sister ashrams, wanting to judge my sanity. You know that an architect must first and forever be true to themselves and their own consciousness. *That* is what guides trajection. *That* is what allows us to enter the Moment, to prevent the Two Visions merging. My absence from my wife was not because my material bonds were loosening, it was so I might understand myself. If anything, those months bound me closer to the ashrams, closer to my wife and our unborn child."

Watch your words, Ahilya had said, and Iravan swallowed, sweat beading his forehead. Never before had he made such pronouncements in the presence of veristem. His heart beat painfully in his chest, wary of a misstep, a mistaken utterance, wary of opening himself so much for so many to see. Ahilya had asked him to delay their decision. That was all he needed to do. The falcon roared in the silence, agitated, flapping against its deathcage. Iravan pushed it away, trying to focus.

"You already know of yakshas," he said quietly. "These creatures of the jungle share our planet, but they are not foreign to us, councilors. They are a part of us. There is a counterpart out there for every architect, forming a missing half. Know this to be true, here with veristem growing as witness."

A quietness covered the Conclave theater. Black veristem still glinted unbloomed, absorbing the light from sungineering glowglobes and blue-green phosphorescence.

Iravan glanced at Ahilya, but she was staring at him, with wonder and curiosity. Despite the growing agitation of the falcon, he took strength from her expression.

"Chaiyya has told you I've studied consciousness. This is true. Consciousness is fluid and mutable. It changes forms through birth and rebirth in ways we do not yet understand. My time in the jungle was so I might find the other half of my own self. A creature that is a part of me, that *is* me. It is what Ecstasy offers each of your architects, too. An anchor to their own identity. It would be disastrous for you to deny your architects that. Their trajection will fail, and they will never fully understand the Moment."

The chamber broke out in mutters. Iravan's eyes met Basav's through the glass.

"We are more," he said quietly, and in his mind, Bharavi lit up blue-green with Ecstasy, speaking the same words. "So much more than we know. So much more than we remember. That is what I offer to you. Not threats, but evolution."

Basav studied him, and for a split second, Iravan thought he'd done it. He'd won.

Then the Senior Architect smiled.

He rose to his feet and strode across the bench. The Senior Architect turned to Chaiyya. "Bring it in," he said.

In the Etherium, the cosmic creatures roared with delight as part of their webbing shattered. Chaiyya exchanged a look with Airav. She gestured to Kiana who stood up and left toward the alcove where Iravan's own deathcage had waited.

Iravan knew then he had made a mistake.

They had wanted him to be dangerous. By admitting to the yaksha being a part of himself, here in front of veristem, he had owned up to it. Terror gripped his heart. He knew, suddenly, why the yaksha had been so agitated in the silence, why it was fighting. They were bringing it here, into danger, and it had known even if Iravan had been too preoccupied. This trial had never been meant for his success. It had always been a trap, a farce for their own records, and he had walked into it, pushed by urgency, like a sincere fool.

His gaze met Ahilya's.

Horror and understanding shone in her eyes, reflecting his own. Iravan stumbled forward, the falcon roaring in his mind, even as a deathcage appeared bearing its massive shadow.

22

AHILYA

A hilya jumped to her feet.

The action sent a stabbing pain through her belly, down to her knees, making her gasp out loud. She moved across the bench regardless to grab Chaiyya's arm even as the massive deathcage that held the falcon-yaksha rolled forward from the alcove.

"What in bloody rages are you doing?" she spat, her grip tight.

Chaiyya's face was grim. She glanced around them, and Ahilya followed the woman's gaze.

Several councilors had risen to their feet across the theater. Their mouths hung open in shock, their faces grown bloodless in the dim. The falcon cried out, a high-pitched sound that sent a thrill of fear through her. Outside of the deathcage, it could spread its magnificent silver-gray wings that would span a hundred feet, wings that would easily cover the theater end to end. Even imprisoned, the yaksha was monstrous. Seen in such close quarters, the creature looked much larger than it had in the jungle. How many yakshas had she seen in her life? Her knees shook as though she were a Junior Architect, first time out on an expedition.

"Do you understand?" Chaiyya whispered. "These people have never seen a yaksha before. They aren't archeologists who are used to these creatures. To most of them, the creature is mythical. They barely believe that yakshas exist, let alone that the creatures can supertraject and that Nakshar has captured one."

Ahilya blinked. "Captured? Chaiyya, the falcon belongs to Iravan, not us. Our agreement—"

"Was only until the Conclave meeting," the Senior Architect completed. "Ahilya, *look* at them. They're stunned. Displaying the yaksha now gives Nakshar much-needed goodwill. This trial has been a debacle for the ashram. Basav is practically ready to call for Nakshar's subsummation."

Ahilya bit her lip, frowning. Her eyes strayed to Basav who still stood in front of Iravan's deathcage. The man's eyes gleamed, reflected by the glowglobes, as he watched the yaksha's cage roll forward.

A hot stab of fury shot through Ahilya's belly, and she suppressed a choke. She had tried to prepare herself for the trial, but the questions had hooked into her, bleeding her emotions. Iravan had seemed ready to commit murder. She and Iravan had been humiliated, but it was Nakshar and the lives of all its citizens, architects, non-architects, sungineers alike, that had been weighed. Basav's allegations and his assertions about Nakshar's fitness to function independently had been another plank to fall, building the ashram's funeral pyre.

Yet, how would displaying the yaksha now help? If the creature attacked, somehow getting past the deathmaze, Nakshar was as good as destroyed.

Unless…

Ahilya spun to Chaiyya in horror. "You're sacrificing Iravan. You've already given up on him and the Ecstatics."

"I've done no such thing."

"Don't lie to me, Chaiyya," Ahilya hissed, and pointed to the mossy floor where black veristem had begun to flower into white at the Senior Architect's words.

The woman followed Ahilya's gaze. Her eyebrows drew together and she shook Ahilya off. "Fine," she snapped. "I made a choice. My priority is Nakshar, Ahilya, not one architect, no matter how much I care for him."

"You're not even giving Iravan a chance."

"Nothing he has said has protected Nakshar so far," Chaiyya replied, her eyes glinting. "He needs to keep his calm, and maybe we'll still get through this, but I'm hedging my bets. You think this is easy for me? Iravan was my friend, and there are Ecstatic children in the cages within the sanctum. But this is what it means to be a councilor—taking tough decisions no one else can. All of Nakshar is in danger—the ashram will be subsumed, our way of life obliterated, our name but a memory—because Basav is right. Three Senior Architects in succession to become Ecstatic? A council with more non-architects than architects?" Chaiyya's lips trembled. "Nakshar is one more mistake away from complete erasure. I will not let that happen."

Ahilya stared at her, the only Senior Architect remaining from the original set. Manav had been excised, Bharavi dead, Airav unable to traject, and Iravan… No wonder Chaiyya had been submissive. Her own position was tenuous, and she had picked her battles for herself too, besides the safety of Nakshar.

Iravan was gazing at the yaksha. Even as Ahilya watched, his skin lit up blue-green, his hands curled into fists. His chest rising and falling too quickly. He had entered the pocket Deepness.

He licked his lips once, terrified.

"You're looking out for your husband," Chaiyya said. "I understand that. If Lavanya was in Iravan's place, I'd be doing the same thing for her. But I need—"

She cut off, as Basav raised a hand.

The falcon's deathcage stopped right next to Iravan's, and the theater quietened.

"So," the Senior Architect of Katresh said. "This creature is what forms a part of an architect's consciousness? Do we all get falcons, Ecstatic, or are the rest of our pets lesser?"

Iravan's gaze flickered to Basav. His body still glowed beneath his black kurta, though there were no creeping tattoos of trajection. He said nothing.

Senior Architect Basav strode forward, dangerously close to the boundary grass of the deathmaze in which both Iravan and the falcon were now contained. The falcon cocked its head, glinting down at him. A ring formed around its eyes.

"Careful," Kiana said, speaking for the first time. "If you enter the deathmaze, it can—"

But the Senior Architect threw the sungineer a contemptuous look. His foot descended over the red grass of the deathmaze's boundary.

No, Ahilya thought.

"No," Iravan whispered, staring at the yaksha.

Basav's eyes rolled back into his head.

The Senior Architect spasmed, a sound like snapping bones echoing in the chamber.

Someone screamed, and Iravan fell to his knees. His palms pressed against the glass and Ahilya met his terrified gaze, even as the yaksha uttered a cry of fury and satisfaction.

23

IRAVAN

Basav *b-r-o-k-e*.

Iravan watched it in the pocket Deepness.

He had entered the blackness the second the falcon had been brought into his own deathmaze. He and the Resonance had circled each other warily, but then the Senior Architect had stepped onto the red grass, and before Iravan could move, the Resonance had sent a jet of silvery light into the shard Moment toward the man.

Basav's eyes rolled in his head, the whites of his eyes stark, the terror of a trapped animal.

In his first vision, Iravan sank to his knees.

Within the pocket Deepness, he struggled against himself.

His dust mote was paralyzed as was his body. He could not cancel out the falcon's Ecstatic trajection. He could only watch in helpless terror, within both his visions.

His eyes grew wide.

He noticed what he hadn't before. The Resonance had shot out more than a single ray into the shard Moment.

It wasn't just Ecstatically trajecting Basav.

It was trajecting Iravan too.

The falcon was rearranging them both—and the horror of it filled Iravan's stomach with bile. He resisted the urge to vomit. But then the urge disappeared because the falcon was rearranging him.

Iravan's eyes met the yaksha's gigantic ringed one. The Etherium *flickered* between his brows, and—

They separated, burning.

They—*it*—found itself flung, terrified, into a storm. Agony sliced through it, and for an eternity there was only pain—the pain of separation, of shrinking, of entrapment—and it knew it was alive because it could feel this.

In its mind, it saw a strange creature, *blink*, a human, a girl, and vaguely it knew—it had been—*her?* Her. She was itself, and when glowing vines grew around her skin, a melody emerged. It wept for her and its own self. Why had they abandoned each other? Where had she, they, it, themselves gone? They had broken. *Broken.*

Blink, and she flickered, became another—the same, but different, a man this time.

Nidhirv, a voice thought in wonder and familiarity, the voice it heard in its head so often. *The falcon is seeing Nidhirv.*

Falcon. That's what it was.

It—the falcon—flew over the bursting trees. Again and again, it heard the melody, a pull—*blink*, and it saw itself in the human; *he* became *she* once more. She called to the falcon, the same melody emerging from her, and it flew, eager; they would know each other, they would *know…*

But the melody stopped.

The falcon roared, it screamed in agony—*blink*—another man, then a woman again.

The melody haunted it, maddening. The falcon leapt into the sky, seeking, forever seeking. It found the velvety blackness and its visions split, but the human was nowhere. *Blink*, another man, *blink*, three undefined in succession, then a woman.

When the falcon slept, it could still hear the aching melody.

When it awoke, it sought, in the skies and the trees and the infinite velvety blackness. It fluttered gaining form, growing alone. Stars became the sun, again and again. It shot out jets of light into the water-droplet universe from the velvety darkness, but no one came. No one answered.

It found a path into the water-globule of lights—*the Moment*, the voice supplied. Inside the Moment, the falcon shuddered. The lights were too big. Fear wrapped around it like its own wings. It made to leave, but heard again the melody, the *call*, louder—and a thrill awoke. The falcon darted toward it, chasing, one star to another, hunting, until it saw, finally *saw* the melody, him—a him, this time.

The man-thing paused and stared, and the falcon's own reflection reverberated on the man, this half-thing, hovering curiously among the lights. The falcon recoiled—it broke away, and the man-thing shot after it. They chased each other between the lights, and it knew it needed to bring him into the darkness.

The falcon crashed into him, and felt his agony. Panicked, it watched the man-thing flail. He would blink away too, he would—

Pain—and it flung the man back into the Moment. The falcon roared in fury as the melody diminished—

Iravan gasped.

He staggered to his knees on the floor of the deathcage, tears flooding his eyes, palms on the glass. Basav shuddered. The falcon was trajecting the Senior Architect, even as it showed Iravan this vision of its own history.

He could barely understand. He'd seen the separation of himself and the falcon, a thousand years in a blink. Each time he or any of his previous lives had trajected—*all* the times they had trajected—they had sent out a raga, Nakshar's Constant, taunting the yaksha. The falcon had shown Iravan his own first encounter with itself, with the *Resonance*, back in Nakshar's temple within the Moment.

How much time had passed since it had begun trajecting him in the deathmaze?

Seconds.

Seconds.

Too… long.

Basav trembled, a spasm that seemed to disintegrate him. Whatever the Resonance was doing to him was destroying him.

Iravan's eyes met Ahilya's through the glass of the deathcage.

Help…

him, he thought.

Did he think it? Everything was slow, lethargic. It took all of Iravan's sense of self to form a desire.

He stared… at her.

A hil ya

help

him

Her eyes grew wide. She tugged at Chaiyya, whispered something.

Chaiyya's body lit up blue-green.

Beyond the grass of the deathmaze, a thick vine grew from the floor and curled around Basav's body. Chaiyya heaved, but in its deathcage, the falcon fluttered its gigantic wings lazily.

Iravan's breath grew shallow, his hand against the glass, holding, *holding*. The pull was too great. Any moment, the Etherium would take over again, but there was something Iravan needed to stop… Something to do with the architect frozen in front of him.

Distantly, he was aware of commotion, of screaming and councilors rising, muttering. Chaiyya pulled, and Basav moved slightly.

What, Iravan panted. *What*
do you
want?

His eyes returned to the creature in the deathcage, his dust mote frozen in the pocket Deepness.

The silence *burst* awake, in the manner of an eye opening.

       want, the falcon whispered, a growl in his head.

Iravan's eyes widened.

This was the first time the creature had formed words, that it had *replied* to him, not through a flutter of wings, or by taking over his mind, or through arbitrary emotion felt in the Deepness or the Moment or the Etherium or the silence. No, it had *spoken*. He hadn't even known that it could, and they—

plunged into the Etherium, into

the horror of a caged intelligence; the *realization* of being caged

The falcon roared, and its own fear rushed through the man as they realized that they had once been able to speak, once been able to *think*, and they were shocked by how much they had lost.

They circled each other surrounded by mirrors, saw themselves, neither man nor falcon, but something else, something greater, shapeless, infinite.

Want gripped it, and the falcon *thought*, it *planned*—it had never done that before, or it had once, a long time ago, when it had been something else. It watched itself flying through the skies, even as the skies exploded. It shot out a webbing of light into the darkness, for it could see the globule where the *others* came from, those creatures of the cosmos—

Blink, and it was back in the jungle, and fury coated it because for an instant, it had seen, it had remembered *everything*, and the knowledge had been taken away. It flew low in the jungle and wrapped a vine around the man's throat, and the man choked.

The falcon pressed, its vast infinite fury pushing the man down, for all those years of silence and abandonment. It knew that this time, the man would not become something else. This time, the falcon would be free of the melody, of the man, even if it were alone.

But threaded through it was the instinct that without him, it would be trapped into seeking, not knowing, *never* knowing.

The memory of that numbing life was excruciating.

The falcon released him.

In the pocket Deepness, the Resonance stopped Ecstatically trajecting.

Tears blurred Iravan's eyes. He let his Two Visions collapse, and vomited over and over again until his stomach was entirely empty.

Basav crumpled over the vine encircling his waist, even as the rings around the falcon's eyes disappeared. Architects rushed toward the deathcages, and Chaiyya pulled the man away and laid him carefully outside of the deathmaze.

Iravan watched all of this occur distantly, his heart pumping a shallow beat. The falcon's fury, the extent of its pain, its anger and hatred toward him and the cosmic creatures, all of it made sudden sense.

He had been born and reborn, into Nidhirv, Askavetra, Bhaskar, and Mohini, and a thousand others, until he had become Iravan. He had reincarnated into one intelligent life after another with will and identity and intent and desire, no matter how damaged.

But the yaksha had been stripped of it all.

It hadn't had anything except a vague memory, nothing except its silence. It had lived in a remembrance of its intelligence captured within this rudimentary form. All complex emotion, desire, or thought had been stripped away by their separation, returning only because of their union in the vortex.

At the back of his mind, Iravan felt its heavy presence, and he stared at it with blurry eyes. Hatred, belonging, and betrayal reverberated between them, as they both realized that finally, *finally*, they understood each other. The falcon had shown him what separation had been for itself through all those years.

want, the falcon whispered again, tasting the word.

Iravan could say nothing in return.

He stared at the creature. Distantly, he heard someone say, *Prepare them for excision*, but too horrified and exhausted to care, Iravan remained unmoving, staring at the falcon, the sounds of Ahilya's screams echoing in his ears.

24

AHILYA

Ahilya moved as though in a dream. The Conclave had burst into furore the second Basav had stepped into the deathmaze. Architects and sungineers surged to their feet, voices raised, fists shaking, and she was surrounded by angry bodies. Her own voice drowned in the chaos, but she stumbled forward, pushing through the sudden press, trying to follow Iravan and the falcon.

Someone—Ahilya thought it might be Garima—called out an order for excision, and Chaiyya confirmed it, but Ahilya's mind could not comprehend it. Basav had stepped into the deathmaze seconds ago. Iravan had fallen to his knees, *seconds* ago. She glimpsed the deathcages retreating, her husband on the floor of his cage, staring into nothingness. Ahilya pushed harder, past the bodies, her stomach cramping, and fell to her knees next to Chaiyya.

"You can't do this," she pleaded. "Please, Chaiyya. You know this isn't right."

The Senior Architect did not even look at her. Her body blazed blue-green, and her eyes were on Basav who lay on the floor covered in vines. Basav twitched, his breathing erratic. Under closed lids, his eyes moved slightly. Kiana, Laksiya, Dheeraj, and Jyothika kept the rest of the Conclave back, their palms raised. "You are safe," Kiana was saying. "You are safe."

Dizziness gripped Ahilya, and the theatre swam in her vision. "Chaiyya—please—"

"We need to get him to Katresh," Chaiyya said. "He needs to be near its core tree." The Senior Architect stood up, and Ahilya scrambled to her feet too. The tattoos on Chaiyya's skin changed, and the ground under Basav raised and firmed. For a bizarre second, Ahilya thought of Bharavi and how she had built a similar platform to take Iravan to the rudra tree, when they had returned from a disastrous archeological expedition in the jungle a few months before.

Her hand tightened over Chaiyya's wrist. "Please—" she heard herself beg. "This isn't right—you know this—"

The Senior Architect shook her off. "Kiana," she commanded, still not looking at Ahilya. "Take care of this. Airav, my vote is yes. Run the proceedings."

A vote for what? What did she mean? Someone pulled at Ahilya, and then she found herself marched away from the angry councilors of the Conclave, Kiana on one side of her and Laksiya on the other. Airav led the way on his wheelchair, clearing a path among the chaos. He stopped when they reached a quieter corner among the now-empty benches.

Ahilya's eyes darted to the wall where the deathcages had disappeared. The falcon had trajected Basav—a terrible loss of control on Iravan's part that would never be forgiven. Iravan was going to be excised. The falcon was going to be excised too. She had to do something—but what? Stop it from occurring—but how? Her stomach spasmed, so violently, so suddenly, that her mind slowed for an instant. She gasped, the pain radiating down her thighs and knees, making her shiver.

Around her, Nakshar's councilors were muttering, and she heard them say, "Yes, I vote yes."

"What in rages are you doing?" she bit out. She was leaning on Kiana, she realized. She tried to straighten, but her legs throbbed unnaturally. Bile rose, and she clenched her teeth, suppressing the urge to vomit. What was happening to her? The pain in her stomach reminded her of her monthly bleeding, but it couldn't be—it couldn't be—Tears spilled down her cheeks, unchecked. She could not grasp the gravity of what was occurring, not now, not when Iravan needed her.

"I'm sorry, Ahilya-ve," Airav said. "But we've voted unanimously to dismiss you from the council of Nakshar. We've passed a vote of no confidence. Your rudra beads, please."

Ahilya did not understand. She stared at them, Airav on his wheelchair with his hand outstretched, an expression of deep regret on his face, Laksiya, her mouth pressed in a thin line, her eyes narrowed in displeasure. And Kiana, who still held Ahilya up as though she knew how weak she was. The Senior Sungineer's eyes glinted behind her spectacles, but she said nothing.

"No," Ahilya whispered, aghast. "No, you can't—"

She took a step back, but her legs shivered, and there was nowhere to go, not when she was surrounded by them.

"Return your beads," Laksiya said coldly. "Or they will be taken from you."

"Why are you doing this?" Ahilya whispered. She swallowed, trying to staunch her tears, but they ran unchecked, and somewhere deep within her a grief built, a grief she could not look at right now. Pain lanced through her again, leaving her momentarily breathless.

"Nakshar requires it," Airav answered, and Ahilya understood—something she should have seen already, something she already knew. She had failed as a councilor. Her gambles, her plans, all of them had been useless. Iravan and the falcon had hurt Basav in front of an assembled Conclave. There would be consequences. Iravan's excision, Ahilya's dismissal, these were only the beginning of what the council would do as reparation in an attempt to stop Nakshar from being subsumed. What would be next? Her exile? The use of the energex on all the Ecstatics? The agony in her stomach sharpened, and she gasped as another spasm shot between her legs.

Ahilya didn't move, but Kiana and Laksiya were already removing her rudra bead bracelets. Airav looked away, mortified, as though she were being stripped naked—and Ahilya thought distantly that she *was*. They were taking away all her power. She couldn't believe this was how it would end: Iravan left drooling in his cage, herself discarded from the council. She had lost this fight. They had both lost.

"Your necklaces, too, Ahilya," Laksiya said. "Unless you want us to remove those for you, too."

Her hands shook, but she obeyed mechanically. Airav studied all the beads, counting them as though wary that Ahilya had kept some, but then he nodded. His gaze met Ahilya's.

"I'm sorry," he said quietly. "I truly am. You will be debriefed once we have excised Iravan, but until then—" He tapped at some of his own beads, and the wall behind them creaked open. Two Maze Architects waited ready. They strode forward at his gesture, their skins lit, placing themselves on either side of Ahilya.

"Geet and Raksha will watch you," Airav said. "Only until Iravan's excision, you understand. We cannot have you mounting another rescue."

A sense of unreality descended over Ahilya. She blinked, the tears falling relentlessly over her cheeks, but past the pain and the sorrow, past her struggle to breathe, she felt someone squeeze her arm in comfort. Ahilya looked up and saw Kiana. The sungineer said nothing, but her eyes glinted again, and Ahilya thought, slowly, wonderingly, *She's trying to tell me something. What?*

Then she was being led away through the wall, the two Maze Architects on either side of her. The wall closed, cutting out the councilors and the chaos of the Conclave, and Ahilya stumbled into a tunnel.

She began to shiver, each step sending a fresh throb of pain through her. Thoughts came to her slowly, but she knew there were two things. She needed to help Iravan first, and then, and then—

Tears flowed down her cheeks. She wanted to feel between her legs, to see if she was bleeding, but she didn't dare. Terror filled her mind.

"Where are you taking me?" she asked, but short of exchanging a glance, Geet and Raksha said nothing. They kept pace with Ahilya, their bodies still lit, providing the only illumination in the dark tunnel, so that it seemed like none of them were really moving at all.

A fresh stab of pain pierced through Ahilya, and she stumbled to her knees.

"Oh, please," Geet said, their voice skeptical. "We were warned you might try to escape. We know you're faking it."

"I don't think she is," Raksha replied, and her troubled face swam in front of Ahilya. "She's pregnant, and I think something is wr—"

Her words cut out.

Ahilya stared. Raksha spun out of her vision, and she heard both the Maze Architects cry out. Ahilya lurched, her legs trembling, but the architects flickered, thick vines around their chest and legs restraining them against the wall as though they were caught in a grotesque green spiderweb. *Iravan*, she thought abstractedly—this looked like something he had made once when he had tethered himself to Ahilya's breaking house. This was *his* design, but that was impossible. He was still in his deathcage, wasn't he? Bound within the deathmaze—then how—

The floor shifted. Vaguely, Ahilya realized that the ground had hardened and was traveling forward, taking her with it. She glimpsed Geet and Raksha struggle behind her, still flickering blue-green. She tried to push herself up, but something heavy and wet was moving inside her. She couldn't stop crying.

Abruptly, the ground stopped moving. Through the blur of her tears, Ahilya saw Naila lean forward, her face concerned. "Are you all right?" the Maze Architect breathed.

"Naila," Ahilya whispered. "Iravan—the falcon—"

"I know. We have to hurry. Geet and Raksha will break through their binding any second." The Maze Architect hauled Ahilya to her feet, but stopped, her face pale, when Ahilya cried out. "Ahilya-ve," she gasped. "Are you—what is happening?"

Tears still fell down Ahilya's cheeks relentlessly. She could not have stopped even if she'd tried. It was as though she had no control, like a dam within her had broken. It was unlike anything she had ever felt before. It made no sense, and far too much of it. She clenched her teeth as another spasm rocked her.

"We have to—have to help Iravan," she gasped out, leaning on Naila.

"But you—"

"Please—" Ahilya clutched Naila. "Please, Naila."

The Maze Architect studied her for a long second, her face troubled. Then she hefted Ahilya and wrapped an arm around her waist. Her skin grew blinding blue-green, and Ahilya closed her eyes. She felt the earth under them harden again. Naila's grip remained strong, and when Ahilya squinted her eyes open, white healbranch vines were growing over her feet, wrapping themselves around her calves.

"Where—are we going?" Ahilya whispered.

"I'm not sure where they're being taken," Naila said. "Kiana messaged me on my citizen ring, telling me what had transpired in the Conclave. My guess is Iravan-ve is being taken back to the courtyard where they held the falcon. It's the only other place big enough for the falcon. They are likely going to be excised there, but even if we get there, I don't know how we can—"

Ahilya wheezed, as another spasm wrenched through her. Naila swore and Ahilya felt the healbranch climb higher up her legs, wrap itself around her waist. There was something there, she knew, a decision Naila had taken. Healbranch was in scarce supply. Naila was redirecting it from architect spaces. And Kiana had messaged Naila? What was the Senior Sungineer's game? She had voted to dismiss Ahilya but was now helping her. Whose side was she on? Ahilya shook her head, her vision swimming, nausea rising in her. She received a sharp glimpse of Iravan on his knees, sobbing. How was she to help him? She didn't have Chaiyya's bead anymore, the one with all overarching permissions, but... but...

"Your rudra beads," Ahilya said, gritting her teeth. "Permissions from—catching—"

Naila's eyes grew wide. She understood.

The Maze Architect had caught Iravan and the falcon when they'd fallen after the skyrage. She had built the deathcage around them. She still had those permissions. Naila tapped at her beads, then nodded to confirm.

They continued in silence. The ground had stopped moving under them, but surely they were going to the courtyard? How was Naila doing this? Had Ahilya thought this before? In her mind's eye, a memory of a then-Junior Architect Naila shimmered, asking her to return to the temple on Iravan's command, so many months before. This was similar trajection. Ahilya had never truly understood it. The pain built deeper, and Ahilya suppressed a cry. *Find Iravan*, she thought, condensing all her thoughts into that one. *Release him.* Terror throbbed at her, at the thick wetness between her legs, but she cringed away from it, unable to look at it, unable to examine it. *Release Iravan*, she thought again. It would all be fine if she only did that. It would all be fine.

The floor lurched, and Ahilya stumbled again, but Naila held on tight, steadying her. The wall in front of them creaked open.

Cold air slammed into Ahilya with the suddenness of a slap.

She gasped, breathing it in, feeling the rain that fell on her. Her vision cleared for an instant. She and Naila stood within a small copse of trees, and through her unyielding tears, Ahilya glimpsed blue-green light flickering within the foliage. Naila had grown dark again. When had she stopped trajecting? The Maze Architect led Ahilya forward, but stopped at the edge of the copse, parting the leaves with her hands. Ahilya leaned against a tree trunk, her breath shallow.

Hidden among the trees, she saw that they were back in the courtyard where Iravan had landed. The falcon was in its deathcage, its monstrous wings flapping, its gaze up to the sky. Rain poured down, slicking the glass, reflecting the blue-green glow of five Maze Architects who stood sentry, looking out into the wet night, their cloaks drawn over their heads.

"Fuck," Naila said. "What do we do?"

Did Naila mean the architects? Ahilya had expected sentries— the yaksha and Iravan would be under guard—they'd have to create a distraction.

But then Ahilya noticed.

The falcon was in its deathcage.

Iravan was not.

The Maze Architects had separated Iravan and the falcon, perhaps expecting interference in their excision. Ahilya would never be able to save them both. Whimpering, she slumped against the tree, each breath painful. *Where are you?* she thought frantically, and the falcon cried out, a bloodcurdling sound. *Where are you?*

25

IRAVAN

Iravan blinked as sungineering lights flooded into his deathcage.

His ears rang, a high-pitched whine, and he closed his eyes tightly, slowing his breath. Still the lights spun, and behind his eyes the falcon cocked its head at Ahilya as she approached it. Was he dreaming? But no, he was not asleep.

Something terrible had happened… something about his own history. Iravan probed at it gently, but heartache so strong seized him that he retreated at once, feeling sickened. Now was not the time. He stilled himself, focusing only on keeping his breath shallow.

Eventually, he realized that his cheek was wet.

Sourness filled his mouth. His body hurt, like he had been beaten, the muscles sore and complaining. He moved his fingers and his toes, but they responded lethargically. A thirst so fierce grew in him that for the next few minutes all he could do was work his mouth to generate a little spit. What had happened? Where was the falcon—and Ahilya? He could see them both in his mind, in the place where the silence had been. Was he there with them? Was she coming to him?

Iravan squinted his eyes open.

He realized he was lying on the moss floor. His face was pressed against the damp earth and a pool of his own vomit. Revulsion gripped him, then receded. How long had he been lying there like that? Why had they let him?

Iravan pushed himself up slowly, and brushed at his face with the edge of his kurta until he had cleaned enough of the filth off himself. The feather cloak was heavy on his shoulders, but he pulled it closer, breathing the smoke of the falcon that lingered on it.

Slowly, very slowly, he stood up, blinking against the lights.

Shapes moved beyond the glass. He was in a courtyard full of Maze Architects in their brown uniforms. Groggily, Iravan noticed Viana, Brinda, and Savar among them. All the architects present belonged to Chaiyya's crew, but they were not the only ones around. Sungineers amassed as well, nearly twenty of them, and their voices were raised in argument. In the distance stood four other cages, an Ecstatic in each of them. Trisha looked at Iravan with concern, but Pranav's eyes were darting around, and the two young children stared about them, their bodies trembling.

Iravan understood then. He was back in the sanctum.

He could hear Dhruv's imploring voice, the intermittent words, "Excision... Energy X... Nakshar's *future*..."

A chill trickled down Iravan's spine.

He straightened, despite the protest of his cramped muscles, and knocked on the glass.

Someone called out, and then everyone in the courtyard was turning to him, wariness and contempt in their eyes. The sungineers exchanged glances with each other. Dhruv stirred, but Maze Architect Viana strode forward and held up a hand.

Iravan and the people outside his cage just stared at each other. Within their deathcages, the four Ecstatics jerked forward, hope and fear on their faces.

Pieces clicked in his mind, memory returning, of the trial, of Ahilya's screams, of Basav's questions. The falcon thrashed in his head, pushing against its deathcage, but the yaksha was nowhere in the sanctum. They had said they'd excise it. Had they done so already? Surely he'd have felt it. Sweat broke out over Iravan.

"Let me out," he said hoarsely. "Let me go, and I'll fly away. I will take them away with me, too. You don't have to do this. You will never see us again. Please."

The sungineers muttered among themselves. Dhruv turned to Viana, speaking rapidly, too low for Iravan to hear. In the Etherium, the cosmic creatures pushed against the webbing of their imprisonment. Somewhere far away, thunder crashed.

"Please," Iravan said again. "You don't have to excise—"

He cut off, with a gasp.

The images in the Etherium had changed, grown sharper, from the cosmic creatures to the architects in their deathcages. The architects were screaming. It was the same image he had seen in the jungle habitat, the one that had spurred him into returning to Nakshar in the first place.

Iravan's legs began to tremble. His heart beat so hard that he could hear the thrumming in his ears.

It was going to happen. He knew it.

That vision in the Etherium was going to come true.

He had seen the images turn sharper right before the skyrage too, taking over every other picture in the Etherium. Tears prickled at him. He had seconds.

"Let me out," he said louder, his voice pleading. He could not shatter the deathcages like the Ecstatics had done earlier—not without access to the whole of the Moment—so in desperation, he entered the pocket Deepness. The red grass in his deathmaze trembled as he Ecstatically trajected. He tried to strip it, turn it into vines, tried to thicken it so he might wield it to attack his deathcage, but nothing happened. The grass didn't react to his supertrajection.

Someone snickered, a Maze Architect, and Iravan knew.

The grass was not ordinary grass. It wasn't merely coloured differently to visually mark underlying deathmazes. Perileaf was special, perhaps of the psyche-phyta class of plants, designed with one specific purpose: not to respond to Ecstasy. The architects had likely created it after the yaksha had trajected them that first time, when Iravan had landed in Nakshar. They had done it so quickly. To them, he and the falcon had always been the real enemy.

Iravan released his ray of light.

In her deathcage, Reyla let out a quiet sob.

Dhruv tapped at his citizen ring and a golden hologram grew over his palm. The tall sungineer pointed at it and turned to the Maze Architects. "Why else would Kiana tell me this?" he asked. "Why else bring him here where the battery setup is? You know she cared about the battery."

"We don't take instructions from the Senior Sungineer," Viana replied, though she frowned.

What were they talking about? What had Kiana done? In the Etherium, the images grew sharper, each individual face of the screaming Ecstatics sharper. One was little Reyla. Tears choked his throat. In the silence, he watched the Maze Architects surrounding the falcon covered in vines, writhing. Everything was confusing, and in the Etherium Reyla screamed.

"Enough," Viana said, cutting Dhruv off. "We'll try it, but only for a few minutes."

Dhruv's shoulders relaxed. "Thank you. That should be enough to judge success."

"Not him, though," the Maze Architect pointed at Iravan. "He remains."

Dhruv's eyes met Iravan's. "Fine," the sungineer said.

Viana nodded, and the sungineers retreated from Iravan's cage. He watched them hurry across the courtyard to the far end. Dhruv gave Iravan one last look loaded with meaning, then followed them out. The deathcages moved, all but Iravan's. Reyla and Darsh began to weep, and Pranav's skin lit up with the light of trajection, though nothing happened either inside his deathcage or outside it. Unlike before when the forcefields had fallen, now the Ecstatics were returned to their pocket Moments. They would be unable to shatter their deathcages like they'd once done.

"What are you doing?" Iravan asked, frantic.

In the Etherium, the architects flickered. He saw both Reyla and Darsh, their skins blue-green then dark again, as though malfunctioning. In his first vision, the four cages rolled toward the bend where the sungineers had gone. Viana gestured to her team and Maze Architects surrounded each cage, leading them away from Iravan.

"Where are you taking them?" he shouted, scrabbling against the glass with his fingers. Iravan zipped in the pocket Moment, through the Conduit into the pocket Deepness, back and forth, looking for a way out. He trajected the stars within his deathcage, but nothing happened. He trajected Ecstatically from the pocket Deepness, but the perileaf lay limp.

The Maze Architects were leaving. Only three remained in the courtyard. Lights dimmed. *No*, Iravan thought.

The Etherium blinked.

The screaming began.

"*No*," Iravan shouted hoarsely. "*Please!*"

Frantically, he trajected in the pocket Deepness, but the grass did not give. He flew through the pocket Moment, spinning out constellation lines, but though the moss under him grew, it did not sharpen.

The screams sounded again, and this time he heard Reyla. In the Etherium, he saw them—all four of them—and lights flashed golden in the night sky, like lightning emanating from the ashram.

Iravan began to sob. *No, no, no.*

He saw the children, and the trust in their eyes when he had walked away from them, when he had told them to stand down. *I won't let them hurt you*, he'd said, but he had done nothing, when the Etherium had warned him of this from the beginning. He had done nothing in the trial, instead allowing Basav to bait him. Were they being excised? Excision required a Senior Architect, but perhaps Chaiyya had shared the secret with Viana.

More screams split the air, louder, accompanied by sobbing.

In the silence of his mind, the falcon roared and thrashed its wings against the deathcage, looking up into a thunderous sky. It looked like it was free—but how?

Iravan flew back into the pocket Moment and found the stars of everdust—the green dust of pure possibility. He had not dared to use it so far, but it was the only way out. He could not afford to waste it; they needed it to stop the earthrages, and using it now could doom them all, it could deplete this precious element when humanity could ill afford to.

But Iravan strung together constellation lines between the stars of everdust. He trajected pure possibility, knowing it to be a mistake, knowing he was condemning himself and the rest of the world. He did not know what his trajection would create, but desperately, he wished only for the strongest substance possible, for something that would help him attack and defend.

The trajection completed itself. A thin sharp blade of sparkling gray rock formed in his trembling hands, appearing out of nowhere. It weighed down his hand, heavy despite its small size, and light reflected off it as though it was not made of one single rock, but a billion tiny ones, latticed together to give it its strength.

It was not enough. He'd need a thousand such blades. He stabbed at the earth, at the glass pane in front of him, trying to rupture them both. A small crack appeared in the glass deathcage, but it did not give.

Outside his cage, the three sentinel architects moved.

Under him, the ground shuddered.

Another scream rent the air.

"Please," Iravan begged, and in his mind, he saw not the children, but Bharavi as she was strangled. He heard her call out his name, ask him to help her. Tears flowed down his cheeks, settled into his beard. Ecstatics spasmed in the Etherium, even as golden light flickered in his first vision. He heard Ahilya say, *You won't be here... You'll make an even worse father*, and he sobbed, "Please, listen to me. You don't have to do this."

None of the three Maze Architects moved.

The ashram juddered again.

In his second vision, Iravan moved desperately but he could do nothing with the grass. In his first vision, he dug into the earth, trying to escape. He smashed the blade into the cage, and more cracks appeared, splinter thin. It would take too long. It would be too late. All his power of Ecstasy, all his unity with the falcon, all his foresight with the Etherium, none of that had mattered. He had lost.

The screams of the children filled his mind and ears, ricocheting through the Etherium and the courtyard. Iravan wept on his knees, the blade slicing his palms, trying frantically to escape.

26

AHILYA

The Maze Architects swayed in front of the falcon's deathcage. Their dark skins glowed blue-green, and vines writhed under their translucent robes.

"They're trajecting," Naila whispered.

Trajecting, Ahilya repeated slowly in her head. *Yes.*

Her vision swam, and she held onto lucidity by a fingernail. Her stomach cramped so hard that her legs shook uncontrollably. Ahilya clutched the closest tree and took a deep breath. Rain slicked her hair back and the night was cool, but warmth grew between her legs. She pressed a hand to her inner thighs, feeling the fabric of her black trousers past the healbranch twined around her. Her fingers came away wet. She brought them to eye level and stared. Blood.

Distantly, she understood the blood meant something—something she already knew, something she had expected—but she couldn't look at that thought too closely, not right now. If she did, she would break completely. Ahilya wrenched her eyes away from her fingers, the rain washing away the dark red, and tried to focus on Naila's words.

"It will be tricky," the Maze Architect was saying. "They will be expecting us. It depends on whether Geet and Raksha have recovered, and whether Chaiyya-ve knows you aren't under watch anymore. We'll have to move fast. All right?"

Ahilya nodded. Chaiyya. The woman had been busy with Basav. She had taken back her borrowed rudra bead. She had ordered away all of Ahilya's beads. She had probably asked for Iravan and the falcon to be separated during their excision. Had Iravan been excised yet? But that thought led to many others, each scarier than the last. The effort was too much. Ahilya blinked as her mind clouded. She returned her focus to Naila. The Maze Architect was speaking slowly, as though she knew Ahilya found it hard to follow the words.

"I think I can contain them," Naila said, her gaze still on the guards. "But I won't be able to hold them for too long. Gaurav is powerful, as is Megha, and they've been Maze Architects longer. They're more familiar with the stars of Nakshar than I am. But if you can let the falcon out quickly, I'll give you as much time as I can."

Ahilya nodded again. *Release the yaksha.* Yes, that was what she had to do. The only thing she had to do. They had been over this plan already. This was the second time Naila was saying it. The two of them had come up with the plan to rescue the falcon because that was all they were capable of doing. In one hand, Ahilya clutched one of Naila's rudra bead bracelets. The Maze Architect had told her which bead to tap. That was all she needed to do—tap the bead and *desire*—but Ahilya's body shook violently, tears falling down her cheeks, mingling with the rain. Salt prickled her tongue.

Tariya had bled too, hadn't she? Yes, she had, and maybe... maybe it was hereditary. Tariya had bled, but Arth had still been born healthy. Ahilya swallowed, feeling the heavy wetness slide inside her. She was fine. She was all right. Her chest caught in a tight sob. Through the trees, the falcon cocked its head toward her.

"Ahilya-ve?" Naila asked, quietly.

"It's—good plan," Ahilya whispered. "You should—" She gasped as something slid inside her body, lower. More wetness ran down her thigh—blood, she knew. *Don't look at it*, she thought in terror. *Don't think about it. Do it later, not right now, you can't right now.* But she couldn't help touching her trousers, anyway. When she raised her fingers, the blood felt slick.

Ahilya heard a gasp. Naila's eyes widened, reflecting her own horror as the Maze Architect noticed the blood, too. *Not now*, Ahilya thought desperately, *don't think of it now.* "F-find your p-position," she whispered. Any louder and she knew her voice would shake hysterically at the unreality of this situation.

Naila stared at her, opened her mouth to speak, then closed it again. Tears glistened in her eyes. Abruptly, the Maze Architect hugged Ahilya.

"Watch for my glow," she whispered, then she was gone, slipping quietly through the dark trees.

Clutching one tree after another, Ahilya staggered through the foliage. Her legs trembled, and without Naila's trajection, the ground did not firm. She slipped over the mud, pain piercing through her, and edged closer to the falcon. The yaksha thrashed its head, pushing against its deathcage. Its guards jumped, and one of them muttered something. All of them glanced behind, their gazes directed to the floor as though to confirm they were still outside the deathmaze's boundary.

Naila struck.

Within the trees, her body glowed blue-green directly opposite Ahilya. Vines grew out of the floor like thick tentacles, wrapping the Maze Architects and dragging them away from the cage.

"*Now, Ahilya-ve,*" Naila shouted, and Ahilya thought slowly, *Yes, now.* That was the signal.

She emerged from the trees, staggering, crawling, lurching to her feet. Blue-green light swam in and out of her vision. Something clutched her—a hand—then it was gone, wrapped in a vine. Shouts and screams echoed in the courtyard, sounds of battle and pain. Distantly, Naila screamed, urged her forward. A Maze Architect broke through his vines, reaching.

Ahilya fell to her knees. Red grass gleamed wetly under her palm. She was in the deathmaze, she realized. The architects would not follow her inside.

Blood pooled around her, thick. Behind her, sounds of fighting resounded, Naila screaming, lights flashing. Ahilya emptied her stomach. *Free the yaksha*, she thought. That's all she had to do. Tears fell down her cheeks, and she stared up at the creature looming over her. She gripped Naila's bracelet between wet fingers and pressed the correct rudra bead and thought, *Open*.

The glass around the falcon's deathcage whisked down.

Ahilya saw herself reflected in it, dark hair disheveled, undone to her waist, her body shaking and wet, her face raw and defeated. Her eyes traveled up, through the pouring rain.

The falcon-yaksha screamed, looking up into the rainy sky.

It flapped its monstrous wings, and wind slapped at Ahilya as the bird launched itself into the sky, water glittering on its silvery-gray feathers. *Help him*, she thought, at the dark monstrous shape. *Help him. Please.* Hope blossomed in her chest. Surely now that the falcon was free, it would go to rescue Iravan. She had felt a camaraderie from the yaksha. It had responded to her ministrations in the cage while it had been injured. Surely it would listen to her now? She hadn't imagined their moment of understanding. She had been able to calm it. It trusted her.

The falcon hovered in the air, cutting out the rain, its wings a rush of wind.

Then it pivoted, streaking through the night sky, away from Nakshar and the Conclave.

No, she thought in anguish, *Come back. You have to—you have to—*

But a fresh burst of pain spasmed through her. The blood moved in her in a final shudder, and she felt something slide down her legs, her body emptying itself. The ground shook like the ashram breaking.

Ahilya's last thought was of regret, that she should have saved Iravan first instead of the falcon—that she should have protected their child before she had tried to help him.

Then the grass rushed up to meet her.

Ahilya lost consciousness.

27

IRAVAN

Iravan fumbled in the pocket Deepness.

His hands were a mass of bleeding wounds from where his stone blade had cut to the bone.

Minutes had gone by. He had stopped sobbing, but silent tears still fell with every fresh scream that erupted from the darkness at the other end of the courtyard. In the Etherium, the sungineers moved between the cages.

In his second vision, he frantically supertrajected, even as he plunged the blade into the soil, as he smashed at the glass pane itself. He knew the futility of his actions. He could not dig his way out of the cage. The glass was too strong, it would take forever, and trajection worked only on the possibilities of plants. Ecstasy could change the nature of a star, but it could not redefine possibility itself. Normal plants had infinite possibilities, but the architects of Nakshar had cultivated this perileaf for a single one—to be useless to an Ecstatic.

Still, Iravan did not stop.

Another scream rent the air. His bloody hands shook, even as his vision blurred.

The ground trembled as though trajection were failing in the ashram again. Iravan couldn't care. He hurled his ray of light from the pocket Deepness. He spun constellation lines within the pocket Moment. Tears stung his eyes, each scream giving him a fresh burst of energy: dig, traject, slash, traject, smash, traject.

Blinding sungineering light burst through the courtyard.

Iravan paused, confused, and raised a bloody hand to his eyes.

The three sentinel Maze Architects jerked and exchanged glances. As one, they sprinted toward the end of the courtyard where the Ecstatics and sungineers had disappeared. Iravan squinted, but the light from that end was too bright; he could see nothing.

But whatever was happening, the Maze Architects guarding him were gone.

He had a distraction.

He could use this. But how? What could he do?

In the Etherium, the images pounded him. Darsh clutching his hair, Pranav and Trisha sobbing quietly, Reyla almost comatose, and the colorless images of Bharavi with her children, Ahilya heavily pregnant, his parents. In his first vision, he gripped the stone blade with bloody fingers, turning in panicky circles, while he raced through the Conduit, hurtling between the pocket Deepness and the pocket Moment, trying to think of a way out, trying, trying.

He would go mad, he knew. The screams would never leave him. The images would forever haunt him. In his memories, Bharavi said, *Remember who you are*, and he thought in anguish, *I'm not ready, Bha*, but she only leaned forward, as she asked Manav about his poetry. *Dangerous*, Manav whispered. *Dangerous, dangerous*. Iravan clutched at his hair, head spinning, even as sobbing sounded from the courtyard. Bharavi said, *Two roads in sleep*, and the yaksha tilted its head in the silence to study Ahilya and Naila, and Iravan thought, *No more, please, no more*. His legs shook, and his mind began to break.

It was too much. These visions, these memories, and Bharavi said *Awakening... beyond time; in undying separate illusions... I've found acceptance... Acceptance—*

He gasped, his eyes growing wide.

His bloody hands stopped clenching the sparkling gray blade. He stopped spinning in the deathcage.

Just as easily as that, he knew what he had to do.

In his second vision, he hovered within the Conduit, the space between the Moment and the Deepness. He had always thought the Conduit a tunnel that connected the two caverns of the Moment and the Deepness, but that was because he had been viewing it from the outside.

Iravan changed his perception, willed the Conduit to reveal itself. The Conduit transformed

—into the Moment, the Deepness, the Etherium—the three realms *EXPANDED*—became each other—and his visions merged, the first into the second into the third—

and Iravan froze as familiarity filled him.

He had seen this happen once, seconds before tumbling into the vortex within the habitat, little over two months before. He had not understood then. He understood now.

His three visions had never been separate paths.

They had been the same all along.

The divisibility had been *his* conditioning, not the nature of what he had been seeing. He forgot to be terrified, forgot that there was a pressing urgency. *See*, he/they/it thought.

And he saw the citizen spaces of Nakshar malfunctioning, and Tariya and his nephews clutch each other in terror. He saw the Disc Architects shriek in confusion as their constellation lines in the Moment disintegrated. He saw Chaiyya and Kiana and Laksiya and Airav frantically tap at their rudra beads, even as the entire

Conclave shook, caught on a precipice. He saw the architecture wobble, the soil break away, the glass shimmer and weaken, the sister ashrams quiver, all fifty of them.

Iravan stared, unable to understand, yet somehow seeing it all, knowing it to be true.

Acceptance, Bharavi said—

And Iravan looked into his present imprisoned reality, and saw himself in the deathcage, tangled hair, matted beard, bloody, wild the falcon flying into the darkness, leaving him abandoned Ahilya bleeding, collapsing, the child they made dead before it could live.

Iravan howled then, an echo of pain that resounded through his three combined visions. He wasn't in the Moment or the Deepness or the Conduit or the Etherium anymore, but he didn't need to be, not when there was no separation between any of the realms. He willed it, and light shot out of him like a billion constellation lines.

All the glass cages within the courtyard burst into powder.

Beyond, blinding sungineering light exploded a second time.

Yes, Iravan thought, through his wonder and his grief—then laughed, because the force of these actions had dropped him back to his knees, face into the earth. Only a few seconds had passed since the sentinel Maze Architects had sprinted from view. He tried to rise, but his muscles screamed. Iravan retched, but the motion produced only spittle. He tried to push himself up, but his arms trembled.

The earth under him roiled.

Footsteps vibrated on the earth.

Someone was coming. Panicked, Iravan thought, *No, I can't go back in there.*

Terror gave him purchase. He stumbled to his knees, even as hands gripped his arms and pulled him up. Iravan found himself looking into Dhruv's anxious face. Rudra beads dangled from the sungineer's fingers. Iravan recognized them. They belonged to a Maze Architect.

"What happ— how did you—" Dhruv stuttered, his words dying.

Iravan followed the sungineer's gaze, back to his own arms, and froze.

His skin glistened, but not in the manner of entering the Moment or the Deepness, no—Iravan was lit from within, and he saw his veins and tissues, he saw the blood flowing within himself, the fibers of his muscles, the fluids within his form. If he took his kurta off, he knew he'd be able to see his lungs and heart and all his organs, the tapestry of his own body alive, as though he were translucent. It was too much, this effort of maintaining the vision, as a deathless void grew inside him, sucking in the energy. His sight trembled and he knew whatever this was, this merged vision of everything, it would kill him if he stayed in it any longer.

With effort—painfully—

Iravan let it collapse, wrenched himself away from this perception.

At once his body darkened. His visions returned, settled back to normalcy, and he found himself hovering back in the Conduit, between the Moment and the Deepness.

He slumped on Dhruv, all his energy disappeared.

The sungineer hefted him with a grunt, draping his arm over his shoulder. "We don't have time." His voice was low and terrified. "The Maze Architects are probably recovering already. I could only create two flashes of light, one to distract Viana, and the other to blind your guards who rushed in, but it will wear off any second. They'll be back."

"Who—excise—" Iravan whispered.

"No one yet," Dhruv answered, helping him along, pulling him forward.

Iravan tried to straighten. He knew he was dead weight on the sungineer.

"We intervened," Dhruv went on, still supporting him. "The sungineers. Kiana sent me information right after the trial, telling me excision was going to happen."

Iravan gripped Dhruv's arm and pushed himself up. "She told you—to stop it?"

"Not exactly," Dhruv responded. "I don't know for sure. Kiana has always only told me what she wanted me to know, but I think she wanted me to make a decision. The sungineers and I convinced the Maze Architects to allow us to attempt the Ecstatic battery before any of you were excised. Maybe that's what she wanted me to do? I don't know—she's always been invested in the battery, but " Dhruv stumbled as the ground under them shook again, and Iravan slid, his eyes widening. "I don't know what happened though," Dhruv continued, even as they staggered over the trembling earth. "The battery, it didn't work, despite the care I took. The spiralweed is harder on Ecstatics for some reason, worse than it was on Airav, and I don't know what is happening to the ashram now—"

His words cut out.

A sudden coldness had gripped Iravan the instant Dhruv began speaking, because he understood now—the screaming of the Ecstatics, the vision of them in the deathcage he had seen while in his Garden in the jungle.

He hadn't seen excision.

He had seen the Ecstatics being harvested for the battery—the very thing he and Ahilya had fought for. The thing Dhruv had created.

Fury climbed in him, and blue-green light suffused him as he trajected. A thick vine climbed from the earth, curled around

Dhruv's neck, and lifted the sungineer off the ground. "You did this," Iravan snarled.

"I didn't know," Dhruv choked. "I—didn't know it would hurt them."

Iravan warped the vine and brought the sungineer to eye level. "What did you do? Talk fast, your life depends on it."

"They were going to excise you! I was trying to help. The battery was never my idea." Dhruv's fearful eyes darted behind his spectacles, reflecting the blue-green light from Iravan.

"The Ecstatics weren't trained," Iravan spat. "They weren't ready for the battery. You knew this."

"It was all I could do to delay the excision." Dhruv gasped. His hand fumbled in his pocket, and he withdrew a velvety black leaf. "Please—I'm—not—not lying."

For a second, despite the veristem in the sungineer's hand, Iravan didn't move.

Then he let go, and Dhruv collapsed on the ground, coughing and choking.

Iravan nearly fell alongside him. The effort had sapped him of his remaining energy.

Next to him, Dhruv faltered to his feet.

"You've been carrying that around?" Iravan grunted, nodding to the unbloomed veristem still clutched in the sungineer's palm.

"Troubled times," Dhruv answered, rubbing his throat. "Look, are we—"

He could say no more.

The ground under them shifted and groaned as the architecture changed. Iravan swayed on his feet, his knees trembling. More screams came from the courtyard, but even as he watched, the courtyard shrank. The others appeared much closer to him, Pranav stumbling out of the remains of his deathcage toward Trisha, Darsh grabbing hold of Reyla and pulling at her. Iravan's explosion of his own glass cage had broken theirs too—he had willed it, but he had not changed the ashram's architecture to do it. Still, with the strange change in the architecture, the four Ecstatics were only a few feet away from Iravan and Dhruv now, while around them, Maze Architects lurched to their feet.

"What are you doing?" Dhruv asked, frightened.

"This isn't me," Iravan replied—and it was not. Neither was this another skyrage. The ashram rumbled under them, and soil ruptured, but the Etherium returned no image of the cosmic creatures or another skyrage.

Yet somehow the constellation lines in Nakshar's Moment were breaking. Trajection was failing in the ashram. This wasn't him or the cosmic creatures, but the Conclave was still collapsing, a failure of the architecture itself.

Viana had risen to her feet. "What did you do, Ecstatic?" she shrieked, glaring at Iravan. Around her, the other Maze Architects rose too, their bodies lit blue-green as they entered the Moment. "You, sungineer," she commanded. "Find other deathcages. What in rages is happening—we need to get these Ecstatics back—"

She didn't get to complete her sentence.

From within the Deepness, Iravan aimed his ray of light at her in the Moment. Viana froze, her eyes darting in fear, and he felt her awareness pushing at the edge of his own, terror in it. The tattoos on his skin changed, turning discordant. He thought as he trajected her, *Leave. Walk away. Now.*

But Viana's eyes grew crimson. They began to bleed. She screamed, but blood choked her, sprayed like rain. Bones cracked along her body, pierced her like roots ripping through her skin, sharp and white.

Horrified, Iravan stopped trajecting. He heard the sound of retching. Shocked, he stumbled forward to Viana, *No, no, no*—he'd only meant to send her away, but he had Ecstatically trajected her in his fury, and now roots grew from the earth to drag her body away. Iravan stood staring at the ground where she disappeared, and he couldn't comprehend it, *I killed her I killed her I killed her*—

How had the falcon done it? It had supertrajected the architects when it had landed in the ashram too, but it hadn't done what Iravan had done. What *had* he done?

He heard gagging and turned to see Dhruv wipe his mouth and stare at him in horror. In the distance, Maze Architects fled, screaming, but closer Reyla was openly crying, and Pranav cringed away from the scene, while Trisha clung to him, weeping. Only fifteen-year-old Darsh stared back, as though fascinated. Beyond them all, Iravan remembered Ahilya, and her bleeding, and the child they had lost tonight. She had known this would happen. She had anticipated her miscarriage, but she hadn't told him, because she hadn't thought him capable of learning the news, of being there for her, involved as he was with the falcon and his own agenda.

She had been right. After all this, after everything they had promised each other and learnt, she had been in pain and alone, trying to save him. He had done nothing for her, again. He had failed her. Again.

Something within him cracked with the weight of all these realizations.

Iravan grew cold all over, and then the coldness vanished, leaving behind nothing but fatigue.

He turned to Dhruv. His voice was emotionless. "Time for you to leave, too," he said.

The sungineer stared at him. "Will you kill me if I don't?" he asked quietly.

For a long instant, Iravan considered it.

He knew a part of him wanted to. It was shocking how badly it wanted to. The horror, pain and fury of the trial and the last few hours, the last few *months*, rolled through him in waves, but at the front it was not emotion that pushed him. He had killed Viana, he had killed Bharavi, he had killed Oam. He could do it again, this time neither by accident nor in desperation. The sungineer might even deserve it for what he'd done to the Ecstatics. Iravan could make that decision. The exhaustion pounded in him, everything he had lost tonight, everything he had experienced, the weight of it, the futility.

Dhruv could see it, he knew, the deadly calm.

Absolute silence covered the courtyard, except for the soft weeping and retches of the four Ecstatic architects. Iravan stared, coolly thinking, examining the thought of killing Dhruv, the pros and cons, the logic of doing so, the deliberation and consequences. His eyes passed over Reyla and Darsh, over Trisha and Pranav, and back to the sungineer.

In the end, the troubled weeping of the Ecstatics broke the moment.

Iravan looked away from Dhruv. "Your life depends on the manner of their recovery," he said coldly.

The sungineer shuddered. His entire body relaxed. "Then I'll take my chances with you," he said, wiping his brow. "After what I did here in abetting you, my life in the ashrams is over."

Iravan began to hobble toward the center of the courtyard.

"What are you doing?" Dhruv called out.

What I should have done two days ago, Iravan thought, but his body jerked unwillingly. Is that all it had been? Two days since he had been in the jungle? Since he had flown to Nakshar, and the Conclave? Two days?

He fingered the blade of pure possibility, still in a ruined hand. Blue-green light *exploded* out of him.

The roof above them split open, letting in the cleansing storm, washing away his blood and tears. The earth under them shook, contracted, bringing the four Ecstatics and Dhruv closer to him.

Iravan raised the architecture.

With a groan, the patch of soil the six of them stood on began to ascend. Next to him, Dhruv swore as they rose into the storm. Darsh whooped, even as Pranav and Trisha cried out—and then all of them staggered to their hands and knees as gravity pulled on them. His stomach lurching, Iravan remained standing. The viney tattoos on his bleeding skin grew dizzying, fractalizing, so many, so complex, that even he could not keep track.

The courtyard ascended through the storm, rain pelting them, drenching them as they rose high above Nakshar. The Conclave shook, minuscule blue-green lights flashing everywhere in the darkness, as Maze Architects of each ashram undoubtedly panicked. Iravan saw the dark shapes of every city, how Nakshar was at the center of it all, and how *he* was now at the center of Nakshar, the column of the courtyard rising, ever rising.

Iravan steadied in the Deepness. He shot out jets of light into the Moment, and trajected the core trees. The Conclave responded to his Ecstasy.

With a loud groan that could be heard even past the storm and their height, the Conclave *split*. Each ashram separated from Nakshar and wobbled in the air. Leaves and branches grew out of every city rapidly like thick ropes. The ropes transformed, knitting themselves and attaching to Iravan's courtyard, even as the ashrams detached. Faintly, he heard screams echoing from every direction, but he did not stop.

He trajected Ecstatically, and they watched the fifty sister ashrams rip apart from Nakshar and each other, and fly independently while still being connected to Iravan's courtyard in the center. The Conclave was laid out around them, long walled tunnels of green building from each ashram toward Iravan's courtyard like spokes through a gigantic wheel.

Frantic blue-green light flashed everywhere in the wheel. The others rose shakily to their feet, joining Iravan. He trajected, and a roof grew over their heads, shielding them from the rain. Healbranch grew on the floor, and the patch of courtyard they stood on grew larger, transformed into shade and calm. When he glanced at them, they stared back at him in terror and awe, four Ecstatics and one sungineer—these people who would make the first citizens of Iravan's new ashram. Iravan turned away from their stares.

"See to them," he commanded Dhruv.

The sungineer stumbled away, and Iravan heard him speak to the Ecstatics. He tuned them all out, and strode forward into the storm, away from the shield of the bark roof.

Standing alone in the night, the feather cloak billowing behind him, Iravan clutched his impossible blade and surveyed his doing.

Earth and leaves flew around, tightening and safeguarding the Conclave's new design, but every single architect in those ashrams knew what this construction meant.

He controlled the Conclave now, its architecture, its flight, its existence.

Iravan stared into the sky, rain pounding him, feeling nothing but a grim purpose. He had come here for a reason.

He would fulfill it.

28

AHILYA

S he awoke to emptiness.

It felt like weight in her chest, a gravity in her stomach, ready to pull her under a sea of grief. Her eyes were closed, and she was on something soft, but Ahilya lay as still as she could, watching the grief build in her mind like a wave, like an enemy. She needed to keep it at a distance. If she didn't it would overtake her, filling up this diminishing space of sacred numbness. She would have to face the reality of what had occurred, of what she had done. *Don't wake up*, she thought, with a kind of frantic slowness. *There is nothing to wake up to, no reason to wake. Just go back to sleep. That's all you need to do.*

Still, tears leaked out of her closed eyes. A sob built in her chest as the grief edged closer over the breaker of emptiness, the wave of it rearing its head. Ahilya wrenched her lids open desperately before it could crash over her. She cast her gaze about, and realized she was in an unfamiliar room.

Yes, she thought. Yes, this was a better problem to focus on. Her immediate whereabouts and what she was doing here.

She struggled to a sitting position on the cot. The chamber was large, though Ahilya was the only one in it. Voices rose in argument coming from one side, perhaps an adjoining chamber. The design, especially the walls, so full of twinkling phosphorescence… all of it reminded her of the library alcove she and Iravan had shared during their courtship. Iravan had… he had…

Her eyes filled with heavy tears again, blurring her vision. The images returned unbidden, of Iravan in the Conclave, his sight unseeing as he knelt in his deathcage. Of Garima calling for his excision. Of the falcon-yaksha Ahilya had set free. A choked sob filled her as a small ripple of grief lulled her closer toward the building wave.

Ahilya's fingers curled into the sheets. What had she done? She had led them to this, played a game she was unfit to play, forced him to present himself in front of the Conclave, and led him toward excision—and the choices she had made—in entering the vortex while she was pregnant, in releasing the falcon before saving Iravan. She had bled, she had *bled*, and that which had been growing inside her had slipped away.

Her body curled into itself. She began to cry softly, unable to hold herself back from the monstrous surge of grief anymore.

Had she chosen to become pregnant? She had felt the pressure behind Iravan's need to be a father. She had consumed the right herbs to make her body pliable, to aid her fertility during those seven long months of his absence. She had fought the need for a child, but in a passive perverse way she had wondered if having children would save her marriage. She had *prepared*, an unconscious decision, in the hope that giving Iravan what he wanted would get him to return, get him to *stay*, even if she had fought against it out loud. She had fallen into bed with him, knowing perhaps she would bear a child. Had she brought this on them? *I want to be a father, Ahilya*, he said in her mind, and she choked as she saw herself leaping after him into the vortex.

Distantly, voices grew outside her chamber, but she could not dissect them. Overwhelming shame filled her, making her body shake in spasms. It was over. It was done. Ahilya heard hurried footsteps on the hard floor, and shrank on her side, closing her eyes, trying to quieten herself, hoping to be left alone—but a gentle hand landed on her shoulder and she flinched, giving herself away.

"You're awake," Naila said, her voice filled with relief. "I thought I saw movement."

Ahilya shook her head, unable to form any words. Hot tears blocked her throat.

"Please, Ahilya-ve," Naila whispered, so close that her breath fluttered Ahilya's hair. "I don't—they'll be here soon. Iravan-ve is all right. He hasn't been excised. He's escaped."

At first, the words didn't register.

Then Ahilya sat up, so abruptly that Naila took several steps back. The grief retreated, in the face of shock. The Maze Architect threw a glance behind her where the voices had grown louder. Shadows shifted along the phosphorescence.

"H-how?" Ahilya said hoarsely.

"I'm not sure," Naila said. Her words came faster. "He escaped with the other four Ecstatics last night, at the same time as we released the yaksha—but Dhruv is missing, and rumours are growing about Viana's disappearance. There has been trouble in the solar lab too. Senior Sungineer Kiana is incensed—I've never seen her so angry with the sungineers. Nakshar's architecture, the *Conclave's* architecture—he has done something, Ahilya-ve, but—"

The Maze Architect cut off. A wall behind her shimmered and formed into a doorway. Kiana and Chaiyya strode in, Kiana's eyes traveling from Ahilya to Naila before returning to Ahilya again.

Naila had said Kiana was incensed, but there was only the same coolness and wariness in the Senior Sungineer's gaze as always. *You helped us*, Ahilya thought abstractedly. She couldn't recall the details, but it had been Kiana who had sent Naila to her rescue when she had been stripped of her rudra beads.

Even as Ahilya thought this, she noticed her beads were back on her wrists, and there were more against her chest. They had returned them to her, all her councilor permissions.

As for Naila… The Maze Architect moved to stand beside Ahilya, and under her brown kurta, Ahilya glimpsed *her* rudra beads. Neither of them had been punished for disobedience and treachery. Why?

Ahilya straightened on the cot as the two councilors approached. The grief settled, heavy and patient, in the back of her mind. The two women took a seat next to her silently. A thousand questions built but Ahilya held her tongue, swallowing her tears.

"I'm truly sorry," Chaiyya said finally. "It should never have happened like this. How are you feeling?"

They knew about her miscarriage. Of course they knew. Heat pooled in Ahilya's stomach, and in her mind she tracked the blood that still flowed between her legs into the bandages. Someone had undressed her and changed her clothes. She still wore black kurta and trousers but they were a different set, looser, without any embroidery. Shame built in her again.

"What do you want?" she whispered. "Why are you here?"

Chaiyya and Kiana exchanged a glance.

The Senior Sungineer shifted uncomfortably, her eyes blinking behind her glasses. "Chaiyya, perhaps we shouldn't—"

"We don't have a choice. The situation is too dire." Chaiyya pressed a hand to her head then dropped it. "I don't know how much Naila has told you, but whatever you know, it isn't the whole truth."

"What *is* the whole truth?" Ahilya asked in a low voice.

Chaiyya took a deep breath. "The use of the battery was unsanctioned. It was a rogue action by a few sungineers. We have them in custody, and they will answer for what they did to Iravan and the other Ecstatics. You have my word on this."

Kiana nodded gravely. "I'm sorry—but yes, it was the sungineers. Several things have been happening in the solar lab without my knowledge. Soon after Iravan recreated the Conclave's architecture, the emergency protocol kicked in, and Laksiya *did* change it back, just as she had confirmed. But some sungineers hacked her security clearance to change it again. She has resigned for this error, though I have asked her to continue to assist with the lab." Kiana noticed Ahilya's widening gaze and shook her head. "I know what you're thinking. It wasn't sabotage—not really. Those sungineers were trying to steal emergency power to redirect it to citizen spaces, to the homes where their families live. They didn't do it to damage Nakshar, but of course, it amounted to the same. They are being questioned."

Ahilya blinked. Her heart began to race. She recalled the strange purplish-black light from Umang's glowglobe. She thought of how she herself had changed permissions to protect citizen spaces using Chaiyya's rudra bead. She could practically feel Naila bursting to speak.

"Iravan is angry about what happened with the battery. We can understand that." A bead of sweat trickled past Chaiyya's ear. Underneath the Senior Architect's careful words, Ahilya detected a tone of desperation. "But what he has done in retaliation is madness. He has rendered our trajection useless in his fury. Not just Nakshar's architects, but those of every single ashram in the Conclave. Our Disc Architects are attempting to break through his trajection, but we have no control over our ashrams anymore. Sungineering has become inoperable, with nothing to power it. Ahilya, he has trajected the core trees into *submission*. It's insanity. If he loses control, if he *desires* it, he could plunge us all to our deaths. He has already abducted the Ecstatics and Dhruv, and what he's done to Viana—" Chaiyya shuddered. "I dare not believe it, but the Maze Architects who witnessed it all tell the same story."

"He helped the Maze Architects," Naila blurted out, clearly unable to keep silent. "The Disc Architects of all the ashrams finally have a chance to rest."

Chaiyya did not chastise the Maze Architect for speaking out of turn, but her eyes hardened, and behind Ahilya, Naila stilled, clearly abashed. Ahilya said nothing, unable to keep track, unable to understand it all.

The Senior Architect took another deep breath and leaned forward. "There is no way for us to reach him. But Ahilya, he would not deny you entry. You are the only one who can convince him to release us. He would not hurt you, surely, or us if we were with you."

Ahilya's head spun. Through the returning grief, she registered a few things. Iravan had escaped. He had taken the other Ecstatics with him. Although he was not in Nakshar or the Conclave any longer, he was not far away. He hadn't left her to return to the jungle, despite his escape.

She threw the covers back and staggered to her feet. Naila was there in an instant, helping her. The Maze Architect leaned forward, her voice a low whisper. "Ahilya-ve. You don't have to do this."

"She's still bleeding," Kiana said at the same time, frowning. "She can't go now. She needs to heal."

But Chaiyya shook her head. "I know what it's like. I've been through two miscarriages myself. I am not unsympathetic, but one slip from Iravan is all it will take for utter devastation. Already many architects are burning crimson, their tattoos mutilating. And what happened to Viana—what he did—there's a pattern. He's out of control and he's clearly tied with all this, perhaps even causing this—*all* of this—"

Ahilya stumbled past them in the direction they had come, not truly hearing their words. Her bare feet guided her through the corridor until a wall opened where rain slashed in.

"Wait," Chaiyya called out. "We need to prepare you."

"We don't know if you will be let in either," Kiana began, but the rest of her words were carried away by the wind.

Ahilya walked into the storm, barely aware of the three women trailing her.

Cold rain and thunder greeted her like a slap, and she was drenched within seconds. The scent of water on earth filled her nose, clearing her mind.

She had emerged onto a balcony that ran in a long, gentle circle. Ahilya gripped the smooth wooden railing, looking down into gray mist. She knew they were still airborne, but she could *feel* the jungle as though they were close to landing, as though she was readying for an expedition. Heavy dark clouds rumbled overhead, lightning flashing through them every now and then. Beyond was burgeoning daylight—*daylight* chasing the last darkness of the night, which meant it had only been hours since Iravan's presentation in the Conclave, hours since she had begun bleeding so fully, hours since she had lost… since she had lost…

Ahilya couldn't complete the thought. Her mind shied away from it, and instead she heard Iravan say, *I want to be a father*. Tears streamed down her cheeks, mingling with the rain, and she moved again. Movement was good. She just had to place one foot in front of another until she found him, until she explained.

The wind pushed at her, but Ahilya gripped the wooden railing and pulled herself along. The narrow ledge-like balcony ran along the green wall of the ashram's construction on one side, the other side open to the elements. Ahilya followed it, going where it led her, until the view opened up suddenly, and she gasped.

Shock and awe gripped her, buried within the throes of vertigo.

A few feet away the balcony came to an abrupt end, a green wall of curling leaves blocking it. The wall extended sideways into the sky, converting into an open bridge that sloped forward and upward, disappearing into the rain and clouds. Far beyond the bridge, Ahilya glimpsed a giant structure—another ashram, she realized, its design cut by dark clouds, and more ashrams beyond it in either direction.

The Conclave was arranged in a circle, blocked bridges from each individual ashram leading up to the center, where a massive diamond-shaped mountain grew in the sky, roots and waterfalls streaming from its jagged edges. As far as Ahilya could tell, all the other ashrams hovered around this mountain, connected by the bridges. But no ashram was connected to another.

Iravan had built this? All alone, in one night? How? It should have taken a whole Conclave to do this, hundreds—no, thousands of architects working together. During the creation of the Conclave two days before, Airav had said that the Conclave was a set of barely connected ashrams, which was a dangerous construct. What would this structure mean now, when everything was connected to Iravan's mountain, unsupported by any of the other cities? What would happen if his mountain failed?

Ahilya faltered forward, closer to the green wall that blocked the entrance to the bridge. The clouds shifted along Iravan's mountain, rain and mist and flowing green.

Then she saw him through the wisps of morning fog.

He stood on a ledge on the far mountain, a shape wavering in and out of her vision, still wearing the same black kurta and trousers from the Conclave, his feather cloak billowing in the breeze behind him. He looked half a bird himself, or perhaps part of the lightning, only visible because of the brilliant blue-green light that emanated from him like a sun.

Ahilya paused, in fear and shame. The grief that had retreated reared again, the wave about to break, and she felt her legs tremble, felt the warm blood fill the bandages she wore. The angry words she had once hurled at Iravan burst in her mind, *You will make an even worse father!* And his heartbroken echo, *I didn't just want a child, Ahilya, I wanted* our *child.*

Ahilya pressed a trembling hand to the railing, her eyes still on her husband. She wanted to go forward, but the green wall blocked her approach. How could she face him now? After what she had done, after what she had said? She had failed to protect their child. Her body had failed her, and she had failed him, and she could not bear his pain. He'd built a dream of her and their family. It had been her own dream, too—but would they be able to fulfill it? Ever? Tears rushed down her cheeks and Ahilya choked back a sob, blue-green swimming in her vision.

When Naila spoke, it was a shock. Ahilya had forgotten that the three women had followed her outside. She had forgotten that Chaiyya and Kiana had wanted to speak with Iravan.

"He has been standing there all night," Naila said quietly. "Ever since he made this. I think he is waiting for you."

Ahilya extended a shaking hand to the green wall. Leaves curled and uncurled, responding to her touch. "H-how?" she whispered. "How do I…"

The Maze Architect understood. "I think you just desire it, Ahilya-ve."

Her gaze on her husband, her hand outstretched, Ahilya wished with all her being to be reunited with him.

The wall of leaves creaked open, a gateway to the bridge.

Iravan's head snapped toward them.

Ahilya felt him move, imagined his eyes widen. Even from this distance, she read the gesture, the urgency and the impatience as he descended from his ledge in a swirl of green and gray as though carried by the storm. Then he was running, his long strides bringing him toward her, his feather cloak streaming behind him. Dhruv hurried behind him over the bridge, wiping his glasses.

She didn't realize she had begun running too.

Cries sounded behind her; Kiana and Chaiyya were held back by vines growing from the green wall, though Naila seemed to follow without restriction.

Then the wall closed again, and she had turned away, running away from Nakshar, from Chaiyya's questions and Kiana's protests, because she couldn't take it, she couldn't think about them and their concerns or the Conclave and its architecture, not right now when the guilt threatened to break the fragile dam she had built, and the only thing that would stop her from going under was Iravan.

Then he was there and she crashed into his hard chest, weeping bitterly against his neck as his arms encircled her.

"I'm sorry," Ahilya sobbed. "I'm so sorry, Iravan."

"No," he whispered, tears and rain running down his cheeks as well. "No, Ahilya, please, no."

"I—I lost our ch-child. I—I did this—my-my fault—"

Iravan crushed her to him, and Ahilya sobbed harder, the sound of thunder and rain mingling with his racing heartbeat. She felt him move, and something heavy and smoky draped around her shoulders. Ahilya blinked her tear-filled eyes open and realized he had wrapped her in his feather cloak. Thunder cracked again, and her legs trembled.

Bending slightly, Iravan lifted her in his arms, cradling her to his chest. Her tears dampened the skin on his neck, and her forehead pressed against the vine he'd hung like a necklace around him, a strange stone blade hanging from it. Iravan shuddered once, as though holding back a sob, and began walking.

Distantly, Ahilya heard Dhruv and Naila speaking. She knew they were walking behind her and Iravan, but though their voices were low and urgent, Ahilya could not focus. She closed her eyes, trying to comprehend this—the extent of what had happened. She had blamed Iravan for being unworthy of becoming a father, but the truth was *she* had been unworthy.

Iravan held her closer as though he could hear her thoughts. She pressed herself to him, unable to still her tears. All other concerns fled from her mind. She only knew that she needed him now, that there was no one else in the world who could help her.

Through blurry tears, Ahilya discerned that they had crossed the bridge. She was inside the mountain now, within a rainy courtyard. A hundred trees towered around them, and balconies lined the courtyard. Ahilya was reminded of Nakshar's Architects' Academy, that time Iravan had brought her in there to interview Naila. Her body shuddered. They had nearly fought about children then too. Only an accident with trajection had prevented that.

Iravan headed into the trees, but stopped at once. Ahilya watched as Dhruv blocked her husband's way, Naila next to him. She averted her gaze, unable to meet theirs.

"We have a problem," Dhruv said.

Iravan's weight shifted. "Deal with it."

"But—"

"I said, deal with it," Iravan repeated, his voice hard.

He began striding again toward a leafy wall. She saw Dhruv take an urgent step forward, but Naila whispered something to the sungineer, and his startled eyes darted to Ahilya. Then the leaves of the wall parted to reveal a wooden elevator, and she and Iravan were alone again. The platform began to rise through the mountain.

Ahilya stirred. "Do you—" she whispered through her tears. "Do you need…"

"No," Iravan said quietly. "I don't need to do anything except take care of you."

The elevator came to a stop before she could form a reply. The tattoos on Iravan's skin briefly grew like vines, and the wall opened again.

Ahilya found herself placed on a bed in the middle of a large chamber. There were no sheets or blankets. Instead, Iravan had trajected the softest moss, woven it somehow into silken strands that covered the wooden bed, so that when he placed her on it, Ahilya sank into lushness. He disappeared for a second to bring back a bowl of water, and Ahilya studied the chamber.

A balcony opened on one side, perhaps the exact one he had been standing on when she'd seen him. The roof was wood and rock, though a massive skylight revealed the gray storm. Gossamer-thin green lines intersected each other blocking the rain but letting in the light. How had Iravan done this? He could change the nature of the plants altogether, but it seemed that with the control of the core trees, his own Ecstasy had matured.

He sat across from her, his eyes grave and tired, studying her as she studied the chamber, a chamber that, for all its differences, reminded her of the home they'd once had in Nakshar in happier times, right after they'd married. They'd been so young then. They could never have imagined where life would lead them.

Tears trickled from her eyes. She wiped them away but they were replaced with more, and in her mind's eye, Ahilya saw herself leap into the vortex after Iravan. What if she had permanently damaged her body by being in the habitat for so long? She had neither eaten nor slept in that place of sentient green dust—and she had done that while pregnant. This… this loss could happen again. It could keep happening. The bowl of water slipped from her hands, and she wrapped her arms around her knees, shaking.

"Please," Iravan said softly. "Tell me how to make things better. Tell me how to help you."

"Traject me," Ahilya replied hoarsely. "Heal me so this never happens again."

But Iravan recoiled with something like horror on his face. He shook his head wordlessly, and his hand trembled as he touched her face.

"I cannot," he said. "It would only hurt you."

"Why not? You can heal yourself with Ecstasy. Surely you can heal me too. Make it so this never happens again."

"It's not that simple."

"Please, Iravan. *Please*. It's my body. I'm giving you permission. I don't know what I did to it. I don't know how I damaged it."

But Iravan only shook his head again, and his hands fluttered down to hold Ahilya's own. She jerked back, angry. For all his power and Ecstasy, that he would deny her this—when it could relieve her agony, when it would ensure she never had to feel this, or make this mistake again. She pulled away. Was he punishing her? But Iravan only folded her into his arms once more, holding her captive, stroking her hair and murmuring soft words, until sorrow replaced her anger and she shuddered against him.

"You said this would happen," she said, her voice cracking. "You said that entering the vortex was dangerous, that it could—that I did this—it was not my choice to make alone."

"Ahilya, *no*," he said, and she heard the heartbreak in his voice. "No, my love, that's not—that has nothing to do with this."

"Then help me. Please—I can't—I don't—I don't know how to make sense of it."

Iravan pulled away from her, but his grip on her hands was tight. He kissed her cold fingers one by one, and she could feel him think as he tried to answer her.

Finally, he took a deep breath and met her gaze. "It may not comfort you."

Ahilya nodded and stared back into his eyes.

Iravan sighed. "Birth and rebirth," he began reluctantly, "are mysteries even for architects who study consciousness for years. I've seen my past lives, which is unusual and perhaps only open to Ecstatic architects, and even I cannot detect the exact time a consciousness enters the body. But I do know this much. For a consciousness to enter a body—a *host*—the body must be ready for it." He tipped her chin up. "Do you remember those carvings in the cave? Ordinary creatures that suddenly changed to hold the broken consciousness of a cosmic being?"

"The yakshas," she said hoarsely.

"The only available host." Iravan paused again. Lightning flashed overhead through the skylight, and his brow furrowed as he glanced at it. He took another deep breath. "Ahilya, you were pregnant only for a few weeks, three months at best. I don't think the fetus your body was building was ready to hold consciousness. It wasn't ready to be a host. It wasn't physically prepared, it was a… a…"

"A mass of cells," she whispered. She had made the same justification to herself when she'd decided to rescue Iravan from the jungle all those months ago. In her heart, she knew what he was saying was true, but her body could not control the grief, the tears that still poured inexorably.

"It doesn't lessen your pain, I know," he said quietly. "Nor does it mine. But Ahilya, it wasn't because of the vortex. It's nothing you did or didn't do. It just… *happened*. Life is more mysterious than we can know, and consciousness is subtle. Some consciousness out there will choose us, the environment and the energies we create. Next time, the fetus might be ready to be a host to that consciousness. If you want to be a mother, you will be—one way or another."

He fell silent and pulled her to him, resting them both against the wall. Ahilya quietened, the tears still falling. But eventually, her breathing eased as she considered his words. She had hoped for him to traject her, but Iravan would not lie to her. His words circled her. *Consciousness is subtle. It's nothing you did.*

She lay on the bed all day, staring at the storm through the skylight while he lay next to her, his skin still glowing with tattoos, one hand holding hers, the other occasionally flipping through Bharavi's book. The events of the Conclave washed over her, and Ahilya did not try to parse them; instead, she let them sink in, saying nothing, while Iravan rose occasionally to bring her something to eat.

She awoke twice during the night. The first time it was only for a few seconds, her body too tired to move even though she could tell that her clothes had become stained and bloody again. She blinked her eyes open, her mind already searching for Iravan, but he lay right next to her, his fingers interlocked under his head, staring up at the ceiling where the storm continued relentlessly. His skin glowed blue-green, tattoos forming and dying in intricate patterns, and vaguely Ahilya wondered if he had stopped at all, if he had rested; but then she drifted again, before the thought could complete itself.

The next time she awoke, she was naked.

Iravan was not in the chamber, though he'd covered her with his feather cloak. All her rudra beads had been removed too; they lay neatly atop her folded clothes by the foot of the bed.

Ahilya pulled her clothes close. They smelled of earth and lavender. She'd bled into them, but Iravan had undressed her and washed them for her. He had even placed bandages between her legs. Soft moss tickled her thighs, absorbing the blood better than any linen could. Warmth radiated on her skin, and Ahilya pressed his feather cloak to her, breathing his scent in.

One by one she placed all her rudra bead bracelets back on her wrists. Her healbranch bracelet as a councilor was gone—Iravan had removed the burden of keeping the council's secrets, perhaps cracked it clean with his Ecstasy. She couldn't believe she had slept through it all, slept through the violent storm that still raged outside, and the comfort and love her husband had given her. How long had it been since they had spent time together like this?

She climbed off the bed, and a shape moved outside on the balcony. Ahilya wrapped the feather cloak around herself and approached on soft feet. Iravan glanced at her, and opened his arms. He waited for her to settle between them, then continued to survey the Conclave, his arms braced on either side of her.

Neither of them spoke. Ahilya pulled the heavy cloak closer as droplets of rain slashed down on them. Thunder still rumbled, dark angry clouds rolling as far as she could see. Another dawn was breaking, but it was hard to tell with the storm. The Conclave cut in through the hurricane every now and then, a glimpse of a bark wall, white in the distance, a ropey bridge dangling precariously.

Ahilya cleared her throat. "The others are concerned," she began, then stopped.

Iravan didn't say anything. He didn't move.

"Chaiyya tried to tell me," she started again, then shook her head. The Senior Architect had implied that Iravan had changed the construction of the Conclave in his fury, but there was nothing furious about him now. If anything, her husband appeared detached, at peace.

"Iravan," she said softly. "The Ecstatic battery. Did they—are you—"

His wrists tightened on the balustrade, the muscles in his arms cording. "I'm unhurt, my love." The patterns of blue-green tattoos on his arms changed, spiralled, grew more complex like a maze interlocking. Something in his tone sent a chill down her spine.

Ahilya turned her head slightly to see a muscle in his jaw twitch. "Iravan, what happened?"

"We don't have to talk about it," he began, but then he sighed. Iravan released her so she stood next to him. His palm rested atop hers protectively. "Your dream—*our* dream—with the Ecstatic battery didn't work. They tried, and it hurt the Ecstatics."

Ahilya grew cold. She remembered Airav bucking in his chair. She thought of her insistence to use the battery, of her agreement with Kiana to continue experimentation despite Iravan's reservations. Of course, she and Kiana had known the dangers of using a battery again—but they had thought the sungineers would use safeguards, that was always implied. It was why they'd needed Iravan's help with the battery in the first place, to allow for checking it.

Had Kiana wrought this? Asked a few rogue sungineers to test the Ecstatic battery instead of excising Iravan and the other architects? The Senior Sungineer had nodded along, when Chaiyya had mentioned that the sungineers who had done this were under custody, that they had acted without sanction. Kiana had even provided her own apology. But no matter the actions with the emergency protocol and the rogue sungineers, Kiana had something to do with what happened last night—of that, Ahilya was certain. What had happened to the Ecstatics? Had their energy been drained like Airav's?

Her question must have shown on her face, for Iravan nodded.

"They're all right now," he said. "The Ecstatics are healing—that is in their nature. But I—I did something terrible." His gaze met hers and he swallowed. "I killed Maze Architect Viana."

Ahilya stared at him. *It's insanity*, Chaiyya said in her mind. *What happens if you find out he is not as safe as you think he is?*

She heard her own response. *Then he will no longer have my defense. If that happens, I will stop Iravan myself.* Her hands trembled, and Oam screamed. Bharavi writhed as spiralweed strangled her.

"I didn't mean to," Iravan said, his eyes red. "I—I was trying to escape the deathcage, trying to stop what the architects were doing—and everything that happened last night—I'm trying to make sense of it myself. But I—I trajected her, and—"

He had killed a Maze Architect. It had been an accident, but he had trajected Viana, taken control of her body, without the Maze Architect's permission or consent. Horror seized Ahilya, and she couldn't grasp the enormity of it.

She tried not to shrink back from her husband. "Iravan," she whispered. "No."

"I—I didn't mean it, Ahilya. I didn't—I wish I could take it back." Tears shone in his eyes, and he took a deep breath. She saw the passage of emotions—terror and grief and a deep trauma at what he had done. And beyond it all something else, something alien and cold that felt like a grim defeated acceptance of who he was becoming. That, of all things, frightened Ahilya more than she could say.

"What's done is done," Iravan said, taking another deep breath. He looked away from her, back to the clouds. "I cannot undo it, Ahilya, but I can make sure to never do it again. This is why I cannot traject you. You do not need it, but even if you did… I don't know how to traject a higher being safely. I don't think even the falcon does. Each time it has trajected even me, it has been… painful."

"You see the dangers of your power, but you still changed the Conclave. What did you do exactly?"

Iravan's voice was toneless. "I took control. All the architecture, all the ashrams. I supersede the privileges of every architect."

Ahilya watched the shadows on her husband's face. "What does that mean?"

"It means the ashrams are frozen. The architects cannot break or change my constellation lines. Their trajection is useless against mine. The Conclave remains connected to this—to *my* ashram. I'm altering the permissions of every core tree as we speak. I'm prioritizing complete beings—non-architects—so that the ashrams protect them before they protect the architects. When that is done, I will return the ashrams to the jungle. To the habitat. Whether they like it or not."

Shock so great seized her that Ahilya was rendered speechless. She did not like the inbuilt permissions of the rudra tree. But what Iravan was doing—rewriting thousands of years of permissions on a whim… Airav had been worried about Nakshar being subsumed, but Iravan was subsuming *everyone*.

She swallowed. "There are conditions to making an ashram."

"And I meet them. Citizens, society—I don't have much but it will grow."

"Yes, those, but also legitimacy. The support of other ashrams and the Conclave. They won't give it to you, Iravan. They won't trade with you. Or do you expect to be fully self-sufficient?"

"They won't have a choice but to help me." Iravan's voice grew hard. "No one can do anything about this architecture unless they become a trained Ecstatic—and given how the rest of them feel about Ecstasy…" He shrugged again, the gesture cold.

It sent another chill down her spine. Ahilya trusted Iravan, she *had* to, but could she trust him with the fate of the world? Chaiyya had warned her that he could destroy them if he wished, and already he was dismantling every permission he did not like. In the past, Iravan had not liked the idea of her being on the council. He had not liked her research on the yakshas. In his desperation, he had *trajected* Viana.

"You disapprove?" he asked quietly.

Ahilya's voice was low. "This is dictatorship."

"I know that." Iravan's fingers tightened over hers. "Do you think I want to control all this? It was my idea to decentralize the Conclave architecture, but now I have bound them all to my city, and their lives are tied to mine. Control by any one entity is treacherous, at the whim of their desire, and desire is unreliable, it mutates and changes. Even if a person were trustworthy it would be dangerous, and I—I am not."

"Then return it. Give the power back to the ashrams. You can let the architects rebuild again."

"I can," Iravan said slowly. "But to what end? So the ashrams remain in the skies, and kill everyone? Life in the skies is doomed, not least because of the skyrages. We've tried asking them nicely but that Conclave meeting was a disaster. They don't even recognize the Ecstatics' right to exist, let alone supertraject."

"So you're taking away their choice. You're doing the same thing the architects did to you by forcing material bonds, the same thing architects once did to non-architects."

"This is not about arbitrary traditions. This is about survival. Once, the architects made a decision to go to the skies to escape earthrages. Now I will take everyone to the jungle, back to the habitat, where they belong."

Ahilya shook her head vehemently, and thought again of Viana. "This is not the way—"

"This is the only way—"

"No. It's not. We don't need to like it, Iravan, but life in the skies has a right to exist. It is not just architects who live here, but citizens too, sungineers and weavers and artisans. This is a thousand-year-old history you're erasing."

In her mind's eye, Tariya and Arth and Kush smiled at her. Tariya had never fully felt comfortable in the landed jungle. Dhruv had been afraid there. Only recently had citizens like Umang tried to popularize the idea of living in the jungle, and even that had been protested. Her gaze went toward Nakshar, but little of the ashram was visible, mere bark and leaves, distorted by the clouds.

"You would defend this way of life, Ahilya?" Iravan asked softly. "It was once your idea to return to the jungle. You know what this system is built on—lies and fabrications and the falsification of history. The erasure of your own kind."

She pressed his hand, staring into his eyes. "I'm not defending it, Iravan. I agree with you. The days of civilization in the sky are numbered. But what you're doing, this decisive action, it will not end well. I've fought against the architects all my life, but you're setting yourself up as an enemy ashram. Do you see where this will take you? War will be imminent. You will learn more of Ecstasy, and they will keep perfecting their technology, and in the end, you will only continue fighting each other, trapping each other."

"They cannot attack me," he said quietly. "If they attempt to damage my ashram of Ecstatics, it will only backfire on them tenfold. I hold their core trees, the basis for their flight. It is what is giving my ashram its flight now."

"And who will this affect? In your war with the architects and the Conclave, it is the non-architects who would suffer. The people you are trying to save. The *complete* ones."

Iravan stepped away from the balcony and ran a frustrated hand through his hair. "Then what would you have me do? The skyrages are going to get worse—another one is imminent. It's not going to be like the last time. That was a... a *rehearsal*. The cosmic creatures are plotting something, the webbing is weakening, the falcon has disappeared, and I don't know how to traject like it did. If everything breaks now, there's nothing I can do to stop it, and I am trying to save everyone."

"*Without* everyone?" she asked. "Iravan, you cannot end the rages alone and you cannot take everyone to the jungle, not against their desire. They will fight you. You know the power of pure desire. You've seen it."

Iravan turned away from her. Thunder cracked long and loud, and clouds rolled over and under them. Wind buffeted Ahilya, and she pulled the feather cloak closer, but Iravan seemed unaffected by the cold. He gazed at the storm, frowning as though it had something to do with his decision.

"You're right," he said finally. "I can't do this alone. But they are holding Ecstatics hostage, and I hold their core trees. I'll agree to a fair exchange, but I won't have another Ecstatic excised ever again. They have the means to test all their architects with the radarx—you told me that before. I'll give them until the end of the week to turn all those who respond to it to me. I will use the Conclave's core trees to take my Ecstatics back to the habitat. Then, and only then, will I return the permissions of the trees to the ashrams."

"This is a bold thing you ask, Iravan, and you give them little time."

"There *is* no more time. And I don't trust them."

"Yet you will be the judge of their arguments?"

"We both will," he said, smiling humorlessly. "Together."

He reached out a hand and clasped hers in his tightly. His trajection tattoos glowed brighter, and between her brows, Ahilya received a startling image of fifty trees, each different from the other. The trees turned toward her, their trunks coiling, then they were gone.

"The permissions of the core trees are not safe with me," Iravan continued. "But they will be safe with you. I'm instructing the core trees to obey you, Ahilya. To supersede anyone's permissions. Including mine."

She could not imagine it—the authority and responsibility he was giving her. Only a few hours before, she'd had all her power taken away from her with the stripping of her rudra beads. The council of Nakshar had returned it to her, but this?

She had made too many mistakes—with the battery, by trusting Kiana and Chaiyya, with even the non-architect citizens when she had forgotten them in her pursuit to save the Ecstatics. Her error with the battery had already allowed the four Ecstatics of Nakshar to be tortured.

"That is far too much power for me, my love," she said quietly.

"I trust you," he replied. "More than I trust myself. I know you will do what is right."

"Iravan, you and I cannot hold absolute power over all the lives in the sister ashrams. That in itself is not right."

"Yet who better, Ahilya? We know more than the ashrams about our combined history—we've already put an end to an earthrage. We are an archeologist and an Ecstatic. A complete being and a broken one, both of us bound by the lies of our history and the future of our survival. We sum up the problems of our world perfectly. Our mistakes are anchored in our truths. We don't deny ourselves honesty, at least, no matter how difficult the truth is to bear."

"And if we don't agree between us? We've fought before—seen things differently—we're doing it right now."

"I'm counting on it. You will try and protect them all. I will try to end the earthrages and the tyranny of trajection. Between us..." He shrugged. "Between us, we may come to some sort of balance."

Ahilya looked away to the Conclave, the floating orbs of bark and the thin viney bridges connecting them to the mountain. She felt the weight of responsibility settle on her shoulders again, the one she had shirked off briefly when she'd run away from Nakshar.

"When do you intend to speak to them?" she asked.

"Whenever you are ready," Iravan said. He hesitated, running a hand through his hair, then dropping it. "Ahilya, I know you need time to recover. But I would ask that you be my emissary. I trust no one else."

Ahilya remained silent. It was the same thing Chaiyya had said, to plead Nakshar's case, the *Conclave's* case with Iravan. Ahilya had done it not for the Senior Architect but because it was right. Now Iravan wanted her to do the same for him. The power that both Iravan and Chaiyya had handed to her was heady and seductive and frightening. Ahilya glanced at him, the anger and regret and fear in his eyes, the promise of a better future still within him, if only lurking below the surface. She had his love and trust, but her negotiations now might not please him. What would he do then? What if her decisions cost them again—not just the Conclave, but her and Iravan, personally?

There was only one way forward.

Ahilya squared her shoulders and turned to face him. "I'm ready."

29

IRAVAN

In what had once been the courtyard of Nakshar's sanctum, Iravan trajected a dome.

He wasn't entirely sure if he was using Ecstasy or trajection proper, or what this new combined form of the power ought to be called, but it transformed the courtyard in ways neither of the individual powers could.

The trees that had sprung all around sank back into the earth. The walls clambered higher, becoming thin, translucent. He could sense the participation of Nakshar's rudra, and Yeikshar's asoka, core trees that were nearly sentient. A power flooded in him, one he had never felt before. The core trees were communicating with him, reading his desire and intent, tapping into his memory.

The patterns on his skin changed, thousands and thousands of them riddling his body, marking even parts of his face. He was giving Ahilya the power to manipulate the core trees, but apart from her, *he* still had the most power. Where once the non-architects had been at the lowermost tier, he had elevated them. It was the least he could do. The desire to make amends burned in him, even brighter, now that he had endured the last few days.

Images from the night before flashed in his mind, the way Basav had interrogated him, the humiliation he and Ahilya had suffered, all to protect the culture of the architects. That culture had allowed for the criminalization of Ecstasy. It had nearly excised Iravan last night. Undoubtedly, several Ecstatics waited even now within many ashrams for their own excision. He would not let that happen.

And so he trajected, continuing to transfer the permissions of the core trees to Ahilya, taking away the power from the architects; taking it away, in a manner, even from himself.

He could feel the difficulty of doing so. Core trees were not mere foliage, they were sentient beings, coded a thousand years ago, and he was changing their nature. He was not the first Ecstatic to traject a core tree, of course. Bharavi had landed Nakshar by changing the rudra's permissions. Manav had paved the way for his own excision with the same action. Yet no one had manipulated the core trees to this extent. This power Iravan used, a combination of Ecstasy and trajection, had once closed the rift; it now seduced the core trees. He gave the trees his emotion, he gave the trees his terror, his exhaustion, his grief. And they responded to him.

There was so much he did not understand. In the last two days alone, he had learned more about his own abilities than he had in two months of being in the jungle. His Ecstasy and that of the yaksha were so different that he could see now his delay in approaching the ashrams had been a mistake.

Within the silence of his mind, Iravan glimpsed the falcon flying low over the jungle, searching. The Resonance fluttered in the Deepness right next to his dust mote, but they had both been wary of each other, maintaining their distance, trajecting their own separate lights. The falcon had an agenda, and sooner or later, they would have to face each other. The creature had *spoken* to him—but for now, it seemed as content to leave him alone as he was it.

Still trajecting, Iravan began down a garden path, thin trees growing on either side, their branches meeting above to form a wavering canopy. He had left Ahilya in their bedchamber to think through his proposition, and had promised to send Naila to her. The Maze Architect was likely on the tier that would become his ashram's Academy, along with the four architects Iravan had rescued.

A part of him wondered how the Ecstatics were faring, but it was a disconnected, distant thought. They had refused to abandon him in his fight with the falcon, a fledgling loyalty he had done little to deserve. They had been tortured because of his mistakes. They had seen him murder Viana. Too much had changed for them, and now they were plunged into a world of his making, ripped from everything they knew. He arrived at the Academy and paused, taking another deep breath, trying to relax his shoulders, slow the beating of his heart.

The space formed a quadrangle, with heavy gnarled trees rising like pillars surrounding a small courtyard of lush green grass. The ceiling was exquisite, the same kind of skylight as in his bedroom growing in gossamer-thin strands high above, letting in dim daylight but not a single drop of the storm. He had barely begun it, and the constellation lines in the Moment had nurtured it of their own accord, taking shape from his intent. A giant tree had grown in the center of the courtyard. Bark stools, so like the ones in Nakshar's Academy, had formed under it. The four Ecstatics sat in a small circle, Dhruv and Naila with them. The Maze Architect had her arm around little Reyla, and Dhruv was speaking to Pranav and Trisha, all of them leaning seriously over Dhruv's dead solarnote tablet.

Iravan approached silently, but even as he did, another seat began to grow among the stools—a chair, similar to the one he had created for himself in the jungle habitat, a throne with its carved armrests and high back.

Trisha nudged Pranav, and then they were all rising to their feet. Naila followed, and Dhruv arose too, his every movement reluctant and forced.

Iravan silently took his seat and waited for them to take theirs.

He had not desired this chair. He had meant to sit on one of the stools. But this new form of trajection was sensitive to half-formed thoughts, discarded ideas, and buried fears. The plants had behaved in surprising ways already, from the strange skylight to the way they had prevented Chaiyya and Kiana from entering the mountain.

Pranav scratched his chin, Trisha rubbed her arms, and Darsh and Reyla darted surreptitious looks at him. Iravan had seen the Ecstatics only once to check if there had been any lasting damage from the battery experiment, but they had recovered surprisingly fast, an effect of ascending too quickly. There was no way to control their power, not up here in the skies. He resisted the urge to rub the back of his neck.

"I understand you've begun to settle in," he said at last, leaning forward. "I'm pleased to hear it. Nakshar is dangerous for you, and you cannot go back there. This needs to be your home now."

None of the architects spoke. Naila shifted on her seat, and Dhruv warily removed his spectacles to wipe them. The sungineer's hands shook slightly.

"This doesn't mean your families cannot come here," Iravan continued. "Tell me their names and I will ensure they arrive from Nakshar. They can be a part of this new home we are building. I won't sweeten the truth—it will be a big change. I am making agreements with the Conclave, and eventually all of you will come with me to the jungle to live there. But it will be easier if your families come too. If you want them there, I will find a way to make it happen."

Pranav and Trisha exchanged a glance. Reyla buried her head in Naila's shoulder. Darsh studied the floor intently.

"My parents won't want to come," the boy mumbled. "They're both Maze Architects."

Iravan suppressed the jolt of anger that ran through him.

It was not Darsh's parents' fault, whoever they were. This was what the council of Nakshar, the entire Conclave, had decided. Ahilya's words returned to him. *You cannot end the earthrages alone.* He gritted his teeth and waited a second before replying.

"They will still have the option," he said. "Them, but especially anyone else who cannot traject whom you want here. I will personally extend a formal invitation to them. You will have family, parents, friends, teachers, from Nakshar and from other ashrams. I will welcome them to begin life anew should they wish it. This I promise you."

The four Ecstatics exchanged more glances, the question clear on their faces, searching for the reason behind his magnanimity, especially after last night's terrible events, but he did not elaborate.

The truth was that Ahilya was right. He could not end the earthrages alone—not the current one, nor any in the future. For all that the traditional ashram structure had gotten wrong, one thing was true. Each Ecstatic architect had to be accompanied by a complete being to end an earthrage. That complete being would have to be someone close, someone attached to an Ecstatic by a material bond. It was imperative that complete beings filled his home. He had understood this even when he'd left the Garden only days ago to fly to the Conclave.

Pranav cleared his throat. "Dhruv-ve said this will be an ashram for the Ecstatics."

Dhruv-*ve*.

Iravan noted the respectful suffix and stored it away in a corner of his mind.

"Primarily only for architects who respond to the radarx," he said. "Nakshar has already shared the devices with others. Each Ecstatic will be sent here for training. That is going to be a part of my agreement."

"What about other architects?" Trisha asked. "The ones who want to be trained too?"

Iravan raised his eyebrows. "There are others who *want* to become Ecstatic?"

The woman drew back as though she had let slip a secret. Naila shifted, her arm still around little Reyla, and met Iravan's questioning gaze.

"There are many, Iravan-ve," she said quietly. "At least in Nakshar. When Ahilya-ve announced the truth about the cosmic creatures and Ecstasy, several Maze Architects refused their Disc duties afraid of becoming Ecstatics, but half of those *on* the Disc trajected because they understood Nakshar's Constant and the call to their own yakshas. They trajected to become Ecstatics."

Iravan frowned, pursing his lips. He himself had found the Resonance accidentally while in Nakshar's temple, a raga that had manifested in the Deepness as a silvery mercurial particle, the falcon's form as melody made solid. To think of Maze Architects deliberately seeking Ecstasy without training? It was astounding that only four Ecstatics had yet been discovered in Nakshar.

"Any architect who wishes to learn the ways of Ecstasy is welcome," he relented. "Them and their families. We're building a new kind of ashram. One different from what you know. When we land in the jungle, we will all be a part of the Garden, but until then we'll need a name for all our treatises and contracts. I'm here to ask for suggestions."

For once, their silence seemed thoughtful.

Iravan glanced up at the storm, visible through the leafy canopy and the strange skylight. Heavy gray clouds rolled overhead, a welcome sign. Within the silence in his mind, the falcon flew lower in the jungle, surrounded by dust and earth. In the Deepness, the Resonance trajected a ray of silver light.

The yaksha had not spoken, not since that time in the Conclave, but Iravan could almost discern its intent. It was searching for something—but what? Did it have anything to do with the cosmic creatures? Their image grew slowly sharper in the Etherium, terrifying him, as the creatures pushed against the webbing the falcon and the incorporeal yaksha had built. If only there was a permanent way to stop the cosmic creatures from splitting…

"Irshar?" Naila said, startling Iravan. He transferred his gaze to her, and she blushed and looked away. "It's a combination of your name and the suffix of an ashram," she muttered.

Dhruv rolled his eyes behind his glasses. Pranav looked vaguely amused. The two younger children nodded and Trisha shrugged in a noncommittal gesture.

Iravan's cheeks grew warm.

Irshar.

It had the right sound, but that was all he needed—an ashram literally named after himself. That would certainly convince the Conclave and Ahilya that he had no grand plans of dictatorship.

"Any other suggestions?" he asked, looking around.

"Oh, just take it," Dhruv muttered. "We need to call it *some*thing. If we're all going to this Garden anyway, then it is only temporary."

Iravan sighed. "Fine. I suppose it will do."

He stood up.

"Recover," he said. "In a few hours, the migration from the other ashrams will begin, and I'll need your assistance to welcome them. Your training will start shortly, too. You are the first true Ecstatics, the representatives of Irshar, and you will have to guide and teach the others. You'll be getting new uniforms like mine—black for the Ecstatics. We'll start negotiating with the other ashrams soon, and if there is anything else you need, tell Dhruv. We'll make it happen."

He left to a flurry of bows.

Naila and Dhruv followed him out of the garden. The sungineer fell in beside Iravan. His hands still fidgeted with the solarnote and his citizen ring, neither of which would work here, not with the part-Ecstatic part-trajectory power that Iravan was using. Dhruv would have to learn how to build a new technology unless Iravan changed the architecture into using one or the other energy. For that, the sungineer would need a team. Irshar—or the Garden, truly—would need a solar lab.

"Ahilya is preparing a treatise to take to the Conclave," Iravan said. "She could use your help. You already know what I intend with the Garden and this ashram. With Irshar."

Dhruv did not reply, but he replaced his useless solarnote back into his pocket and removed his glasses to polish them again in a sheepish gesture.

Iravan stopped walking and faced him. "I don't know what happened between the both of you, but you need to fix it. Unless you want to return to Nakshar."

The sungineer stared at him.

They both knew that with Iravan, Dhruv would control the direction and manner of all technology. He'd be a Senior Sungineer, *the* Senior Sungineer. But in Nakshar he would be imprisoned, perhaps exiled. There was really no choice at all.

Naila looked from one to another, biting her lip.

Dhruv narrowed his eyes. "Is this how it's going to be? We all follow your commands all the time or you threaten to evict us?"

Yes, Iravan thought, but he could see Ahilya's withdrawn face, and hear her words, accusing him of tyranny. A weight built in his chest, pulling his shoulders down.

I'm tired, he thought suddenly. *I need to rest. This is all a mistake. I shouldn't even be here, doing this, building a fucking* ashram *from scratch*—no, this was Bharavi's task. *She* had wanted to rebuild. She had wanted to raze it all down to start again. All Iravan had wanted was Ahilya. He'd wanted to father children. He'd wanted to raise a family.

The dream he'd nurtured flashed in his mind, of Ahilya and two children, a home and a family that he could have had perhaps in another life. Iravan was building this city, and Ahilya would speak to the Conclave on his behalf, but was a life with their children available to him at all? He had seen her face when he'd told her about Viana. He had felt her disgust and shame in him—it was his own disgust with himself. Even if she could overlook such a horrific offense, would they ever be happy? Would they be able to have children?

Ahilya had wanted him to traject her, a risk he refused to take, not after what had happened to Viana. She had blamed herself, but the miscarriage was not her fault. Rages, perhaps it was no one's fault. Yet Iravan could not forget how the cosmic creature he'd trapped in the Moment had erased his own possibilities of fatherhood in the vortex. *Nothing is more important*, he had said to her, when he had spoken of their child—but he had let her suffer alone. A corrosive hatred grew in him for all the cosmic beings, for what they had done to him and by extension to Ahilya: the pain they had caused, the suffering they had inflicted.

He had rebuilt himself and the yaksha, but who knew how permanent their reconstruction had been. Was that why he and the falcon were estranged still? How would he teach other Ecstatics to rebuild themselves if he understood nothing himself? How much of their own innate knowledge could he count on?

The truth was that for all his knowledge and power he was moving in the dark only through feeling, and that terrified him more than he could admit. They wanted him to build a legacy, but he could barely put one foot in front of the next, and each step was a mire, a hole in quicksand, pulling him under, leaving him breathless and panicked. Irshar was magnificent, an architectural marvel, but it was a mistake—a mutilation of freedom. He knew this as well as he knew his own name. *I can't go on like this*, he thought, but what were his choices? He had set foot on this path and there was no going back. Was he truly going to become a tyrant? An out-of-control Ecstatic like everyone feared him to be?

Dhruv and Naila still watched him, and he shook his head.

"No," he said at last, a reply to Dhruv.

As much as the urgency of the situation demanded it, Irshar had no longevity. Iravan had meant it for the Ecstatics, but it would not be like other ashrams—Ecstatics *had* no purpose beyond uniting with their yakshas and ending the earthrages to make amends to the complete beings. Once that was done, their lives were over. There was no more rebirth, nothing else to be born into. Iravan had known this ever since he had chosen the path to clarity instead of the future lives open to him. If Irshar was a destination for Ecstatics, then every architect would end up in it, one day now or in a future life, until there were no more architects or trajectors at all.

Which meant that, if anything, Irshar would become an ashram for *sungineers*.

That would be its legacy.

Iravan studied Dhruv, noticing the dark circles under the sungineer's bespectacled eyes, the hunch in his shoulders. It had been a long night for them both. While Iravan had kept his vigil in the storm for Ahilya, Dhruv had come to him twice to discuss how to make this new ashram work, intermittently checking on the Ecstatics. Iravan had listened to him carefully. There was something to be respected about a man who could do his job even if he didn't like who he was doing it for.

Who better to lead the sungineers than Dhruv? The man had helped Iravan, against his own allegiances to Nakshar. He had tried to stop Iravan's excision. Dhruv had invented the radarx and the energex. He had once vied for a councilor's seat. He understood politics—enough that he had convinced the four Ecstatics and Iravan himself that he was on their side, even though *he* had been the one to put them through the experimentation on the battery.

Irshar's existence would not be countenanced easily by the Conclave, in that, Ahilya was right. War with the other ashrams was a real possibility, and it would be complete beings like her who would suffer most. Yet the Conclave could not harm him—not even if they updated their own trajection or built new plants like the perileaf. The architects were not dangerous. But the sungineers were.

Undoubtedly, no sungineering devices worked in the Conclave now, not with the new kind of trajection Iravan had used—but it was only a matter of time before something was invented. Sungineers had already progressed beyond his wildest imagination with the invention of the radarx, energex, and deathmazes. Whatever else he overlooked, Iravan could not forget that sungineering devices had once trapped him completely.

In order to prevent war with the sungineers, Iravan would need to win them over to his side. He would have to make it so that no sungineer ever willingly betrayed him or the Ecstatics again. The other ashrams had always treated sungineers as second-class citizens, but Iravan would welcome them to Irshar. Kiana had wanted relevance for her kind; he would give them more than relevance. He would give them power unlike any they'd had before—more than even the Ecstatics. Irshar would one day belong to them.

"I want you to add an invitation to the sungineers to the treatise," Iravan said now. "Those who helped you, but any others who wish to come. The Conclave won't like it, but make this a non-negotiable condition. The sungineers all have my protection and my welcome—but monitor the technology they bring. I will not have deathmazes trapping us again. Conduct a veristem test to make sure they mean no harm to the Ecstatics and we will proceed."

Dhruv shrugged as though he had worked this out himself.

The sungineer glanced at Naila then said, "There's something you should know. Naila and I tried to tell you earlier. The way Nakshar behaved, the fragility of the Conclave last night, I think it was because of the Ecstatic battery. I've gone over it, and I don't think Ecstasy can be stored at all, not like trajection. Experimenting on the Ecstatics caused the shaking of the ashram. I'm convinced that Ecstasy is not sustainable for building."

Iravan nodded slowly. He had already considered this. Spiralweed had reacted differently both to him and to Bharavi when they'd each used trajection and supertrajection. If the battery had used that dangerous plant, then it only made sense that the effect was different.

As for Ecstasy being unsustainable for building—Ecstasy didn't build. It transformed. That was its power and its danger.

"If you hadn't taken over the construction of the Conclave as you did last night, sir," Naila said carefully, "the Ecstatic battery would have damaged all the ashrams. We're still assessing the effects, but it's possible that none of the ashrams would have survived."

Iravan raised his brows, but Dhruv made an irritable sound in his throat.

"Yes, yes," the sungineer said scathingly. "It all sounds like excellent news, but tell him the rest."

Naila hesitated, but at Iravan's gesture she continued. "Since the experiment, Nakshar has had many incidents of architects burning crimson instead of blue-green when they enter the Moment. Last count was one-hundred-and-fifty, though more may have happened since. They're being contained, but whatever this is, it is similar to what happened during the skyrage. No effect has been noticed except for their tattoos changing colour though, and while we can't communicate with any other ashram, it's likely this has happened there as well."

Iravan froze. "This is because of the cosmic creatures. They can affect architects in the Moment."

"Chaiyya-ve and Airav-ve think you made it happen because of what you did to the core trees."

"*I* think it was because of the battery," Dhruv said stubbornly.

The three of them stared at each other.

Iravan considered each of the possibilities.

The cosmic creatures had interfered with the world for ten thousand years, causing the earthrages. Yet there had never been a record of *sky*rages, no record of architects burning, not even in secret architect histories. He and Ahilya had thought it a retaliation for trapping one of the cosmic creatures and ending the last earthrage, but that was not necessarily accurate, was it?

Earthrages had been ended by Ecstatics and complete beings before, even if that history had been erased. But surely no account of skyrages would have been erased, not when it left architects so vulnerable. No, trajection would have evolved to counter that threat somehow.

Which meant that the last skyrage was the *first* skyrage, the *only* skyrage, a freak new phenomenon in the history of their world.

Only one other event had occurred for the first time ever before it.

The sungineering battery that had drained Airav.

Iravan's mouth fell open a little.

The battery had always been dangerous. Experimentation on architects was banned by the Conclave precisely because of an architect's connection to consciousness in the Moment. Could the first battery which had allowed Ahilya to arrive in the jungle have precipitated the skyrage? Had the battery weakened the Moment itself, allowing the cosmic creatures to *shake* the universe—something unheard of during all the years of earthrages? Had it somehow broken the Moment's collective consciousness, thus allowing the cosmic creatures to burn the architects?

He had no way to prove it, but in his heart, Iravan knew this was exactly what had happened.

The Ecstatic battery that Dhruv had tried a day ago must have only worsened it all.

Bloody rages.

He pinched the bridge of his nose with a forefinger and thumb. "That battery was a fucking mistake from the start."

"It was your idea," Dhruv pointed out.

"And it was a bad one. I didn't account for a lot of things."

Back in those days of being a Senior Architect of Nakshar, Iravan had wanted a way to remove reliance on trajection to give the Maze Architects a rest. He hadn't known about Ecstasy or the cosmic beings or the possibility of a skyrage. He had never known how badly a battery could backfire. He had forced Kiana and her team to make one—and Kiana had taken to the idea since then, resulting in her deal with Ahilya and Ahilya's own deal with Iravan.

"This," Dhruv said with a certain malicious relish, "is what happens when architects interfere with things they don't understand."

Iravan said nothing, but he remembered the arguments in Nakshar's council when Kiana had once said the same thing to him. In the silence, the falcon circled above the jungle. A dust cloud grew within the earthrage, too symmetrical to be anything but the falcon's trajection.

Wordlessly, Iravan trajected as well, and tiny phosphorescence glimmered along the grass of the canopied corridor, lighting the way back to his bedchamber where Ahilya was. He gestured at it, a clear dismissal. Dhruv and Naila glanced at each other and began down the path.

When they were out of sight, Iravan crossed his arms over his chest.

"You can come out now," he grunted.

Something moved in the bushes, then Darsh emerged, looking half abashed, half mutinous.

Iravan gestured and the boy began walking next to him. He reminded Iravan of Kush. Once, Iravan had spent a lot of time with Bharavi's son, watching him grow, hoping for a son one day himself. Grief and rage burned in him as he remembered again the cosmic creatures ripping his possibilities apart.

"Why aren't you resting?" he asked. "Your training will begin soon enough."

"What you did," Darsh said, hesitating. "The glass cages and then with that Maze Architect—will you teach us—"

"No."

"But... I want to help."

"I'll teach you to unite with your yaksha and stop the rages. That is all."

Darsh scowled. He continued to match Iravan's pace, casting glances at the intricate tattoos on his arms. Within the silence, the falcon circled the dust in the jungle, then took to the sky again, satisfied.

Iravan braced himself.

The yaksha was returning.

He stopped walking down the canopied corridor and waved a hand. A narrow ramp grew underneath his feet, winding up through the hallway toward the ethereal gossamer ceiling. Darsh followed him as he climbed.

Iravan did not tell him to leave. He'd seen the boy's fascination when he'd done what he had to Viana. He had seen such eagerness in students before, right before they discovered something new and dangerous about trajection themselves.

But trajection had been understood for thousands of years, it was a known entity. Iravan had barely scratched the surface with Ecstasy. The others would discover more of it, whether he liked it or not. What if they used everdust, the green dust of pure possibility? What if, when presented with the two paths of their future, they chose to be reborn instead of choosing clarity of their own selves? He could not force their choice, not when he had no idea of what would happen to his own consciousness on death. Consciousness recycled into birth and rebirth, everyone knew this, but for an Ecstatic, joined with a yaksha as he was—what would happen to them? What had happened to all those others in the jungle, thousands of years ago? If a cosmic being split to create a yaksha and an architect, could it be that Iravan's own death would return him to becoming a cosmic being in some form again?

The thought was so disgusting that Iravan faltered on the ramp, tripping.

Darsh leapt forward, stabilizing his arm, but Iravan barely noticed. His free hand clutched the stone blade he'd hung around his neck, as a warning never to misuse everdust again. Fingers splayed across his palpitating heart. He could almost see the organ like he had in the sanctum, his skin translucent and clear. The terror built in him, heavy and stark. All his lives, Nidhirv, Mohini, Askavetra, Bhaskar, and now Iravan—lives lived in mistake, only to eternally make the same mistake again. What if this last death was only another death for the cosmic being he had originated from? His breath came in short bursts. His kurta was drenched in sweat. Oblivion would be better. Erasure would be better. He could not return to becoming a creature like that. He would not.

"Are you all right?" Darsh asked, his eyes wide.

"I'm fine," he rasped, and shook the boy off. Iravan staggered the last few feet off the ramp straight into the storm.

At once, his clothes and cloak were soaked. Wind blew his hair back and he stood there in the maelstrom, opening his face to the elements. The scent of smoke surrounded him despite the rain, emanating from the feather cloak.

Within the silence, the falcon flew steadily in the sky, and Iravan took a few more steps forward on the terrace top. He couldn't see the yaksha, but he knew it was flying toward him. It could be here in minutes, or days. Iravan could not read its mind.

What if the falcon's plan interfered with what he was attempting with Irshar? Even if everything worked in the way Iravan planned, this city alone would not solve the problem of the cosmic creatures. All architects would one day become Ecstatic, they would die out in their last lives, no longer able to reincarnate, and a day would come when there were no earthrages at all, and no Ecstatics either. But then another day in the future, the cosmic creatures would split again, restarting the cycle of earthrages. Perhaps Ecstasy would be allowed then, perhaps Ecstatics would find themselves ending the earthrages. But perhaps Ecstasy would be outlawed again.

Iravan could not rely on the transience of culture to ensure earthrages were allowed to end. No, *he* needed to end the earthrages at the source—not merely trap the cosmic creatures in the Moment like he and Ahilya had done, and not a simple delay like the falcon-yaksha had performed with its webbing, either. He needed an enduring solution. *That* was how he would make amends to the complete beings. That was how he would ensure that when he died in this life, he would die forever. That he would never return to becoming one of *them*.

Was such a trajection even possible? Did the falcon know of it? Surely, if the falcon knew how to stop the cosmic creatures permanently, it would have done so. He could feel its hate of the cosmic beings; it was his own hate. Its fury grew inside him.

Iravan turned to Darsh who still lingered behind him. "There *is* something you can do to help. Come with me."

Darsh straightened. His eyes glittered in anticipation. "Where are we going?"

Iravan pointed at the disparate ashrams, still connected to Irshar. Already, architecture was forming between the cities so both Ahilya and Dhruv would be able to fulfill their tasks as they negotiated with the Conclave. The ashrams changed too, and though it was nothing he was consciously doing, Iravan could sense his intent rendered within the design.

"We're going to begin freeing Ecstatics from their imprisonment."

He had sent Ahilya to take his demands to the Conclave to test every architect with the radarx. Dhruv would demand that sungineers be freed. But several Ecstatics were already imprisoned in deathcages. Several had come to his rescue in his battle against the falcon. Ahilya was going to negotiate their release, and Iravan trusted her despite the mistakes she had made—the mistakes *both* of them had made. But he did not trust the Conclave, and Iravan was no longer asking permission to take the Ecstatics. Ahilya and Dhruv's missions were a formality, a politeness he was showing to the Conclave that meant little beyond politeness itself. He was not going to risk the Ecstatics being kept hostage, risk any wayward experimentation on them, risk their excision. He had abandoned them once. He would not abandon them again.

Iravan trajected, a swirl of leaves and green fibers. Wind lifted the two of them up, carrying them into the air, a torrent of roots and earth bearing their weight in exquisite trajection.

30

AHILYA

Ahilya paused on the bridge back to Nakshar.

The storm had grown worse, although it was hard to tell with the constant downpour. She shielded her eyes from the stabbing rain and gazed up into the thunderclouds. Dhruv and Naila had stopped too, their gazes following hers back to Irshar, to the top of the diamond-shaped mountain.

They could all see it, the architecture transforming in a way that had never happened before. Bridges rippled out, now connecting one ashram to another, where before there had been none, yet there was a deep violence in their formation. Each of the ashrams changed even as they connected. Where once they had been a different shape, some resembling boulders, others flowers, now the ashrams grew homogenous, each one shaped like a bark oblong hovering in the sky.

The effect was magnificent, uniform, yet there was a profound loss there, a contained rage as bridges raced too swiftly to do anything but smash into one another as they formed. A rock fell from the labyrinthine construction, caught midair by a vine, before being absorbed into a part of another bridge far from where it had begun. A thousand vines flicked in and out of the clouds, carrying boulders at high speeds. Ashrams merged and fed off of each other, with no regard for their plants contaminating each other, the concern obliterated by Iravan's Ecstasy.

Goosebumps erupted along Ahilya's arms. *He's hanging on by a thread*, she thought.

Iravan had taken the news about their miscarriage too easily, but his grief rippled out through the formation of Irshar. Chaiyya asked again, *What happens if you find out he is not as safe as you think he is?* Ahilya swallowed, the rain pricking her face.

He needed to heal. They both did. He had wanted to take the time to talk it out—he had asked her twice—but she had deflected. Had they missed their chance? What would have happened had she confided in him about how she felt during the pregnancy? Perhaps Iravan would not have been able to take the news, like she'd thought. But perhaps the two of them could have weathered the storm together.

Something flickered, and two dark shapes moved from the mountain in a swirl of green, angling toward one of the newly constructed ashrams. Ahilya recognized one of them even from this distance, the constantly glowing skin, the leanness, the billowing cloak.

"Rages," Dhruv said, hurriedly wiping his glasses. "Is he *flying*?"

Next to Ahilya, Naila's mouth had dropped open. "Yes," the Maze Architect breathed. "But it's still trajection—or Ecstasy. He must have tapped into the core trees' flight permissions to use it for himself. This is… this is incredible."

Ahilya met Naila's uncertain gaze with her own, and knew they were both thinking the same thing. She had more power than she knew what to do with now, with his transference of the core trees to her, but he would not be pleased with what she planned. Yet wasn't she supposed to be a check on him? That was her role from the beginning, even when he had been a Senior Architect and she an unknown archeologist.

It was what she'd said to Dhruv and Naila when they had all drawn up the treatise in Iravan's bedchamber, scribbling in Bharavi's book. Ahilya held the pages now in her pocket, safe from the rain. She stole a glance toward Dhruv, but he was staring into the pouring skies, wiping and squinting through his glasses. Dhruv had not joined the conversation between her and Naila except to grunt every now and then, his mouth a thin line. It was an expression she knew well, so endearing that Ahilya had felt the pain of their estrangement again. Their meeting had been awkward, the sungineer looking like he wanted to say something several times, but then holding his tongue.

It didn't matter.

This was her task—to build peace between the Conclave and Iravan.

She began hurrying along the bridge again. The leafy wall opened and the three of them hastened through the rain and wind onto Nakshar, circling the walkway.

Kiana and Chaiyya emerged from a break in Nakshar's wall. The councilors had seen them coming, of course, and the group hurried back in, Ahilya, Naila, and Dhruv following the other two into a chamber much like the one Ahilya had woken up in yesterday.

She clutched the papers in her pocket as all of them settled, shaking off the rain from their clothes and cloaks, wiping their faces with proffered linen napkins. Iravan had demanded the impossible, with an ultimatum for all new Ecstatics to be delivered to him by the end of the week. After what he had endured, she could not blame him, but opening negotiations with a dagger to the throat would end badly. She had a decision to make now, about her own future with him, and that of the Conclave.

Ahilya took a seat on one of the tree-trunk stools that had begun growing in the chamber, and Chaiyya sat opposite her. Phosphorescence glimmered on the walls, and Ahilya felt Iravan's presence in the plant, his intention, his attention.

"You've been gone a whole day and night," Chaiyya began. The Senior Architect looked tired, her round cheeks wan, her long braid unkempt. "Tell us what is going on. What does he intend?"

Dhruv sat stiffly, as far away from Ahilya as was possible without being rude. Iravan had promised the sungineers sanctuary and power, but Ahilya knew Dhruv did not like being answerable to her. He had hoped to be second in power in Irshar, answerable only to Iravan.

Her own uncertainty twisted within her. She had begun down this road, hoping to find compromise, playing both sides from the day Iravan had landed in Nakshar, but she had never imagined this. Iravan had presumed she would return to Irshar to live with him. By making her his ambassador, he had made her a citizen. But could she abandon everything she had begun in Nakshar, now when her rudra beads had been returned to her? When there was no one else who could do what she could? Where would her loyalties lie?

She would have an answer now.

Ahilya leaned forward and fixed Chaiyya with her gaze. "Why did you make me a councilor?"

The Senior Architect blinked, but rallied quickly. "We dismissed you under duress. We regret it."

"I don't mean being reinstated. I meant before, two months ago. Why did you do it, when you must have guessed the Conclave would treat me the way it did? When you knew it would give you more trouble having a non-architect on the council instead of an architect?"

The only sound was the restive wind outside.

Ahilya felt Dhruv's attention pique. He had been in line for the council seat Ahilya now occupied; Naila too, each a potential nomination from Iravan.

Chaiyya opened her mouth, but it was Kiana who spoke first. "How much do you truly know of Nakshar's history, Ahilya?"

Ahilya transferred her gaze to the Senior Sungineer. "Is that a serious question? I am an archeologist. I know everything I am permitted to know. Everything that isn't a part of privileged architect records."

Both Chaiyya and Naila flinched. A stab of vindication passed through Ahilya.

Kiana nodded thoughtfully. "Then you know Nakshar was the first ashram to induct sungineers into its council. It was the largest of the sister ashrams to understand the desire of non-architects, thereby raising their status. It was one of the first to open architecture to manipulation by citizens. It *asked* for architects to be allowed to marry non-architects, and was the first to allow the secret of excision—the earlier secret of excision, of excised architects being rendered senseless—to be shared with spouses. Nakshar asked for a five-year timeline to select new councilors because that was the only fair way to judge a candidate, the only fair way to ensure stability. Since its inception, food, shelter, and medicine, all of it was made available to everyone, ready to grow and use because of the permissions of the rudra tree, presented at an instant's notice should citizens desire them. Why do you think that is?"

Ahilya raised her eyebrows. "I think you are eager to tell me why."

"It's because Nakshar was built on the principles of equity," Chaiyya said. "It was built on the idea of freedom—and freedom for *all*. Airav and I are the oldest councilors in tenure, and our actions might not have always made sense, but we would die a hundred times over before letting anything ruin Nakshar or subsume it."

"And you would sacrifice Ecstatics too," Ahilya said, crossing her arms over her chest.

"I would not take back the decision to excise Iravan if it led to Nakshar's freedom," Chaiyya said evenly, meeting her gaze. "I know Airav would allow excision to happen too. My stance was clear from the start—I had to protect Nakshar, but we truly tried to let you change the power structure, Ahilya. We *saw* the need for change. It was why Airav supported you on the council, even against my own wishes. At the heart of it, we agreed with the things you have been trying to achieve, even if our methods were different. We *wanted* you to succeed, but we feared you would not. It's why we needed to prepare alternate plans. Sacrificing Iravan and the Ecstatics *was* such an alternate plan."

"And you, Kiana?" Ahilya asked. "Is that why you've been so insistent about the Ecstatic battery too? Why you helped me and Naila? Why you told Dhruv about Iravan's planned excision?"

The Senior Sungineer glanced from Dhruv to Ahilya. Her mouth grew thin. "I seconded your nomination, you know," she said quietly. "I could have nominated Dhruv to the council seat."

"But you did not," Dhruv snapped, his eyes burning into hers. "After everything I did for the lab, you chose to forsake me. I was your best raging sungineer, Kiana! I invented things that no one else did—things that directly helped survival!"

"It was never only about the sungineers, Dhruv," Kiana responded tiredly. "You've learned this, haven't you, Ahilya? That once you come into such power, you can no longer protect only one group? You began down this path to protect the non-architects, and look at you now—look at all the people you made promises to. The people you're beholden to."

Ahilya flinched. She couldn't respond.

"I wanted the Ecstatic battery because with such a device, one day we could *all* truly have freedom," Kiana continued. "If the battery worked, then perhaps we would have a future where mere survival was no longer a priority. A future where all groups, including other non-architects, could flourish because energy would be in surplus, where sungineers could create independently, and Ecstatics could unite with their yakshas, and people like you, Ahilya, could do whatever they wanted to do because none of us would be worrying anymore about something as foundational and essential as *being able to live*. Iravan could have remained a councilor in Nakshar—not just a Senior Architect, but a Senior *Ecstatic* Architect."

Ahilya's breath caught in her throat. Suddenly it made sense why the council had not passed a vote of no confidence against Iravan in the beginning when they'd known he was an Ecstatic. It made sense why they had agreed he was a citizen of Nakshar, why they had counted him as a councilor during the Conclave meeting, even though doing so had incurred the wrath of Katresh. Basav had held Iravan's Senior Architect status against Nakshar's hold on its own sanity, but Chaiyya and Kiana and the others had *hoped* for Ahilya's success, wanting to build on it by including an Ecstatic on the council. The falcon's trajectory of Basav had ruined it all.

"Do you understand now?" Kiana asked softly, watching the play of emotions on Ahilya's face. "I helped you because I believed in the future you were trying to create. When it became clear Iravan had lost the trial, that future died—but don't forget, I seconded Iravan's own nomination on the council years ago, too—I saw the potential in him to change things as well. I did not wish to see him excised, Ahilya, but I couldn't openly do anything about it, not when it would jeopardize Nakshar's safety and position with the Conclave. You could. You and Dhruv." Her gray eyes went to Irshar's Senior Sungineer. "I only intended you to free Iravan, however," she added dryly. "Using the battery on the Ecstatics—I'm afraid that was *your* decision."

Dhruv said nothing, but he pursed his lips and his eyes glinted angrily.

Whatever Kiana's reasoning, Dhruv did not like being manipulated any more than Ahilya herself did. By letting him take the fall for Iravan's escape and the rogue Ecstatic experimentation, Kiana had protected her own position as much as Nakshar. By dismissing Ahilya from the council, all of them had let her take the heat for their own gambles.

Chaiyya leaned forward as though she could see Ahilya arrive at this conclusion. "Making you a councilor was a risk we calculated, ready to dismiss you should we need to. But underneath it all, Ahilya, you were made a councilor by unanimous vote because we saw that you would protect Nakshar like we do, no matter the cost. Your actions with Iravan showed us you would protect that which is yours even unto death and calamity. We gambled on giving you the entirety of Nakshar to protect."

Ahilya stared at the two other councilors, and on his stool, Dhruv's face grew confused. *He didn't enable your selfishness*, the sungineer had said about Iravan, right before Ahilya had rescued her husband. *Do you think he'd want you to do what you're doing right now?* She glanced at him, the frown on his face, the guilt, the uncertainty. *You two deserve each other.* Pride, absolution, and shame lanced through Ahilya, making her mouth dry.

"We judge a councilor on fit," Chaiyya continued. "That ultimately is how we decide. You proved your love for Nakshar time and again. Did you think I had not noticed you changed the permissions of the ashram when you were sent to re-form councilor communication? You gave the citizen spaces a higher priority, didn't you?"

Ahilya stared at her. "You knew?"

"I noticed it, yes. I couldn't have made that decision myself, not without angering the architects I represent on the council, but I saw that you did it, and that action likely saved the citizens when the construction failed after the attempt with the Ecstatic battery. I noticed it and I allowed it."

Ahilya said nothing. Chaiyya might have allowed Ahilya to change the permissions of Nakshar's priorities, but if Basav had demanded Ahilya's own resignation in return for Nakshar's sovereignty, Chaiyya would have used Ahilya's meddling with permissions as an excuse to remove her. The council had done that from the very start—use Ahilya for their own devices. Kiana and Chaiyya had admitted as much, and in her mind, Airav said, *What makes you think I don't have my reasons?* She thought of how easily they had stripped her of her power. She thought of how they had reinstated her when they'd needed her. Her strings had always been pulled, a marionette for their games. Had this happened to Iravan, too? As a member of the council, had she become like that herself? After all, she had tried to manoeuvre Iravan too, by giving him Bharavi's book, by asking for his cooperation in return for the Ecstatics.

"If we had veristem that we could access," Chaiyya said, "we would swear on it. We would prove to you the purity of our intentions."

She could make them, Ahilya knew. She herself had the highest priority now for any core tree, and Dhruv could retrieve veristem too—Iravan had loosened the permissions to allow him to clear the sungineers. But Ahilya stayed unmoving, watching the other two women.

Because it was not about the veristem, nor about whether they were saying this now to manipulate her. Once again, she was caught in the middle as the one to bring peace between Iravan and the Conclave. She'd done it for Nakshar first, and now she represented Iravan—but this was about none of them.

This was about her. Not their truth, but her own.

She had held back the cosmic beings from rupturing into an earthrage with the pure power of her desire. She had gambled and risked and paid the price for trying to protect them all as a councilor. It had almost ripped her apart, but that had still been the only right thing to have attempted. As hard as her choices had been, she was not about to forsake anyone, and now she would take back her power, from Iravan and from the council, because in the end, she had not done it for them. Nakshar was hers to protect, as was this world.

She would do it for *herself*.

Ahilya stood up. She felt the papers in her pocket but dismissed them for now. "I need to go to the rudra tree."

"We have a treatise," Dhruv said, frowning. "The sungineers and the Ecstatics—"

"Will have to wait."

"Iravan's commands were clear."

"He put me in charge," Ahilya said. She met the sungineer's eyes and took a deep breath. "I am returning some measure of control to the architects. I am returning their trajection to them."

A shocked silence greeted her words. Naila's mouth dropped open. Dhruv's eyes widened behind his glasses. Before Chaiyya could speak, he stood too, facing Ahilya.

"You cannot," he breathed. "This is explicitly what Iravan didn't want. He *took* their control away. You would trap the Ecstatics, you would trap the sungineers too. The minute you return trajection to them, they could excise the Ecstatics, they could begin using the energex to drain them, and sungineers would have to be party to such an atrocity."

"Iravan sent me here to negotiate, Dhruv. I mean to do it in good faith."

The sungineer loomed over her. "If you give the architects back their power, it will undo everything he wants to achieve. Nakshar's justifications are all well and good, but do you really trust the rest of the Conclave? Cities like Katresh and the Seven Northern Sisters? They've never wanted a rosy future of equity."

"Look at the Conclave," Ahilya said quietly. "Look at what he has done with their architecture. These ashrams no longer pose a threat to him. Besides, Iravan needs each ashram to check every architect through the radarx for Ecstasy. The radarx works on trajection, does it not? How will it work if no architect is able to traject anywhere in the Conclave?"

Dhruv opened his mouth, then frowned before closing it.

It was clear he had not thought of this. Like everyone else, he was used to trajection. With Iravan's new construction of the Conclave still resembling its power, its absence had not hit him— not fully.

The others stood up too.

"This way," Chaiyya said, relieved. She led them through a curtained doorway toward another corridor shaped like a ring, this one on the inside of Nakshar's construction. They took a path lit by glowing moss toward another balcony looking down into Nakshar. The design reminded Ahilya of when the ashram had been on reserve energy, right before she had flown to the jungle to rescue Iravan. Shaped like a giant beehive with hundreds of narrow hallways leading away from the central balconies, Nakshar spread out before her, a massive orb.

Yet unlike the last time, the design looked expansive, healbranch growing so abundantly that Ahilya smelled its woodsy scent. Far below, the rudra tree flourished, so massive that the tops of its canopy reached the highest floor from where Ahilya and the others leaned. Tiny birds twittered from its branches, and a light breeze shook its sharp leaves. Blue-green light flashed on the tree, useless attempts at trajection from the Architects' Disc that was still undoubtedly trying to break through Iravan's control. Ahilya studied the tree, and a creeping sensation grew over her, that the rudra was watching her. Sweat broke out over her lip.

They began to descend a curving ramp. Every now and then, Ahilya glimpsed citizens within their homes—no longer the cramped quarters she had seen Tariya in, but something more luxurious, bark windows and lush grass and multiple chambers for each family. Iravan had equalized it all again, architect or non-architect, and the lower they descended, the more of his architecture she made out: playgrounds on some levels, gardens and courtyards, all of them glimmering with phosphorescence, all of them smelling like healbranch.

The garden at the bottom reminded her of the one Iravan had built for her the day she had left him and the habitat. Ahilya glanced up and citizens leaned on balconies all over the structure. More citizens walked through the lower gardens, parents with their children sitting on benches, their faces half relieved, half wary; clusters of architects glowing blue-green despite not being on duty; sungineers in their orange robes, conspicuous because of the absence of holograms surrounding them. It all looked peaceful now, yet how were the citizens truly faring? So much had happened; they were unused to architecture changing this dramatically so fast. It was undoubtedly beautiful, but Iravan's leash on himself was loosening, the things he had suffered too much to bear. She could not gamble the safety of everyone on his temper.

Chaiyya led the way through a flower-lined promenade toward the rudra tree. A ramp led high up to the Architects' Disc, but even as Ahilya made to climb it, Dhruv blocked her way.

"You have permissions from Iravan, but I have instructions too. Do what you need to do—I won't stop you—but I intend to invite the sungineers to Irshar, just as Iravan wants. I intend to make sure that any architect who wishes to learn the ways of Ecstasy is welcome in Irshar along with their family."

Iravan wished to make Irshar a haven for sungineers. Who was Ahilya to stop that? She ought to encourage it; with sungineers in Irshar, a war between the ashrams would likely never happen, not when Irshar's sungineers built their own technology to prevent it. At best, there would be cooperation and harmony. At worst, the war would be a cold one—with damage that could be contained, negotiated, even mitigated with time. As for the architects... if she wanted freedom for all, she would not stand in the way of architects willingly going to Irshar. She nodded, and Dhruv turned to Chaiyya.

"Who is in charge of the Conclave? I will need to speak to them."

Chaiyya pointed toward a private alcove a little away from the base of the rudra tree. A thick curtain of sound-repelling fronds covered the entrance, and Geet and Raksha, the same Maze Architects who had been charged with escorting Ahilya after her dismissal, stood outside the alcove on guard.

"The tribunal represents the Conclave in this matter," Chaiyya said. "Basav is leading it. Kiana will take you there."

Dhruv turned toward the alcove, his posture determined, and Kiana made to follow, but Ahilya arrested Nakshar's Senior Sungineer with a hand.

"We don't have time for subtlety," she warned. "Iravan's commands were clear. Impress this upon Basav, Kiana. As a show of Irshar's good faith, I am returning trajection, but if the tribunal refuses him, Iravan will just take what he wants with violence. The tribunal needs to work with me. I am on your side. Give Iravan what he has asked for. It is only fair."

Kiana exchanged a glance with Chaiyya. "I understand."

"Naila," Ahilya said. "Go with them. They might be able to use your help."

The Maze Architect nodded, and Ahilya watched her and the two sungineers stride toward the alcove, push aside the curtain of leaves, and enter. She turned back to the ramp.

"Do you mean it?" Chaiyya asked quietly. "About being on our side?"

Ahilya met her gaze. "Do not misinterpret me, Chaiyya. No single person or group will have absolute control, not if I can help it." Without another word, she began climbing the ramp, toward the Disc Architects. Behind her, Chaiyya silently followed.

31

IRAVAN

They landed on a bridge connected to a dim courtyard within one of the ashrams.

Iravan led Darsh in, the rain pelting his feather cloak. If he tracked his trajectory of the core trees, he would know which ashram this was, but he did not bother with such unnecessary knowledge. What did it matter? He had homogenized the construction; all of them were now the same. They had allowed the tribunal to do what it had done. They had been about to excise him. Fury still throbbed in him at his humiliation, at *Ahilya's* humiliation. He was no longer beholden to upholding the architects' culture.

The courtyard resembled Nakshar's sanctum, but not the one he had recently been trapped in. This looked like the one Bharavi had brought him to in order to study Manav all those months before. Her voice echoed in his ears. *You're meant to define the rules. To create them.* He had certainly done that now. Would she have been proud? He picked up his pace, and moss lit up the courtyard, glowing along the floor and in patches on the wall. A few feet away from the bridge, he and Darsh stopped as they came to a dozen deathcages.

In all but one, men and women sat extremely still, some of them staring into the distance, others silently weeping. These were the excised architects, those who had found Ecstasy long before Iravan had. He studied them silently, and Manav shivered in his mind, his face contorted. The once Senior Architect of Nakshar had emitted a weak Ecstatic signature—how? The question still lurked in Iravan's mind, but excision itself would soon be a thing of the past.

He turned toward the last cage, within which stood three people—two men and a woman, muttering to each other. Caged Ecstatics, as yet unexcised, bound within a single deathcage. Iravan hadn't known for certain he would find any here. He had taken a chance; now he'd found three.

The blue-green light of trajection suffused their dark skins. With sungineering dead in all of the Conclave, the deathmazes had stopped working. The loss of sungineering had dropped the forcefields around the cages, but it had not dropped the glass. Like every other architect, these locked Ecstatics were clearly trying to manipulate the Moment in order to escape.

They would not be able to. They were limited by his power like everyone else.

Iravan drew forward, heeled by a silent Darsh, and the three Ecstatics in the cage paused in their muttering, turning to him. Lightning flashed over and over again.

"Enter the Moment," Iravan commanded Darsh. "Watch."

He had taken the idea from Pranav and Trisha. The two Maze Architects had shattered the deathcages in Nakshar as soon as they'd had access to the Moment. It had been a planned move, a smart move. Iravan adapted and replicated it.

Within the Moment, he spun out a dozen constellation lines, each of them connected to a different star. He picked the strongest, sharpest plants—Katresh's white locust, Yeikshar's ravine cactus,

Auresh's blackthorn. Using one ashram's plant in another had once been dangerous—but that was for normal architects and normal trajection. Iravan's new power superseded these concerns. The entire Conclave now was built of whatever materials he desired, and he had already changed the nature of the plants to not damage one another. Spinning the constellation lines into a tight weave, Iravan grew a dozen vines. The Ecstatics' deathcage trembled and they retreated from the edges, eyes wide, as thin veins of plants grew under the surface of the glass, expanded, grew bulbous until the glass itself appeared to be made of thick, sharp, veined foliage.

The deathcage vibrated. It shook.

It shattered.

Iravan exhaled softly. Next to him, Darsh's eyes glowed, and a smile formed on his face.

The three Ecstatics staggered forward. They watched Iravan warily, both in their first visions as they approached him, and in their second within the Moment. With the Conclave working on the new part-trajection part-Ecstatic power, these Ecstatics were as helpless in the Moment as other normal architects, but unlike those others, Iravan needed them now. The falcon was coming. He could see its wings flash in the silence.

"Brace yourselves," Iravan commanded.

The three of them exchanged startled glances. The young woman gulped.

Converting his ray of Ecstatic light into delicate constellation lines, Iravan spun the lines around the dust motes of the three architects within the Moment. They shuddered in his first vision, the two men clutching each other's hands, the young woman gasping.

As gently and carefully as he could, Iravan pulled them through the Conduit.

Once, he had tried to teach four other Ecstatics how to find the Deepness. Naila's voice flashed in his mind. *You might have more success if you comfort them first.* But *he* hadn't found the Deepness because he had been guided to it gently. The Resonance had slammed into him in Nakshar's temple and dragged him there unceremoniously against his will. Iravan had not thought to try it before, but now his trajection tightened. He and the three Ecstatics remained suspended in the Conduit, the universe of the Moment and the velvety darkness of the Deepness surrounding them, blurring their second vision—

Then Iravan pulled, and their second vision snapped, coalesced.

They appeared in the Deepness alongside him, hovering in the velvety darkness.

A stab of satisfaction went through Iravan.

The short man looked close to hyperventilating. The woman's face grew pale. All of them stared at him, wide-eyed, shocked, but still coherent, perhaps because he hovered there in the Deepness right by them, a steadying presence.

Iravan himself had leaned on Bharavi during his first encounter with the Deepness. He had told her what had occurred, and she'd been alarmed—because despite being a hidden Ecstatic herself, she had not expected him to find Ecstasy. Behind his eyes, colorless images grew again, of Bharavi with Tariya and their children, before the images converted into sharper ones of the cosmic creatures shrieking. He blinked and dispelled them.

"My name is Iravan," he said. "I am—"

"A Senior Architect of Nakshar," one of the men said. "An Ecstatic Architect."

Iravan turned to him. "You know me."

"We all do," the woman replied. When Iravan transferred his gaze to her, she blinked. "We heard rumors... that Nakshar claimed to have an Ecstatic Architect in control of his power. That he had been a Senior Architect once."

"Mukthi said you know how to balance Ecstasy with material bonds," the man said, gesturing to the woman. "Is it true?"

"Was that you in this darkness before?" the other man interrupted. "The shape that bound us while we fought a silvery particle?"

"Is this the Deepness?"

"Can you teach us?"

"What happens to us now?"

Iravan held up a hand.

The cities had clearly wasted no time in using the radarx Nakshar had distributed in order to imprison their Ecstatics. He had not expected the three here to be part of the group that had shown up to help him when he had battled the falcon from Nakshar's sanctum—but for all he knew, by helping him, these architects had unleashed their own Ecstasy. Perhaps until then, they had been hidden, like Bharavi. Perhaps after the battle in the sanctum, they had found the Deepness again and again, until they had energized the radarx, until they had been imprisoned. The ascent of an Ecstatic was fast, and as far as he could tell, the battle, the distribution of the radarx, his trial, and the creation of Irshar had been mere hours apart. Perhaps the only reason these three here had not been excised yet was because Iravan had changed everything with his reconstruction of the Conclave.

What had triggered their arrival in the Deepness when he'd needed them? He only knew that his own arrival in the Deepness, all those months back, had been because the falcon had sought him—it had *shown* him how it had sought him through lifetimes. Perhaps these architects had been pursued too by their own yakshas. Perhaps the incorporeal yaksha that had come to his rescue against the falcon belonged to one of them.

Had that yaksha not swept in to take his place in the linking, the Resonance would have taken Iravan over, of that Iravan had no doubt. The falcon had strangled him in the jungle in its rage; it had trajected him multiple times, always for a different reason. The last time it had shown him a vision of its own desolation, but even that had a purpose. Certainly, the falcon had wanted Iravan to know what life had been like for a thousand lonely years. But it had also wanted his acquiescence.

A grim, cold understanding washed over Iravan as he accepted this. The falcon was a brute creature, but it was not only a brute creature. It understood him, his guilt, his shame, his regret, and it had shown him that vision of itself to provoke these feelings so he would comply with its desire to subsume him. So he would stop fighting.

In the silence, Iravan felt the yaksha's determination and fury, as it came ever closer in the storm. The falcon needed him. Perhaps its understanding of itself was as incomplete as Iravan's own, but more than that, it needed *him* to amplify its own power. It had resigned itself to using the incorporeal yaksha. As fledgling as Iravan's power had been in the battle, the falcon had wanted it. Perhaps only such a combined power of a single self could permanently delay the cosmic creatures. What would happen if Iravan simply let it take him? The thought made him nauseous. The creature would not release him. If he let it, he would become a thrall. Irshar, Ahilya, everything he had set into motion… all of it would be lost.

Iravan studied the nervous Ecstatics in front of him who shivered in the cold breeze. "Mukhti," he said, addressing the woman. "And?"

"Kamal," the shorter man said. He gestured to the other man next to him. "And Nagesh."

"It is clear you have some measure of control in the Deepness," Iravan said, nodding at them all. "You are handling your arrival into it well. But there are dangers in this realm." His hand went to the blade of pure possibility hung around his neck. In his mind, Viana's eyes grew crimson and begin to bleed. The glass blade and Viana. Two terrible mistakes he had made that stood out among so many others. Iravan turned to Darsh. "Did you see how I broke the cages?"

Darsh nodded nervously. "Pranav and Trisha… they did something similar."

"Can you replicate it?"

"Yes. I think so."

Iravan loosened his power in the Moment, attuned it to Darsh and Darsh alone, and pointed to the cages where the excised architects sat, staring into nothing. "Show me."

Darsh's dark skin began to glow blue-green. From the Moment, Iravan watched as the boy spun out his own constellation lines, replicating the knots between the same stars Iravan had. Within the courtyard, sharp, pointed vines grew under the glass of the deathcages of the excised architects. Darsh strained—his constellation lines vibrated. Iravan thought he was pushing the boy too far. He was only a Junior Architect. *You might have more success if you comfort them first—*

But the lines snapped close, and the glass on the deathcages cracked.

The glass shattered, spraying into fine dust.

Darsh turned to Iravan, his face split by a triumphant smile.

"Good," Iravan said. "Go to the other ashrams. The moss will light your way within the cities, and you won't encounter anyone. Tell any bound Ecstatics who I am and what I offer. Take them to Irshar."

He took in the excised architects, who now had no cages around them. They hadn't noticed. Most of them stayed where they were, staring ahead of themselves, drool collecting around their mouths, their forms limp and disinterested.

"Start with Nakshar," Iravan said to Darsh. "Make sure you release Manav in the sanctum. He is—"

Iravan cut himself off.

His gaze went to the open sky, visible over the bridge. In his first vision now, a speck moved in a straight line in the rain and storm. The yaksha. It was here. It had come to him.

He moved past the Ecstatics in the courtyard toward the bridge. Rain thrashed him instantly, but he could still see into the sky. There was something else behind the falcon—a gigantic cloud of dust, too spherical to be natural.

Iravan shielded his eyes with a hand. In the Deepness, the Resonance shone bright, and he felt the three Ecstatics jerk, as though only just noticing the silvery particle.

One by one, as if summoned there, more shapes appeared in the Deepness right next to the Resonance. The Resonance spun out links of hair-thin light, and each of those shapes attached themselves to it, making it flare brighter.

Iravan's eyes grew wide as realization hit him.

That was no dust cloud.

It was a swarm of yakshas.

Next to him, Darsh gasped too. The others had joined Iravan. They could all see it, the monstrous birds flying toward them with the falcon at their head. The skies were endless, but the creatures filled them up, wings and beaks, talons and feathers, a crow-shaped yaksha, a raven-like monster, a swift among them. The Ecstatics cried out, astounded, pointing up.

Iravan turned to Darsh. "Go. Now. Quickly."

Darsh's wide eyes moved from the sky to Iravan. He nodded wordlessly and ran toward the closest bridge leading to Nakshar.

Iravan turned to the other Ecstatics who stared at him. "I need you to trust me."

They looked at each other, then glanced at the yakshas in the sky. One by one, they nodded.

Taking a deep breath, Iravan spun out three intricate braids of linked trajectory within the Deepness toward them. Kamal and Nagesh gasped. Mukthi staggered, but Iravan braced her before she could fall. Awe filled their features, as undoubtedly they felt their own Ecstatic power, linked to Iravan's. The three straightened as he arrayed their dust motes behind his in the Deepness.

"I won't hurt you," Iravan promised. He pointed toward Irshar. "There are other Ecstatics there waiting to welcome you. You will be safe. Take these excised architects and go."

"What about you?"

"That is not your concern. Go."

Fear clouded their features, but they bowed. He watched as they led the excised architects by the hand, then disappeared into the rain toward the mountain city. Their Ecstatic forms in the Deepness remained bound to him, amplifying his power.

Iravan turned his gaze back up to the skies. In the Deepness, the Resonance flickered, its mercurial surface rapidly blinking. In his first vision, the falcon flew toward him too quickly, but Iravan knew with sudden certainty it was not going to land, not going to stop, and it was leading those other bird-yakshas past the Conclave, far higher into the skies, in a fulfillment of its own agenda. Once, that agenda had been to traject Iravan. Once, it had been to kill him, to link with him, to try and take him over.

Iravan was done with such surprises.

He rose into the skies to meet it.

32

AHILYA

Out of habit, Ahilya made to press her councilor bead to access the chambers at the top of the rudra tree, but even as the desire formed in her, the bark whisked open, an indication that her permissions had been restored to the highest level. A large circular room greeted her, and she strode in with a silent Chaiyya.

A hundred architects in their brown kurta uniforms sat on a floor of thick, soft moss, their eyes closed in deep meditation. No trajection tattoos climbed up their dark skins, but the chamber itself was illuminated by the blue-green glow that emanated from everybody as they undoubtedly wandered the Moment, trying to break through Iravan's constellation lines. They weren't trajecting, not truly, but this was the Disc, and the ashram had archival memory. She could feel the power within the chamber, like a current under her skin. Chaiyya had said that the tree was most powerful at the Disc, and Ahilya sensed it now, as her own emotions and her hold on herself blurred, visions flashing through her mind of herself as a young girl, of saying goodbye to her once-lover Eskayra, of the last goodbye with Dhruv before she flew to find Iravan.

Ahilya picked her way through the seated architects to the rudra tree's trunk in the center. Taking a deep breath, she reached out a hand and touched the tree.

Instantly, gravity sucked her in. Architects were arrayed on the Disc, but superimposed behind them, a thousand citizens glimmered around the ashram, their forms like shadows and smoke, pinpricks of light growing and dying inside of them, too many to keep count, each light flickering and burning like the briefest glow of a firefly.

Desire.

She was looking at the citizens' desires.

Iravan's voice sounded in her head: *Desire is unreliable, it mutates and changes.* The rudra's own sentience grew behind her eyes, a terrible age to it. She thought she could hear the tree talking, rhythms that sounded like language, like words she could understand.

Raga, her mind supplied. She could hear ragas.

All trajection released that byproduct, and base ragas dissipated— or so architects had always thought—but suddenly Ahilya knew, base ragas were absorbed by the core tree. They *created* the archival memory of an ashram. All the citizens that she could suddenly see, all their desires that formed and died, this was what happened when a desire was fulfilled—it became a part of the core tree, part of its memory and sentience. In many ways, the core tree *was* the life of an ashram, an amalgamation of the many lives lived within it. Ahilya witnessed the strength of Nakshar for the first time, more so perhaps than any architect sitting on the Disc ever had.

Tears sprang in her eyes. Was this what the architects felt in the Moment? This was not that dimension, but suddenly she could understand why the architects had needed material bonds. The seduction of a realm like this… the peace she felt…

Let me in, she thought, instinctively knowing what to do.

The rudra tree responded.

The lights within the people grew brighter even as other lights faded. A complex tapestry grew, shaped like the oblong ashram. The tree's roots reached everywhere under Nakshar, seeping into the soil, drinking the desires of the citizens, and the tree acknowledged her.

Ahilya saw herself through the rudra tree's eyes, a figure standing by the trunk, surrounded by the shapes and shadows of the architects. She felt the tree's intention. *Ask*, the word sounded in her ears as leaves and foliage shook on the Disc, a breeze forming. A memory came to her from a lifetime ago of Airav saying, *You will have to be specific with your desires. The more abstract your desire, the fewer chances there are of success.*

She fed that memory back into the tree, and the tree blossomed in her mind like a flower unfurling. Ahilya thought of what she truly wanted—the balance of power between sungineers, architects, Ecstatics, and non-architect citizens of the ashram. She formed that desire, a burning bright light within her, and fed it into the tree. She thought, *Return trajection to the architects. Let them form constellation lines within Nakshar again.*

Something relaxed in the tree, a massive exhalation that sent a cool breeze susurrating through the chamber.

Her desire stayed unmutated. A radiance formed from her shadow, ricocheting across the ashram, feeding and flaring the desires of several citizens—architects, she knew.

Then those desires sparked, fulfilled. Light burst, then disappeared. Ahilya opened her eyes and dropped her hand away from the rudra tree, and the images behind her eyes faded.

She was back on the Architects' Disc, and around her Maze Architects glowed blue-green. This time trajection tattoos climbed over their skins. Several had their eyes open. They were staring at her, awe and disbelief in their features. A low murmuring began as they whispered to each other.

"It works," Chaiyya breathed. "We can build constellation lines again." Vines grew over her arms and face as she trajected, and Ahilya felt her own rudra beads hum slightly as sungineering began to work once again in the ashram.

Immediately, Ahilya searched for Tariya, Kush, and Arth on her beads. Among the thousand people in the ashram, their forms blinked safe and sound. Her breath slowed in relief. They were fine. She hadn't known how much she needed to see Tariya and the boys, how much she had worried for them, through all that she herself had endured.

Next to her, Chaiyya studied her own sungineering beads and frowned. "I can build," she said slowly. "But I still cannot change Nakshar's design. I cannot disconnect from Irshar."

"No. You can make certain alterations to his constellation lines based on your trajection, the same as citizens can with their desire, but your trajection will still be a subset of what is allowed within the bonds of Iravan's construction."

Chaiyya stared at her. "This is not freedom for architects. I understand you don't know how to build truly, but let me help you. Turn control to me, and I will rebuild Nakshar."

"I won't give power to you alone, Chaiyya."

"But you would give it to Iravan?" the Senior Architect countered, her voice echoing on the Disc. "He still supersedes it all."

"Irshar is in flight because of the Conclave's core trees. I would not take that away, even if I could. With what I've done, Iravan no longer has absolute control."

"Only in name, and you know this." Chaiyya's eyes bored into Ahilya. "If you do this, then you leave architects with no purpose. We become useful only for the sungineering we can power. It is an enslavement of its own kind."

"You are not enslaved, Chaiyya. You just have equal power to the sungineers now, to the citizens. You can work together, no group being more than the other, no group worrying about *survival*. This is what Nakshar was aiming toward. You said it yourself."

She paused.

Chaiyya, who had opened her mouth to respond, closed it too.

Both of them turned back to the Architects' Disc. A hush had fallen over the murmuring architects, but this was not reverence at the return of their power. Instead, the assembled people stared at the one man whose dark skin glowed not with blue-green light but a hazy crimson. The man's eyes were wide in terror.

"Chaiyya-ve," he whimpered, in a small voice. "I don't—I can't—"

The Senior Architect hurried over to him, fear in her face. "What is Iravan doing?"

"Not him," Ahilya breathed, joining her. "This is the cosmic creatures."

Between her brows, Iravan rose into the stormy skies to meet the falcon. Other bird yakshas flew with the falcon, and awe overtook her to be witnessing so many yakshas at the same time. Somewhere in her archeologist brain, she was already drawing the creatures, tracking every line, sketching every beak and talon.

She and Chaiyya knelt beside the crimson architect, and Chaiyya's skin radiated with the light of trajection as healbranch began to creep up the architect. Chaiyya pulled the skin under his eye and peered into the pupil.

"Rajesh. What do you feel? Tell me."

"A strangeness in the Moment. My constellation lines are mine, but—" He shook his head as though to clear it. "They feel different, like they are not mine at all."

Chaiyya exchanged a glance with Ahilya. "The Moment isn't thrumming, though. And there's no skyrage, as far as I can tell."

"Iravan said the cosmic creatures could affect the architects. They may not need the skyrage to do so."

Ahilya cut herself off a second time. Shouts grew over the Disc. She and Chaiyya turned as one to see more architects burning, their tattoos growing crimson instead of blue-green, terror in their faces.

The Senior Architect rose to her feet. "Leave the Moment. All of you. Now."

The Disc Architects obeyed instantly. Light faded from of all of them, even Rajesh, who breathed in relief. Blue-green light vanished along with the crimson. Gloom grew over the chamber, the only trajection light now coming from Chaiyya.

"What are you planning?" Ahilya asked, her quiet question carrying in the tense silence.

"I'm going to examine the Moment. Should anything happen to me, I want you to take back the permissions you have given to the architects." On Chaiyya's face, Ahilya could finally see the acknowledgment that Iravan was not the greatest danger. The cosmic creatures were.

She pressed a hand to the rudra tree, feeling its sentience, feeling its own desire to respond to hers. "Ready."

Chaiyya closed her eyes, and her skin burst into light.

33

IRAVAN

He leaned into the air, hair slicked back, and met the falcon halfway.

The thrill of flight rushed through his veins. Wind billowed through his hair and clothes. Wisps of cloud and moisture cut in and out of his first vision as rain stabbed every inch of him. Iravan laughed out loud in wonder and release.

The Conclave was becoming smaller and murkier with every second, but it was not the ascent that brought him joy. It was this new form of trajection—if it could even be called that. He had tapped so deeply into the permissions of all the core trees that flight itself had become available to him. A tornado of wood and leaves bound together in no cohesive pattern carried him up through the storm, the leaves churning so fast that they created an airflow propelling him upward. He floated and shifted his weight by instinct, pressing his shoulders down, leaning forward in an upward dive, streamlining his body.

So close to the falcon, the silence in his mind retreated to a muted buzz, showing him not the creature in its physical form but its mood. A raw purposefulness had seized the yaksha, angry and pinpointed, just as it had been right before it had trajected him. Iravan angled forward, his own intention giving him speed.

The yaksha did not stop. Carried by the wind stream of the leaves, Iravan rippled through the rain and clouds to intercept it. Feathers filled his eyes. He shifted and swung away from its monstrous wings, under then over them, and found his position. He reached his arms forward to clutch at the falcon's neck.

The storm of leaves gentled, slowing him into a descent. His cloak ballooned behind him as his momentum relaxed. His extended fingers tightened on the falcon's neck. He clutched, landed with a soft *whump*, and slipped—he *slipped*, and now his fingers were scrabbling, stomach lurching, his mouth widening into a cry of horror. The silence in his mind considered his demise. He felt its dismissal as his legs lost purchase. The falcon was going to let him fall.

Then the yaksha shifted and Iravan felt himself swing in the opposite direction, steadying on the falcon's back. His legs tightened, trembling fiercely, and his entire body shuddered.

He buried his head in the smoky feathers, unsure whether he was laughing in relief or hysteria, if he was laughing at all or really sobbing. Exhilaration and terror swept through him in waves, the thrill and giddiness of his own recklessness frightening him.

The falcon wove through the clouds, its wingtips sharp and cutting, swirling ever upward in and out of the mist, as though to outpace the storm itself. In the Deepness, the Resonance fluttered, the other yakshas arrayed behind it, awaiting its command. Head still buried in the smoky feathers, Iravan dared a glance behind him to see the other monstrous birds still following. Beaks and talons waved in his vision, cutting through vapor. A terrifying sense of age and intelligence surrounded him. The raven-yaksha's black glinting eye settled on him, the eagle-yaksha let out an ear-splitting scream of anger. A whimper escaped Iravan as he turned away. A part of him registered how incredible this was. No one in living history had ever seen such an aerial flotilla of yakshas. He counted eight birds behind him, eight other forms in the Deepness besides himself, the Resonance, and the Ecstatics he had bound. The falcon, linked to these other yakshas, intended to use them, surely, like it had the non-corporeal yaksha.

He and Ahilya had once discussed what other forms the split of a cosmic creature could take. There were not enough corporeal yakshas in the world to account for every architect's counterpart, but these gigantic birds, like his own falcon, must have belonged to the first crop of cosmic creatures that had split—the ones who had begun the earthrages. It was astonishing the falcon had found them when Iravan himself had not seen a single yaksha besides his own for so long. The falcon had some power over them, something he barely understood even now.

Wind and rain whipped at him, and he bent low over the yaksha again, chilled to the skin. Within the infinite velvety dark of the Deepness, the nine forms of the flying yakshas began to shimmer, nascent jets of light building inside them. The cosmic creatures stretched, pushing.

Part of the webbing holding them cracked.

The falcon shrieked, the sound unearthly.

Iravan tensed. A skyrage, then.

He had expected one soon. It was going to erupt in the next few minutes, and the falcon was going to spin another webbed pattern to delay it. The cosmic creatures had been pushing against their bonds this entire time, but it was not that which concerned Iravan.

The storm was still raging—he still had time. Had the weather become anomalous, he would have been more fearful, but that presence of dark clouds was an indication the weather was still balancing whatever the cosmic creatures would do. The creatures were surely important, but they were not the immediate threat. The falcon was.

The last time the yaksha had stemmed a budding skyrage—the time in the sanctum when Nakshar's sungineering had failed—it had nearly subsumed Iravan. It would likely attempt to do so again. The falcon had never truly seen him as anything but an instrument to be used and discarded. It even made a perverse kind of sense. The yaksha had existed for thousands of years. Iravan in his current form was the newcomer.

The Resonance fluttered next to him. He staggered back as far as he could without losing sight of it in the Deepness. *We have to end this*, he thought desperately, shaking in the rain and wind, unsure if that was his own body's reaction or one being forced on it, unsure what it was he needed to end exactly.

The falcon climbed higher into the storm. Another glance behind showed Iravan that the birds were still following. Lightning glimmered within the clouds—not the anomalous one of a skyrage, but pure, clean, *normal* bolts. The scent of electricity climbed up his nose. His fingers tingled as though sparking.

Then they flew clear of the storm.

An ocean of dark clouds swam underneath them, lightning captured within the waves of angry rain. Iravan turned his head forward again, and the sky cracked open, an unnatural slit within it, eyes forming like shards—and in the Etherium, the push of the cosmic creatures, stronger than ever before, snarling, ripping, screaming. It was the pressure not of merely one or two, but of a hundred, several hundred, *all* of those beings who had ever existed.

A deep horror grew within him. One cosmic creature could create an earthrage. What would *all* of them do if they were released?

The cosmic creatures are a hive mind, he heard himself tell Ahilya. Perhaps the webbing the falcon had created would have been enough to contain a few of them, but they knew how to weaken it—with simple strength in numbers. This was why the falcon had brought its own army. This, Iravan finally understood, was what it had been trying to tell him from the start in its own convoluted way. It had shown him the webbed trajectory back in the jungle to align their strengths, but Iravan had not learned quickly enough, and so the Resonance had tried to simply link with him and *take* his power. It was going to do so again.

Within the Deepness, the Resonance began to traject braids of radiance growing from the tips of its mercurial shape.

Iravan didn't wait. He didn't think, he didn't plan, he didn't pause.

Using the power of the Ecstatics, he trajected his own braid of links, spinning it around the falcon before it could hit him with its jet.

The falcon screeched, a blood-curdling sound, enraged and desperate, and its words poured into Iravan suddenly, *stop no weak break want kill become BECOME*, even as the Resonance and all the other yakshas tied to it ricocheted in the Deepness and bound themselves to Iravan.

Power unlike anything he'd ever known before filled him.

His back arched. His head snapped up to the skies. Blue-green light flooded his throat, his eyes, his body. Fire rushed through his veins as his breath turned molten. He thrust his arms out and light emerged from him, flooding the clouds in an unearthly radiance, a halo of brightness surrounding him and the yakshas.

The silence *screamed* with fury and terror in his mind, but for the first time Iravan had control of the falcon instead of the other way around. Under him, the bird grew frenzied, shaking, trying to buck Iravan off, but he held on, feeling its desperation, knowing it to be his own. *See*, he thought grimly. *I do learn.*

Alarm radiated off the Resonance, infecting the bound Ecstatics. Iravan released them, one by one, and they vanished from the Deepness.

He did not need their power anymore. Besides, he had sworn to protect them.

The Resonance jerked, trying to break free from his binding. The yaksha screamed, and the sky cracked open and more shards of lightning formed within the blueness. Iravan kept his mind focused; he could not let go now. There would be a reckoning later. The falcon would not forget.

But the skyrage was coming.

Converging the combined power of all the yakshas, Iravan started to build the webbing, one ray of light at a time.

34

AHILYA

On the Architects' Disc, Ahilya watched Chaiyya anxiously. The Senior Architect still glowed blue-green, vines climbing over her skin in radiant tattoos as she trajected the plants of Nakshar. White wood slithered across the floor and wrapped across the architects who had burned crimson. Chaiyya was examining them to see if the burning had damaged them. A memory flashed in Ahilya's mind, of Airav and Chaiyya under the same rudra tree, trying to heal Iravan after the terrible expedition where Oam had died.

The Senior Architect's eyes met Ahilya's. She shook her head slightly. "I don't see anything irregular with them. Nothing that separates them from any of the other architects assembled here. Why would the cosmic beings affect them alone?"

"I don't know..." Ahilya frowned. "Iravan said that the cosmic beings knew we were trying to stop the split from occurring. Perhaps it is these architects who would stop the split with their complete beings?"

"Or it could be the beginning of *every* architect being affected,"

Chaiyya said, her gaze fixed on all those who had healbranch growing on them.

"Either way, you have to remove them from the Disc. Naila told me there were others like these who had burned, who were being contained."

"Because I was studying them. I didn't imprison them."

"No, but you don't know what is happening to them." Ahilya dropped her voice further, just a murmur. "Whatever this is, Iravan likely knows more. Perhaps he can stop it. Perhaps it will help him learn about the cosmic creatures. You have to send these architects to Irshar."

Chaiyya drew herself up. "I won't send anyone who doesn't want to go least of all if they are not an Ecstatic."

"I won't ask you to. But Iravan has already asked for every architect to be tested. He has sent an open invitation. You will have to adhere to that."

"That is for Basav to decide," Chaiyya said. She tapped at her rudra bead bracelet, and Ahilya watched as a message hovered there next to Kiana's face. "You can make your case to him. Kiana says he has requested to speak with you at once."

Ahilya sighed. She had sent Dhruv to the Senior Architect, but it was too much to hope that she'd never have to deal with that odious man again. This was, after all, what it meant to be an emissary. The tribunal still did not know of the cosmic creatures. If Basav did not believe her now... Iravan had been ready to murder that man even before he had created Irshar. He would not be patient, no matter Ahilya's counsel.

"All right," she said wearily. "We best get it over with."

35

IRAVAN

The Etherium churned with the cosmic creatures.

Thousands of them pushed against the webbing. Remembering what the falcon had done, Iravan spun out hair-thin light in the Deepness, weaving strands of it in and out of each other. The power of the bound yakshas supplemented his own. The Resonance strained against him, attempting to break away, even as he used its Ecstasy. The silence reared in his mind, *destroy, break, escape, ESCAPE.* In his first vision, the face of the skyrage morphed, lightning already beginning to flash in the cloudless sky.

The trajection completed itself, and Iravan did what the falcon had shown him many times now. He shot the webbing out into the darkness of the Deepness, as far as it could go. He pushed all the power out, focusing—

The trajection unraveled. His webbing fell apart, individual tendrils of light winking out of the Deepness, the power within them dissipating.

Desperation clawed at Iravan.

He had copied the Resonance exactly. He had woven his light the same way it had done. He had thought he had enough power.

He tried to spin the webbing again, but in his first vision, the face of the skyrage grew larger. Lightning cracked close to Iravan, singeing the air. The falcon bucked, and Iravan lost his balance. He clutched at the bird, momentarily blinded. The Resonance strained against him, and Iravan's focus broke in the Deepness. His second web faltered.

The pause was all the cosmic beings needed.

A dozen bolts emerged from the clouds, heading toward Iravan and the yakshas. The rest of the birds scattered, but for a second, the falcon remained suspended within the cloudless sky, bolts dazzling in every direction, unnatural, aberrant. Iravan whimpered, eyes tightly shut, mind spinning, his head low over the yaksha's smoky feathers.

They would die here. He would never see Ahilya. *MOVE*, he shouted at the silence.

And the falcon obeyed.

Iravan's stomach dropped as the creature streaked through the unnatural lightning. He squinted his eyes open a fraction, and a jagged bolt crackled where they had been fluttering a moment ago. The falcon uttered a high-pitched yarp, and plunged through the bolts, twisting and turning, stopping only to change direction or retreat. Electricity chased them, and Iravan bent his head low until the falcon emerged through the clouds, regrouping with the other yakshas as the clouds recharged themselves.

Part of the webbing that had held them until now cracked.

Iravan watched the cosmic creatures push through, a wisp of air that became a claw, a hand pushing through the earth, a dying being trying to resurrect itself. His mind was forming these images, trying to interpret the abstract into something knowable, and in the silence the falcon murmured low and angry, seeing the same thing, sensing the urgency.

More hands appeared through the webbing around the cosmic creatures, decrepit forms pushing, pulsing.

Lightning flashed, too close, and charred air entered his nose, choking him. Something sizzled, burned wings, and one of the forms in the Deepness flickered before returning. Head low, he glanced back; the raven-shaped yaksha had barely missed being hit.

The skyrage was beginning.

A powerful ray of combined light in all the colours of the rainbow emerged from his dust mote and shot into the velvety dark of the Deepness, haphazardly aimed, arbitrarily fired.

In the Etherium, the cosmic beings paused, startled.

For a brief second, Iravan thought that it had worked, that he had somehow repaired the webbing, stemmed the skyrage.

Then the cosmic creatures roared in delight. A massive part of the webbing broke in the Etherium, unaffected by his trajectory.

Iravan's blood chilled. Horror seized him, his breath coming out in short bursting gasps.

He could see now that he would never learn to create the webbing in time. That he would never know where in the Deepness to shoot such an Ecstatic trajectory. It would not be enough—*he* would never be enough. In the Etherium, another image sharpened, and the Conclave broke apart between his brows as though in real time.

The cosmic beings roared again in delight, more webbing around them shattering. Dead arms emerged from the earth, up to the elbows. The storm of the last few days flickered—

and disappeared.

Terror consumed Iravan, as the cackle of the cosmic beings rang in his head. He watched as shoulders appeared, thin and scaly, smoke-like, pushing through the breach. Rain still pounded, but the skies had become sunny, instantly clear. Around him, the birds shrilled, agitated, a flurry of feathers and wings, high-pitched cries echoing through the air. Iravan had a single instant of warning, an image of all of the Conclave's architects burning crimson—

The cosmic creatures attacked.

36

AHILYA

"D o you know, Ahilya-ve, why architects outlawed Ecstasy?"

It was late afternoon, high in the skies. Ahilya had climbed down from the rudra tree, exhausted and weary, and made her way to Basav in the private alcove. She had thought that perhaps Dhruv had been unsuccessful in convincing him of Iravan's demands, but evidently the tribunal had accepted the release of sungineers instantly, almost submissively.

More surprisingly, it had accepted the testing of all architects, with the intention of turning them over to Iravan. The migration had already begun. Dhruv and Naila were overseeing it from Nakshar even now. Basav had acquiesced without a murmur, according to Kiana.

The Senior Architect leaned forward, his night-black skin ashen, the clothes hanging off his form loosely. Withdrawn and tired, he sat on a bone-white healbranch wheelchair, much like Airav's. He should have returned to Katresh, to get healing from his own core tree, but Basav had wanted to speak with Ahilya first. All of Nakshar's council now clustered in the tiny garden alcove at the base of the rudra tree, along with the four councilors of the Conclave's tribunal.

Ahilya studied the man from Katresh. It was absurd that Basav was questioning her on Ecstasy after she had fought so hard for it, when she was here as Iravan's emissary, and he had given in so easily to Irshar's demands. She noticed the respectful suffix he granted her, but after all that had occurred, Ahilya was no longer in the mood to play political games.

"I think," she said flatly, "it is you who does not know about Ecstasy, and it is my turn to educate you."

"You mean regarding the cosmic creatures?" Basav said dryly. "We call them the Virohi. Yes, we know about them. They're ancient knowledge that a select few architects are privy to, preserved and passed down only through whispers in the ear."

Ahilya's own shock was replicated on the faces of Airav and Chaiyya, on those of Garima and Jyothika and Dheeraj of the tribunal. They stared at Basav, their mouths hanging open, eyes wide.

"You knew about this?" Airav sputtered. "You knew and you kept it from all of us, for *generations*, you sent Ecstatics to their excision—" His voice cracked, fury swallowing the rest of his words. In all her time knowing the Senior Architect, Ahilya had never seen him so angry.

Basav's voice was contemptuous. "You were not told because you did not deserve to know. Now, with Iravan-ve taking over everything, the situation has changed, and we must adapt."

Ahilya ground her teeth. The man had known about the cosmic creatures, about the *Virohi* and their association with the Ecstatics. He had known it during all those generations of stepping on non-architects, during Iravan's trial, and during Nakshar's proposition when he had walked so callously into the deathmaze. Perhaps he had counted on being trajected, had intended to discredit and excise Iravan. The man caught her stare and shrugged. He *shrugged*, as though all of it had been a small price to pay.

"You bastard," Ahilya said softly.

Basav smiled thinly. He leaned back and interlaced his fingers.

"Ecstasy was outlawed," he said, answering his own question, "because architects from time immemorial understood the power of desire. When an architect becomes Ecstatic, a desire burns in them—a single desire fueling everything else, every waking and sleeping action."

Ahilya's fingers slowly released their tension. Iravan had said something similar once. He'd said Ecstasy changed an architect. She lifted her chin.

"A desire to make amends. I know this."

"No, Ahilya-ve. Not a desire to make *amends*. A single burning desire. A capital desire, as we have historically called it. What form that desire takes, that is up to the consciousness of the Ecstatic architect, dictated by a lifetime of choices. Perhaps for your husband, it culminated in wanting to make amends to the world."

"It is why he is building Irshar, why he wants to train the Ecstatics."

Basav nodded indulgently. "And in the fulfillment of that desire, he will break the world. He will not stop. As a near fully realized Ecstatic architect, Iravan-ve is not just powerful, he is *all*-powerful. But I suppose that is clear for anyone to see. Imagine a world of Ecstatics like that, each with their own singular capital desire guiding them. Imagine a world of superbeings intent on nothing but the fulfillment of their individual will."

Silence fell over the gathering.

Airav and Chaiyya exchanged a startled glance.

Ahilya's gaze narrowed. She did not have to imagine a world of superbeings. She had been aware of her own powerlessness since birth, seen the privilege of others closely.

"Do you see the problem?" Basav leaned forward again. "Iravan-ve wishes to train the Ecstatics, unite them with their yakshas, but the minute they unite, their own capital desires will become apparent. He will not be able to control them. Whether any of them intend it or not, they will become competitors to each other with their own agendas."

Who will this affect? Ahilya thought, remembering her own words to Iravan. *In your war with the architects and the Conclave, it is the non-architects who would suffer.*

Basav held her gaze. "Make no mistake, Ahilya-ve. Ecstasy is anti-civilization. Not anti *this* civilization, but anti *any* civilization. An Ecstatic architect who is united with their yaksha is at the end of their cycle of birth and rebirth. The only thing tethering them to the world is the fulfillment of their capital desire. They will do anything to make that happen, because for them it is not about a result or consequence. It is about fulfilling a need. Until it is fulfilled, the Ecstatic architect can never be free. And that freedom—in the end, that is the only thing an Ecstatic seeks. There was a time when Ecstasy was encouraged, and there were architects who united with their yakshas. They held simple capital desires, and they achieved that freedom easily. But there were others too, who in the pursuit of their capital desire wrought fire and pain. A great battle occurred. Humanity barely survived. It was then that Ecstasy was outlawed, that architects were taught to fear the jungle, that yakshas were forgotten. Because our culture learned. For an Ecstatic architect, the capital desire is a final roadblock, an ultimate obstacle in their path toward freedom."

"Iravan won't let such a battle occur," Ahilya countered. "He wants to teach the Ecstatics to *end* the earthrages. His own capital desire is to build a world which is freer, more equal."

"An easy conflation of ideas, but no." For once, Basav's contemptuous smile was gone. He looked deeply tired.

"You must understand something," he said. "Desire—even a capital desire—is not a clear-cut entity. By its nature, it grows seeds, it branches off into smaller desires. Yet for every branched desire that Iravan-ve now has, the world will remain hostage. His smaller desires will feed into the formation and nurturing of his capital desire. He will continue to chop away at the branches, even as he feeds and forms the roots. Sooner or later, he will determine an ultimate action, a capital *event*, one he will deem as the fulfillment of his capital desire. When he fulfills it, when he completes that action and wrenches the desire from its roots, the path to his own freedom will be clear. I believe the consequence for the rest of us, for survival and civilization through all this will be—"

"Devastating," Chaiyya breathed. The Senior Architect was shaking. Airav put an arm over her shoulders.

Basav nodded. "*That* is why material bonds were put into place. *That* is why Ecstasy was outlawed. *That* is why we excise Ecstatics."

Another long silence greeted his words. Ahilya glanced around her. Dheeraj of Reikshar held his head in his hands. Jyothika of the Southern Sisters was rubbing her sweaty palms over her clothes. Garima of Iravan's native ashram had covered her mouth with her fingers. And the councilors from Nakshar—Chaiyya was still trembling, Kiana frowned deeply, and Airav met Ahilya's gaze, his eyes heavy with worry.

Ahilya remained unimpressed.

Basav had spoken matter-of-factly, but why had Iravan not known this, even though he had trajected the green dust of pure possibilities for answers when they'd seen the carvings in the habitat? She watched them now, these people who were Iravan's friends, his teachers and mentors, his rivals and enemies. How quick they were to judge him. How soon they had decided he would choose the wrong path.

"You're saying Iravan is the enemy," she said coldly, turning back to Basav. "I will not believe it."

"I'm saying he is a threat. He has built Irshar, but that is only a small branch of his capital desire, and even that arrested our core trees, left us powerless, killed an architect. What happens when he finds the true shape of his capital desire, finds the one capital event that he will accept for himself as the ultimate action for the fulfillment of making amends?"

"He will save us."

"He will destroy us."

"No," Ahilya said. "He will not. You paint a drastic picture. You doubt Iravan's morality. But his morals are what truly define him. His integrity means everything to him. If he has decided his capital desire is to make amends, then he will *make amends*. You should be considering this an opportunity—finally, an all-powerful Ecstatic architect who wants to make civilization a beautiful, equal haven for everyone. Instead, you sit here condemning him."

"He has condemned himself," Basav began tiredly.

"Has he?" she snapped. "You mistreated him, humiliated him, trapped him, and punished him. If you had heard him with trust and respect right from the beginning, how different would our situation be now? You are willing to blame him for everything, but I do not see you taking any responsibility for what *you* did."

Basav stared at her, for once lost for words. His forehead creased.

Ahilya ran her scathing gaze over the rest of the assembled councilors, her voice shaking with fury. "All of you are to blame for this. So don't you dare sit here asking me to help you, asking me to *join* you, in accusing my husband. You have done nothing but push him toward this."

Basav stirred, but it was not he who spoke next. Airav's voice was hesitant, his tone laden with a quiet grief. "You're right, Ahilya-ve. You are right on every count."

"Then do what you should have done from the start. Treat with him in good faith. The acceptance of his demands is a good beginning, but if you truly want to protect civilization, then talk to him with that shared, common goal."

"I'm afraid it is not that easy," Basav said. "All of what you said would be the obvious path if we were dealing with a normal, rational person—but he is an Ecstatic architect at the end of his rebirth cycle, tethered only by his capital event. Perhaps if he were a simpler, less arrogant man, his capital event would be a more manageable thing. But do you think he will hand over control once his role in it is over? Or will he want to control it himself?"

Ahilya frowned. "What do you mean?"

Again, it was Airav who explained. "Letting civilization take its course, setting it on the path to freedom... these things can be recorded into events—things that we can all collectively point to and proclaim as a fulfillment of his amends. But it is not about any of these actions at all, Ahilya-ve. It is about what *he* thinks his mistakes are worth, what *he* must do to make amends."

Basav nodded. His gaze grew more considering as he studied Airav.

Airav's attention remained on Ahilya. "You are closest to him. Surely you must have an idea of how he would measure himself? How far he would go?"

She imagined it. A treaty between the ashrams that would end in peace. A life for all citizens here in the skies and perhaps in the jungle too, where everyone lived in harmony and perfect symbiosis. An ecosystem in precise balance where earthrages were controlled.

Would Iravan stop? Surely after Irshar, after training the Ecstatics… Yet the self-condemnation that had buried itself deep, the freedom he had always sought… Did she not fear these things she saw in him, too? He *had* killed Viana. Irshar, for all of its magnificence, had changed their culture irrevocably. She herself had been shocked by how he manipulated the core trees. She trusted Iravan; she *had to*, but she had altered his demands from the Conclave, even while acting as his emissary—*because* her trust could not be blind, not when it meant the future of all the ashrams. She had intended to balance him, because even before all this had begun, her husband had never done anything in half measures.

If Basav was right, and if hundreds of lifetimes of desire truly ruled Iravan's capital desire, then Iravan might never forgive himself the things he had done, both as Iravan and as the cosmic creature he had once been. He would determine the price of his failure, and it would be a personal war, encompassing his anger and pride, his shame and regret, his entire personality into one decisive action. He would almost be compelled, his capacity to do damage the greater threat than his intent.

She stood up. "If Iravan truly is the most dangerous variable in this equation, then he needs to know so he can determine his own part in this. So he can find a way to reconcile with his guilt instead of trying to atone for it. We need to help him through it, *heal* him."

She paused, frowning.

Noises wafted in from outside. They shouldn't have been able to hear anything, not with those silencing fronds covering the alcove. The others exchanged glances, and Ahilya moved forward and snatched the leafy curtain aside.

Chaos had overtaken the garden.

Shouts and screams echoed from different corners, and flashes of red flickered in the air.

The Maze Architects standing guard were on the ground in a fetal position, their dark skins riddled with crimson tattoos. Ahilya dropped to her knees, placing a hand to Geet's shoulder. They turned, their eyes bleeding. Appalled, Ahilya stumbled back, and someone gripped her arm.

The other councilors had followed her out. Chaiyya pulled Ahilya to her feet, but the Senior Architect was looking beyond her. Architects all over the garden were spasming, the tattoos on their skins crimson, citizens clustering around them in concern, trying to help. Ahilya glanced up at the rudra tree, saw the glimmering of the Architects' Disc flash red. Airav and Chaiyya hurried toward the rudra tree, leaving her behind.

Thunder rumbled long and harsh, and the rudra tree shook, dispersing leaves. Wind gusted through the garden. The roof opened, letting in the downpour, and Ahilya staggered, pushed back by the gale as all around her people screamed again, this time because of the surprising rain.

Then, without warning, the storm disappeared.

It didn't clear. It *disappeared*, as though it had never existed.

Ahilya straightened, her pulse rushing in her ears. She stared up, horrified.

Thunderclouds vanished. Rains still fell, slicking down the back of her neck, but blue, blue sky looked down at her, the first she had seen in days, filling her with dread. Lightning struck, once, twice, thrice.

"What—" Basav began, but his words became a shriek as the floor under them cracked open.

Ahilya staggered back, pulling the Senior Architect's wheelchair with her. All over the courtyard, massive gaping holes were opening into nothingness, reminding her eerily of the time Iravan had threatened her and Dhruv in the solar lab. Screams grew, and she watched people scramble back in terror even as the impossible rain drenched them. At the center, the rudra tree stretched, its leaves vibrating in the gale.

Nakshar's architecture transformed.

Walls broke down in a clatter of dust and roots. Coughing, Ahilya squinted to see dozens of viney bridges form directly toward Irshar, rapid constructions of wood and roots. With no more boundary walls, the mountain appeared clearly, a massive split down its front. Far more bridges than the ones that had opened for the migration now connected Irshar to the ashrams, a dozen levels of them dangling across the sky.

Basav clutched her arm. His skin glowed blue-green though no tattoos had yet formed. "What is going on? The Moment—it thrums."

"He wants everyone in Irshar. Not just the architects and sungineers he's invited. Everyone."

"*Why?*"

Lightning cracked again, this time farther away, as though aiming for something else. Ahilya received a vivid image of Iravan flying through a storm of electric bolts. *Another one is imminent*, he said. *It's not going to be like the last time. That was a rehearsal.*

"A skyrage," she said, surprised at how calm she sounded. "Irshar must be the only safe place now. He's offering refuge to the Conclave."

The Senior Architect's eyes grew wide. "Then we must mobilize all the citizens toward it." He skimmed forward on his wheelchair, a determined look on his face, and Ahilya followed, waving people through the destruction toward the bridges.

37

IRAVAN

The power of Ecstasy surged through Iravan, breathless, intoxicating. Bound to him against its will, the falcon-yaksha cried out in terror and fury. In the Deepness, it struggled against his linking, but Iravan held on. All of the yakshas' combined power flowed through him now, and he strengthened his own jet of light, redirecting it to the Moment and the constellation lines he had built there to sustain the new form of the Conclave.

Words echoed in his mind, constant, horrifying. The falcon whispered, *release, kill, free, want*, as the words converted into Iravan's own lexicon, strung together in sentences, *I have waited, I will take you, I will remove you, you are me, you are mine, you infant, you no one, you nothing, release me, free me, take me, end me*, until he was unsure if it was he or the falcon who thought them.

Through the crackling sky, he guided the falcon's flight with a squeeze of his knees, with a tug on its feathers, with their connection in the silence and the Deepness. Sweat and rain soaked him— then lightning sizzled by Iravan's shoulder, crashed behind him, morphed into a fearsome air tornado.

The shockwave was too much. His Two Visions nearly collapsed and he held on with the force of habit. The yaksha balked, the scent of char in the air, and Iravan was grateful for its distraction. He knew that if he lost control now, the falcon would subsume him completely.

Holding onto the Resonance, he directed all their combined power into the Moment toward the core trees, forcing the ashrams to stay their construction. Around him, bolts crashed angrily. Rain whipped his body, piercing his feather cloak. Steam and smoke burned in a clear sky, and Iravan's stomach twisted as the yaksha wove past another slew of bolts.

Surrounded by the other birds, the falcon flew lower. The Conclave grew clearer in his first vision. Dozens of bridges materialized from each ashram toward Irshar, and tiny forms of people stampeded toward the diamond-shaped mountain. Iravan had a second's thought to wonder how those bridges had formed, he had only asked for the construction to be safe—

Lightning struck again, and he ducked. He forced the falcon to fly lower, and it resisted, *stop, release, fly, end, I will kill you, I will end you—*

"Do as I fucking say!" Iravan screamed, and the falcon screamed back in fury and obedience.

It circled lower, evading the bolts. More of the Conclave's architecture changed.

Bridges strengthened as Iravan poured Ecstatic energy into the Moment. From this vantage point the entire construction was contracting slowly, becoming one with Irshar. He was not building the bridges, not actively, nor was he contracting the Conclave to merge with his own city, but a corner of his mind registered this was the same trajection as had happened in Irshar before—something between an idea and an action, tied to his intent without his active command. Irshar was likely the only place that was safe.

He pressed his eyes shut as another jagged bolt fell too close. The falcon wove around it, and Iravan squinted his eyes open just in time to see another bolt smash into one of the bridges. Wood popped and cracked, catching fire. Bodies hurled out into the open sky, burning.

No, Iravan thought, aghast, and the ashrams responded to his anguish. Immediately, plants swelling with rainwater grew around the fires, smothering the flames. Fires were doused all over the bridges as the construction reknit, and people scrambled, still heading toward Irshar.

In the Etherium, the cosmic creatures paused.

He saw another image of the architects on their knees, writhing, their tattoos crimson and burned.

The image transformed. The burning architects rose to their feet. Iravan watched the cosmic creatures surge into the architects, their dying hands gripping the humans—a construct of his mind, but nevertheless true. The burning architects trajected, but it was not trajection, it was a mutilation of the power, and sharp thorny weeds grew around them, attacking the citizens. The cosmic creatures were taking control of the architects, using the architects' trajection. His own words to Ahilya resounded in his ears. *They are evolving. The architects are in danger.*

No, Iravan thought desperately, *break you, end you, years, years I have waited*—

In the Etherium, the cosmic creatures laughed again.

Iravan realized this had been their plan all along. With the Moment weakened, with the architects vulnerable, the cosmic creatures could manipulate the architects directly. Iravan had aided that plan by changing the permissions of the core trees. He had moved architects to the lowermost priority, elevating the non-architects, but that had only made the architects vulnerable, taken the protection that the core trees would have provided against the cosmic creatures. It opened them up to infiltration. He watched the Etherium in horror as more men and women burned, attacking the citizens and destroying the architecture. Lightning struck and the falcon spun once more, evading it. Iravan screamed.

Still tied to the Resonance, he flung himself into the Moment. The universe *thrummed*, and dust motes of architects flickered, but Iravan pulled the architects to him, and thrust them through the Conduit into the Deepness, the same thing the Resonance had done to him in Nakshar's temple so long ago. He knew the cosmic creatures could not affect the Deepness, but in the Moment, the architects were vulnerable.

His distraction cost him.

The Conclave broke, dropped altitude too quickly, falling instead of descending.

Cries echoed up to Iravan even as lightning crashed over and over again, and the falcon swerved. In his mind, Iravan heard it growing louder, matching the power of his own thought, frightened and furious, *Wake you, break you, no more, no more—*

More people ran toward Irshar, some glowing blue-green, others red, even as holes opened up. The bridges lurched, their altitude dropping too swiftly as the ashrams responded to Iravan's panicky desire instead of his controlled trajectory.

Frantic, Iravan halted the Conclave's hurtle, controlled his Ecstatic trajectory—but the cosmic creatures infiltrated more architects in the thrumming Moment. He tried to yank the architects through the Conduit into the Deepness, but the Conclave plummeted, unrestrained. He forced the falcon to obey and spin past the lightning even as it tried to break apart, but it raged in his head, *free you, stop you, unmake you—*

It was too much. It was too fast, too continuous.

He could not fight the battle on three fronts. It was only a matter of time before one of those bolts hit him, before his own desire was mutilated, and then it would all be over. He would have to make a choice—save the architects against the cosmic creatures or save the civilians from the architects.

Iravan froze, paralyzed by indecision.

38

AHILYA

Nakshar shattered.

Ahilya saw whole chunks of the ashram break apart, people stagger, bodies tumble into the open air. Architects flickered blue-green then red, their eyes turning crimson. Bloody trajection tattoos climbed up their arms, necks, and cheeks, like hideous creepers. The soil fragmented where they trajected. Under a thin veneer of calm, Ahilya observed all this, her sorrow and fear buried deep.

Her gaze caught on Basav, his face sooty and grim, his wheelchair right next to her. She and the Senior Architect waited on a patch of steady ground, surrounded by three Maze Architects, Ridhhi, Karn, and Gaurav.

They had gathered this contingent to accompany them through various floors. Their mission was simple—to escort frightened citizens across the bridges that had sprung up around Nakshar. Ahilya had already deployed as many architects of Nakshar as she could to perform the same duty through the disintegrating ashram.

In her sinking heart, she knew this was a flawed strategy.

Any one of those Maze Architects was likely to turn crimson

and attack the people they were escorting. She could already see flares of red on the bridges, more gaps opening, bodies falling. Somewhere a fire burned, smoke curling, too thick to be put out by the constant downpour. She glimpsed sungineers banded together, throwing down strange devices to trap the burned ones, and for a second her heart seized. Where was Dhruv? Where was Naila? Were they all right?

She had done this. She had returned trajection to the architects after Iravan had taken it away. If she had not meddled with the rudra tree, then perhaps the architects—despite their burning—would not have been able to traject to *harm* the ashrams. She should have understood what the signs in the Architects' Disc meant. She should have calculated the risk. The terrain heaved then steadied again.

Basav asked her, "Are you ready?"

Ahilya gritted her teeth and nodded. She and Basav had noticed something on their third round of rescuing civilians. The ground beneath Ahilya's feet did not pitch. Every step she had taken was on steady terrain. It was clearly because of her own priority level to the core trees of the Conclave, but just as the architects could now traject, Ahilya controlled some part of Nakshar's stability.

They began to descend back to the ashram away from the bridges, Basav careful to slide his wheelchair where Ahilya stepped. Nakshar tilted. A rooftop section fractured amid screams, Maze Architects glowing blue-green, bark expanding into shields, while they snatched citizens away from the fissure using vines.

She started toward them, but Basav gripped her arm. "We have our own task."

She shook him off, but he was right. They had already divided the ashram into zones. She had to sweep her floor methodically before moving on. She signaled to the accompanying Maze Architects and they trajected. Thick twirling vines grew from the ground, pushing aside debris, clearing the path amid the torn bushes.

The group followed a pattern with Ahilya in the lead. It progressed a few steps, searching carefully, and moved on again, floor by massive floor. It was slow grim work, and all thought fled her each time the architects upturned another boulder, discovered another body. She dreaded finding Tariya or Arth or Kush, injured or worse. Iravan had changed the permissions of the core trees to protect non-architects first, but there was only so much that the rudra could do when crimson architects were deliberately attacking everyone. Deep within Ahilya, a slow horror was building—this was the end of Nakshar, of all the ashrams, the number of bodies they had found far outnumbered the survivors—but she kept moving. *The next floor*, she told herself. *I'll find Tariya in the next one, and she and the boys will be safe.*

She brushed wet hair and tears out of her eyes and rounded a corner around broken earth, only to bump into Airav on his wheelchair, accompanied by Chaiyya and Megha.

"Ahilya," Chaiyya gasped. "We heard you were here."

"Oh thank goodness," Ahilya said at the same time. Gaurav abandoned his position and leapt toward Megha to embrace her. Lightning cracked and all of them winced, shading their faces, as the ground wobbled again, the wind keening across the splintered ashram.

"We're rescuing the citizens," Ahilya said, before the others could speak, her eyes still shaded. "The earth stabilizes under me."

"We are too," Chaiyya said, on the heels of Ahilya's news. "We've finished this floor, but we haven't seen Lavanya or—"

The Senior Architect stopped. Her blue-green trajection tattoos sputtered.

Ahilya recoiled, and the others did too, tense; they had seen this happen right before an architect turned crimson. But then Chaiyya started screaming, her body bent on itself, her head in her hands. The sound sent a chill down Ahilya's spine. She stumbled back.

Airav leaned forward, horrified. "It's not the red tattoos—not the burning—but I've seen this. A few of us unable to traject, but still glowing. It's—"

"Ecstasy," Ahilya finished. She knew the signs. Chaiyya's skin still sparkled blue-green though there were no tattoos anymore. The Senior Architect had likely found the Deepness. In her second vision, she was perhaps tumbling through infinite velvety darkness, lost and alone. What had brought this on so suddenly? But they had no time to wonder. Not right now.

"I'm taking her to Irshar," Airav said, gripping Chaiyya's arm as she continued to scream. Rain slashed down, and lightning reflected in his glasses. Ahilya coughed, the smog-filled wind choking her.

"You'll need help," Basav was saying. "I will accompany you. And Ahilya, you should come with us."

"No," she said, at the same time as Airav. In her mind's eye, she saw Tariya and the boys again, cowering behind a rock, hiding behind the next bush, buried under debris waiting for help. It was the only thing that kept her going. She would not abandon them. Not again.

Airav shook his head too and tears glinted in his eyes. "Our families," he said, when Basav opened his mouth to argue. "Ahilya, please. My husband and my children—and Chaiyya's family, Lavanya and the twins and the older boys. We haven't seen them. Please."

"I'll find them," she said. Chaiyya's screams had subsided into whimpers. The Senior Architect shuddered, her mouth covered by her fingers, tears still streaming down her cheeks.

Airav took a quivering breath. "Thank you. I'll return here after I get Chaiyya across."

"You must stay in Irshar," she said before he could complete his thought. "Both you and Basav. You can't traject, Airav, you won't be any help here, and Nakshar's citizens in Irshar are likely terrified. They'll need a councilor to calm them down. When all this ends, Nakshar will need you. I haven't seen Kiana yet."

"You can't do this alone."

"I'm not alone, and we don't have time to argue." Ahilya took in Basav with her scrutiny. "You are all liabilities right now. If the Maze Architects are wreaking so much havoc, what do you think will happen if a Senior Architect's tattoos turn red? We can't take unnecessary risks. This could be worse than untrained Ecstasy."

The two Senior Architects exchanged a glance. She saw them think the same thing. For the first time, each of them was as dangerous as an Ecstatic architect, their power likely to turn devastating in an instant. Beyond, a dozen more Maze Architects turned red. A fiery bridge dangled, and civilians fled, trying to escape the double onslaught. Tariya. Was she safe? Was she already in Irshar? Surely the permissions that Iravan had created to prioritize citizens had saved her. Tariya had to be safe. She had to.

"You know I'm right," Ahilya said, her fists tightening.

Rain poured down from clear skies, and Senior Architect Basav nodded curtly, his gaze on the same broken bridge Ahilya had been watching.

"We'll see you in Irshar," Airav complied. The two men aligned their wheelchairs across the mud to better support a whimpering Chaiyya between them, helping her along as they skimmed carefully over the debris.

Ahilya turned away from them and faced the others. "Right," she said, keeping the quaver from her voice. "Maze Architects. You're with me."

39

IRAVAN

Forgive me, Iravan thought, *end this, break this, no more, no more—* Tears streamed down his face, mingling with the unnatural rain. The weight in his heart became heavier. A great distance built in him. He felt cold, defeated, tired. Iravan pushed his Ecstatic energy into the Moment. His first vision filled with smoke and blood. He spun through the lightning bolts, the falcon and the other birds weaving and swirling through steam and smoke. How many people had already died? There would be no redemption for him.

He had thought there had been a choice, but he didn't have enough time to release all the Maze Architects into the Deepness. He couldn't stem the cosmic creatures by recreating the webbing. He didn't *know* how to create the webbing, and the only way to do it would be to release the Resonance, when the yaksha would lash out and take him over permanently this time.

There was only one battle he could win. He started to land the Conclave—aimed for the habitat—hoping it would be enough. Despair built in him even as he trajected.

This was his fault. He should have done this from the very start, as soon as he'd arrived in Nakshar. He should have found a way to permanently end the rages and the cosmic creatures, before he had attempted anything else. The hatred for them grew in his mind, and the Resonance shimmered, pushing against its restraint. The falcon said, *break you, take you*, and Iravan swallowed the thickness in his throat.

The cosmic creatures broke through the webbing, free entirely.

Around Iravan, the air transformed into a massive whirlpool, a tornado of terror and dust, rippling in every direction.

Rain fell down his cheeks, salty, and men and women flickered red, as the cosmic creatures took over their bodies and minds, forcing them to attack the ashrams and citizens they were sworn to protect.

This truly was the end. The skyrage would grow to epic proportions, worse than it was now, worse than ever before. It would take an army of Ecstatics and complete beings to trap all the escaped cosmic creatures. It would take another millennium. They were entering an era of neverending earthrages, and there would be no safety except the habitat, and the habitat itself—

Iravan blinked back tears, still directing his ray of Ecstatic light into the Moment. He could not think of the futility of the habitat now. It was all he could do to land the Conclave in the jungle. In the Etherium, the rudra tree cracked, smoke emerging from it, as it fought with its last breath. Iravan felt the core trees extend themselves from the Moment, trying to bear the weight of the Conclave's safety.

The Resonance smashed against him, trying to separate. *I will end you*, Iravan thought. It was a cold thought. It was *his* thought. They could not continue like this.

In response, the Resonance did something, and the power of his Ecstasy dropped. The light from his jet lessened. In his first vision, the other yakshas scattered, their giant forms flying in different directions through the clear storm. Iravan spun in his second vision, to see them leave the velvety darkness of the Deepness. His chest tightened in fear. Where had they gone? Were they going to attack him? He had taken over their leader, the falcon; perhaps they were going to mount a defense. The Resonance had unlinked them, that was why his power had dropped. Had it figured out how to unlink itself too?

In his first vision, the Conclave plummeted, smoke swirling. The jungle became visible.

Iravan gritted his teeth, bent low over the falcon, and shot out all his power to control the hurtle of the Conclave.

40

AHILYA

"Ready?" Ahilya asked.

The short-haired man nodded nervously, clutching his taller husband and their little baby. Screams echoed all around them, but Ahilya locked away her own terror and focused on the family in front of her.

"Hold hands," she said. "Step where I step."

The father obeyed, and his trembling fingers clasped Ahilya. She blinked the rain out of her eyes and nodded to the Maze Architects around her, Aditi and Bhavna and Sanjay, architects she had not known the names of until a few minutes ago. They were all bloody, mud-streaked and soaked, same as she was. Their trajection tattoos still glowed blue-green, the colour so comforting that Ahilya nearly cried in relief.

Her hand tightened around the citizen. She and the Maze Architects moved as a unit through the debris toward a bridge. Red flashed around them, but Ahilya kept her focus and her desire strong—to get this next batch of citizens across to Irshar.

She had escorted at least fifty citizens so far toward the bridges, accompanied by her contingent of Maze Architects. Somewhere she had lost Gaurav, Megha, and the others, and they had been replaced with these men and women. She'd started with five, but Jaya had fallen, her eyes glassy when Rana's tattoos had turned crimson and he'd attacked them all. Ahilya and the others had barely escaped.

It'll be all right, she thought dully, the same litany she had been repeating in her mind. *It'll be over soon*. She had to believe that.

The earth rumbled and another breach opened up by her toes. The man behind her gasped, but Ahilya held his hand tightly, shifted her stance, scrambled away from the chasm toward where the earth was still solid. A bridge swayed less than ten feet away. Somehow, the Conclave had begun merging with Irshar, as though all the ashrams were being folded into Iravan's own. This group of citizens had been cowering among fallen rocks, unsure of movement, but escape was close now, the bridge filled to the brim with rushing people, and she picked up her pace.

Next to her, Sanjay shuddered. Their mouth fell open and their eyes grew wide. Their trajection tattoos blinked blue-green then red.

"*Run!*" Ahilya screamed at once, and then she was pulling the family behind her. The other Maze Architects were already trajecting to bind Sanjay up in vines, but Ahilya saw the architect burn crimson, saw a feral look on their face, saw the vines around them break and splinter as they fought off the Maze Architects easily.

Ahilya ran past the fighting architects and leapt over exploding earth, pulling the family of citizens along with her. Close by, a fire singed the air and fumes filled her mouth. She choked, but by instinct she thrust the citizens toward where the bridge still held.

"*Run!*" she screamed again, and then they were sprinting, joining the rush toward Irshar.

Across the other bridges, Ahilya caught a glimpse of other familiar shapes, Laksiya and Kiana, leading citizens toward Irshar. She spun back toward Nakshar. She had lost her group of Maze Architects, but the rudra tree was visible once again. It trembled uncontrollably as though at the limits of its own power, a fire snaking up one of its branches.

Frantically, Ahilya searched for other Maze Architects in the crowd. There were many more citizens hidden among the rubble. Perhaps the next time she'd find Tariya and the boys. She could not rescue them all alone. She needed architects to protect her from their own kind.

A green uniform flashed, and Ahilya whirled, looking for the Junior Architect. Her hand reached out to grab a shoulder.

"You," she gasped and the Junior Architect stumbled into her as the earth roiled again.

Beyond, more people screamed and the ashram shuddered. Ahilya felt the breath knocked out of her, and then she was screaming too—*trying* to scream. Her belly swooped, and wind rushed in her hair, pulling it upward and she tottered against the Junior Architect even as her ears rang and her knees felt the force of gravity.

This had happened a couple of times but only for seconds. This— whatever this was—this plunge—

This wasn't just the Conclave wobbling, trying to sustain itself in the air.

They were landing. Nakshar was descending, too fast, too dangerously. She saw the mountain on Irshar shake, then the stampede toward it began anew, citizens frantically trying to clear the bridges as the same realization undoubtedly hit them.

"We have to help them," Ahilya shouted at the Junior Architect, her eyes watering, her belly still squirming. "I need your help!"

The frightened architect nodded, and belatedly Ahilya registered they were so young, barely out of adolescence. Nakshar plummeted again, and she thought once more of Naila. Where was she? Was she all right?

"Come with me," she managed to yell, but the Junior Architect in front of her blazed crimson, blue-green, then crimson again.

Ahilya reeled back, the soil underneath her firming. Wood burned, flesh burned, and she gagged, her scream half formed, her frightened look still on the architect whose skin had turned red. The Junior Architect gazed at her with their unearthly light, and vines grew toward Ahilya, sharp and thorny, ready to pierce her. She moved back by instinct, horrified.

But her feet found no purchase, scrabbling over nothingness. Her arms flailed, eyes widening. She lurched, the crimson architect filling her vision.

Ahilya fell into the storm.

41

IRAVAN

The Conclave plunged too swiftly, too dangerously.

Iravan chased it on the falcon, rain beating him down, lightning hunting him. Bound to him, the falcon's constant muttering filled his mind, *kill, rage, die, DIE,* but Iravan ignored it.

All his attention was on the Conclave. In his first vision, he saw the bridges pull the ashrams closer to Irshar, saw the mountain in the center expand, growing taller as it amalgamated one ashram after another into its fold.

In the Etherium, the cosmic creatures roared, even as more and more architects turned crimson, attacking the architecture. A massive chunk separated from the mountain and fell into the earthrage. Iravan saw bodies hurtle in the air, panicked action in their limbs. In his mind, Oam flipped end to end, and tears rushed down his face. *I'm sorry*, he thought, *I will kill you, I will take you.*

The earthrage ballooned, gigantic swirls of dust rising from the jungle. The mountain of Irshar wobbled. All the ashrams were enclosed within it now, the bridges all but disappeared, and Iravan and the falcon dove lower, splitting their ray of Ecstatic trajection toward the jungle. Branches whipped at him. Grit filled his mouth and eyes. He was out of reach of the lightning as he entered the forest of breaking wood, but the earthrage was fiercer than he had left it. Iravan and the falcon wove in and out of branches and giant dust balloons, keeping Irshar in their sight as it plunged toward the habitat.

Iravan's Ecstatic trajectory transformed, and the mountain of Irshar changed. Its diamond shape sharpened, becoming more pinpointed, and it plummeted through the jungle, a gigantic structure containing the entire Conclave, cutting across dust and mounds of earth like a comet, slicing through flying debris and ricocheting boulders.

He followed in its wake, leaning close to the falcon, mud swirling in the wind through his hair and eyes, even as he trajected the mountain toward the habitat with the last of his energy. The cosmic creatures shrieked and Iravan glanced behind, seeing their face in the earthrage, a hundred shards of branches like jagged teeth, bark ripping like flayed skin, darkness tearing like dead eyes.

Just as suddenly, the face was gone.

Iravan flew into everdust, the glittering green dust of the habitat, and underneath him Irshar landed with a terrifying, echoing sound. It ripped the soil of the courtyard, its pinpointed base smashing into the earth so it stood like a giant rocky diamond, balanced on its tip.

The falcon circled lower, round and round the gigantic diamond-shaped mountain. Inside, citizens, architects, and sungineers of every ashram were undoubtedly injured. For all Iravan knew, the burned architects were destroying the architecture of the habitat even now.

His hands shook as he directed the falcon toward the courtyard. Relief, terror, and homesickness throbbed in him. He was here. He had brought them all to his habitat like he had wanted to ever since he'd left. They had survived, but they had lost. After everything they had endured for so many years, they had lost. *He* had lost.

Iravan climbed off the yaksha as the bird landed. At once, the falcon took to the air again screaming to get away from him. In the Deepness, the Resonance throbbed, attempting to break through his linking. It shrieked at him, *Ruin, break, take you, wake you.* A part of the link frayed, and the Resonance exulted. All around Iravan, the green dust of pure possibility coalesced, surrounding Irshar.

He glimpsed the cosmic creatures again in his first vision, pushing against the barrier of everdust, attempting to break into the habitat. They were pacing outside, testing the limits of the everdust, pushing and pushing. Sooner or later, they would break through.

Another image sharpened in his Etherium, his fathers with their arms around his mother, the three of them holding each other close. Had they survived? Were they alive? Iravan clenched his fists, staring at the mountain of Irshar that loomed in front of him, the last sanctuary of the sister ashrams. Wind ruffled his hair, the everdust swirling.

Iravan braced his dying power in the Deepness and entered his ashram.

42

AHILYA

The storm surrounded Ahilya.

She flipped through the air head over heels, over and over again, wind rushing through her, nausea climbing, belly roiling. Her eyes darted everywhere, and the Conclave shifted in and out: lightning, other bodies, boulders, crimson light.

Something reached for her. A vine tightened around her waist.

She gasped, not understanding, but even as the vine coiled around her, buds grew from it, spreading over her like a nest. The buds grew harder, turned into bark. Out of the corner of her panicked eyes, she saw the same thing happen to the other bodies that had tumbled out with her.

Ahilya's breath came in quick gasps. For a disorienting second, she thought of Oam and herself and Iravan back in the earthrage, wearing the magnaroot armor, shooting back toward Nakshar. The wood around her hardened, and she smelt the sharp scent of the rudra tree. Bark cocooned her, and Ahilya's body curled in on itself. Her arms rose over her head, her knees pulled up to her chest. She felt herself being heaved up.

Ahilya closed her eyes, lulled by the movement. In her mind, she saw herself a child again. She and Dhruv had once been caught in the foliage between rock and bark when the ashram had landed. His words came back to her when she'd left Nakshar to go find Iravan a few months ago. *You protected me because I was yours to protect.* What had happened to them? He barely spoke to her anymore. Tears streamed down, and she huddled within the armour, shaking. Where were Tariya and the boys? Had Naila survived? Was Iravan all right?

She could see nothing out of her cocoon, there were no eye slits—but something shuddered and trembled outside, and her belly swooped in the familiar sensation of landing. Ahilya gritted her teeth and tried to curl further, but she couldn't move her arms and legs anymore. She couldn't even move her neck. A whistling wind came to her, the rustle of leaves in a hurricane, audible past the armor.

Then everything juddered, and her bones shook painfully. A roaring filled her ears, blood rushing to her head, and her insides vibrated.

Everything came to a sudden rest.

Ahilya felt it in the unfurling of the armor as though the wood had completed its final task. The vine around her waist withered away. Light glimmered from between sharp-pointed leaves, and she stared. She was in a tree—within the *rudra* tree. Somehow it had grabbed her mid-air, pulled her up to it. For a few minutes, she could do little else except spit dust and earth into her palms, and swallow in turn to control the ringing in her ears.

Then another sound came to her through the rustling. Whimpers. Crying.

She was not alone. The rudra tree had saved others too. Ahilya clutched the closest branch next to her, and arose on shaky feet.

In response to her desire to descend, a narrow ramp grew by her feet. Ahilya brushed the dirt off her clothes, wiped the blood off her mouth, and hobbled slowly down the incline. Other slopes circled the vast tree, shapes and shadows moving as people climbed down, but Ahilya met no one else.

She emerged into green light.

It took a long second for her eyes to adjust.

She was in the habitat. How? Iravan must have done it. She stumbled forward, waving her hand to dispel the dust.

Behind her, the rudra tree loomed, more people emerging from it looking dazed and shocked, all of them non-architects. The tree shrank, even as Ahilya watched. It was like seeing a tall man crumple. Branches withered away. Vines and creepers crumbled into ashes. Leaves darkened, brown and sickly, and the tree grew smaller, the ramps visible around its thin trunk.

Dazed, Ahilya turned away to the scene in front of her.

She was in a courtyard. It looked remarkably like Irshar, the tall thin trees forming a perimeter—but no, those were not plants, it was more of the habitat's strange dust. It swirled and pooled into familiar shapes, its construction weaving in and out, so she was unsure if she was really seeing anything at all, or if her mind was playing tricks on her.

Hundreds of people lay on the floor, some of them sitting, some kneeling, all of them weeping either in relief or terror. Others like her stood, their eyes roving as they looked for their friends. This was what was left of the Conclave, then? Grief bound her chest tight. In her archeological mind, Ahilya remembered the pictures in historical records, of humanity's rise into the air, the first ascension of the ashrams when architects had discovered flight to escape from just such a devastation. Tariya and the boys haunted her mind: where they were, if they were here, if they were safe.

Slowly she wove her way across the crowd to search for them. The courtyard extended for miles in either direction, filled with people.

She floundered past a weeping family clustered around a young Maze Architect. More architects littered the ground, uniforms ranging between green and gray. All appeared unconscious, with citizens leaning over them, trying to rouse them. A tall shape caught Ahilya's eye in the distance, and she hurried over to the man in a long coat, pushing his spectacles back up his nose.

"Ahilya," Dhruv said dully, looking up as she approached him. His voice trembled. She had never seen him so lost. Sweat covered his brow, and behind cracked spectacles, the sungineer's eyes were wide. He had never wanted to be in the jungle, but surely he understood as well as she did where they were.

Then the shape he was leaning over grew clearer, and Ahilya forgot about Dhruv.

"Naila," she gasped, falling to her knees, pushing Dhruv's hand away to check the Maze Architect's pulse.

"She's alive," he said. "We were fighting some of those red architects, but then everything fell apart. I can't revive her."

"Did she burn too?" Ahilya asked, her throat tightening. She cradled Naila closer, pushing the hair out of the Maze Architect's face.

"No. Her tattoos remained normal. But it's *all* the architects, they dropped the minute we landed, and—"

Dhruv broke off and stared beyond Ahilya. She turned and followed his line of sight. There, walking slowly among the citizens, his hands clenching and unclenching by his sides, was her husband.

Iravan looked as though he'd fought the storm itself. His entire body shook as his vacant gaze roved over the crying people. His shoulders were hunched, and he looked ready to fall on his feet. His sleeves were rolled back as always, and blue-green tattoos still covered his dusty arms, but they appeared weak, the vines thinner, the shade lighter. The feather cloak over his shoulders was scorched and burned. Not even after news of Bharavi's Ecstasy had Iravan looked so defeated.

She was not aware that she was on her feet until Iravan's head snapped toward her. His eyes grew wider. He waved a limp hand, and then he was hurrying toward her and Dhruv, weaving past the dust and the scores of people clustered together.

Iravan reached Ahilya and pulled her to him. His grip was weak, and through his kurta, she felt his shallow breath.

"Your parents," she said softly. "I haven't seen them yet."

"They're by Yeikshar's asoka tree," he replied, and his voice shook. "The mountain, this courtyard. It extends far into the habitat. Ahilya, someone saw Tariya and the boys. They're closer to the heart of Irshar. They are unhurt."

Relief so strong washed over Ahilya that she swayed. Iravan took a shuddering breath, and leaned his forehead against hers, closing his eyes. His hands trembled around her waist.

"What's going to happen to them?" Dhruv asked, interrupting "To her?"

Iravan's face changed. He bent to his knees to check Naila's pulse, but there was no relief on his features. Sorrow, wariness, and unease flashed across him in quick succession. Iravan brushed a trembling hand over his face, shaking his head.

"What?" Dhruv asked, his voice alarmed. "What does *that* mean?"

Iravan said nothing, but she understood the look. Whatever had happened to Naila and all the other architects had shaken him too much to speak. This nightmare was far from over.

Iravan shook his head again.

"Let's talk," she said quietly, pulling her husband aside.

43

IRAVAN

She led him away through the rising green everdust, past weeping citizens and unconscious architects. Iravan followed like a child, his hand in hers, aware only of each step that he placed in front of another. In the back of his mind, the silence had returned. He saw the shrieking falcon fly low over the raging jungle. The Resonance squirmed and fluttered in the Deepness, as another part of the link binding them frayed. The urgency built in Iravan to drop his Two Visions and retreat from the Deepness before the Resonance broke free completely, but he was still trajecting the diamond of Irshar into something more stable before the cosmic creatures broke through the defense of the green dust.

Every step so far had been a disaster. He couldn't be in the Deepness when the Resonance was free. The Resonance would subsume him this time. Perhaps he could never return to the Deepness at all. What had he done? Yet, it didn't matter anymore. The cosmic creatures pushed against the habitat, trying to force themselves in, reminding him of how little anything had mattered over the last few months.

Ahilya stopped by Nakshar's rudra tree. Iravan let her pull him down to sit by her. Glittering green everdust swirled around them, alive and conscious, but she didn't seem to notice. She traced the everchanging blue-green tattoos on Iravan's dark skin, on his arms and neck and cheek, and her brows furrowed. The tattoos were too complex. Her light fingers couldn't keep up. Her touch raised goosebumps on his skin. Iravan gently covered her hands with his. She took a deep breath and rested her head on his shoulder.

It was so like her, he thought with a twisted smile. She had been hurt too, but her attention was on him. How much love did she have for him? How much of it did he deserve? He'd told her what he had done with Viana, but what if she had seen the brutality of it? This moment of stolen peace—he could feel its fragility, its lie. A great sadness grew in Iravan. Tears burned the back of his eyes. He thought of Ahilya as she had been in Irshar, distraught after the loss of their child. *I couldn't give you what you wanted*, he thought. *And that will be my greatest regret. Regret, REGRET*, the falcon echoed, blasting in his mind.

Iravan took Ahilya's hand in his own. He turned it over to see the cuts sealing, the injuries healing. Blood dried and flaked off, and the skin had already reknit itself. The habitat had restored her, just as it had him. But there were others to whom the habitat would not respond so easily. *Break them, wake them*, the falcon said. Iravan trajected Ecstatically and thought, *Heal them*, and the green dust of possibility within the habitat obeyed him.

It swirled and coalesced into smaller swarms, a hundred, then a thousand clouds of light. Each tiny ball of glittering green light flew toward a prostrate form on the ground, toward a weeping civilian or an injured architect.

Iravan and Ahilya watched from under the rudra tree as people started, mouths dropping open. Murmurs filled the courtyard among the weeping, as each ball of green dust settled, planted itself in an approximation of healbranch. The familiarity of the plant, of its intention, seemed to calm the citizens. Something like comfort and relief filled their eyes. Iravan had commanded the everdust to do much the same in the other parts of Irshar he had walked through. It had transformed into mediweed in Yeikshar, amelaus in Kinshar, yararoot within Katresh.

He had asked for healing, but it was a scratch on the surface. They'd have to rebuild from the beginning. Iravan gripped Ahilya closer, nausea rising in him. Irshar alone had been monstrous to think about as a functioning society, but this? This confluence of all the ashrams together? Was rebuilding even a possibility? They only had minutes until the habitat collapsed. Maybe a few hours, if they were lucky. The cosmic creatures pushed at the walls, the earthrage furious and devastating. In the silence, the falcon cried out, circling the jungle, even as the Resonance flapped against the link in the Deepness. Some more of the link frayed.

Iravan sat up. There was no more time.

"Did the everdust respond to you?" he asked.

"Are you doing this?" Ahilya said at the same time.

They both nodded slowly, warily.

"I don't know," Ahilya said. "About the everdust, I mean."

"Try," he urged. "Try now. Give it a command."

Ahilya bit her lip and extended a hand to the dust around them. Her face grew intent, and then the green dust turned, converting into a small jasmine. She glanced at Iravan and nodded.

Relief weakened Iravan. He took a deep shuddering breath and closed his eyes in a long blink.

Ahilya watched him, frowning. "What does it mean?"

"Pure possibility. It has become a part of us. Of you and me."

"Because we were the first ones here in the habitat after so many years?"

Iravan shook his head. "Because of what we did here together when we trapped the cosmic being in the Moment. The entrapment was an explosion of our desire. Mine with my trajection, and yours with clear, uncontaminated desire. We somehow *trained* the habitat's everdust. What we did—it was unlike anything the habitat had seen in a long time."

Ahilya shifted her weight, and glanced back toward the people. Several were on their feet, slowly moving through the crowd, calling out names, hugging each other as they saw familiar faces. But no one was in charge yet. This would devolve into chaos soon enough as citizens demanded answers. They would turn to her as a councilor. They would turn *on* her. Iravan watched her, willing her to understand what he was saying. The green dust would hold against the cosmic creatures, but not for long. Not without Ahilya's help. Iravan had lived here for two months, called it his home, but the everdust had only responded to him in half-measures. He needed her.

"The everdust responded to me before we trapped the cosmic creature, though," she said. "Back when I came looking for you from Nakshar after the falcon had taken you away... It brought me to you. It listened to me, it *understood* me, like it was sentient and intelligent, and I was something to be learned."

"It *is* sentient," he said. "Everdust is an artifact from the time the rebels created this habitat. That group of architects and complete beings, you remember?"

"I remember. There were more habitats like this where now only one remains."

"Yes. These habitats were created for a single purpose. To respond to the combined desires of Ecstatic architects and complete beings. When you and I discovered this place, the everdust reacted to both of us, but it was as though we had guest privileges. It didn't let us do everything we wanted to do. It didn't let us leave the habitat, and while it protected us by healing our injuries, it did not obey us. But when we ended the earthrage—when we trapped that cosmic creature—we... *conditioned* the dust to respond to the both of us. To *only* the both of us. It recognized us as residents of this habitat as though we were one of its original creators. It's as though ancient protocols and permissions kicked in. You and I, we own this place, my love. It will never be anyone else's as much as it is ours. The dust will obey us."

Ahilya was silent for a long instant. The Resonance struggled and another part of the link between it and Iravan broke away. He rested his head back against the tree trunk, trying to control his breathing as he approached something close to panic. *Be calm*, he told himself. *Be methodical. You need to do this right.*

You need to break, the falcon said. *I will take you, wake you, make you*

His breathing grew rapid despite his control. Shallow panicked gasps escaped him. He felt the cosmic creatures' assault again outside the habitat. Not long now. But she had to understand. Once the falcon unlinked itself, he would be vulnerable in the Deepness. The dust would respond only to her. He'd be more helpless than he had ever been.

"It sounds like the way the core trees were designed," Ahilya said quietly. "The way the ashram would respond to the desire of anyone with a rudra bead because the tree was coded for its residents."

Iravan opened his eyes.

A swell of surprise and admiration filled him. How had she made the connection? Then again, she was a councilor and an archeologist. She was *Ahilya*—beautiful, brilliant, amazing Ahilya. Pain lanced through him as he considered her. She deserved so much more.

"It's *exactly* like the core trees," he said. "Whatever technology was used to create everdust, I think the same was used for the core trees, or at least something similar. As far as I can tell, flight happened around the same time as these habitats were created. Technology must have grown in similar directions even if the rebels were separated from the ashrams. Regardless, this dust was once in plenty, that's why there are—there *were*—stars everywhere in the Moment belonging to everdust."

"But?" she asked, clearly sensing his hesitation.

"But it is depleting," Iravan said grimly. "Once everdust is fully gone, the earthrage outside will have no barrier." He brushed a trembling hand across his face. There was already barely a barrier. The survivors were in a siege that would only end in their destruction. The others just didn't know it yet.

Was that what he'd done? Saved them only to destroy them? Iravan was under no illusions. His parents, Tariya and the boys, Naila and Dhruv and people he had cared about or needed in some capacity had not survived because of arbitrary coincidence. They had survived because of his latent desire to protect them, first and foremost— because the core trees had *recognized* that desire, and he had changed the permissions of the core trees to obey him and Ahilya.

How many others had died? How many more would die before this was over? Had any of the higher bands of ashrams survived at all? It was impossible. Not with architects attacking people, breaking the structures they were supposed to build. Whoever was left within the habitat… these were the last of the human race. The thought was so horrifying that Iravan gagged on his own tongue. He had been a Senior Architect once; his duty had been to protect *all* the citizens of his ashram at any cost. What had he become now? This was not a battle he would win.

Ahilya had raised her eyebrows. "How do you know all this?"

"I asked the everdust. And in doing so, I depleted it."

It had taken irreversible mistakes to learn all of this. The blade of possibility pulsed against his throat, reminding him of the danger of using the green dust frivolously. He remembered how his skin had lit up, how his three visions had merged, how the deathcages had shattered. He had thought the green dust of possibility endless. In the last two months, he had asked it innumerable questions about himself and the falcon, about his past lives, about Ecstasy and his path forward, about the cosmic creatures. He had tried to learn, but he hadn't realized what he had been doing. By the time he'd found out, it was already too late.

"Can we recreate everdust?" Ahilya asked.

"When I asked, the dust indicated it rebuilds itself when parts became a whole again."

"Like you and the falcon?"

"That's my understanding, yes." But Iravan was not sure. There was more there, something he had missed, a question he had not asked and clarified. Besides, there were no clear answers with everdust, only interpretations, just like the carvings he and Ahilya had seen together.

In the Deepness, the Resonance fluttered farther away as some more of the link frayed and ripped. It was going to happen. He could not rebind it. Iravan straightened, preparing to unlink the Resonance and drop his Two Visions.

Ahilya stood up and began pacing, her movements agitated as she grasped the gravity of their situation. "So. We need everdust because otherwise the habitat will fail and the earthrage will consume us. We need the unified power of an Ecstatic and a yaksha to rebuild everdust. But we don't know exactly how to rebuild it, or if that unification will work at all, and we can't ask everdust because we might end up depleting it when we can't afford to, and anyway, we don't have the time to sit around interpreting its cryptic clues." She paused and looked at him. "You are an Ecstatic, and I am a complete being. What if we ended the earthrage like we did before? That would take away the problem altogether. We could rebuild the green dust later, when the urgency is over."

"It won't work. We're not just dealing with one cosmic being anymore. There are hundreds. Thousands. This attack is from every single one of those creatures who ever existed."

Iravan pushed his sleeves back and stood up.

His voice was dull as he told Ahilya of how the Moment had been infiltrated by the cosmic creatures, of the Resonance and the subsummation it would unleash onto him if he lingered in the Deepness, of the bestial creatures hunting and waiting outside, circling the habitat trying to enter in at this instant.

Ahilya's eyes grew wide. Her fingers covered her open mouth, and she shook her head over and over again, her horror growing with his every word.

"You and I cannot put an end to so many," Iravan said. "We cannot trap them all in the Moment. Even trapping one nearly killed us both, and this—" Overwhelming shame filled him. His fingers curled into a fist and he slammed his hand against the rudra tree. "This is my fault," he grated, staring at the glittering green floor.

Ahilya lifted his chin so his eyes met hers. "Don't be foolish."

But Iravan shook his head. She didn't know. None of them did. He had pieced it together himself only in the last few minutes.

That first skyrage was not the first time the falcon had created its webbing to stop the cosmic creatures. It had done so for thousands of years. *That* was how it had known to do it at all; but doing so had only resulted in longer earthrages, growing through time, because the cosmic beings had not been allowed to split. Each time the webbing had broken, a lull finally had occurred, and the cosmic creature had birthed itself into an architect and a yaksha—but then the cycle began again, of another cosmic creature beginning to split, of the yaksha creating more webbing, of longer earthrages and delayed lulls, until finally the cosmic creature broke through the falcon's trap to birth again. The falcon could never trap the creatures in the Moment by itself, and the cosmic beings had learned of the webbing and how to break through it. The falcon's last few efforts had been short-lived. The yaksha had needed help—from Iravan, and the other yakshas—but it was a futile effort with the cosmic creatures becoming stronger. With them evolving.

And now, because Iravan had failed to learn the webbing by ignoring the greater threat of the cosmic creatures, the sister ashrams had been brought to their own destruction. He would never be able to make amends. The desire chafed at him, deep beneath his bones. Revulsion filled him for all his lost promises, for all his broken words.

"This is not the time to place blame," Ahilya said, forcing him to meet her gaze. "We need to focus and plan. Can we fly again? Is that possible?" She tapped at the rudra tree's trunk, but Iravan shook his head.

"The skyrage is still out there, much worse than ever before. It might never truly end. The core trees have rooted." Iravan could feel it, a relaxation and a burden shrugged by the core trees as though putting down a weight of centuries. He had seen it in Katresh's neem as he had passed it; he had seen it in Reikshar's bael. He took hold of Ahilya's fingers with his own cold hands.

"Ahilya," he said, quiet grief in his voice. "I think we are all that's left of humanity. There is no way that the other bands will survive the endless skyrage happening with the release of so many creatures. If they haven't already fallen to their deaths, it is only a matter of time. It could be happening even now." Tears leaked out of his eyes. "Ahilya. We will never fly again."

Shock plastered her face. Sudden tears welled in her eyes and began spilling down her cheeks. Iravan did not try to brush them away. They had spoken about the end of their civilization throughout the last few weeks. They had both even desired life in the jungle, but this realization, this irreversibility of circumstance...

There would be no more flight or escape from any future rages. There would be no more Conclaves, or trade, or views of freedom floating over the earth. Iravan had destroyed their thousand-year history in a blink. The loss of the other ashrams, those that had not belonged to the Conclave or Nakshar's sisters... Each time he tried to contemplate it, his mind gibbered. He could not even begin to imagine the magnitude of it. He had only saved a few. He had saved so few.

To her credit, Ahilya said nothing. She wiped away her tears with her knuckles and nodded once, her lips trembling. Iravan wiped his own away, tried to steady himself.

"They're breaking through now," he said in a low voice. "The cosmic creatures. Whoever created the habitat ensured that the earthrages wouldn't be able to enter. That's why the architects are now all comatose. They are liabilities in the Moment, easy vessels for the cosmic creatures to manipulate. The habitat is keeping the cosmic creatures out for now, but this place was weak even when we found it. It's only a matter of time before the creatures rupture it. Before they take over the architects again."

A breach opened in the defense of the habitat even as Iravan said these words. He saw it happen in the Etherium, saw the cosmic creatures make to enter, snarling, rasping—a second's lapse, then the breach closed. Sweat broke out over his forehead.

"There's only one thing we can do," he said, his words coming faster now. "What I should have done from the start. I must train the Ecstatics somehow, force them to unite with their yakshas.

I take the four from Irshar to find their counterparts—we do it now, immediately, and maybe that will rebuild the everdust."

He knew the impossibility of this strategy, the miniscule chances of success. He could barely function in the Deepness anymore, not with the Resonance almost free. He would have to guide the four Ecstatics theoretically, or risk the falcon subsuming him.

Besides, he had not seen any corporeal yakshas for months. The only hope was that the four Ecstatics had non-corporeal yakshas, but how would they ever find those when they barely understood the Deepness? In his heart, Iravan knew he had already lost. By the time he did this, the cosmic creatures would have ravished the habitat. This was why he needed Ahilya. To protect the habitat with her desire while he did what he could.

But she was shaking her head, agitated.

Ahilya began to pace back and forth, muttering, "*No, no, no*. This can't be it. Iravan, you can't train the Ecstatics now. They cannot unite, not now, not like this."

"Why not? That had been our plan from the beginning. The one thing we agreed on."

She came closer, fear clouding her eyes. "I've learned something since then," she began, her hands clutching his sleeves, and this time it was Iravan who listened as she told him what Basav had told her, about an Ecstatic's capital desire, about their endless power, the end of their rebirth, the freedom they sought, and the capital event standing in their way.

Against his wont, Iravan stiffened as she told him about the cosmic creatures.

Virohi.

He tasted the word, as the anger that was always so close to the surface rose in him. His vision blurred and he was only aware of the blood pounding in his eyes. One part of the anger was his own, cold, calculating, surprised. That bastard Basav had known all of this. He had forced Iravan and the falcon to react during the trial. He had stepped into the deathmaze deliberately.

But another part of the anger was the falcon's. A fury so harsh filled Iravan that for a second the Resonance stopped struggling. He felt the falcon's attention in the silence, as it watched him, still circling the jungle. The anger united them, and Iravan gritted his teeth. He should have let the falcon traject Basav into obedience. He should have attempted to destroy the cosmic creatures—the Virohi—when he'd had the chance. Iravan thought, *When did I have that chance?* Memory was murky, flitting from life to life, his own past merging with the falcon's. He swallowed, trying to understand his own self.

Ahilya watched him, her face withdrawn. "You can't train the Ecstatics now. We might never survive this, not if their capital desire is something else entirely. We don't know anything about the four Ecstatics. We don't understand their motivation or their fears or their history. What if they turn on you and the habitat after their union? What if they traject everdust into something else instead of safety for all of us? It's too dangerous."

"Then what do you suggest we do?" he asked, though he knew the answer. He had known it all along—he had feared it. This was why he had wanted to abandon the Deepness.

"What *can* we do?" Ahilya asked, rubbing at her eyes in desperation.

"There's only one option," he said. His voice was emotionless, dull. Gigantic wings flapped as the falcon read his intention, as it returned toward the habitat. The Resonance stilled, wary, watching him.

"I find the falcon," Iravan said. "I find a way to link it to me forever. I learn from its memories, everything it knows about Ecstasy, everything it knows about the Virohi, all the ways to block them forever, and I force them back into a webbing just like it once did. I use the other Ecstatics and I delay the rages—indefinitely if I have to."

Terror and inevitability grew in him, like a war he knew he'd always have to fight. *What have you lost?* Bharavi asked in his mind, and sudden anguish filled him, leaving his knees trembling. *I miss you, Bha*, Iravan thought, his throat choking. *I've failed you.* And she whispered, *I know you're tired. What have you lost?*

Ahilya was staring at him. "Iravan, you just said if you're in the Deepness any longer, the falcon will subsume you. That you chose to land the Conclave instead of rebuilding the webbing because you didn't know *how* to create the webbing. How do you expect to learn now when your last attempt failed? When the falcon will undoubtedly fight you?"

"What else is my choice, Ahilya? You said I will have a capital desire, a capital event—well, this is it, this is what I want. This has been my task, to stop the cosmic creatures—the Virohi—somehow."

"I don't think that's how it works. You can't just pick your capital event on a whim."

"You said I had to choose it, that Basav said I would determine it."

"I don't think he meant it like that," Ahilya said, shaking her head vehemently. "It's a choice, yes, but there is an inevitability to it. You choose your capital event, but it is an ultimate action rooted within lifetimes of desire in the depths of your consciousness. We need to find Basav, ask him to explain."

"We don't have the time. He's probably unconscious like the other architects."

"We have time to train the Ecstatics but not to speak to Basav? Don't be ridiculous."

"Ahilya," Iravan said quietly, taking a step toward her, but she shook her head and backed away, terror growing on her face, denying him what he needed to do, denying his intention.

He followed, enclosing her in an embrace. She struggled but he held on tighter until she relented. Her body trembled and her arms encircled his waist. He breathed her in, and he felt her desperation, her helplessness even as she shook her head over and over again.

"With training the Ecstatics, I intended to leave the Deepness forever," he said softly. "But if I can no longer do that, I need to act now, before the Resonance unlinks itself completely and takes me over."

"It can still take you over," she said, her voice muffled against his chest. Iravan felt her tears dampen his kurta. "You might not win this."

"That is a risk worth taking."

"Iravan, please."

"Ahilya, there is no more time."

She shifted, and her face lifted. Tiny teardrops glistened in the corner of her eyes. "I'm coming with you, then."

"You can't. You're the only other person the habitat responds to. You have to protect the others. Shield them. If I'm successful, things will have to be rebuilt."

"And if you're not?"

Iravan shrugged. If he was unsuccessful, he would be gone. The falcon would subsume him. A great terror grew in him, a yawning emptiness making his heart pound—but that terror was edged with a wondering relief. To be no more... Was that not freedom too? He would fight the yaksha—he had to, for himself and Ahilya, and for the rest of the world. If the falcon subsumed him, there was no telling what it would do to the survivors of humanity.

Yet the alternative... To be subsumed himself. To be erased. That did not sound so terrible. That sounded like rest. He was so desperately tired now.

Ahilya trembled in his arms. They knew he was going to his demise, but was Ahilya's own situation any different? If he failed, she would die too, slowly, and more painfully than he could imagine, the cosmic creatures eroding everything.

That, more than his own end, frightened him. That was why he had to try and win. He pressed her closer, unwilling to let go. There was so much still that they had to do together. So much they hadn't said. How had they come to this? How had it happened so quickly? The falcon raced back toward the habitat, and the Resonance thrashed again, breaking another thread of Iravan's link, and he thought of the seven months when he had kept away from Ahilya. He had been such a fool. He had been *such* a fool.

He stirred, and Ahilya pulled apart, perhaps knowing the moment was here. He wanted her to ask him to stay, to not leave, to tell him that if this was the end, they would face it together. He wanted her to promise him that he would return, to tell him that *he*—the way he was now, this version of him—*this* was what she wanted back. But her eyes were dry now, a determined look on her face.

She didn't say any of the words he wanted to hear so desperately. She didn't ask him to return safely, to fight with desire, to not give in. She merely kissed him, her lips just a brush against his own. Both of them knew that the words and the instruction were unnecessary. It would only highlight their loss, lay it naked and acknowledged, too much to bear right now, opening the wound to bleed freely. He touched her hair with a light hand, and stepped away.

Ahilya stepped back too and nodded slowly, like she understood. She swallowed once, her fingers twitching restlessly, the only sign of how much pain she was in, how much she was trying to control. Her gaze met his unflinchingly, giving him strength.

"All right," she said quietly. "What do you need me to do?"

44

AHILYA

Iravan had walked away from the rudra tree; he had walked away from her, *again*, and this time she had let him. She had *sent* him to his death. Hot tears clogged her throat, making it difficult to breathe or swallow. Ahilya nursed her grief like a precious thing. Green everdust swirled and collected around her in a hazy swarm before rushing past her to obey her furious command.

His shoulders had been bowed under his smoky feather cloak, his fists clenched hard by his sides, his face to the ground, defeated and lost. What would happen to him? Would he return? In what manner? Grief turned into a hot anger, but it was not anger at him, or at herself. It blazed at the circumstance, at the need to be strong. She could barely understand how their lives had come here to this instant, but she had agreed to his plan. It was the *only* plan that would work. She thought to the everdust, *Keep him safe*, knowing her wish was for possibility itself, a thought that would drive her to hysteria if she gave it too much weight.

The everdust swept past her in a low wave, knee high. From a lifetime ago, she heard Airav say, *Don't tell it what you need it to* do. *Say what* you *want, and the design will fulfill it in its own best manner.* Ahilya rolled her shoulders back and stood up straighter. She had her own fight coming. *Lead them all to safety*, she thought grimly. *But do not deplete yourself.*

The dust transformed into flickering vines and flowery stems. People gasped and pointed, but they had been brought up to trust moving architecture, and this was familiar. Even as Ahilya watched from under the rudra tree, they obeyed the everdust, slowly shuffling forward. Stretchers, litters, and wheelchairs materialized as the green dust coalesced, and unconscious architects levitated forward within the crowd as though carried by some sorcery.

Ahilya moved from under the rudra tree and joined the press of muttering people. She did not know where the dust was taking them. Iravan had said that Irshar extended for miles now, a gigantic city, with the survivors from every sister ashram within it. But if she had formed her desire right, then all the citizens were likely moving deeper into the mountain toward Irshar's heart. Was someone managing the crowd in Irshar? She had sent Airav and Basav there, but perhaps they were unconscious too. It could be chaos inside.

Someone stepped beside her, and Ahilya looked up to Dhruv keeping pace easily. His eyes behind cracked glasses were narrow and he held Naila in his arms, although everdust swirled and pooled around him, intent on helping him carry her. If the situation weren't so grave, Ahilya would have laughed out loud, but she could still remember her own panic on first encountering the green dust. It had shimmered and changed, contradicting her senses. She had not trusted it—and, it appeared, neither did Dhruv. In his arms, Naila breathed erratically, her eyes moving behind closed lids.

Dhruv followed her gaze, and the expression on his face changed slightly to fear and concern. "What did he say? What is going to happen now? To her and all of us? What is happening here? What *is* all this?"

Vaguely, Ahilya thought of how once Dhruv had shown *her* the consideration he was showing Naila. They had left that behind now—a lifetime of friendship washed away because of one poor decision. How much could she tell him now?

"They'll wake soon," she said. "All the architects."

That would be a sign, Iravan had said. The architects had been hit worse than the civilians in some ways, their bodies desecrated and invaded, their trajectory mutilated. All of them had been knocked out because of their connection in the Moment, but the unburned ones—those who, like Naila, had not turned crimson—would likely wake first, and that itself would be an indication the Virohi had broken through the habitat's first level of defense. Ahilya glanced at Naila, motionless in Dhruv's arms. Her heart ached to see the Maze Architect so defenseless and small, but for now, it was best she was still comatose.

The landscape changed.

Green everdust was still everywhere, a shade of leaf, a blink of wood, but amid the haze a massive courtyard appeared, wide and strong.

Irshar.

Despite the destruction of all the ashrams, the central courtyard within Irshar had retained its shape, with trees interspersed and the grass lush and soft beneath Ahilya's feet. If it weren't for the swirling dust and the thousands of citizens milling everywhere, frightened and wary, Ahilya would have thought they were still in the skies. *But there's no going back now.* Her heart sank and shuddered, shying away from the enormity of the event. She could not comprehend it, not right now.

A few more steps in, and several people moved through the crowd, urging others into lines and pressing everyone to continue moving forward. Someone had organized the survivors. Ahilya rose on her toes to see, but Dhruv was much taller. He cleared his throat.

"Pranav and Trisha are at the front of two of these lines," he said softly. "The Ecstatics from Nakshar—from *Irshar*—they seem to be ushering people in, taking names. They must have been organizing refugees within Irshar."

Form a defense in Irshar, Ahilya thought to the everdust. *Once everyone is inside, close the mountain and strengthen yourself into a shield.*

The green dust shimmered. More of it dissipated from the courtyard, and floated past her back the way they had come. Some of it flew higher, and people pointed and murmured even as they moved forward in their lines. Cradled in Dhruv's arms, Naila remained comatose, but her eyes flickered faster. She was waking.

Ahilya's heart grew cold. If Naila was regaining consciousness, then the Virohi had come one step closer to entering the habitat. Suddenly frantic, she thought of whether she should break the line, push past these people to find who was in charge. But even as she thought it, the everdust responded to her panic, and the dust whooshed around them, became pinpointed as though to jab the citizens out of her way, and she thought, *No, don't do that!*

The dust settled again. It had happened too fast for anyone to notice, and Ahilya took a deep breath, wiping her sweaty palms on her clothes, willing herself to be patient. She moved forward one step at a time, following the people in front of her.

It seemed to take forever.

By the time they arrived at the head of their own line, Naila's eyes had blinked open though she still looked dazed. The Maze

Architect stirred in Dhruv's arms, and he muttered, shifting his weight. Ahilya stumbled into the person in front in her haste.

Then *they* were the ones heading up the line, and she recognized a familiar face triaging the survivors.

"Ahilya-ve," Umang said as he saw her. Relief grew on his features. She could hardly believe that the last time she had seen him, they had all been in Nakshar. He had been protesting the treatment of the citizens. He had been trying to popularize the idea of living in the jungle. Umang looked as tired as she felt now, sweat beading his brow, his forehead furrowed.

"Your sister passed through a while ago," he said, and his voice trembled. "I sent her to one of the highest homes. She didn't want to go, wanting to stay and search for you, but I was told you were alive. I said I'd send you to her. Ahilya-ve, my family—I haven't seen them yet. I don't—I can't—I'm doing—"

"Umang," Ahilya said, grasping his arm and stopping him. He seemed close to tears, at the edge of his tether, only working by automation. She knew the feeling. How much horror had he seen already? How many people had he helped during the Conclave's terrible landing? He looked more childlike than she had seen before, just a boy, brave and powerless. Oam flashed in Ahilya's head. They would be the same age. So young, still.

"Listen to me, Umang," she said slowly, carefully. "Is someone organizing all this? You need to take me to them, all right? This is important."

Umang paused, staring at her uncomprehendingly.

Then he nodded, and called out. Another young woman took his place, and he led Ahilya and Dhruv through clustering people beyond the courtyard, down a narrow garden path.

The weeping cut out. Above her, canopy waved in and out, green dust dancing. They hurried along the path. Naila stirred, murmuring, and Ahilya's heart skipped another beat. She picked up her pace, nearly running, and Umang hastened too. Dhruv called out, asking to slow down, but Ahilya ignored him, terror giving her speed.

They emerged into a quadrangle with gnarled trees standing like pillars all around. The courtyard was filled with Maze Architects, all of them stirring and sitting up, looking dazed. Ahilya's heartbeat quickened. She hurried behind Umang toward the gigantic tree in the center. Out of the corner of her eye, she glimpsed Dhruv setting Naila down and placing an arm around her waist. The two of them staggered forward—Ahilya wanted to pause and ask Naila if she was fine—but terror chased every other thought from her mind, and she pushed past stirring architects to the tree.

Airav sat there on his wheelchair, Chaiyya next to him on a bark stool. Other sungineer councilors sat on similar stools, speaking commands to messengers, gathering reports, flipping through papers that looked like names of the survivors. The Conclave's assembly—whatever was left of it—was working hard, but it would all be meaningless if Ahilya did not do her own duty.

Airav looked up at her as she approached. Chaiyya's skin had turned dark again—clearly, she had found her way out of the Deepness—but the woman looked like she had seen the face of death. Ahilya gestured to them, and Airav skimmed his wheelchair away from the gathered councilors toward a more private corner, Chaiyya following him numbly.

"What is going on?" he said as soon as they had gathered. "Is this the habitat? This green dust—Ahilya, only the Ecstatics and non-architects were conscious a moment ago, though more are waking now. What—"

"I need to spread word," Ahilya interrupted, her voice soft.

More and more architects around them were reviving. For a second, she considered asking the green dust to separate the citizens from the architects, but was that even possible? She had no idea how Airav and the others had organized the refugees—the *refugees*, that was what all of them were now, refugees from the sky—and for all she knew, Airav had sent families to be together. That was what she would have done in such a time of crisis. Besides, trying to separate the architects from the citizens would only deplete the dust. Ahilya had deliberately kept her commands simple so far.

"I need citizens," she continued. "Not architects, but complete beings. Anyone willing to volunteer."

Her gaze met every one of theirs: from Umang's terrified stare to Dhruv's wary one, from Airav frowning on his wheelchair to a still-numb Chaiyya. As quickly as she could, Ahilya appraised them of the situation, of her command of everdust and the infiltration of the cosmic beings. Fear grew on their faces, the same fear that had embedded itself within her.

"I need to keep the shield up, the dust strong," she ended. "This is our last stand against the Virohi."

"You're readying for battle," Dhruv said, his brows furrowed.

"Yes."

"And Iravan?" Airav asked.

Ahilya closed her eyes briefly. "He's already fighting."

Was he? How would she know if he was succeeding? There was no way to tell.

Ahilya shook herself. She needed to focus. "The Virohi are coming. I asked the dust to form a barrier at the entrance of Irshar. I'm going there so I can see its defense and change it should the need arise, but I cannot stop the Virohi alone."

"You think the non-architects can help?" Umang asked, pushing his hair out of his eyes.

"Non-architects are complete beings," Ahilya said. "They're unbroken by the split of a cosmic creature. The last time I held back a Virohi it ripped through me, but it could not bypass me. If the everdust fails, then the citizens will be the only defense against the Virohi, and I need beings of pure, unadulterated desire to hold hundreds of Virohi back. Enough to give Iravan the time he needs to repair the webbing through Ecstasy."

"Y-you're asking the citizens to protect *us*," Chaiyya said, her voice trembling.

"Yes." Ahilya met her eyes. "Volunteers only. They will be told what they're up against. It will be painful. They may not make it out alive. We don't have trajection, but we have our unsplit consciousnesses."

There was a silence.

Airav appeared close to tears, and Chaiyya swallowed convulsively, the only two Senior Architects among them, helpless now, liabilities for the first time in their lives.

Airav gestured to someone, another messenger, and issued quiet instructions. The young person nodded and disappeared to spread the word.

"Send the volunteers outside," Ahilya said. "I'll ask the dust to light the path toward me." She turned away, preparing to return to the edge of Irshar, but someone grabbed her arm and she glanced back to see Chaiyya.

"I'm coming with you," the Senior Architect said. Her skin had begun glowing again, and for a brief terrifying second, Ahilya thought she had entered the Moment—open and vulnerable to the Virohi—but only Chaiyya glowed in the courtyard; none of the other architects had recovered. "If this is Ecstasy," Chaiyya continued, lifting her arms limply, "then it could be helpful."

"You don't know how to use Ecstasy," Ahilya began. "Can you even summon the Moment from the Deepness?"

"No. But I wasn't knocked out when we entered the habitat like the other architects, and the other Ecstatics of Irshar weren't either. It must mean *something*. You could use us. Use *them*."

"You are, all of you, untrained Ecstatics. You're still a danger yourself. If you lose control of your Ecstasy—"

"Ahilya, please. You don't know what you're up against—not fully—and you might need help, *some* architectural help, even if it is to build and direct this everdust. Let me come."

Ahilya opened her mouth to refuse, then paused. She had been so preoccupied with the events of the last few hours that she hadn't realized that she'd been performing the duties of an *architect*, in asking everdust to build a shield and a barrier. What did she know of construction? Perhaps with Chaiyya's advice, she could fortify the shield somehow. They might not need to use the citizens at all. She nodded, and a relieved look crossed Chaiyya's face, a look that was only too familiar—to not be powerless, to finally be of some use.

"I'm—too," another voice whispered, this one barely audible.

They all turned toward Dhruv, but it was Naila who had spoken. The Maze Architect still leaned heavily on Dhruv, her face wan. She tried to push herself up, but staggered and flopped against the sungineer, though her listless eyes remained on Ahilya.

Ahilya moved to gently cup her face. "You can't. You are vulnerable in the Moment. You've done enough."

"Not enough," Naila whispered. "Earthrages. Our fault. Architects' fault." She took a breath, tried to push against Dhruv again, before collapsing once more. "Can—indicate burning—inside—"

Ahilya's eyes widened as she understood. Dhruv inhaled sharply, and Airav and Chaiyya exchanged a wary look.

"She's not wrong," Umang said. Some of his fear seemed to have left him, replaced by determination now that they were all here at the precipice of their purpose together. The others nodded too, even Dhruv whose eyes had grown considering.

Still, Ahilya hesitated. It was not just concern for Naila that tinted her reluctance, but the Maze Architect's connection to the Moment. Chaiyya had found the Deepness somehow, she was immune, but Naila would become a weapon for the Virohi. *She* would burn red, her tattoos mutilating, as the cosmic creatures took over her body and mind. She would end up attacking the citizens Ahilya had asked to volunteer as shields.

But already the architects around them were waking. Each one of them could become a living weapon, and once outside Irshar Ahilya would have no idea it was happening, let alone how to stop it. With a single Maze Architect accompanying her, Ahilya would at least be able to tell when the cosmic creatures made their move. Naila would go down first, before any of the others inside Irshar, and the few seconds of delay could mean the difference between destruction and being able to protect everyone.

Naila would be bait. For all Ahilya knew, several Virohi could penetrate Naila simultaneously. The effects of that—

A deep sadness filled Ahilya and tears burned her eyes. "Are you sure?" she asked.

Naila nodded, a jerky movement. "Dhruv—will—"

"Take her out," he completed. "If she starts to burn. And yes, this means I'm coming too."

Ahilya glanced at them, this group they had made, sungineer, architects, archeologist, civilian—all of them citizens. They gazed back, terrified, grim, resolute. None of them knew what they were up against—Ahilya barely did, *Iravan* barely did—but in the end, here they were, standing with her to protect those they loved. Gratitude, awe, and admiration filled Ahilya. After all their differences and all their arguments, after all the machinations and subterfuge, she could hardly believe that she was here leading them in this battle, that they had come together somehow, that they were *united*. She could not fail.

"Very well," she said. "Gather the others and meet me outside. The Virohi are already here."

45

IRAVAN

He stepped into the earthrage.

Wet earth entered his mouth and nose, settled into his hair and beard. The earthrage clawed at him, attempting to pierce the small bubble of protection he had trajected for himself. In the distance, a glittering green dome arose, the largest he had ever seen, extending for miles and enclosing the vast mountain of Irshar inside it. Irshar itself stood on flat ground, a small ring of grass circling it, adjacent to the Garden Iravan had lived in for two months. He had built that Garden for Ahilya when they'd first found this habitat. He had wanted it to be their home. Now this habitat was everyone's home, and the dust solidified and coalesced into a protective dome not because of his desire, but hers.

From where he stood on a trembling hillock, the dome appeared like a thousand beams of intersecting light, part wave, part plant, wholly ethereal. Its construction modified with every blink, a whisper of a leaf, a bud of a flower, the coarse grain of wood. The dome undulated and rippled, a hundred rainbow colours trapped within so much possibility, as though possibility itself had never known to be so unified, as though unity was against its nature.

Ahilya had done this, converting possibility into reality. Did she understand her own power? Sorrow and love corded around Iravan's chest. He should have told her she had given meaning to his life. The dome changed, jasmines blooming on its wavy surface, disappearing in a blink, responding to his grief.

Iravan turned his gaze away from it all, back to the earthrage.

The tattoos on his skin brightened, even though the Resonance had almost broken away from him in the Deepness. It was only his Ecstatic power he relied on now—and he remembered how he had been in such awe of the falcon for all the trajection it could do before they had flown to Nakshar. He had learned from the yaksha since then. Before this night was over, he would learn it all.

In his first vision, the earthrage screamed.

Wind entered the protective bubble of his trajection and furled Iravan's feather cloak behind him. Dust and earth ground between his teeth. The falcon was returning; he could see it in the silence, the fury in its flight, its purpose and intent. Neither of them would emerge from this clash unscathed. The Resonance struggled, and another part of the link between them broke.

Iravan trembled. *I don't know the limits of Ecstasy*, Bharavi had said once, and he thought, *I don't either, Bha. But I think I'm about to find out.* In his mind, she shook her head wryly. A dark smile formed on Iravan's lips. He was about to face a monster, a *master*, and all he could think about was how she would be curious and calculating right now. She would see a way to win this, if she were here. He had been alone for so long.

The earthrage pushed against his bubble again. Water droplets entered despite his trajection, flicking at Iravan like blades. A twig scored him, then another. A face appeared—the face of the cosmic creatures, the Virohi—and just for a second, Iravan did not see the jagged teeth and the flayed skin, no, he saw *themselves*, he and the falcon back when they had been a Virohi too. A memory spiked, of splitting voluntarily, of burning incessantly. He saw their face and it was formless, unformed, a smoke-like memory that wove in and out like a dream of an alien entity.

I am the fury, Iravan thought. *I am the storm.*

The words were disjointed, part himself, part the falcon, reverberating in his skull.

I am completion. I am destruction.

He had accepted it now, the way the yaksha could affect him and take him over without even trajecting. It was a part of him, and that had been his mistake. To see it as separate from himself. To see the Virohi as separate from himself.

I will destroy you, he thought to the falcon and to the cosmic creatures, and this time it was his own thought, tinged with desperation and unfounded confidence. He held onto it—he *had* to—for beyond lay the seductive relief of oblivion and erasure—and if he gave into *that*, he would lose any will to fight. The anger within him grew hot and feverish. The wind cut him, the gale loud despite the bubble.

The last cord of light tethering the Resonance to him shattered. Iravan stiffened.

In the Deepness, golden light burst out of him, and rays crisscrossed around him in a shield. In his first vision, the falcon dropped down from the sky, talons and beak and pure fury.

The everdust responded to Iravan's Ecstasy, some of it seeping away from Irshar's dome.

A grim smile of anticipation grew on his face.

Iravan ascended into the air to meet the falcon.

46

AHILYA

They arrayed together, sungineers, artisans, civilians—the last survivors of humanity, its heroes, its offenders, its martyrs, ten thousand of them assembled behind the translucent dome of twisty green everdust.

On Ahilya's command, different messengers led by Umang moved through the crowd, ordering everyone to form up into two rows, stretching themselves thin but making a full circle around the mountain.

They had come empty-handed, for what use were weapons and tools against an enemy they could not see and barely feel? They were here to fight the *earthrage*. Ahilya almost grinned at the incongruity of the circumstance, the sheer absurdity. Her own fear and disbelief reflected on their faces: in beautiful Lavanya who stood with her wife, Chaiyya, both murmuring to each other; in Reniya and Vihanan, Shreya and Hiral, who looked determined yet nervous; in people whose names Ahilya did not know, who had gathered to her call to arms.

Umang had told her that several of these people were either

married to architects or were related to them in some way. Had their spouses and children, cousins and friends who could traject survived? Were they reviving even now, ready to be used by the Virohi? Or had they burned already, tumbled out of the skies, gone forever?

Ahilya swallowed as her gaze roved over the civilians. She knew so many of these people. She had grown up with them. Their desire was strong. It had once kept a group of them from sinking into a hole near the Academy in Nakshar; it had supported the trajection of the architects. These people likely understood their power, but none of them had faced anything like a Virohi before. The cosmic creature had ripped through her, tapping into her worst memories, her greatest failures. The pain had been excruciating, sloughing off her flesh, burning her insides, and Ahilya had felt death a million times. And that had been one single creature. These were *all* of the cosmic creatures.

She moved toward the citizens to warn them when a shape caught her eye among the press. Ahilya's heart jumped in her chest. She pivoted toward her sister, and Tariya turned to her, sensing her coming. They hadn't seen each other since that time in Nakshar. Both Umang and Iravan had told Ahilya they'd seen Tariya safe, but Ahilya had not gone to her—and Tariya was perhaps thinking the same thing, for her face morphed into anger, her lips tightening, chin lifting.

"You cannot be here," Ahilya said, closing in and gripping her sister's arm. "It's too dangerous."

"I have a right," Tariya replied, shaking her off.

"Ta—please. What about Arth and Kush? They cannot be alone."

"You asked if I wanted to see them die. I don't. That's why I'm here."

Ahilya drew back. She had said those words in a moment of provocation. She had never wanted Tariya to do this. The boys had already lost one mother, they could not lose another—and there was no guarantee anyone out here would survive. She opened her mouth to speak, but her sister forestalled her.

"Don't waste your time. I've already decided," Tariya said bluntly. "Talk to them—*they* still haven't and you have a job to do."

Ahilya followed her gaze, and sweat broke out over her forehead. The citizens had assembled, but fear and despair were rife in the assembly. They had crashed into a foreign jungle only hours before. Their ashrams were gone, dissolved as though they'd never existed. Their core trees had shrunk. Nakshar had seen terrible days recently, but for many of these citizens from the other ashrams, this was their first taste of such an ordeal.

They were terrified.

What would such fear do to their desire?

Ahilya strode forward closer to the edge of the dome. The earthrage ripped and snarled at her, the pressure of the wind just beyond pushing her back. A face leapt on the dome, then more, a hundred snarling creatures, ready to break through. She got the distinct sense that the cosmic creatures knew her, that they recognized her as a threat. When she turned her back on the dome, a chill ran down her spine at the thought that she had made herself so conspicuous to a predator. She repeatedly wiped her sweaty palms on her sides, trying to concentrate on the people in front of her.

Let them hear me, she thought, and the dome shimmered and morphed like a wave. People pointed and muttered, and the grass under Ahilya tightened into a disc and began to rise. Vertigo gripped her. She swallowed, resisting the urge to drop to her knees and hold onto the disc.

The disc carried her above the crowd. Faces turned up to her and silence built among the waiting people. They stared at her, Tariya, Dhruv, Reniya, Vihanaan, Naila, and a hundred others.

Someone pointed, someone else muttered, and a familiar unexpected face—Eskayra, her mind supplied the name—shone from the crowd grimly, so that Ahilya did a double-take and nearly fell off the rising disc. She had climbed fifty feet now, still only a fraction of the height of Irshar. The people on the other side of the mountain would not be able to see her, but perhaps they would still hear her. The disc stopped and hovered in the air, solid beneath Ahilya's trembling knees.

She cleared her throat and gazed down at them all. Fear gripped her. What was she doing? She was no leader. She had no clever words to address an assembly of this size and make them fight for their lives.

Then her eyes fell on Naila and Umang—and Ahilya thought of Oam, who had been so brave. He had been scared, but he had accompanied her nonetheless, and she had failed him. She would not fail these two.

"We've all lost so much," she said. Her voice was quiet, yet amplified by the dome it reverberated around the gathering. "Our homes, our friends, our families. A time will come to grieve it all, but today give me your anger and your desire. Out there is the real enemy, the one that has brought us to this point."

She flung a hand out, and as though to emphasize her words, the earthrage roared. A hundred jagged faces pushed through the dome, snarling, reflected all over the green dust. People gasped, staggering back.

The roar subsided and Ahilya dropped her hand.

"They fear you," she said louder, her heart beating rapidly. "They *FEAR* you. Your greatest power is your uncontaminated desire. It is what allowed ashrams to fly before. It is what allowed us to land during an earthrage. It is what keeps this dome between us and these creatures. You have relied on it all your lives. The *architects* have relied on it for their trajection. I ask that you rely on it again, this one final time."

Muted cheering grew over the gathering. People clapped. Shouted their defiance against the earthrage. Shouted their acquiescence to their own power.

Ahilya's eyes fell on Tariya again, and she swallowed, pushing past the choked feeling in her throat. "Focus on the people you are doing this for," she said quietly. "The ones you love and are trying to protect. This is it. We are here now, at the edge of our purpose together as the survivors of the sister ashrams. Stay strong. Keep your desire pure. We *will* survive this."

The disc began to descend. Cheering grew around the heroes, and someone shouted "*Nakshar!*"

And then they were all clapping and yelling the names of their ashrams and Ahilya's own name. She smiled despite herself.

Reflected on the undulating dome, the earthrage pounded—but something like courage now ran through the crowd, potent and powerful. The green everdust shimmered as the snarling continued, but a rush of exhilaration filled Ahilya, the same giddiness that took her over when she went on an expedition in the jungle. She jumped down the last few feet off the disc, and it blinked out behind her. Her step was lighter than before as she returned to her spot in the first row between Dhruv and Chaiyya.

The sungineer still held Naila next to him. Naila gave Ahilya a watery smile, but closed her eyes, almost fainting again. Dhruv hoisted her up.

"Nice speech," he said in a low voice. "But what does it mean? We just stand here and stare at this dome? *That* is our last stand?"

A smile formed itself on Ahilya's face. He made it sound so ridiculous. "Yes. More or less."

"That should be dramatic."

"Better this than a bloodthirsty battle."

He snorted, and his eyes met hers. For a second, the distance between them disappeared, as though the events of the last few months had not happened at all…

Then Dhruv looked away, his lips pursing, and steadied Naila once more.

Ahilya thought, *Not yet. He hasn't forgiven me yet.* They were here together at the end of everything, but matters were still unresolved between them. She turned back to the wavy dust dome and the earthrage beyond, her mouth filled with bitterness.

Another roar reverberated beyond the dome, unearthly and bestial. The mountain of Irshar became translucent. She saw it from the corner of her eyes, the core trees shimmering and waving, the citizens inside scared, and Ahilya thought abstractedly of how Iravan had said the green dust and the core trees were made of the same technology, and how both of those obeyed her.

And then she glimpsed him, an image so vivid, so sharp, that her mouth dropped open. He and the falcon circled each other, and she could tell he was weakening, that he wouldn't win. Iravan dodged a flying tree trunk; he swirled in the air, arms outstretched, and the yaksha pivoted.

Cracks appeared in the dome.

Ahilya blinked, the image of Iravan forgotten.

Wisps of air pierced the dome, and to Ahilya's eyes, they took gigantic shivering form like mist made solid, arms and hands like branches spread apart, feet like murky roots, a hundred screaming faces that distorted and eddied before melting away.

"Get ready!" she called out, her frantic voice echoing inside the dome.

The words had barely passed her mouth when the dome shattered.

The earthrage attacked.

47

IRAVAN

They collided into themselves in the storm.

Carried by a tornado of everdust, Iravan spun in the earthrage, dissecting the branches and heavy tree trunks the falcon trajected at him. A vine flipped through the air, wound itself around his neck, but this was a familiar trick. He was ready.

A jet of light shot out from his shield within the Deepness, found the plant in the Moment, shattered it into splinters. He flew through the debris-laden jungle, unleashing his own vines. It was so quick that the air around him crackled, the wind of passage searing his own bubble of protection.

The yaksha screamed, the sound bloodcurdling. Its words were meaningless in Iravan's head—*break, split, gouge, kill*—but it spun in the air, its gigantic wings like blades. The vines Iravan had unleashed shredded into a thousand little tubers and were swept away by the wind.

The falcon didn't stop. Its shape was just a blur, and Iravan was sucked in by the strength of the vacuum. He tried to resist, but it didn't work. The falcon was going to let him smash into itself.

It was going to pick him apart like carrion. Its fury and vindication reverberated in his head.

Desperately, Iravan trajected. His ray of light became constellation lines in the thrumming Moment—and *something* responded, the core trees or the green dust, he didn't know. The constellation lines connected. Vines grew from a passing tree trunk and anchored him. He half staggered, half flew in the opposite direction, away from the falcon's powerful vacuum.

The creature shrieked and pivoted, chasing him.

Iravan sent more jets of his Ecstatic light into the Moment toward the jungle. When he glanced behind him, the falcon had easily dodged his onslaught of boulders and tree trunks.

Manic laughter built in Iravan's head. The creature was enjoying this.

In the Deepness, the Resonance bolted, and a thousand hair-thin rays of silver light burst out of it toward the Moment—not the linking, but something else.

A second later, the bubble of his own protection grew sharper, turned inward at him in spikey thorns. The bubble shattered, a million tiny spikes aimed toward him to pierce his body like arrows.

Iravan abandoned his assault. Frantically, he trajected his own light, and twisted. A shard swept past his right eye, gouging a cut in his cheekbone. He cried out, forcing his own trajection in the Deepness against the Resonance. Some of the wooden blades formed into armor. Iravan floated for a dizzying second, spinning in panicky circles, trying to find the falcon.

Where was it? The Resonance still trajected in the Deepness, but the falcon had gone. He looked up, squinting through his eye slit, waiting to see if the falcon would drop from the sky.

The jungle itself roared, and Iravan glimpsed a ringed eye, too close—the creature had *camouflaged* itself.

The falcon and the Resonance smashed into him in both his visions.

The world tilted, and Iravan gritted his teeth within the armor. He ricocheted through the darkness of the Deepness. Both of his shields—the one in the Deepness, and the one in the jungle—cracked as he tried to break the hold. A hundred rays of light spun out of the Resonance toward him in a powerful linking even as it continued to ram him. Iravan cut them with his own beams. If even a single ray of light linked with him, all his Ecstatic power would transfer to the falcon. He would be helpless. He struggled, attempting to break through its momentum, even while he trajected, trying to find his own opening.

They crashed through the jungle, past spinning boulders and hurtling debris. All of his attention in the Deepness was in keeping the yaksha from linking with him. Iravan could do nothing to stop their plunge through the jungle. The creature's wings beat at him, enclosed him, and his armor groaned. Iravan couldn't breathe. The yaksha was going to crush him.

The cosmic creatures entered the dome of Irshar.

Iravan glimpsed Ahilya freeze, and desperate fury pounded at him. He was wasting time when the real enemy was out there, when Ahilya needed him.

His fury at the Virohi mirrored itself in the falcon.

Its hold loosened involuntarily.

It was all Iravan needed.

He twisted and spun out of its grasp in his first vision, trajecting a complex beam of light in the Deepness at the same time. The falcon shrieked, but Iravan did not aim to link with it. Instead, he flung his beam into the Moment toward the falcon's stars to traject it.

It intercepted his beam with its own—

The two beams collided and merged, and—

Nidhirv blinked.

He stood with the other architects, readying for another birthing ceremony, but something irked him. In his third vision he could see—was that *himself*? Flying and struggling with a giant bird, and was that the jungle, so violent, whiplashing? He had not sought completion with his yaksha in this life—deliberately—so he could live more lives and find Vishwam in them. But this image, this memory—if the future could be called a memory, except it wasn't the future, it seemed to be happening *now*—this image showed not completion, but annihilation.

He blinked again and excused himself from the preparation circle. Vishwam threw him a concerned look, but did not follow, and Nidhirv strode to a water barrel. The cup trembled in his hands, and he saw his own reflection, except it was another man, and that same gigantic falcon.

The cup dropped into the barrel with a loud splash. Nidhirv choked, an anger rising in him, alien yet so familiar. He slid down to the ground, the anger taking over everything, the feeling that everything he had done so far was so wrong, *so* terribly wrong...

And Iravan hurled himself away from the falcon in the relentless jungle.

He gasped, tried to banish the memory. He could not give it attention right now. The falcon roared, unleashing a hailstorm of debris at him. Iravan ducked, pushing his hands up. Debris dust coagulated into a bark barrier, taking the brunt of the falcon's attack.

The Resonance chased him in the Deepness.

Iravan leapt into the Conduit and to the thrumming Moment to evade it. The universe was vibrating, crimson dust motes unleashing destructive constellation lines. He thought desperately, *I need to help Ahilya. The Virohi are killing them.*

The bark shield splintered, the force of the falcon's attack tossing Iravan back. Thorns and rocks ripped at him. Iravan's body *spasmed*, his bones screaming, his eyes bleeding.

He realized his mistake at once.

He had left the Resonance alone in the Deepness to Ecstatically traject as it wanted.

In his second vision, he flew out of the Conduit and back into the Deepness, hurling trajection light to his own stars to heal himself. His body righted itself, and he thought in horror, *I can't do this. I need more time.*

The Resonance shot out another beam of linking, and Iravan *screamed*, his own beam colliding and merging again with the Resonance's—

Mohini stopped mid-sentence.

What had she been saying? She stared at her husband and their wife, and their faces were curious, caught in laughter, like she had said something particularly witty.

But Radha's eyes grew worried, and Taruin frowned and took a step back from her. She lifted her arms as though to take flight. She saw herself, a bird in the sky, shooting a webbing into the dark realm. *This is not who I am*, she thought, and a massive falcon said those words in her head at the same time.

Radha and Taruin were backing away. They picked the twins from the cradle anxiously, and she knew the rage was taking her again, this anger at the cosmic creatures who birthed themselves in her ashram, who would destroy the world. She would need to end it—

They broke apart from each other again.

Iravan gasped and ascended in a whirlpool of dust. Far opposite him the falcon did the same thing, its giant wings beating heavily. Iravan saw his own shock mirrored in its mind, and he knew, neither of them had trajected to see this. The first one with Nidhirv had been a mistake, but understandable—they had once done a similar trajection to see their past. But the one with Mohini, that fury and rage at the cosmic beings? For it to make itself apparent through so many lifetimes?

What are you

doing? the falcon completed.

Get out of my

head, it thought.

A terrible cold fatigue grew over Iravan.

He and the falcon stared at each other. His own breath drummed in its heart.

What, he began—

Between his brows, the mountain of Irshar trembled and Ahilya screamed, and Iravan suddenly remembered the real fight. He was here to control the yaksha, to link it with itself, to stop the Virohi with the webbing.

This is a

distraction.

Iravan howled in fury and confusion. They crashed into themselves again.

48

AHILYA

Dust and earth pelted her skin, and Ahilya thought, *This is the end.*

She braced herself for destruction, but nothing happened.

She was still alive.

How? The dome had shattered. The Virohi had pierced through the citizens' flimsy protection. They should all be dead.

No.

The everdust still held the cosmic creatures back—only not in the domed structure she had desired. Thick smoke curled around her, dimming the light of the green dust. Where had the smoke come from?

Ahilya realized with a chill that it wasn't smoke. Those were the Virohi, wandering among them all like living things. Those were the Virohi, wanting to take form.

The smoke grew thicker, more of the cosmic creatures pouring in, mixing with the green everdust. The Virohi would be unable to enter Irshar proper, but they were here in the courtyard. The combined desire of all the citizens had not stopped them, not completely, but it had done something else. It had inhibited them from taking over the architects in Irshar.

Her hand reached out nervously toward Dhruv, but emptiness greeted her. Ahilya moved forward a few steps, and her touch encountered something slippery, but it dissolved instantly. She retched in terror and disgust. The fog grew around her, and she thought to the everdust, *Let me see.*

It did not respond.

The miasma swelled thicker, and she groped blindly, taking a step into the thickening mist. Her legs and feet grew wet, like she was in water up to her knees, but when Ahilya glanced down her kurta was dry. A chill grew over her. She suppressed a whimper. This was just the green dust. It had played with her senses before. It had contradicted perception.

She took a small step forward, terrified she was suddenly alone. A cry came to her from somewhere on her left. She moved toward it, her shallow panicked breath resonating in her ears.

Reform, she thought desperately, but the green dust of possibility shivered and did nothing. Ahilya could feel it trying and failing. She needed simpler commands, she needed to—

The earthrage roared at her, dust and earth flicking at her, twigs stabbing her. Ahilya staggered back. Somehow, she had wandered to the edge of the habitat. Iravan had warned her to stay inside. She could hear the earthrage beyond, despite the mutilation of her senses. Ahilya edged away from it, rain still spitting, leaves and wet earth climbing her nose and throat, until she was surrounded by the thick smoke and green everdust again.

Reality shifted.

She blinked as the fog next to her cleared a little. Above her, she glimpsed Dhruv supporting Naila. More figures appeared around her, wavering in the fog and dust. Chaiyya screamed a silent, open-mouthed scream. A man slashed at an unseen tendril of smoke with his arm. Tariya ran away in fear from something that chased her. It was as though the dust had finally understood her command to see, and Ahilya's teeth chattered. Everdust was still obeying her, like Iravan had said it would, but it was slow.

Under her, the ground hardened then wobbled, then hardened again. She held her breath, too afraid to move, sweat pouring down her forehead as she began to ascend. Everdust had reformed into a disc, similar to the one she had made her speech on minutes ago. The disc wobbled as she rose through the mist and fog, and Ahilya forced herself to clamp down on her fear. A part of her wondered at what would occur if the disc failed now, but she could not afford to think like this. Everdust was unpredictable. It would react to her fear, not her desire. She needed to to be careful.

The disc carried her higher. Tentatively, Ahilya reached a hand forward, careful not to disturb her balance.

As though her touch in the fog had disturbed something this time, Ahilya saw *everything*.

The citizens below her were frozen in motion, their eyes darting everywhere, while others ran unseeing through the fog. The mountain of Irshar splintered and cracked in an explosion of earth, the people inside screaming, the architects burning, as ceilings fell apart and floors disappeared. Naila spasmed in Dhruv's arms, her eyes rolled back, appearing so close that Ahilya could touch them. But then the breeze whipped the image away, and the fog rolled back in. Ahilya trembled where she stood, unsure of what to do.

The Virohi had entered Irshar. They had attacked the architects.

They were even affecting the citizens in their smoky form, something that shouldn't have happened. The complete beings, the non-architects, were supposed to have been a shield, but she heard Iravan's voice from before.

The cosmic creatures are evolving. Those creatures now know that people like you exist. The architects are clearly in danger. Complete beings like you are vulnerable too.

Ahilya tried to think. She lowered herself to her knees, trembling. Her sweaty palms clutched at the disc, and even though her eyes told her it was solid, she felt as though she were touching rotten fruit.

Frantic images grew above and around her, as though space and position had no more meaning. Reniya battled a twirling tendril of fog that tried to strangle her, then the image was swept away. A man shuddered and fell to his knees, weeping, before a breeze carried him beyond Ahilya.

She took a deep breath, close to tears. Iravan had said everdust would respond to her will. But the dust had been weakened by the onslaught of so many cosmic creatures. Had everyone's desires crumbled in the face of the fog?

"Stay strong," Ahilya called out, her voice trembling, but the mist swallowed her words.

So that was useless.

She had only one thing at her disposal, she knew. This little disc of green dust that had formed under her, still reacting to her desire.

Take me toward Chaiyya, she thought, willing the disc, her hands clutching it.

It crumbled slightly, and Ahilya realized it would break away any second now. Each command she gave depleted it.

Terror overtook her. The plan to go to Chaiyya, to ask her to use Ecstasy, was ludicrous. The Senior Architect didn't know *how* to supertraject. Ahilya opened her mouth, to countermand her own command.

But the disc made of everdust was already moving.

It stirred slowly in the air as though cutting through quicksand, and Ahilya gripped the edge, as images of the survivors churned around her in the fog.

49

IRAVAN

Iravan held nothing back.

All his fury, all his wrath, everything that had happened in the last few months erupted out of him. In his mind, Ahilya bled again, their child lost. Viana burst into mutilated shards of bone. Trisha, Pranav, Darsh, and Reyla were tortured for their Ecstatic energy. His own split happened again, as he and the falcon destroyed the earth around them.

Iravan roared in anger and agony and unleashed it all.

In their first vision, he and the falcon were flung around each other in the shattering jungle, branches, roots, and vines whipping and scoring them. The falcon spun, its wings like blades. Iravan leapt away, hurling boulders at it. It broke out of its spin and dove upward, but he chased it, ricocheting trees at it, each trunk a massive arrow.

The yaksha screamed and circled back for an attack.

Iravan met it head on.

Light erupted out of him and the Resonance in the Deepness, bladed toward the Moment, each beam its own complex construct.

Iravan's skin was blinding blue-green, and the rings around the falcon's eyes grew in number, not one but a hundred.

They smashed into each other, and the momentum flung Iravan back, spinning head over heels, his armor cracking. He glimpsed the falcon's wing tear, felt its excruciating agony, but they rose again at the same instant.

The Virohi distorted reality even as the falcon pulled him into battle, and he thought, *I will fight you in every realm and in every memory.*

The thought was for the falcon and the cosmic creatures together. He heard it in the yaksha's mind even though it was he who had thought it.

He screamed and golden light *exploded* out of him in the Deepness, a billion filaments that lashed out toward the Moment and the Resonance.

The Resonance responded in kind.

Its shape changed. It expanded, the silvery mercurial particle no longer an abstract form but resembling a giant falcon even in the Deepness. Wings made of silvery light overpowered the prickly lights of the Moment. They faced each other in the storm of their first vision and the blackness of the second: two entities, mirrored infinitely, warring forever, except this time one of them would win and subsume the other.

The earthrage *adapted* to them.

It shifted as though they were suddenly in a vacuum. The bubble of protection Iravan had built for himself extended to the falcon. He reached out toward the earthrage with his Ecstatic power and yanked a passing tree trunk into the bubble of protection. He *hurled* it toward the falcon where it splintered into dust. The falcon shot toward Iravan, its speed blinding, and Iravan rotated in the air, barely missing its sharp wingtips.

In his second vision, his beams of light grew harsher, more brilliant. His dust mote altered.

Iravan saw himself through the Resonance's wild eyes, a human-shaped construct of golden light, as big as the Resonance's new falcon shape.

Then, with the full power of his Ecstasy acknowledged, the Deepness transformed.

For the first time, the infinite blackness was no longer as black.

A million droplets of light blossomed in the darkness as though each were a separate Moment. And Iravan finally understood.

The Moment was a single world, *this* world, *his* world.

But infinite such worlds existed: a world of fire and water; a world of mountains and chaos; and finally, the world the Virohi had come from.

Suddenly, everything was clear.

This was how the Resonance had always seen the Deepness. This was how it had known to shoot its webbing into the darkness to stop the Virohi. It hadn't shot it into an arbitrary part; it had shot it at the Virohi's world. Iravan reared in the jungle and the Deepness, facing his own self, and thought,

I know

what you know, now.

The Virohi had plundered whole planets in their attempt to take form. They had scattered themselves, uncaring of the damage they wrought. Iravan had been one of them once. He and the falcon had been the precursors, the first ones to do it, the first ones to split in their arrogance, and all of Iravan's lives, all his forms, centered on this instant—

An older Askavetra looking up at the sky, furious at her incompletion—

Bhaskar shuddering against his trajection, memory searing—

Agni falling to their knees, rage taking over their limbs—

Iravan and the yaksha clashed with each other again within the vacuum of the storm. They hurtled around in the Deepness, the globules of the different worlds flashing by so rapidly that everything was a blur. The Two Visions combined in Iravan's mind, as he and the falcon flew through the jungle and the Deepness, whipping in and out, and Iravan *roared* as Ahilya trembled on a disc of green dust.

The force of their combined trajectory flung him and the falcon together. Iravan and the falcon screamed in defiance, each proclaiming their supremacy over the other.

The universe—all the universes—blinked.

The Deepness flashed.

The jungle exploded.

The thousand beams of their golden and silvery trajectory combined and intersected into a vortex, and Iravan and the falcon physically rose up through the jungle, a whirlpool of light surrounding them. The worlds of the Deepness disappeared. The storm quietened.

> *I am*
> > *the rage.*
> *I am*
> > *the earth.*
> *This will*
> > *end now.*
> *You will*
> > *be mine.*

Each thought was closer, mirrored and completed in rapid succession, so Iravan could barely distinguish himself from the falcon.

They existed in a place of pure desire and consciousness.

And Iravan knew, the real war between them was just beginning.

50

AHILYA

The disc disintegrated under her.

She fell through the fog.

She had anticipated it, and her mouth did not form into a scream... but in the back of her mind, a slow terror built... before it melted away...

She found herself on all fours.

A desperation pinched at her, right by her temples. She thought, *I should get up. I am here for a purpose.*

She rose to her feet, unsteadily.

Around her, smoke curled thickly but it did not smell charred, and she thought, *I have desire.* It was important she remember that. *I have desire.*

It was only when she paused that she realized she had been walking.

She had been heading toward her home in Nakshar, hadn't she?

Iravan was waiting. He was with their children, Eesha and Viran. He and Ahilya took turns at the council, barely making one councilor between the two of them these days, but Iravan had wanted to stay at home more often. She smiled as she thought of how she had left them this morning, Iravan wrangling a squirming Viran with one hand while chasing Eesha. They were all likely resting now, tired from play. Were they supposed to meet her outside the council chambers? Ahilya couldn't remember. She turned to the architecture, to ask it to weave a path, but smoke filled her vision, burning the leaves...

She staggered.

Someone was pulling her up.

This was not Nakshar. This was a lonely, haunted place with glittering green dust and wisps of smoke.

Ahilya stumbled to her feet, and stared into Tariya's grim eyes. There were others collected around her sister, Chaiyya cradling her wife, Dhruv clutching a spasming Naila. Ahilya's eyes drifted to them, then dully returned to her sister. Memory seared Ahilya—of Tariya flinging her out of her house, her desire so strong that it had superseded the trajectory of the Disc Architects.

It should have been you, Ahilya thought, tears in her eyes. *You and Bharavi were meant to protect us all. You both had always been more capable.* What was her own desire compared to Tariya's? Her sister had always been a silent warrior. The world had deserved her and Bharavi. Instead, it had gotten Ahilya and Iravan, poor seconds in this cosmic crusade.

Tariya's face softened. Her voice came to Ahilya from afar. *Come on, Ahilya.*

We conditioned the dust to respond to us, Iravan said. *It will never be anyone else's as much as it is ours.*

That desperation in her forehead grew stronger. The everdust was weakening.

Naila writhed in Dhruv's arms, red tattoos climbing up her body.

To respond to us, Iravan said.

To only the both of us.

Ahilya's eyes widened.

She understood their mistake.

She and Iravan had thought they'd strengthen the green dust of pure possibility by decentralizing its command, sharing it with the other citizens. But that was not how everdust worked. In sharing her permissions, Ahilya had only absolved her own responsibility. She had weakened everdust. That was why the dome had shattered.

This was her battle, hers and Iravan's alone.

They had made it so, right from the beginning.

Braced against Tariya, Ahilya thought, *Return to me. Only obey my command.*

This time, the dust obeyed.

It swirled around her, thick and glittering, blocking out Tariya and the others.

Along with the dust came the smoke, and Ahilya felt the Virohi's attention on her. She shirked beneath it, but the gathering green everdust acted like a beacon for them now.

She felt all of their weight, and all of their immortality. A profound sense of smallness filled her, as the cosmic creatures stared at her, assessing her. She was a woman alone against a hundred planetary storms. Her own fledgling desire caved and throbbed in her ears, a gentle rhythmic sound contrasting with the roar of the cosmic creatures.

Then the Virohi moved.

Ahilya had a second's glimpse in her mind, of the architects within Irshar curling to the ground, their tattoos no longer burning;

a second's glimpse that took in Naila who had stopped spasming, citizens for whom reality was no longer distorted.

Her desire peaked within her against her will, and the cosmic creatures responded in a feeding frenzy.

The Virohi came for her.

51

IRAVAN

In the realm of pure desire and consciousness, Iravan saw themselves reflected in a thousand mirrors as one.

The image expanded, dissipated, exploded—and he and the falcon separated again, but not truly. He thought a thought, and it reflected back to him, so he could no longer tell where his—

beginning, merged, since eternity,
much greater than I have been;
we could be broken, and yet
we watch incessant, the division
between existence and its death;
begin here, now, you I will erase;

so endless; we became, will become
more complete, reunified, where
we will see that which sees us
shatter and unite amid spaces and
death. I must become, and it will
reveal to us ourselves in completion.

He wrenched himself apart, breathless—but the falcon followed, even as it pulled itself away from him too.

I am

the falcon

Iravan, he thought desperately.

Iravan

That was his... name...
Victorious laughter, for it was winning.

Ira
He couldn't...
remember
not... fully.
It grew mightier. Words flowed into
it faster. Language and thought, that
had once belonged to *him*.

Ir
There...
had been...
more...

I
Am not, it thought. *Only* I *remain*.

The falcon subsumed him.

52

AHILYA

Beyond the pain and agony, Ahilya wandered in an unfamiliar circular chamber, mirrors surrounding her on every side. The mirrored chamber grew between her brows, encompassing her, taking over her reality. The jungle, the habitat, the glittering green dust, all of it was gone. She knew she had not physically moved. She knew that if she focused her mind, she would return to the habitat, and see herself frozen in anguish.

But the thought was distant.

It was as though she had been dreaming of the jungle and the habitat, and her Etherium was her only reality.

The Virohi reflected in the mirrors.

She became one of them.

Their desperation cascaded through her—

They descended, took form, for this one final time when they would escape erasure.

But the form shattered. It could not contain them, not for long.

They wept, frantic, caged and terrified.

But even that fear was removed from them. How could they *feel* when there was no form to express it through?

They tried, again, and again, and again.

Yet through all the worlds, and all of time, there was no eternity, no immortality. Forms by their nature were finite. Forms could not contain them, though they needed to be contained so they could *know* themselves.

But wait.

Here was a solution of a kind. A continuity of a kind.

They descended, took form again, and the form transformed, from one life into another, the same consciousness recycled, a part of it immortal, eternal.

Here was form, finally, a freedom within it. And they shattered the world for it was a small price to pay.

The Virohi let her go. Ahilya still stood in the strange mirrored chamber, but the attention of the Virohi shifted. She felt the weight of her own body, her own existence, return to her in stark clarity.

With clarity came understanding. Her world worked on desire, the most powerful thing there was. Finally, she understood what the Virohi desired. *There is a way,* she thought, *for all of us to win.*

She knew that Iravan was battling the yaksha, that something terrible was happening to him. But she couldn't help him.

She could help the others.

Retreating from her Etherium and the mirrored chambers, Ahilya focused back into the reality of Irshar with a new determination. Perhaps the Virohi understood what she was going to attempt. Perhaps they could see. Their anguish parted from Ahilya. A watchfulness took over, and the pain of her own body, the agony of their desperate attack, abated.

"Chaiyya," Ahilya whispered, and the Senior Architect grabbed her hand.

"What do we do?" Chaiyya asked.

Ahilya swallowed. It was a risk. She did not fully know the consequences. They did not have time. They did not have a choice.

Ahilya lifted her head.

"We build."

53

IRAVAN

Annihilation
crept in.
He held onto himself with a thread.
Memories… washed…
Vishwam's smile
Radha's touch
children born
sunlight
forests

He watched through another's—
        —my *eyes*.
It is… was
            over, a melancholy thought, then—

Then—

Something appeared through the Conduit, a familiar power, amorphous and dust-like.

He grasped
for
it—

And—

All their lives rushed through them—
Nidhirv stared at Jeevan who became Bhaskar who regarded Askavetra who recognized Mohini and became Agni until Iravan

IRAVAN

returned

Possibility blazed in him, and he stared at himself, at all his selves, and the falcon recoiled in shock.

Iravan didn't wait. He gripped the power from the Conduit, in the same linking he had once used on the Ecstatics and the falcon itself, and the power bound itself to him. He thought, *Two roads in sleep, and yet, I rouse to many.* Supported by the power—the incorporeal yaksha's power—Iravan pushed himself away. His vision separated from the falcon and became his own.

It expanded, the Moment becoming the Deepness becoming the Etherium becoming the Conduit.

He surged into all of them at once, invading the falcon's consciousness.

It snapped away from him, retreating in terrified confusion.

Iravan remembered why he was here. He could see, without even trying, the battle between the Virohi and Ahilya. Iravan narrowed his eyes. His mind grew grim.

Now, he thought to the falcon. *You become me.*

54

AHILYA

With Chaiyya's mind supplying the knowledge, Ahilya rebuilt the habitat.

They worked together in seamless trajectory.

Ahilya did not know if Chaiyya was using Ecstasy, or if Chaiyya was doing anything at all. For all she knew, the Senior Architect was simply imagining the habitat in a certain architectural model.

Ahilya did not care. She saw the images in her head, and she directed everdust to carve itself in that form, communing with the Virohi in the mirrored chamber as she bound them.

Around her, a city materialized.

It was a city unlike anything she had ever seen, constructed not of leaves but of the green dust. It was a city more alive than any ashram had ever been, yet somehow unmoving, static. It was a city made of Irshar, Nakshar, all the landed and destroyed sister ashrams and their core trees, a city made of thousands of escaped and desperate cosmic beings, thousands of survivors of humanity.

Possibility and eternity intertwined as one.

The first true habitat of the jungle—the first *enduring* habitat—constructed itself in waves. A massive plaza replaced the courtyard under Ahilya's feet. Grass rippled, lush and thick, and a gigantic tree shot up in the center, its trunk curled and gnarled, its canopy wide and shady, an amalgamation of all the core trees that melted to form this one giant.

Ahilya moved forward to see the rest of the city better, but a part of her knew she needn't have. The entire structure of the city glittered for her, as though the air were a sungineering bio-node, showing her different parts all at once. Dust rippled and gushed beyond the plaza. Arches formed in green stone. Buildings and playgrounds grew, groves and orchards. Roads and paths twined above and over grass-covered hills, and a hundred, no, a thousand different residences formed in flower-covered valleys for miles in every direction.

Ahilya climbed atop a small hill, her pulse beating rapidly. This habitat—this new home for the sister ashrams—laid itself out in front of her as far as she could see; a city of massive proportions, the glittering green dust settling in obedience to her command.

Beyond, the mountain of Irshar cracked, the everdust and Ahilya's architecture overtaking it. The levels within Irshar gently collapsed until the mountain itself was no more. The citizens inside, and those outside who had been her warriors, her shields, her companions, stared around them at this rise of architecture, so like what they were used to, yet so alien.

Ahilya turned as Chaiyya joined her, staring into the jungle-city alongside her. The Senior Architect said nothing, but her skin glowed blue-green and tears ran down her face. Deep within the mirrored chambers, Ahilya sensed the cosmic creatures breathe and relax—and with that breath, the architecture of this new city glimmered and stabilized.

And then the Virohi were gone, blinked away from the mirrored chambers.

The earthrage—the *earthrages*—all the hundreds that had been unleashed shimmered and came to an end. Beyond the vastness of the city, the jungle undulated in earth and dust, and green formed as foliage began to grow slowly. Within the wild jungle that was reforming, the city existed as an oasis of possibility. Ahilya had not expected the jungle to rebirth so quickly, but it was as though the final resting of the cosmic creatures had freed the planet itself.

Chaiyya trembled where she stood. "I have never built like this. I have never built without trajection."

Tears fell from the Senior Architect's eyes. She pressed Ahilya's hand, then pulled Ahilya closer and enveloped her in a tight hug, a sob escaping her.

"Thank you," she whispered. "Thank you, my friend. You—you saved us."

Ahilya felt her own wonder and awe mirrored in the woman. She hugged back just as fiercely before disengaging. Giving her an exhausted smile, Chaiyya nodded and joined Lavanya at the foot of the hill. Ahilya watched them go, and they were soon lost in the crowd that had formed in the plaza.

She turned away, back to the jungle. Chaiyya and the others would direct the survivors. The newly formed city would soon be inhabited. This, in the end, had been her destiny—to provide a home to the peoples of the ashrams in the jungle like she had always intended.

She turned her attention to the blue-green light in the distance, barely visible past the growing dawn. She had noticed it when the architecture began building, a vortex that was dimming even as she watched.

Iravan, she thought, her heart beating rapidly. Her battle was done, but his? How had he fared?

A shape moved in the sky, carried as though by wings.

Ahilya stared, her fists clenched, all her desire concentrated on her husband's return.

55

IRAVAN

He annexed the yaksha.

Iravan didn't think; he didn't try. The event happened on its own, and he watched, detached, as the falcon shrank slowly the more his own vision coalesced.

Its mind darted somewhere within his own, inarticulate terror, diminishing rage.

The boundaries of its consciousness collapsed slowly—then too fast, like a drop of water that became one with a river, watched in slow motion, occurring in a blink.

He did not know where he existed. This was neither the Moment nor the Deepness, neither the Conduit nor the Etherium. Nor was it that which he had once called his first vision, the physical reality of his world. *Two roads in sleep*, he thought in this everspace. *And yet, I rouse to many.*

He rose to many.

All his visions merged in and out of each other, like ripples of water intersecting. If he focused on one, he existed in that vision, but when he surfaced, they all joined together again, never having been separate.

He saw himself, a dust mote in the Moment, a Moment that no longer thrummed, as the Virohi became... something else. He noticed their transformation—and horror and anger curdled in him for what Ahilya had done, but he put it away. He would deal with it later. He would deal with *her*, later.

Through this, the falcon continued to shrink.

He saw himself in the Deepness, in an infinite blackness with a million other worlds and planets embedded into it. He noted them with wonder—then dismissed them. They were not his concern. His own shape within the blackness was. His dust mote altered. It became a silvery mercurial falcon, merging with the Resonance, for the falcon was merging with him, even now, against its will, even as it shrank.

He saw himself in the Conduit, and another shape hovered there. A yaksha that belonged to Manav. Iravan recognized it was his, for he had known the man as a Senior Architect of Nakshar. Now, in this second encounter, he could even sense the man's resonance in this creature.

Manav had been excised, but that excision had only cut him away from one of his yakshas. The other remained. Iravan had not even considered the possibility that there could be more than one yaksha for an architect. Did it mean there could be more than one architect too, for every split cosmic being?

Either way, unlike Iravan's union with the falcon—Iravan's only yaksha—Manav's unity with his own parts had been incomplete, interrupted by his excision. Yet he had found some way to communicate with this other creature; perhaps that is why he had made any recovery at all despite being excised. Manav's yaksha had come to Iravan's rescue twice—first when it had intercepted the falcon during that time of crisis within Nakshar's failing sanctum, and now, when it stopped Iravan from being subsumed. Had Manav somehow *sent* this creature to Iravan's rescue? How? *Why?* Is that why he'd emitted an Ecstatic signature? A dozen questions followed, but Iravan put them aside with his gratitude.

He would find the answers. He would repay Manav, somehow.

The falcon continued to shrink, the boundaries of its consciousness and knowledge pouring into him.

Iravan turned his attention to the Etherium—what he had always thought of as his third vision, though that manner of thinking now seemed laughable. Colorless images poured one into another, Bharavi with her children, Nakshar flying in the sky, a dozen Maze Architects fallen to their knees in the deathcages—and then another image, which had not been colorless before. The Virohi shattering the skies in a violent, turbulent skyrage.

He understood it now. The Etherium had always been a vision of guidance. Yet the images showed only probabilities that existed on a spectrum—ones that *he* converted into reality by his choices. The sharper the images, the more they had moved toward the truth. He despaired in the late knowledge. Shame and regret formed within him, burying itself deeper. He should have understood sooner.

Finally, Iravan coalesced his vision into a singular one—his physical reality. He and the falcon were suspended above the dying earthrage in a vortex of light, but the falcon had shrunk. Where once it had been massive, it was only as big as Iravan now—and shrinking further, now small enough to perch on Iravan's arm.

Its wings flapped limply in the vortex.

Its mind darted in terror, trying to escape, trying to flee.

But Nidhirv/Jeevan/Bhaskar/Askavetra/Mohini/Agni/Iravan pressed the will of their being, the complete power of their desire, the power of their depth-memory that had embedded itself within their consciousness and forced them to make amends.

The falcon screamed, a last hushed echoing shriek full of anguish and confusion.

The silence flickered, grew deep, then was absorbed.

The falcon-yaksha, this ancient creature, the oldest creature perhaps on the planet, burst into a dozen filaments of silver light. It exploded into a billion mercurial dust motes, filling all of Iravan's visions.

He hovered in the vortex, head thrown back, arms spread out, and the silvery dust motes settled on him, were subsumed by him.

A thrill of power and completion filled Iravan.

His being, his essence

magnified

multiplied.

He felt the weight of an ancient consciousness settle and amalgamate with his own, so there was no more separation.

The vortex disappeared.

The silvery light vanished.

Iravan continued to hover in the air, supported by his own power.

He could tell already that his sight had become sharper, that memories of flight and rage and desperation were filling him. The falcon was gone, but it was him now; it was all *him*. He spread his arms and the blue-green viney tattoos of trajection transformed into silver, riddling all over his dark skin. He trajected—he did not know what, whether it was even trajection, or just a simulation of it. He did not know what he trajected, perhaps the planet itself—and wind rustled around him, carrying with it the heightened scent of smoke and a charred jungle. His feather cloak billowed behind him, and he floated down on his own command, descending onto the broken, quiescent earth.

It was done.

It was only beginning.

He turned his head, and saw among the awed, terrified congregation, one distinct face staring back at him with neither fear nor wonder, only sadness.

Ahilya had seen what had happened to him. She had understood it, connected as she was to his own Etherium.

A cold detachment grew within him.

Iravan turned and walked away from the assembled people, toward the lonely Garden that was his home.

56

AHILYA

S he followed.

Ahilya descended the hillock and walked slowly toward
the Garden that Iravan had built all those months ago—the
Garden that he had built for her. Nothing else of the original
habitat remained, not Irshar, not the courtyard, not the glittering
green dome. Yet somehow the Garden and its surrounding square
were untouched, as though the everdust had obeyed her but only
within limits. Unlike the core trees, she would not supersede
Iravan's command. Everdust had coded itself to obey them
both equally.

She understood this now. In building this new city in the jungle,
she understood the consequences. There was no more everdust to
stop the cosmic creatures if they began the earthrages once again.
The only way to prevent the rages from happening was to ensure
the Virohi stayed trapped in this new city forever.

She had to believe that.

She had to make Iravan believe it.

Ahilya made her way past the clustered people. The citizens of the landed ashrams stared at her, their fearful gazes darting from her to the tall hulking shape she pursued.

Something had changed in Iravan in that battle. She could sense it, despite the distance between them. Her husband had always been a forceful personality, but now his presence cleaved through the congregation, and though only his back was visible, she could see the terror he left in his wake.

Ahilya's heart grew cold. Her palms grew sweaty—and then she had passed by the last of the people. She and her husband walked alone, a great distance between them, winding their way through a small copse.

He disappeared into the jagged crack within the stone wall of the Garden, and Ahilya paused, rallying herself. She could almost see the falcon-yaksha resting outside in the yard, a memory from long ago. The creature had not returned. Only Iravan had. That had to be a good sign, surely? He had won—but what had that victory cost him? What would it cost the rest of them?

She entered to find the place almost exactly how she had left it those months ago, wild yet careful. Flowers grew everywhere in a riot of color, and a stream gurgled across pathways. Jasmines blossomed over the walls, and trees whispered though there was no wind. The architecture was acknowledging her presence.

Iravan did not.

He sat on a chair, over a grassy staircase, his head bent low even though he must have felt her there. A bone white battery sat next to him, and Ahilya recognized it as the one she herself had brought when she had rescued him. What did it mean that he'd gone looking for it? What did he intend to do with it, this man who had wanted to erase trajection and elevate the sungineers? Something moved in his hands, the stone blade she had seen hanging around his neck, the one he had created out of the green dust of pure possibility.

The blade transformed into a thin staff, then an arrowhead, then a beaded necklace—and then, finally, a slim iridescent circlet that looked like a crown.

Ahilya stared.

Iravan tilted his head and studied the crown in his hands. He measured its weight. He molded its edges. For one terrifying second, when he lifted it slightly, Ahilya thought he was going to wear it—but then his hand crushed the crown, and it returned to looking like a necklace.

Iravan pulled it over his neck, the only jewelry he wore now.

His gaze met hers.

Ahilya stumbled back.

The strength of his gaze was like a physical thing. She stared at him, noticing what she hadn't before. His hair, that had once been salt-and-pepper, was now wholly silver—yet he did not look any older. If anything, Iravan appeared younger, stronger, more virile, more handsome than he had ever been. His features had sharpened, the angles of his face pinpointed, harsher than before. His eyes were no longer the almost-black they had once been. Instead, they were silvery-gray. Rings surrounded the irises as if he were a yaksha.

Was he trajecting? Ahilya breathed harder, resisting the urge to retreat from that potent, silvery gaze. Her eyes ran over the rolled-up sleeves of his tattered black kurta, over the dark skin of his arms, neck, and face. Tattoos glittered all over Iravan, but the tattoos were not the blue-green of trajection or Ecstasy. Instead, they glowed mercurial, a thousand of them, forming and dying in silvery beams of light. Tears burned in her eyes, and Ahilya blinked them away. She would not come to him in weakness or submission.

It took all her strength, but Ahilya took a step forward, then another.

He watched her, saying nothing, until she was almost upon him.

Iravan smiled.

It was not a smile of affection or welcome, but as though he were acknowledging her as a worthy adversary. It was a cold, twisted smile that chilled her to her bone.

Another chair like his own materialized in front of him, and she sat down.

For a while, they simply stared at each other—an architect and a citizen, a split Virohi and a complete being. Husband and wife.

His relentless power slammed into Ahilya. She wanted to touch him, but an instinct told her that it would be a mistake. He had seen what she had done in constructing the jungle-city. He had seen how she had welcomed the cosmic beings, how she had incorporated them irreversibly into a common life with everyone now, a shared purpose. His eyes glinted like silver moons.

A dozen questions and explanations grew in Ahilya. Where ought she to begin? They had left each other only a few hours ago, in a final goodbye. They had hoped to escape death but that wasn't what had happened at all, was it? They were separated now, more so than ever before.

Iravan smiled again, the same cold smile. He spread his hands out in an elegant, careless gesture. "I won," he said, holding her gaze. "Are you proud of me, Ahilya?"

She jerked back. "I won too. Are *you* proud, Iravan?"

He snorted softly and leaned back.

"What did you do?" she asked.

"What did *I* do? I did what we had agreed. I learned from the falcon. I changed from it. What did you do?"

"I—I improvised."

"You made them a part of us. You gave them eternity. Immortality."

"The plan was to save everyone," Ahilya said, taking a deep breath. "I did that."

"The plan," he interrupted softly, "was to keep them out. Not invite them into our lives and ecosystems. They are not guests, they are murderers. Colonizers. They unleashed the earthrages. They destroyed whole planets."

"To escape erasure. Iravan, you do not understand. I saw their desperation—I understood it, the need to endure."

His eyes glinted again, silvery bright, so powerful that Ahilya cut herself off.

"I *was* them once," he said quietly, and a terrible fury laced those words. "They manipulated you, and you allowed it. You gave them what they wanted. Do you understand the consequences of the kind of city you have built? How that will shape the survivors, their perceptions? Their consciousness will be tainted, they will begin to see the Virohi as one of them, they will *sympathize* with the enemy."

"I—"

"The Virohi will toy with you, Ahilya. I told you that the cosmic creatures had evolved. I told you they had learned about you—*you*, specifically. That Virohi you and I trapped together once in the Moment—did you think it stayed silent? The Virohi are a hive mind; it communicated with the others. The Virohi you faced knew to anticipate you and other complete creatures like you. Now they will corrupt all of you. They've corrupted you already. Soon, they will desire to take form *within* you, and nothing will stand in their way."

"Iravan—"

"You," he said, his voice hard, "could never understand them."

Ahilya recoiled like he had slapped her.

A heavy silence fell between them.

Finally, Ahilya spoke. She clenched her fists, but kept her voice even. "Once you said the same thing about architects. That I could never understand them because I was a non-architect. That I could never understand the Moment or the pressures and responsibilities of being a trajector."

"Back then I didn't know enough. Now…" Iravan gazed at her, and the cold mask of his face slipped a little to reveal his anguish. "Ahilya, listen to yourself. You're defending them. You were innocent once, untainted, but now you will lose yourself. I will lose—I've already lost—"

He cut himself off, and removed the necklace again to begin molding the stone, a restlessness to his actions that was at odds with the stillness of the rest of his body. She watched the necklace became a blade, then a bead, then a crown again, reflections of his intent.

"What happened to the falcon?" she asked.

"I did. It is a part of me now, no longer separate."

"Then you learned everything it knows?"

"That, and more. Within me lies the knowledge of all my past lives, all of the falcon's experiences. Our depth-memories are combined now. We are one, finally. Its form is mine, its consciousness mine." He glanced up and the shock of his silvery gaze took Ahilya aback. "I am its intent. I am its rage."

"Then you subsumed the falcon," she said quietly. "That's why—this physical change."

Iravan's smile grew twisted. "Does it frighten you?" he asked, his voice a whisper. "This is me now—more myself than I have ever been, in any of my lives. There is no more confusion within me, Ahilya, only a deep clarity of purpose. I can see now how much I floundered, how powerless I was within my own mind at every turn. You cannot imagine that kind of turmoil, the sheer paralysis of it, the uncertainty of never knowing whether an action is the right one, whether it is necessary. But all that is in the past. With the falcon and I finally one being, we are more than we have ever been. We are contenders to an unsplit Virohi—richer, wiser for all the experiences we have had in the unnecessary lives full of mistakes we have lived. There are things I can do now that the *falcon* could never have done. I am," he ended softly, "finally in control of myself."

A profound sadness grew in Ahilya.

She stared at her husband and saw not Iravan but an ancient alien creature in the guise of the man she had loved, a man she still loved so deeply. He had defeated the falcon-yaksha. She had saved the survivors of the sister ashrams. But this was no victory. This was… *grief.*

Iravan's hands stilled over the stone blade. Something of her sadness must have shown in her face for he seemed to relent, just a little. "You did what you had to do. Now I must do what I need to."

"And what is that?"

Iravan leaned back. The silvery tattoos on his skin gleamed brighter, and the blade became double-edged. He balanced it on the palm of one hand carefully.

"I never understood my past lives, fully," he said, not answering her directly. "I always saw them as people different from me—and in a way, they were. But their choices, their desires, their experiences— *Iravan* took shape from all that. Now here I am, the last life of this consciousness, of *all* their consciousness. There will be no more rebirth for us after this. There will be no more… anything. That used to scare me, but now I see how there is a kind of freedom in this non-existence. The Virohi feared this. It is why they desire to be reborn endlessly. But what they fear, I have embraced. And that will be their undoing."

Ahilya frowned. "You believe the lives that you lived before— this life, *our* life together—all of it was a mistake?"

"It could have been stopped. If Nidhirv had not been such a coward. He lived in a time where Ecstasy was desirable, where it was encouraged. But he never did seek to find his yaksha, never thought to unite with it, even though he had that knowledge. He was no better than the Virohi. He could have had completion, but instead he chose to become Bhaskar and Askavetra and Mohini and Agni and now me. But I am here now, and I will put an end to it all."

"Choosing life is not cowardice, Iravan."

"Certain as ever," he replied, smiling darkly. "Oh, Ahilya. You are truly an admirable woman. You have gotten used to making things happen by sheer force of will, haven't you?"

The question sounded warped, the words twisted. Ahilya felt her cheeks warm in embarrassment, but she refused to drop her gaze. Instead, anger arose in her, and she clenched her fists over her lap before releasing them.

"I have learned about the time when Nidhirv existed," she snapped. "Yes, that was when Ecstasy was encouraged, and perhaps he should have sought out the falcon-yaksha. But you once told me that you did not know why things changed from his era, why architects began to fear the jungle instead of revering it. I have learned why. It is because they finally understood the limitless powers of an Ecstatic. Basav told me that a great battle occurred between Ecstatics, in the pursuit of their capital desire—"

"You fear that will happen again. You have already told me this. I do not intend to make more Ecstatics with their own individual capital desires. But I do intend to fulfill my own."

"Which is to make amends."

"Which is to destroy the Virohi," he said bluntly. "*That* is the only way to make amends. That is the one way I can ensure this cycle never repeats itself, that matters resolve within my own final lifetime. I will not build systems only for Virohi to split again when those systems are forgotten in time. I have seen this now. I have understood it. The split of a cosmic being is an atrocity against nature and consciousness—one that affected not just our world and Moment, but possibly the Moments of a thousand different planets. No more will I allow them to exist. They will die by my hand, every one of them you have locked into this jungle-city."

Another silence fell between them. In her mind's eye, Ahilya heard Oam scream. She saw Bharavi struggle against the spiralweed. She thought of Chaiyya telling her what had become of Viana, the horrific manner of the Maze Architect's demise, brought about by Iravan.

"Death has become such an easy answer for you," she said quietly.

"Death is inevitable, now. It is only your will that keeps them in this form, my dear. They come from a different realm, a different time of existence; they do not exist in the kind of reality that we do. You might find that out to your detriment." He paused. "It does not matter that you've sheltered them for now. Sooner or later they will break."

In her Etherium of the mirrored chambers, she felt the Virohi that were now in the jungle-city shifting restlessly. "You are talking about genocide."

"I am talking about freedom—freedom for all of you, freedom for multiple worlds the Virohi once infected."

"Twist my words all you want, but this is not freedom, and you are not the dictator of every life on this planet, let alone the lives on other planets. If this is your juvenile solution, then perhaps Nidhirv *should* have found the yaksha in his lifetime. Maybe his capital event would not be as distorted as yours."

Fury shone in Iravan's eyes. He sat up straighter.

"Nidhirv and I are the same," he said coldly. "If I want, I can become him. This desire that burns in me, it is not the will of one life, it is the will of thousands of lives. It is inevitable, a destiny we chose for ourselves, an amalgamation of myself, the falcon, and the

Virohi we once were. You think I am a monster, a dictator, a tyrant, but I am the oldest creature there is now. I am doing this not for myself, but because this world deserves better than the Virohi—it always has. I am doing this to build systems and structures that will never depend on architects and trajection, where sungineers will fill the gap left behind, them and people like you. I am *giving* you power, Ahilya, why do you not see that? Humanity will be yours again."

"So, you will take the architects, then—against their wishes, away from their families—to fight this crusade of yours. You will use them not to give them Ecstasy, so they can unite with their yakshas and find completion again, but to wage your war when peace has already been achieved."

"Your peace is an illusion. You will see that soon enough."

"Iravan, you cannot take the architects against their will."

His silvery tattoos flared, and the rings around his eyes grew sharper. "They will come," he said, smiling that twisted smile again, "of their own accord."

The words, that expression, the suddenly glinting tattoos—all of them sent a chill down Ahilya's spine. At once, she was afraid—deeply, deathly afraid. Iravan had gained incredible powers as an Ecstatic when he had first become aware of his falcon, when he had first united with it. What had he gained now, after subsuming the creature? What were his limits? Sweat beaded her brow. For all she knew, he could warp people, the elements, the very planet without a thought. Maybe he was trajecting all of that even now, while he sat talking with her so insouciantly.

"This is our home now, Iravan," she said, her voice trembling. "I will not allow you to destroy it."

"And I will not allow the Virohi to be a part of it." Anger glittered in those silvery eyes, and his jaw tightened. "You should have never incorporated them into the design, Ahilya. I offered you a place by my side. We were meant to do this together, build something better—that is what I had intended for us in Irshar. But you chose them. You betrayed me. How could you?"

His voice cracked with the question, and once again she saw the deep distress flash in his silver eyes for the merest second before disappearing again behind a cold rage.

She leaned forward. "Please, Iravan. Listen to your own words. We can still work through this together. We can find a way for all the ashrams to endure, and for you to get what you need."

For an instant, a deep yearning reflected on his face, but Iravan shook his head just as sadly. "I wanted that, Ahilya," he said quietly, and this time he sounded so much like his old self that tears sprang into her eyes. "But we cannot have that anymore. What you did with them… you will not remain yourself. All I can hope to do is to stop their infection from spreading into you deeply." His hands shook and he made as though to raise them to her face, but dropped them. "All I can do," he whispered, "is make amends to *you*."

"If I am to be infected, you would abandon me again? You would leave me?"

"I am not leaving you. I am saving you. Even if it means saving you from yourself. What will happen to you, what is likely already happening—" Iravan took a deep breath, and the emotion left his voice. "I will carry that guilt until I end them, until I find the freedom of my own erasure."

His words were so shocking that Ahilya couldn't speak for a few minutes. Basav's voice echoed in her head, *Sooner or later, he will determine an ultimate action, one he will deem as the fulfillment of his capital desire… And when he fulfills it, the path to his own freedom will be clear.* The Senior Architect had implied that pursuit of freedom was inevitable for an Ecstatic Architect, but what her husband said now was not freedom. This was annihilation.

In her mind's eye, she and Iravan sat underneath the rooted rudra tree, holding each other before they went to prepare for their individual fights. The tree was gone, amalgamated with the other core trees into that giant spiraling one in the middle of the jungle-city's plaza. But Iravan was gone too. This man—this creature who was in front of her—was not the man she had loved, not the man who had loved *her*.

She struggled to take a breath. She did not care, suddenly, that she appeared weak. All she could feel was her loss that had embedded itself in both their victories.

"I saw your fight," she said, choking. "I did not understand it at the time, but now with what you've said... The Etherium showed me glimpses of your battle with yourself as it was happening. This is not what I thought it would bring us."

"I would not trust the Etherium," he said quietly. "Yes, our third visions combined in some way ever since we stopped the earthrage together, but the images are unreliable. It is only a vision of probability. Rarely, does the improbable become actuality—and we... We do not have control over any of it."

"You cannot tell me that we cannot choose our own reality. I saw a vision of our futures, Iravan. I saw us—our children. A boy and a girl. Do you remember when we wanted that? When *you* wanted that?" Tears stumbled down her cheeks, unable to be controlled any longer, and Ahilya's sight grew blurry. She could recall it clearly, the feel of her children in her arms, Iravan hugging them all, laughter and joy, family and love. She dashed the tears from her face angrily.

Iravan seemed not to be breathing. His silvery ringed eyes were on her, but he was looking beyond her, into his own thoughts, stunned, frozen. For a second, in their shared Etherium, the same vision glittered for the both of them. Their son sat on Iravan's shoulders, tugging at his silvery-gray hair, while their daughter was cradled in Ahilya's arms. There was laughter on everyone's faces.

"You dreamed of this," she said. "You wanted this, Iravan. We are still married. We can still have this. All you need to do is work with me. You can come back to me."

He blinked. His gaze took her in, and he took a deep shuddering breath. The moment of vulnerability disappeared like it had never existed. "The time for that has passed," he said.

It was the indifference in his voice that undid her.

Ahilya closed the images in her mind within her Etherium, and stood up. Tears continued to fall down her face but when she spoke, her voice did not waver. "I won't let you do this."

"You cannot stop me. You will find them no easy ally and me a difficult enemy. I only need you to fail once."

"Do not count on it occurring. You do not know my power."

"And you do not know mine." He looked away from her, and began to shape the stone once more. "Leave, Ahilya. You have made your choice. Your subjects await you."

She walked away, her last glimpse of her husband on his chair in his Garden all alone—majestic, powerful, misguided.

In the weeks that followed, Ahilya did not see Iravan at all. Perhaps he was avoiding her, or perhaps she was him. Maybe neither of them felt the need to be around the other, when there was so much to be done. Councilors directed the surviving citizens to homes within the jungle-city. Sungineers led by Kiana began gathering every material that had survived the crash. Ahilya helped them, but the irony of the circumstance did not escape her. They had all thought subsummation was the worst possible scenario. Now *all* the ashrams had merged, becoming subsumed by one another, evolving into something new even as the architecture defined and defied their decisions, the freedom they once had in manipulating it but a memory.

Through it, one thing grew increasingly clear.

Iravan had been right about the jungle-city.

The construction she had wrought, this final entrapment of the green dust and the unleashed Virohi, had combined into something completely unlike any architecture she could have imagined.

The buildings were created out of a material resembling glittering green stone, iridescent and opaque in the right light, yet somehow more alive than any ashram. Pathways altered mid-stride as though the design had changed its mind. Walls shimmered and disappeared, and roads suddenly came to a dead end, where only an hour before they had circuited the city. Reality moved and morphed, so that one second Ahilya strode on a flower-covered path, and the next waded in a pool of water.

"Everdust has always played with perception," Ahilya said to the remaining councilors of the Conclave, when they met under the vriksh. "But this—this was never how the habitat worked."

"It has to be the Virohi," Chaiyya said amid mutterings. "They are alive, after all—complex eternal beings. They have accepted the architecture as their eternal form, but eternity is not static. It moves."

"How can we live like this?" Garima, who had once belonged to Yeikshar, questioned. "If the architecture manipulates our senses, with no control from either architect or citizen, then we are at the mercy of the Virohi. They can change and mutate this city as they see fit. They can open a chasm under our feet at any instant, collapse the walls around us without warning."

"It is still architecture," Chaiyya said. "It can be contained and controlled. We were in a battle for survival. You cannot expect the result to be perfect."

"We expect it to be habitable."

The discussion had ended in shouts, the grief of what they had lost in the skies stark.

In the end, Airav had suggested the obvious solution. Everdust had been conditioned to obey Ahilya from the very start. With her communication and understanding of the Virohi during the battle, she had formed a connection with the cosmic creatures too.

"I think the city obeys your desire, Ahilya-ve," the Senior Architect had said. "I imagine only your desire will stabilize it. I'm afraid your work here is not done."

She had listened to his counsel. Every morning for several weeks Ahilya traversed to a different part of the city with an architect to guide her construction, finding different sections to stabilize. She settled disputes when she came across them. She assured citizens of their safety within these new structures. She lied about her confidence.

The architecture responded to her—*only* to her. It was no longer simple desire that she followed, but an exhausting persuasion. Ahilya found herself in the Etherium in the same circular room full of mirrors she had seen the Virohi in, watching herself as she *spoke* to the architecture and the Virohi's sinuous forms, as she induced them to remain a certain way, with promises of evolution several years in the future.

The mirrors showed her the various forms of the Virohi, shifting from stone to stream to grass, until she showed them—through the projection of her will and desire—what they ought to settle in. Ahilya showed them a life she imagined where the jungle-city would grow, where the Virohi could experience what the citizens did, happiness, sorrow, conflict, joy, jealousy, and love, always love. All those experiences would be available to the Virohi, no different from splitting into an architect and a yaksha. Ahilya talked to them every day, holding onto the vriksh in her mind, asking it to anchor her as though the embedded memory of the ashrams within it would remind her of who she was.

She came away from it not knowing how real the city was, or how real *she* was. Sometimes she thought she could hear the Virohi call out to her <*Ahilya, Ahilya*>, but other times, their voices became her own thoughts, and she heard Iravan say, *They've corrupted you. You only need to fail once.*

She did not fail. She remembered that she *could* not fail.

And so the architecture remained still for a time, the cosmic creatures convinced, the citizens of the landed ashrams safe.

"What happens if I lose control?" she asked dully, one time, when she accompanied Airav and Kiana out on a patrol.

"You will prevail," Airav said. "Iravan might be waiting for your failure, but if we can maintain the shape of the city for several years, and continue to make small changes—well, then. It is no different from any other architecture or any other repair. The sister ashrams will be able to live here for a long time."

"But this is not what I intended," she said, saddened. "How does this make me any better than Iravan in his Garden? I have too much control. This is not sustainable. What happens to the city if something happens to me?"

"Then the sungineers will help," Kiana replied. "We are building it back, Ahilya. There are possibilities in the jungle and materials available to us here that we've never had before. We will prepare for an eventuality should your will truly fail."

"Precisely," Airav added. "We will have to begin from scratch in some ways, but with the earthrages at an end, we can look for new habitats in the jungle. We can build anew."

Ahilya grew quiet at that. She was finally getting what she'd always wanted, but she had never imagined it would be like this. Where would they begin? How would they search for places within the jungle when so much in the landed ashrams was destroyed? How would they build when their architects were injured?

Kiana nodded when she asked those questions. "There is work to be done—there will always be work to be done. But I've already recruited several citizen scientists—the people who were once helped by the rogue sungineers from Nakshar's lab. We are united by purpose. That is not to be taken lightly."

"Time is a gift you have given us," Airav said. "We won't take it for granted. We have hard days ahead, but no harder than ones we have already had. You brought us peace, Ahilya-ve. We know it. We see it."

Yet despite the words, Ahilya sensed a quiet, frantic terror in her friends. They were not fools. They knew the dangers of their circumstance, the horrors of it. All of humanity was now leashed to her and Iravan. She and her husband had never been the most stable of people—and now for their whims, their wills, their *desires* to be the only factors in survival... Her breath came out in spasms, her entire body trembling. She had to stop the patrol and kneel for long minutes, panic making her vomit, while Airav and Kiana stroked her back and murmured soothing words.

Ahilya barely heard them She understood their pity for her, their fear *of* her. Had she not behaved in the same way with Iravan, knowing she could not tell him about their child lest he lose his fragile control over himself and destroy them all? Her friends were doing the same to her now—and could she blame them? *They will corrupt you*, he had said, and then in her memory from long ago, *Don't leave me.*

What have we done? she thought in desperate anguish. *Oh rages, what have we* become? *Look where our pride has brought all of us. Look what our choices with each other have wrought.* It seemed as though a hand clutched her heart. She couldn't breathe. She couldn't breathe.

Kiana knelt down next to her, face alarmed and concerned. "Ahilya, please. Trust in the rest of us. The sungineers have always invented with their backs to the wall. This is no different. Do not add to your burden. You are not alone. *We* are not alone."

She said it to be comforting, but not everyone thought like that.

Whether because of Iravan's long-standing invitation, or of their own volition, hundreds of sungineers and architects refused to live within the jungle-city, the city that citizens had begun calling Irshar, even though Iravan had made it plain he wanted nothing to do with it. Her husband had sent proclamations announced by Pranav and Trisha that any sungineer or architect was welcome to his Garden along with their families. While non-architect citizens had refused, wanting to cling to their fragile newfound equality in Irshar, many Ecstatics and sungineers had responded to his summons.

The Garden offered them familiarity, a remnant of how old trajection worked. Within the jungle city of Irshar, architects could no longer traject the design, but within the wild Garden there was control. News had spread of everything Iravan had done— of his power, the inevitability of Ecstasy, the history with the Virohi. Nothing was a secret anymore, and the architects flocked to the magnetism of Iravan's capital desire. They understood the infiltration of themselves; they blamed the Virohi, just as Iravan did. He offered them vengeance, and purpose. Even Ahilya could not deny this deep seduction, though it broke her heart to watch families separated again.

As for the sungineers—Dhruv, Iravan's emissary, his right-hand man, *the* Senior Sungineer of Iravan's Garden, had spoken on her husband's behalf. Ahilya had begged her old friend to reconsider. Kiana had pulled him aside to argue with him, but Dhruv had chosen his side. The sungineer promised the others of his kind prosperity, more than they'd ever had before in the flying ashrams, more than Kiana ever could in this fledgling new city. With support from Iravan himself, Dhruv had walked taller.

She had thought to confront Iravan about all this, but she saw him only once, when he came to the vriksh within the central plaza. At first, Ahilya did not recognize what was happening. The vriksh, the tree within the plaza, loomed gloriously in every direction. Ever since its creation it had not moved at all as though it had never known trajectory, yet suddenly gnarled roots whiplashed in agony, and leaves rained down onto the plaza without a breeze. Ahilya prepared to enter the circular chambers, to confront the Virohi again, then she noticed him stride in, and understood. The architecture of Irshar—including the vriksh—responded to him just as it did to her. It was made of the green dust, and that was theirs to command, even though the dust could no longer change its shape.

But the vriksh was no ordinary tree. It was an amalgamation of all the core trees of the ashrams. Ahilya pressed a hand to it and the vriksh stilled under her, even as Iravan arrived, the black sleeves of his kurta rolled back, his silvery gaze sweeping over the citizens who were collecting under the vriksh's massive canopy.

Ahilya stood there among her people—her *subjects*, as Iravan had called them with careless irony. She stared at him, a recovering Naila on one side of her, and Chaiyya on the other, Basav, Weira, Garima, Airav, Kiana, and so many other councilors arrayed behind her to indicate their support. She could feel the vriksh behind her too, the power of her and Iravan's opposing and equally powerful desires making it thrum in agitation. She still superseded his permissions of the tree, but perhaps the vriksh knew, it *remembered*, that *he* had coded it to obey her.

Her husband gazed at them all, his mouth harsh and unmoving. Hundreds of sungineers and architects detached themselves from the congregation under the vriksh and made their way toward his Garden. Iravan's own parents came to him during the exodus. His mother and his two fathers hugged him and touched his face. Ahilya had hoped that Iravan's parents would speak sense into him, divert him from his desire to destroy the Virohi. But Iravan remained unmoving through their meeting.

Instead, he locked eyes with Ahilya as she watched him. She uttered not a single word, but thought of their shared dream—to build a home, and have children, a family of their own. She hoped, and her silent hope shone in her eyes. Would he ever come back to her? Would he see he had a choice?

Yet Iravan only bowed to her, mockingly, before taking away the architects and sungineers.

For a long time after, Ahilya stood there while the others returned to the city. Only Naila remained by her side, the two of them watching the path to Iravan's Garden. When Naila spoke, Ahilya was surprised to see that the sun had set and fireflies were circling the plaza.

"There is nothing out there for you anymore, Ahilya-ve," Naila said softly, her voice sad.

Ahilya did not reply. Airav had said that she heralded peace, but a storm was coming, one worse than all the earthrages they had stopped. Iravan was going to carry them all into fire and blood.

But for now, the jungle beyond lay silent.

For now, there was life to be maintained.

Ahilya allowed the Maze Architect to lead her away. One foot in front of another, she fortified her heart for the days that were to come. Iravan had limitless power. But she had desire too, unexplored fully, uninhibited truly. It would have to be enough. She and Naila walked silently back toward Irshar, to their home in the jungle, this final abode of the sister ashrams. Dying rays of a silent sun guided their path.

EPILOGUE

IRAVAN

Iravan sat on his chair, unmoving.

He did not focus on the sungineers and architects arrayed in front of him, but he was aware of them in Ahilya's Garden—in *his* Garden. They stood clustered under the trees, by the pathways along the gentle stream, against the rock wall. There were so many that they filled the courtyard. Iravan could barely smell the jasmine on the walls anymore. He studied the stone in his hands that constantly changed shape. He was aware they awaited his pleasure—but it did not please him yet to address them.

Senior Sungineer Dhruv stood on his right, surveying the gathering. On Iravan's left were the first Ecstatics he had claimed for himself. Manav, whose gaze wandered wide-eyed as he clutched a garland of ice-roses Iravan had created for him. Pranav, Trisha, and— Iravan took another deep breath—the two children, Darsh and Reyla.

Do you remember when we wanted that, Ahilya had asked him. *When you wanted that?*

His hands trembled. He had come so close to acquiescing to her words, tempted by the one thing that could take him away from all this, the family he could have with her. But even if his own possibilities for fatherhood had not been erased… what the cosmic creatures could do to Ahilya…what they might be doing already… How could he inflict their new selves on innocent children? Grief pounded at him. Even he did not know how the Virohi would affect her after what she had done. He had lost her already. If he did not end them, she would lose herself too. That torture… He would not allow that.

She flickered in his mind, her sadness, her beauty, her sheer courage. Askavetra shook her head, *his* head. He watched Nidhirv put an arm around Vishwam, watched Mohini, and watched Bhaskar embrace children. That was not his path. How could it be, when he knew so much now? All those people he had been had known about Ecstasy, yet they had delayed the inevitable, choosing their material bonds over finding the falcon. They had left destruction in their wake.

Now it was up to him.

There would be no delay. The falcon roared within him, gone from the material realm but living inside him, its desire violent, overpowering the memories of Nidhirv and the rest. Destroying the Virohi—achieving the freedom that came from it—was the desire of lifetimes. What was Iravan's wish to have children compared to the wish of who he had become now? It was weak. It was nothing. It was laughable.

There was no more Ecstasy or trajection for him, but he had the pure power of uncontaminated desire now, to mold in the manner he had molded trajection once. Plants were still the easiest to manipulate, then the jungle, the wind, and the earth, and finally in some measure the planet itself. People were harder—a part of him still shied away from trajecting them—but no matter, he would learn. He would bind the architects to him. He would understand the limits of what he could do.

Then, when he had figured this new state, he would take the war to the Virohi and wrench the cosmic creatures out of the worlds they had infected. He would release the planets they had destroyed. He would bind the architects and all their power, and he would extract the Virohi's perversion.

Then, when it was done, the architects could be reborn without the part of Virohi that still lived in them.

Then, Bharavi's consciousness would be reborn into a world that did not see her as either the enemy or the hero. She would find completion without the agony.

And then—when all this was done—Iravan would finally rest. He stood up.

At once, a hush fell over the gathering, every eye on him. Behind him, the chair he had trajected—*trajected*—so long ago vanished. His gaze took in every frightened eye, every nervous gesture. They were expecting a speech. He did not have the patience for grand gestures anymore. They were expecting comfort. He had none to give.

He would give them something better.

Purpose.

"Work with me," Iravan said softly. "And I will give you Irshar."

Architects and sungineers exchanged nervous glances. Eyes fell on the thin necklace sparkling around Iravan's neck, on the silvery tattoos on his skin. He acknowledged their fear and their confusion. Then he dismissed it.

"Work with me," he said again. "And I will give you the jungle. I will return to you the skies. I will give you back the entire world."

This time a few people cheered. Disparate shouts grew around the gathering, the energy of his own desire infecting them. Someone clapped, someone else whooped.

"Work with me," Iravan said, one final time. "And the future of humanity will be yours."

At this, applause pounded over the gathering. Architects yelled, and sungineers pumped their fists in the air. It was terror made solid. It was Iravan's own power threading through them. He did not do it deliberately, but the influence of his energy could not be challenged.

"There is only one enemy now," Iravan said. "Work with me. And we will defeat them."

Dhruv moved next to him, but Iravan turned away and strode toward the jagged opening in the wall. Irshar rose in gentle waves around him—Irshar, they had dared to call it, the monstrosity that was the jungle-city. The everdust chain was in his hands again, its texture as smooth as stone.

He willed his desire, and his silvery tattoos glowed on his dark skin, silver circles forming around his irises. The planet reacted, and he ascended into the air in the small courtyard outside the Garden, his feather cloak billowing behind him. The citizens of the Garden, of his ashram, followed him out, gazing up at him. The sungineers and architects of humanity grew hoarse, calling out his name— but Iravan was only dimly aware of them as wind sluiced his hair back. He spread his arms out and threw his head back to the skies, in a gesture of welcome to the freedom that awaited him.

GLOSSARY

- COSMIC CREATURES: Creatures from another dimension who cause earthrages. An earthrage occurs when a cosmic creature splits itself, and only stops when the split is complete. The split portions of cosmic creatures become trajecting architects and yakshas.
- CONDUIT: An extra dimensional reality available only to those who can traject. Often visualized as a tunnel that connects the Moment and the Deepness.
- CORE TREE: Semi-sentient trees that form the heart of a flying city. Embedded with thousands of permissions, which ordinarily cannot be altered, including flight permissions which allow ashrams to float in the sky.
- DEATHBOX: A sungineering device that runs on trajection energy. It is made of glass and creates a pocket Moment. There are two layers of protection on a deathbox—the glass itself which forms a physical barrier, as well as forcefields which can be activated to increase or decrease the size of the pocket Moment. Any living thing that is inside an activated deathbox shows up only in the pocket Moment within the deathbox, and does not show in the Moment proper. Anything inside of a deathbox does not interact with the true Moment and vice versa.
- DEATHCHAMBER: A sungineering invention that runs on trajection energy. It is made of forcefields that create a pocket

Moment. Unlike deathboxes or deathcages, deathchambers have no physical boundaries of glass, thus allowing one to walk in and out of them unobstructed.

- DEATHCAGE: A sungineering invention that runs on trajection energy. Essentially a gigantic deathbox that can potentially contain people within it. Like a deathbox, it also contains two layers of protection i.e. the glass and the forcefields. Deathcages are traditionally used to imprison Ecstatics who are awaiting excision. Architects inside the deathcage can only traject the possibilities of those living things that are inside the deathcage with them by using the pocket Moment. Architects outside of the deathcage can traject only the complete Moment minus the pocket Moment. Separate deathcages create separate pocket Moments. It is possible to have infinite pocket Moments because the Moment itself is infinite.

- DEATHMAZES: A sungineering invention that runs on trajection energy. Recently developed in Nakshar, deathmazes are a true maze where glass is layered in the shape of labyrinth. These mazes can be life size or be embedded in the fabric of a city, so they run underground and cannot be seen. Deathmazes create a pocket Deepness. When an architect is inside a deathmaze, they can only summon a shard of the Moment from the pocket Deepness. See, Shard Moment. Each deathmaze creates its own individual and unique pocket Deepness. Infinite such pocket Deepnesses can exist since the true Deepness is infinite.

- DEEPNESS, THE: An extra dimensional reality available only to those who can traject Ecstatically. The Deepness is an infinite black space where the Moment can be summoned. One can move from the Moment into the Deepness using the Conduit. See also, Conduit, and the Moment

  - POCKET DEEPNESS: A carved out portion of the Deepness

proper, created due to deathmazes. When deathmazes are activated, they cut off part of the Deepness and create a pocket. From this pocket, only a shard of the Moment is available. See also, Shard Moment.

- EARTHRAGES: Cataclysmic storms that destroy the surface of the jungle planet constantly and unpredictably. Earthrages were thought to have been caused by a disruption of consciousness at a planetary level. Recently, new knowledge has been discovered to indicate that an earthrage is caused due to a split of a cosmic creature. Each earthrage begins when a cosmic creature begins its split, and only comes to an end when the split is complete. A lull between earthrages occurs when no splits are occurring.

- ECSTASY: Traditionally considered a state of uncontrollable trajection power, Ecstasy has recently been theorized as an architect's natural state. Ecstasy occurs when architects begin to bond with their counterpart yakshas. Ecsatics function in the Deepness, and this form of trajection is called supertrajection or Ecstatic trajection. Ecstatic energy is also referred to as Energy X. See also, Trajection.

- ENERGEX: A sungineering device that runs on Ecstatic energy. It uses Ecstatic power instead of regular trajection.

- ETHERIUM: A third vision of reality that manifests itself between an individual's brows. Unlike the Moment or the Deepness, this is available to non-architects as well as architects. Unlike the Moment or the Deepness, which are shared realities, each person has a unique Etherium personal to them.

- EVERDUST: Green dust of pure possibility that presents itself in select places as physical glittering green dust, and in the Moment as stars.

- EXCISION: The act of cutting an architect from their trajection, both in the Moment or the Deepness. Traditionally a punishment for Ecstatic architects. It has recently been hypothesized that excision cuts architects away from their counterpart yakshas as well.

- GARDEN, THE: A location in the habitat, shaped like a garden.
- HABITAT, THE: The only known refuge in the jungle from earthrages.
- MOMENT, THE: An extradimensional reality only available to architects. The Moment is infinite, and contains the literal possibilities of all living things within it which are represented as frozen stars. Traditionally, architects are trained only to see the stars of plants in the Moment, which is how they manipulate them. Architects themselves enter the Moment as dust motes. As living things, they also have their own infinite possibilities represented as stars within the Moment, though most architects are not trained to see that.
  - ◆ SHARD MOMENT: Literally a shard of the Moment that is created due to a deathmaze. Ordinarily, the entirety of the Moment can be summoned from the Deepness. However, when the Deepness is constricted due to an activated deathmaze, only a shard of the Moment is available from the resulting pocket Deepness. The shard Moment contains the possibilities of all the living things that are trapped within the deathmaze only.
  - ◆ POCKET MOMENT: Different from a shard Moment, this is the pocket of Moment created due to deathcages, deathchambers, or deathboxes. The pocket Moment is a carved out piece of the Moment. When an architect within an activated deathcage or deathchamber tries to enter the Moment, they have access only to this pocket. It contains the possibilities of all the living things that are trapped in these sungineering inventions when activated.

- PERILEAF: A new plant created specifically to be useless to Ecstatic architects. Red in color. Used to visually mark the boundary of a deathmaze.

- RADARX: A sungineering device that runs on trajection but detects Ecstasy.

- RESONANCE, THE: The falcon yaksha's form in the Deepness, the Moment and the Conduit.

- SUPERTRAJECTION: Ecstatic trajection.

- TRAJECTION: The power used by architects when they build constellation lines within the Moment to connect different stars to each other, which in turn changes the form of those living creatures within normal reality. Trajection energy is different from Ecstatic energy. Trajection is also sometimes used as an overarching term to refer to trajection proper as well as Ecstatic trajection.

- TWO VISIONS, THE: The manner is which an architect splits their vision, the first of which is their normal reality and the second which allows them to interact with extra dimensional realities like the Moment and the Deepness.

- VERISTEM: A velvety black plant that blooms white when in presence of a lie.

- YAKSHAS: The non-human part of a split cosmic creature.
  - CORPOREAL YAKSHAS: Gigantic jungle creatures that live in isolation. They formed when the first of the comic creatures split and birthed in animals. Some examples include: falcon-yaksha, tiger-yaksha, bear-yaksha etc.
  - NON-CORPOREAL YAKSHAS: Amorphous, formless parts of split cosmic creatures. Many brutal earthrages destroyed all wild life on the planet. Future splits of cosmic creatures resulted in human architects and these formless yakshas. Little is known of them.

SUNGINEERING TECHNOLOGY

The following diagrams represent certain sungineering devices and their relationship/access to the extra-dimensional realities of the Moment and the Deepness.

Activated Deathboxes/Deathcage

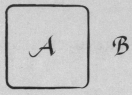

A   *The space within the deathcage only has access to the pocket Moment.*

B   *The space outside of the deathcage can access the full Moment – minus the pocket Moment created by the deathcage.*

Activated Deathmazes

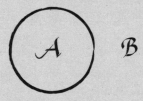

A   *The space within the deathmaze only has access to the pocket Deepness, and through it to the shard Moment. It also has complete access to the Moment through entering the Moment itself.*

B   *The space outside the deathmaze has access to the full Deepness – minus the pocket Deepness created by the activated deathmaze.*

Through the full Deepness minus the pocket Deepness, this space has access to the full Moment, minus the shard Moment within the deathmaze. It also has access to the full Moment itself from the Moment.

Activated Deathcages and Deathmazes

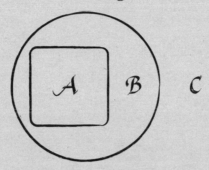

A   The space within the deathcage only has access to the pocket Moment, a pocket Deepness and, through the pocket Deepness, the shard Moment.

B   The space within the deathmaze but outside the deathcage only has access to the pocket Deepness and, through it, the shard Moment.

     Any living thing within this area is visible in the shard Moment, though it needs to be within the deathcage too to show up in the pocket Moment.

     This space also has complete access to the Moment through the Moment itself – minus the pocket Moment that is carved out by the deathcage.

C   The space outside the deathmaze has access to the full Deepness – minus the pocket Deepness inside the deathmaze – and through it to the full Moment – minus the shard Moment carved out by the deathmaze. It also has access to the full Moment – minus the pocket Moment carved out by the deathcage.

     The Conduit is indifferent to all this – as long as one has access to any part of the Deepness and the Moment, the Conduit exists as a bridge between the two.

     The Etherium is unaffected by Deathcages and Deathmazes because it is a personal third vision.

ACKNOWLEDGEMENTS

Weirdly, for a second book, this one was easy to write.

My deepest thanks to my wonderful editors, George Sandison and Katie Dent. You guys are such *nerds*—I love it! Thanks for making edits so much fun, all through the conversations of deathboxes/mazes/cages (good grief), and going down different worldbuilding rabbit holes just coz, and all the many talks about Iravan and Ahilya's character arcs. I considered putting in a bullet list for you in here.

Thanks also to the extended Titan Team, Katharine Carroll, Kabriya Coghlan, Hannah Scudamore, Kate Greally, Charlotte Kelly, Adrian McLaughlin, and the wider PRH sales team, for all the behind-the-scenes wizardry. To Leo Nickolls for this fabulous cover art, and to Julia Lloyd for all the gorgeous interior art, and turning my extremely basic diagrams about sungineering technology into what they are now. Thank you to Recorded Books, for all the audio magic, and to my narrators Pranshu Mishra and Sharmila Devar—what a joy it is to work with such passionate, creative people who put so much love and care into making the performance stellar! Our discussions of all things related to Ahilya and Iravan, and their moods and motivations—we fanpersoned hard together, and it was the best.

To my beta readers, Leon and David, thank you for sticking with me for so many years. Thanks also to my author buddies, especially to those in SFF Powerhouse and the Bunker, for keeping me company and helping me wrangle publishing and life woes. In an industry where there is no certainty, you folks provide the necessary lifeboat. Special thanks to Hannah M. Long, for holding my hand through some of the toughest parts of my life, which incidentally happened during the working of this book. Also thanks to Sunyi Dean and Essa Hansen – you know for what. As always, a tremendous thanks to the many booksellers, bookbloggers, readers, reviewers, and general enthusiasts who are talking about Iravan and Ahilya. I am humbled by how you have invited my disaster protagonists into your life, and how you continue to follow their story. They're a part of you now.

And finally, to Tate and Rohan and little baby X—for managing the house, for giving me time, for letting me be distracted, for feeding me snacks. I love you.

ABOUT THE AUTHOR

KRITIKA H. RAO is a speculative and children's fiction author, who has lived in India, Australia, Canada, and The Sultanate of Oman. Whether writing for younger audiences or adults, Kritika's stories are influenced by her lived experiences, and explore themes of self vs. the world, identity, and the nature of consciousness. When she is not writing, she is probably making lists. She drops in and out of social media; you might catch her on Instagram @KritikaHRao. Visit her online at www.kritikahrao.com.

For more fantastic fiction, author events,
exclusive excerpts, competitions, limited editions and more

VISIT OUR WEBSITE
titanbooks.com

LIKE US ON FACEBOOK
facebook.com/titanbooks

FOLLOW US ON TWITTER, TIKTOK AND INSTAGRAM
@TitanBooks

EMAIL US
readerfeedback@titanemail.com